CHRISTMAS
Seduction

CHRISTMAS
Seduction

Sarah Morgan
Cathy Williams
Michelle Celmer

MILLS & BOON

Published in Great Britain 2014
by Mills & Boon, an imprint of Harlequin (UK) Limited,
Eton House, 18-24 Paradise Road, Richmond, Surrey, TW9 1SR

CHRISTMAS SEDUCTION © 2014 Harlequin Books S.A.

The Twelve Nights of Christmas © 2010 Sarah Morgan
His Christmas Acquisition © 2011 Cathy Williams
Caroselli's Christmas Baby © 2012 Michelle Celmer

ISBN: 978-0-263-25092-3

024-1114

Harlequin (UK) Limited's policy is to use papers that are natural, renewable and recyclable products and made from wood grown in sustainable forests.The logging and manufacturing processes conform to the legalenvironmental regulations of the country of origin.

Printed and bound in Spain
by Blackprint CPI, Barcelona

The Twelve Nights of Christmas

Sarah Morgan

To Kimberley Young:
seven years and forty-two books together.
Thank you. xx

Sarah Morgan is the bestselling author of *Sleigh Bells in the Snow*. As a child Sarah dreamed of being a writer and, although she took a few interesting detours on the way, she is now living that dream. With her writing career she has successfully combined business with pleasure and she firmly believes that reading romance is one of the most satisfying and fat-free escapist pleasures available. Her stories are unashamedly optimistic and she is always pleased when she receives letters from readers saying that her books have helped them through hard times.

Sarah lives near London with her husband and two children, who innocently provide an endless supply of authentic dialogue. When she isn't writing or reading, Sarah enjoys music, movies and any activity that takes her outdoors.

Readers can find out more about Sarah and her books from her website: www.sarahmorgan.com. She can also be found on Facebook and Twitter.

CHAPTER ONE

'I NEVER thought this moment would come, Pietro. Let's celebrate.' Rio Zaccarelli sat back as the vintage champagne was poured into his glass. Across the table, his lawyer opened his case and handed him a sheaf of papers.

'I'm not celebrating until this one is in the bag. How did you get a table here? I've never seen so many rich, powerful people in one place.' Pietro glanced discreetly over his shoulder, his gaze skimming the other diners. His eyes widened as he focused on a man in a dark grey suit. 'Isn't that—?'

'Yes. Don't stare or you'll have security teams swarming over your lunch.' Rio flicked through the papers, scanning the contents. As he reached for his champagne he noticed that his hand shook slightly and he wrenched back his emotions, forcing himself to treat this like any other business deal. 'You haven't eaten here before?'

'I've been waiting a year to get a table at this restaurant and you do it in one phone call. There are times when I wish I had your influence.'

'Complete this deal and I'll get you a table. That's a promise.' *Complete this deal and I'll buy you the restaurant.*

'I'll hold you to that. You have to sign on the back page.' Pietro handed him a pen and Rio signed the documents with a bold scrawl.

'As usual, I owe you—for your discretion as well as your

astonishing legal brain. Order the lobster. It's sublime and you've more than earned it.'

'Thank me when it's all signed and sealed and not before. I've learned not to celebrate until the ball is in the net. It's been a hard fight and this may still not be finished.' The lawyer took the wedge of papers and slipped them into his briefcase. 'The stakes are high. They haven't stopped fighting, Rio. They don't want you to win this.'

'I'm aware of that.' A red mist of anger coloured his vision and his fingers tightened on the delicate stem of the champagne flute. The tension was like steel bands around his body. 'I want to be kept updated, Pietro. Any changes, phone my personal line.'

'Understood.' Pietro snapped his case shut. 'This deal could still blow itself apart. The most important thing is that you need to keep yourself whiter than fresh snow between now and Christmas. Don't get yourself so much as a parking ticket. Not a blemish. Not a rumour. My advice as a friend who knows you? Find an isolated ski lodge and lock yourself away. No liaisons with women, no kiss and tell stories—for the time being, sex is off the agenda.'

Rio, who hadn't gone ten days without sex since he'd lost his virginity, kept his face expressionless. 'I'll be discreet.'

'No.' Pietro leaned forward, switching from friend back to lawyer in the blink of an eye. 'If you want this deal watertight, then discretion isn't enough. I'm saying no sex, Rio. Unless it's married sex. If you happen to suddenly fall for a decent, wholesome girl whose entire objective in life is to love you and give you babies, that might actually help your case—' he gave a faint smile and spread his hands in a fatalistic gesture '—but, knowing you as I do, there's not much chance of that.'

'None at all. There's no such thing as a decent, wholesome girl and if there were she'd undergo a personality change the moment she met me,' Rio drawled. 'Within minutes she'd be thinking about prenuptial agreements and record breaking divorce settlements.'

Pietro picked up the menu. 'I don't blame you for being cynical, but—'

'I understand you. No sex. Sounds like I'm in for an exciting Christmas.' Rio thought of the Russian ballerina who was currently waiting in his apartment, lying on silk sheets, waiting for the visit he couldn't risk making.

He'd send her diamonds and give her the use of his private jet to fly home to Moscow for Christmas. They could pick up their relationship in the New Year. Or not. Realising that he wasn't bothered either way, he frowned.

Perhaps it was a good job he had an urgent business trip to make. He could work off his excess energy in other ways.

His eyes blank of expression, Rio stared out of the glass sided restaurant that had views over the centre of Rome, watching the crazy traffic fighting for space on the streets below.

There was nothing he wouldn't do to achieve the outcome he wanted. Even denying his libido for a short time.

Pietro put down the menu and picked up his glass, a hint of a smile on his face. 'I have a feeling this will be the hardest thing you've ever done. Go somewhere there are no women. I hear Antarctica is sparsely populated at this time of year.'

'I have to fly to London on business.'

'You are confronting Carlos?'

'I'm firing him,' Rio said coldly. 'His appointment was a mistake. I've had a full report from the external management consultant I put into the hotel. I need to deal with the situation before his appalling mismanagement affects the reputation of my company.'

'I don't suppose I can persuade you to wait until after the deal is signed?'

'Carlos cannot affect this deal.'

'In theory I would agree, but—' frowning, his lawyer put his glass down slowly '—this has been a difficult fight and we're not there yet. I'm uneasy.'

'That's why I'm paying you such an astronomical sum. I pay you to be uneasy, so that I can sleep.'

Pietro lifted an eyebrow. 'Since when did you start sleeping? You work harder than I do. Especially at this time of year. I assume you're planning to work right through Christmas?'

'Of course.'

The lawyer picked up the warm, crusty bread roll from his side plate and broke it in half. 'Why do you hate this time of year so much?'

A cold, sick feeling rose in his stomach. Aware that, as always, he was the focus of attention in the restaurant, Rio sat still, his features carefully composed. Catching the eye of a pretty European princess who had been gazing at him across the restaurant since he'd arrived, he gave a brief nod of acknowledgement. Desperate for distraction, he contemplated accepting her blatant invitation, but then he remembered Pietro's warning. No sex. Whiter than white.

Instead, he drained his champagne glass and formulated an answer to the question. 'Why do I hate Christmas? Because everyone uses Christmas as an excuse to stop work,' he lied smoothly, wrestling down his emotions with sheer brute force. 'And I'm a demanding boss. I hate time wasters, you know that. But I appreciate all the hours you've put into this deal and I will heed the advice. Until this deal is closed, the only person sleeping in my bed will be me.'

'It might make for a boring Christmas, but that is exactly the way it should be. I'm serious, Rio. Stay indoors. The only things you should be touching are your laptop and your phone.' Pietro looked him in the eye. 'Don't underestimate how much could still go wrong.'

'Whiter than white,' Rio purred, a faint smile touching his

mouth. 'I can do that if I really concentrate. Anyway, I'm not likely to meet a woman who interests me in London. Shall we order?'

'You can't do this to me! You can't just throw me out of my home! I can't *believe* you changed the locks when I was out. Don't you have any human feeling?' Evie grabbed the man's arm, almost slipping on the snow and ice as he shrugged her off and dropped his tools back into his bag.

'Life's tough. Blame your landlord, not me. Sorry, love.' But he didn't look sorry and Evie felt the panic rise as the enormity of the situation hit her.

'It's only twelve days until Christmas. I'll never find anything else at this short notice.'

The emotions she'd been suppressing for six stressful weeks suddenly broke through the front she'd been presenting to the world.

This was supposed to have been her wedding day. Tonight she would have been flying to a romantic hotel in the Caribbean on her honeymoon to make a baby. Instead, she was on her own in a big, cold city where no one seemed to care about anyone else. It was snowing and she was homeless.

'At least let me get my things.' Not that she had much. The few things she'd brought with her could probably fit into one rubbish bag.

Even as the thought wafted through her mind, the man gestured to a black bin liner leaning against the door.

'Those are your things.' The man snapped his bag shut. 'Good job you haven't got much stuff.'

Evie wondered what was good about not having much stuff. She'd thought moving to London would be exciting and full of opportunities. She hadn't realised how expensive it would be. Everything cost a fortune. And she hadn't realised how lonely it would be living in a city. She couldn't afford a social life. When a few of the girls at work had invited her out, she'd had to refuse.

The snow fluttered onto her head and neck and Evie huddled deeper inside her coat, her spirits as low as the temperature.

'Just let me stay here tonight, OK? I'll try and find somewhere tomorrow—' She felt as though she was holding everything together by a single fragile thread. It had been that way since the day Jeff had texted her to tell her the wedding was off. Concerned about her grandfather's distress, she'd taken refuge in the practical, returning presents with polite notes attached, cancelling the church and the venue, explaining to all the well-wishers who arrived at the house. She'd told herself that she'd shed her tears in private, but she'd discovered that cancelling a wedding was almost as much work as organising one, without any of the excitement to drive you forward. By the time she'd fallen into her bed at night she hadn't had the energy to cry. 'Please—it's going to be impossible to find somewhere else to live this close to Christmas.'

'It's a dog eat dog world, love.'

Evie recoiled. 'I love dogs. I'd *never* eat a dog! And it's supposed to be the season of goodwill.'

'I feel plenty of goodwill. Thanks to landlords like yours, I have a job.'

'Well, it's nice to know I'm supporting someone through the credit crunch—' Feeling a vibrating in her pocket, Evie dug out her phone, her anxiety doubling when she saw the number. 'Just wait there a moment and don't go anywhere because I have to answer this or he'll worry—he's very old and—Grandpa? Why are you calling in the middle of the day? Are you OK?' She prayed he hadn't had another one of his turns. It was one thing after another. Her life was unravelling faster than a pulled thread in a sweater. She'd wanted so badly to make him proud. Instead, all she was going to do was worry him.

'Just checking up on you because I saw the pictures of the snow on the news.' Her grandfather sounded frail and Evie tightened her grip on the phone, hating the fact that he was getting older.

He was the person she loved most in the world. She owed him everything. 'I'm fine, Grandpa.' She shivered as more flakes of snow found their way inside her coat. 'You know I love the snow.'

'You always did. Built any snowmen yet? You always loved building snowmen.'

Evie swallowed. 'I…I haven't had the chance yet, Grandpa. Soon, I hope. There's a huge park opposite the hotel where I'm working. It's crying out for a snowman.' She didn't tell him that no one paused to build a snowman in London. Everyone was too busy rushing from one place to another.

'Are you at work now? I don't want to bother you if you're at work, dealing with some high-powered celebrity.'

High-powered celebrity?

'Well…er…' Her face scarlet, Evie moved away from the man who had just tipped her life into a rubbish bag and wondered whether the lie she'd told about her job was about to come back to bite her. It was one thing trying to protect her grandfather, but she'd probably gone a little over the top. Or possibly more than a little. 'Grandpa—'

'I boast to everyone about you. I'm so proud of you, Evie. I told that stuffy Mrs Fitzwilliam in the room next door to mine, "My granddaughter has got herself a brilliant high-powered job. She may have been left standing at the altar—"'

Evie pressed her fingers to her aching forehead. 'It wasn't at the altar, Grandpa. No one got as far as the altar—'

'"—but she picked herself up and now she's a receptionist at the smartest hotel in London and she never would have had that opportunity if she'd married useless Jeff." He was nothing but a dreamer. And he wasn't good enough for you,

you know that, don't you? He was wet, and you don't want a man who is wet. You need a *real* man.'

'Any man would be a start,' Evie muttered under her breath, 'but fat chance of that.'

'What was that?'

'Nothing.' For once grateful for her grandfather's hearing aid, she changed the subject quickly. 'Are you OK? Are they treating you all right there?' Although he'd persuaded her he wanted to go into the same home as his closest friend, she still wasn't comfortable with the idea.

'My bones are aching in the damp weather and they make too much fuss here.'

Evie smiled. 'It will be summer soon. And I'm glad they're fussing.'

'I wish I could see you at Christmas but I know it's too far for you to come for just one day. I'm worrying about you on your own. I miss you, Evie.'

Flattened by homesickness, Evie felt a lump settle in her throat. 'I miss you, too. And I'll try and come up as soon as I can. And don't worry. I'm fine.' She pushed the words past her cold lips and then waved her hand frantically as the man loaded his tools into his van. Was he really just going to drive away and leave her here, standing on a snowy pavement in the dark? What had happened to chivalry? Her fiancé broke up with her by text and this man was about to leave a vulnerable woman alone in a big, scary city with nowhere to spend the night. Where were all the knights in shining armour when you needed them? Her grandfather was right—she needed a real man. Down with rats, wimps and cowards.

'So how's the job going?' Her grandfather used his most bracing voice. 'I told Mrs Fitzwilliam that you have Hollywood stars staying and that you'll be meeting and greeting them personally. That shut her up. Nosy old madam.'

Evie didn't know whether to laugh or cry. She was going to be struck down for lying to her grandfather. On the other hand, the alternative option was disappointing and worry-ing him. And she *did* 'meet and greet' guests. Sort of. If she met someone, she greeted them, didn't she? The fact that they usually ignored her didn't count. 'The job's great, Grandpa. Brilliant.' She'd been demoted and the slimy hotel manager had made a pass at her but, apart from that, it was all perfect.

The man started the engine and Evie sprinted across the pavement to stop him, her feet slithering on the ice. 'Wait—'

Her grandfather was still chatting. 'I've been watching the shares of Zaccarelli Leisure. They're soaring. You picked a winner there, Evie. At least your job is safe.'

No. No, it wasn't safe. Her entire existence was balancing on a knife edge.

Evie had a sudden urge to confess that the manager had tried it on with her, but stopped herself in time. She didn't want to upset her grandfather. And she also had a sneaking worry that he might somehow get on a train, find his way to London and deal with Carlos Bellini personally. Despite his eighty-six years, her grandfather was a real man.

'My job is…it's…well, it's great,' she said firmly. 'Really good.'

'Going to any Christmas parties? I'm sure you'll be able to have your pick of men if you do! And you won't be able to make it through the Christmas season without singing *The Twelve Days of Christmas* at the top of your voice. You know you always love doing that.'

'No parties planned. And I'm not quite ready to meet an-other man yet, Grandpa.' Dragging the bag behind her, Evie slithered towards the van. As she let go of it, the top gaped open and her tiny silver Christmas tree tumbled into the snow and slush. 'Don't worry about me. I'm fine.' A lump in her throat, she stared at her Christmas tree, which was now lying in a puddle. Her whole life felt as though it was sinking into a puddle.

'Don't hang around, Evie. I'm not getting any younger. Next year I want to be bouncing a great-grandchild on my knee.'

What? 'I'll do my best, Grandpa.' Wondering how on earth she was going to fulfil that particular wish when she couldn't find a man who wanted to talk to her, let alone sleep with her, Evie forced out a cheery goodbye and dropped the phone back in her pocket.

As she retrieved the dripping Christmas tree, the man drove off, showering her with slush.

It was snowing steadily and Evie was just wondering whether it was worth wading through the contents of the bag to find her umbrella when her phone rang again.

'Why am I suddenly the most popular person in the world?' Looking at the number flashing on her phone, she groaned. *Oh, no.* 'Tina? I know I'm late, but I've—' she flinched as her boss gave her a sharp lecture '—yes, I know Salvatorio Zaccarelli is arriving tomorrow and—yes, I know it's important because he's looking at the way the hotel is run and we're all under scrutiny. Yes, I know I was lucky you gave me another chance with this job when you could have fired me—' She gritted her teeth as she listened. 'I—yes, the Penthouse will be perfect, I promise—I'm lucky that Carlos wants me to do the job personally—I do know Mr Zaccarelli is the most important guest we ever have—I know he doesn't suffer fools and won't tolerate anything less than perfection—' *the guy was obviously a cold, heartless pig* '—I feel the same way,' Evie lied, making a mental note not to be anywhere near the scary, ruthless tycoon when he arrived at the hotel. The way she was feeling at the moment, she'd probably punch him. That was one 'meet and greet' that was *not* going to happen. If she saw him coming she was going to dive for cover.

Tina was still talking and Evie slithered her way towards the bus stop, the rubbish bag banging against her legs, her clothes soaked through. Snow landed on her hair and water dripped down her neck. '—Festive? Sparkling? Yes, I'm going to decorate the Christmas tree—I'll be there ever so soon, but I just need to—' she broke off; *I just need to find somewhere to sleep tonight when I come off my shift at midnight* '—catch a bus. The buses are mad because of Christmas, but I'm on my way now.' All she ever did was tell lies, Evie thought, struggling with the bag. She lied to protect her grandfather from more worry and she lied to Tyrannosaurus Tina because, until she'd found something better, she couldn't tell the woman where to stick her job. Maybe she should suggest to scary Salvatorio Zaccarelli that the first person he should fire was the manager of his flagship hotel.

As she sat on the crowded bus, jammed between stressed out Christmas shoppers, Evie wondered if she should have just told her grandfather the truth. That London was lonely. That she missed him. That she'd been demoted after just days in her new job by a boss who hated her. Apparently, she'd been too friendly.

Evie sighed, well aware that she'd probably been a little too desperate for human company. But she still didn't understand why that was a crime. As a receptionist in a hotel, how could you be too friendly? Anyway, she had no opportunity to be friendly now because, as a member of the housekeeping staff, she didn't often meet any guests. She didn't meet anyone. She'd taken to talking to herself as she cleaned bathroom mirrors.

Trying to take her mind off it, Evie picked up a discarded magazine and flicked through the pages, staring gloomily at the slender models wearing the magazine's recommendations for glittery dresses perfect for the party season. Apparently, silver was bang on trend. Absently, she picked the one she would have worn if she had money and had actually been invited to a party. Shimmering silver, she thought, with diamonds and swept up hair. Except that she'd look ridiculous dressed like that.

Face it, Evie, you're a bit of a freak.

Hearing Jeff's voice in her head, she dropped the magazine back on the seat, jumped off the bus and walked towards the back entrance of the prestigious hotel that provided a bolt-hole for the world's rich and famous. She was just wondering where she was going to hide a rubbish bag when a sleek black Mercedes drove through a puddle and muddy water sprayed over her tights and shoes.

'Oh, for—' Hopping to one side, soaking wet, Evie glared after the expensive car, imagining the warm, luxurious interior. 'Thanks a lot. Just as long as you're comfortable in your cosy, rich cocoon.' Her eyes widened in disbelief as she read the number plate. 'TYC00N.' Drenched and shivering, she wondered what it was like to live a life of luxury, filled with diamonds, shimmering silver dresses and ostentatious car accessories.

'Hi, Evie, you're late.' A colleague hurried past her in a cloud of perfume and hairspray. 'You've already missed the staff briefing. Tina said you were to go straight to the Penthouse because she doesn't have time to waste with you. The big boss is arriving tomorrow. Rumour has it that he is going to axe anyone who doesn't fit. Even Creepy Carlos is nervous. Personally, I can't wait to see Rio Zaccarelli in person. He's the most stunningly good-looking man I've ever seen.'

Chilled to the bone, Evie sneezed. 'You've never seen him.'

'I've seen him in pictures. Red-hot Rio, that's what we're calling him.'

'Ruthless Rio is what *I'm* calling him,' Evie muttered and her colleague frowned at the bag in her hand.

'Since when have you been responsible for dealing with the trash?'

'Oh, I like to be helpful. Versatile, that's me—' Evie pinned a rigid grin on her face, refusing to admit that she was carrying her home around. Like a snail, she thought, as she followed the girl through the glass door and into the plush, privileged warmth of a different life. Maybe there was a number plate that spelled out DISASTER. She could stick it on her back to warn people she was coming.

Hiding her bag in the basement behind some large pipes, Evie took refuge in the peaceful elegance of the Penthouse suite. She felt so utterly miserable that, for the first time since her aborted wedding and humiliating demotion, she was relieved that she wasn't on Reception, having to smile and be cheerful. She didn't want to meet and greet. She just wanted to curl up in a ball and not emerge until her life had improved.

The warm, spacious luxury of the top floor suite made her feel instantly calmer and Evie looked around her wistfully. Two deep white sofas faced each other across a priceless rug and flames flickered in the fireplace. Huge floor to ceiling windows gave views over Hyde Park and the elegant buildings of Knightsbridge.

Someone had put a large fir tree next to the grand piano and boxes of decorations were neatly stacked, ready for Evie to create a perfect Christmas.

A perfect Christmas for someone else.

'Imagine spending Christmas somewhere like this,' she murmured, talking to herself as she explored the Penthouse suite. 'Talk about how the other half live.'

Feeling incredibly down, Evie set to work decorating the tree, trying not to think about the times she'd done the same thing with her grandfather. Last year they'd shared a wonderful Christmas. She'd baked Christmas cake and Christmas puddings and roasted a turkey just for the two of them. They'd eaten leftovers for weeks. Turkey curry, turkey soup, turkey sandwiches—

Only a few weeks later, her grandfather had suffered a mini stroke and she'd had no choice but to agree to let him go into the home where his friends were. They'd sold his cottage to pay the exorbitant fees and now she was miles away in a city where no one spoke to anyone except to ask directions.

And she had nowhere to sleep tonight. The thought terrified her and for a moment she considered confessing to Tina and asking if she had any free rooms. Imagining the response she'd get, a hysterical laugh bubbled up from the cauldron of panic that was simmering inside her. Tina would simply remind her that one night in the cheapest room in this hotel was more than her monthly salary.

Merry Christmas, Evie.

She worked without a break, twisting lights through the branches of the enormous tree, hanging glittering silver baubles and filling vases with elaborate displays of holly. Then she started to clean the Penthouse. She was only halfway through when the door opened and Carlos, the hotel manager, strode in.

Evie was immediately on the defensive, horribly aware that she was alone with him and that her mobile phone was in her coat pocket at the other end of the room.

She'd avoided him since the day he'd tried to kiss her and she stood warily, her mind scrambling through her options. They were pitifully few. He ran the hotel and held her future in the palm of his hand. Unfortunately, he'd made it clear that he wanted to hold other bits of her in the palm of his hand, too.

His hair shone greasily under the lights and Evie shuddered, bracing herself for criticism.

Was he looking for an excuse to fire her?

'It looks perfect. Incredibly Christmassy. Just what I wanted for Rio.' Something about his smile made her uneasy.

'You're sure you like it?'

'Absolutely.' His eyes trailed over her body. 'You're wet.'

Evie stood rigid, wondering why the only man to pay her any attention had to be a total creep.

'It's snowing. I had to wait for a bus.'

'I don't want my staff catching pneumonia. Take a hot shower.'

She felt herself blush. 'I can't afford the time. I still have loads to do and my shift ends in thirty minutes.'

'You're on again first thing tomorrow morning.' Carlos frowned. 'Stay here tonight. That way, you can start work straight away. I want everything perfect.'

He was giving her permission to stay in the hotel?

Unable to believe her luck, Evie almost sobbed with relief. 'That would be helpful,' she said casually. 'Do we have a spare room?'

'No, we're full. But you can stay here. In the Penthouse.'

Evie looked at him stupidly. 'Here?'

'Why not? Rio isn't arriving until tomorrow afternoon. Your shift ends at midnight and begins again at seven in the morning. It makes perfect sense for you to stay here. Sleep on top of the bed if it bothers you. I'll make sure you're not disturbed.'

Evie stared at him, her instincts on full alert. 'You're suggesting that I stay in the Penthouse?'

'Why not? It isn't doing anyone any harm and I owe you a favour.' He hesitated. 'Evie, I apologise if I came on a little strong a few weeks ago. I misread the signals.'

She hadn't given him any signals. 'I'd rather forget that.' Evie, feeling horribly awkward, was nevertheless relieved by his surprise apology. Perhaps he wasn't trying to find reasons to fire her. 'How is your finger?'

'Healing.' Carlos flexed his bandaged finger and gave a rueful smile. 'Seriously, Evie. Stay here tonight. It's in the interests of the hotel—you'll get more work done if you're here on the premises.'

What he said made sense.

So why was she hesitating? She'd have somewhere warm to stay and she could start searching for another place tomorrow. 'All right. Thanks. If you're sure.'

'Do you have any dry clothes?'

Evie thought of the bag of belongings she'd left in the basement. 'I have a…a bag downstairs.'

'I'll arrange for someone to collect it. Where did you leave it?'

Flanked by his security team, Rio Zaccarelli left his private jet under the cover of darkness and slid into the waiting car.

'No press—that's good.' Antonio, his senior bodyguard, scanned the area. 'No one knows you're coming. Do you want us to call ahead and warn the hotel? They're expecting you in the afternoon, not at four in the morning.'

'No.' Rio lounged in the back of the car, his eyes hooded as he contemplated the surprise that would no doubt accompany his unexpected arrival. 'I don't want to announce myself.'

Knowing never to question the boss, Antonio simply slammed the car door shut and slid in next to the driver. 'Shouldn't take us long to get there at this hour. No traffic. I suppose it's because it's Christmas. Lots of people have already stopped work.'

Rio didn't reply.

A cold feeling spread across his skin. A feeling that had nothing to do with the dropping temperature and the swirling snowflakes outside the car. He looked out of the window, keeping his expression blank.

Christmas.

Twenty years had passed and yet he still hated this time of year.

If he had his way, Christmas would be scrubbed from the calendar.

Blocking out the endless twinkling lights and Christmas decorations adorning the dark streets, Rio was for once grateful for the endless demands of his BlackBerry.

Anna, the ballerina, had sent him fourteen messages, each one more desperate than the last.

He read the first three, saw the word 'commitment' and deleted the rest without reading them. Christmas, commitment—why was it that his least favourite words all began with C?

The car pulled up outside the hotel and Rio sat for a moment, surveying the elegant architecture. It was the most expensive few acres of real estate in the world.

You'll never make anything of yourself, Rio. You'll amount to nothing.

Rio gave a grim smile as he surveyed 'nothing'.

He owned it. All of it. Every last brick. Not bad for someone who had once watched his life ground into the dirt.

Leaning forward, he spoke to his driver in Italian. 'Take me to the rear entrance.'

'Yes, sir.'

Rio sprang from the car and walked through the rear door of the hotel, his mouth tightening in disapproval as no one challenged him.

Antonio was right behind him. 'I'll go first.'

'No. I want you to go back downstairs and check those security cameras. And time how long it takes them to discover I'm in the building.' Rio sprinted up ten floors and reached the locked door that protected the exclusive Penthouse suite. He entered a code into the pad and the door opened. Realising that no one had changed the code, his mouth tightened and a dangerous spark lit his eyes.

Inside the luxurious suite, it was warm and peaceful.

And decorated for Christmas.

Rio froze.

He'd given strict instructions—no decorations.

His tension levels rocketing, his gaze fastened on the tall fir tree that glittered and sparkled in the elegant living room, taunting him—*reminding him*.

Turning his back on it, he prowled through the suite. His instincts, honed through years of dealing with people, were suddenly on full alert. Something didn't feel right and it wasn't just that his express instructions had been overlooked.

His firm mouth hardened and he walked purposefully towards the bedroom suite, his footsteps muffled by the thick carpet.

Pushing open the door, Rio stopped on the threshold of the room.

Lying on top of the bed was a naked woman, her glorious red hair spilling over the pillow like a spectacular sunset, her eyelashes forming a dark smudge above pale cheeks. Her mouth was a deep pink, her lower lip full and softly curved.

Rio stared at that mouth for a full minute before trailing his gaze down the rest of her body. It wasn't just her mouth that curved. The rest of her did, too, although some of the secrets of her body were concealed beneath all that glorious hair. As he studied the astonishingly vibrant colour, he felt his libido come alive. His mind computed every last detail. Eyes—green, he decided. Temper—hot. Body—*incredible*. She had the longest legs he'd ever seen and, as for the rest of her—

When she didn't stir, he strolled into the room.

Distracted by the full curve of her breasts, he sat down on the edge of the bed and slid a leisurely hand over her shoulder, brushing aside a strand of silky hair.

Unable to resist the sensual curve of her soft mouth, Rio lowered his head and kissed her. He just had time to register that she tasted as good as she looked when her eyes opened.

Deliciously groggy, she stared at him blankly. 'Oh—' Her words were slurred from sleep. 'Is it Christmas?'

If this was Christmas, then maybe it was time he re-evaluated his feelings towards the festive season. Perhaps it wasn't all bad. *Blue,* Rio thought absently, correcting his earlier assumption. Her eyes were the palest aquamarine.

Lust shot through him and he felt himself harden. Because he was staring down at her, he saw the exact moment she was gripped by the same sexual awareness. Those incredible eyes darkened. Her lips parted and he saw the moist tip of her tongue.

Unable to help himself, Rio lowered his head and was about to kiss her again when a light flashed.

He whipped round in time to see a man darting from the room, camera in hand.

Swearing under his breath in Italian, Rio moved with a speed that would have impressed an Olympic sprinter, but the man was already out of the door.

He grabbed his phone from his pocket and speed-dialled his security team but before Antonio could answer the call, Carlos came striding into the room.

'Rio? I was told there was an intruder in the Penthouse. We had no idea you were arriving this early. Reception should have notified me. How was your journey?' He held out his hand in greeting and then froze, his eyes widening as he stared over Rio's shoulder and through the open doors of the bedroom. 'I'm so sorry—I had no idea you had company— how very embarrassing. Rio, forgive me... We'll give you privacy, of course...'

Rio didn't have to look round to identify the reason for the triumphant gleam in the man's eyes. He had his lawyer's words ringing in his ears.

The most important thing is that you need to keep yourself whiter than fresh snow between now and Christmas.

He, of all people, had allowed a woman to distract him and his carelessness could have the most devastating consequences.

He'd been set up.

He'd walked right into a trap.

And now he was going to pay.

CHAPTER TWO

DIZZY from the kiss and fully aware of just how much trouble she was in, Evie scrambled frantically off the bed and then remembered she was naked. She grabbed the silk throw and covered herself, but it refused to co-operate, slipping and slithering through her fingers. Finally she managed to fasten it, sarong-style around her body. She clutched it tightly, praying that it wouldn't fall off. Hurrying through to the living room, she saw Carlos standing there, deep in conversation with a tall, broad-shouldered man. *The man who had kissed her a few moments earlier.*

Still shaken from the explosion of chemistry, a strange heat spread through her body as she took her first proper look at him and immediately her grandfather's words flew into her head—*a real man.*

He dominated the room with the sheer force of his presence, his powerful legs spread apart, his stance unmistakably commanding as he focused furious black eyes on Carlos's face.

Hearing her entrance, he transferred that terrifying gaze to Evie and she stood pinned to the spot, the simmering fury in his eyes acting like a bucket of cold water.

She went from burning to shivering in the space of a glance.

'I…I'd better get dressed,' she stammered and he made a sound in his throat that sounded ominously like a growl.

'You'll stay *exactly* where you are until I give you permission to move.'

Whatever had propelled him to kiss her, it obviously wasn't something he intended to repeat. There was no softness in his eyes. No hint of the sexual promise that had shimmered only moments earlier.

And suddenly she knew exactly who he was and that realisation came with a cold flash of horror. She'd once seen his picture in the back of the hotel brochure—read a statement from the lord and master of the Zaccarelli Leisure Group. The man who had kissed her was Salvatorio Zaccarelli—Rio to the media, who licked their lips over his taste for glamorous women and super-fast cars.

From what she'd read, Evie had already decided that he was a ruthless, cold-hearted money-making machine who didn't give a damn about the human cost of his decisions. When he took a personal interest in one of his hotels the first thing he did was to change everything he didn't like, and that included the staff. He didn't visit when things were going well. Only when they were going badly did he thunder in like an executioner wielding his sword. There was nothing gentle about him. Nothing soft. He treated women the same way as his business. He hired and fired. No one was with him for long.

Evie had planned to keep her head down and stay out of his way.

Realising that her plan had backfired in the most spectacular fashion she stared, terrified, into his smouldering black eyes. He was obviously livid that she'd spent the night in the Penthouse.

Unless Carlos would admit that he'd given her permission, her job was toast.

And so was her dignity.

Evie swallowed hard, wondering why he'd kissed her. From the firm, deliberate seduction of his mouth to the sensuous brush of his hand over her bare skin, it had been a kiss loaded with sizzling chemistry and erotic promise.

Even as she was wondering if it was usual for him to kiss the staff before firing them, a burly man she'd didn't know came sprinting through the door.

'Sorry, boss.' He stared hard at Rio Zaccarelli, as if in some silent communication. 'Lost him. He must have nipped down the back stairs. I've contacted the local police and I'm going to go through the CCTV footage with hotel security. We'll identify him. Do you want me to question the girl?'

Question her? Why would they want to question her? Her crime was straightforward enough, wasn't it?

'You don't know her?' Carlos looked shocked. 'I assumed—why else would she be in your bedroom, Rio?'

Appalled, Evie stared at him. Obviously, Carlos was going to put his own future before hers. Presumably he was worried that if he confessed to having given her permission to sleep in the Penthouse, he'd be disciplined. Feeling intensely vulnerable, she stood there, searching desperately for a way out of this mess.

'Accept my apologies, Rio.' Carlos's voice was smooth. 'We normally screen our staff very carefully but at this time of year when we're so busy—' He left the sentence hanging. 'I'm disappointed in you, Evie. You abused a position of trust.'

'She works here?' Rio Zaccarelli's voice was harsh. 'She's one of your staff?'

Everyone turned to look at her and Evie burned with humiliation. So that was that. No one was going to believe she'd slept in the Penthouse with permission. They'd believe Carlos, not a lowly member of the housekeeping team. She was nothing more than cannon fodder. Whatever happened next, she was doomed.

There was no point in defending herself.

She had no home, no job and it was less than two weeks until Christmas.

Thinking of her grandfather, Evie felt despair seep through her veins. There was no way she could tell him. Not just before Christmas. He was so proud of her new job and the way she'd picked herself up.

You're a real soldier, Evie.

After everything he'd done for her, she'd let him down.

Maybe she should just forget dignity and beg. Or maybe she should try kissing the boss again. Her eyes drifted over his handsome face and rested on his firm, sensuous mouth. *That same mouth that had taken liberties with hers only moments earlier.* Without thinking, she drew her tongue over her lower lip, tasting his kiss.

He saw the gesture and his eyes flared with anger and something else, far, far more dangerous. With a final contemptuous glance, he turned back to Carlos. 'Do you know what you've done?' His voice was thickened with emotion. 'Have you any idea how much damage you've caused?'

Confused, Evie watched as Rio Zaccarelli transferred the full force of his anger onto Carlos. Why? Had he guessed that Carlos had given her permission? Had he seen through the lies? He was rumoured to have a brain as sharp as a blade.

Hope flickered to life inside her. If Rio Zaccarelli knew Carlos had given her permission, then maybe he'd let her off this time.

He had the reputation of being an exacting boss with impossibly high standards, but, all the same—

Sweat shone on Carlos's forehead. 'What damage? I have no idea what you're talking about.'

With a growl of anger, Rio Zaccarelli crossed the room in three long strides and locked his fist in the front of Carlos's shirt. 'Have you no conscience? No sense of human decency?'

Seeing the black expression on Rio Zaccarelli's face, Evie covered her mouth with her hand.

Wasn't he going a bit overboard?

Oh, dear God, he was going to punch creepy Carlos.

And Carlos looked terrified and triumphant at the same time. Although he was undoubtedly afraid, Evie had the strangest feeling that he was enjoying seeing the other man lose control. His expression was mocking rather than apologetic, as if the outcome had exceeded his most extravagant hopes.

Trying to make sense of it and failing, she could do nothing but watch as the drama unfolded in front of her. The two men appeared to have forgotten her existence. They faced each other down like two bulls fighting for territory, but there was no doubt in her mind who was the superior, both in strength and intellect.

While Carlos blustered and bumbled, Rio's anger was cold and a thousand times more frightening.

'If you have lost me this deal—'

'Me?' His voice contradicting the look in his eyes, Carlos sounded shocked. 'You think I had anything to do with this? You seriously think—? Rio, I know you don't need this sort of publicity right now—I know you're at a delicate stage of negotiations. This could ruin everything for you.'

Evie looked on in disbelief, trying to follow the thread of the conversation. This was all about some stupid deal? That was why Ruthless Rio was so angry? What had happened to everyone's priorities? All they thought about was money, money, money.

It was only because she had her eyes fixed on his taut profile that Evie saw the flash of raw emotion cross Rio Zaccarelli's face. For a moment she thought he was going to reach out and grab Carlos by the throat.

Instead, he released him.

'*Vai al diavolo.* Get out of my sight.' His voice was

strangely robotic, his features a mask of contempt. 'From this moment on, I don't know you. You don't work for me and I don't want to hear from you or see you again. Step into one of my hotels and I'll have you removed. My lawyers will sort out the details with you. And if this causes me trouble—if I lose—' He broke off, apparently unable to finish the sentence, his voice thickened with an emotion so much deeper than anger that Evie felt real fear.

How could he be so angry about one stupid deal?

She waited for Carlos to defend himself but the other man shot through the door without looking backwards.

Which, basically, left her alone with a madman.

Evie tightened her grip on the throw. She loathed Carlos, but at least he was a familiar face. If murder was about to be committed, then it might have been useful to have a witness. Or even an alternative victim.

The burly man, who she assumed was a bodyguard, flexed his fingers threateningly. 'Do you want me to deal with him, boss? I reckon I could get the information you want out of him in less than a minute. He's a wimp.'

Another wimp, Evie thought numbly. The world was populated by wimps. Wimps and bullies.

'Don't waste your time.' Rio's tone was ice-cold. 'I know a quicker way of extracting information.'

Realising that she was the 'quicker way', Evie took a step backwards, seriously scared.

'Calm down,' she stammered. 'Take a deep breath—count to ten—or maybe a hundred—' She had absolutely no idea what was going on, but it was obvious that she was in enormous trouble for sleeping in the Penthouse. 'I don't suppose there is any point in saying sorry or trying to explain, but honestly, I don't see that it's that big a deal. I know I did wrong, but I think you're overreacting—' She gulped as Rio Zaccarelli strode towards her.

He stripped off his jacket and threw it over the back of the nearest chair. His white silk shirt moulded to his wide, muscular shoulders, hinting at the power concealed beneath and Evie found herself staring in fascinated horror as he rolled the sleeves back in a deliberate movement. He looked like a boxer preparing for a fight. And she was obviously earmarked as the opponent. She wondered whether he'd removed his screamingly expensive jacket so that he didn't end up with her blood spattered on it.

His eyes dark with fury, he came to a halt right in front of her. 'Not a big deal? Either you are the most insensitive, selfish, greedy woman I've ever met or you have no idea of the magnitude of the trouble you've just caused.'

Up close, she could see the rough shadow that framed his hard jaw. She saw that his eyelashes were thick and dark and that underneath his fierce gaze there were dangerous shadows. Other women talked about his monumental sex appeal, but Evie was too scared to feel anything other than fear. 'I'm not selfish or greedy,' she defended herself in a shaky voice, 'and I honestly don't see that spending a night in that bed is such a big deal. I shouldn't have done it, but I thought the Penthouse was empty overnight. And I didn't even dirty the sheets. I slept on top of the covers.'

'Of course you slept on top of the covers,' he gritted. 'How else could the photographer have taken his picture?' He fisted his hand in the front of the throw and pulled her hard against him. Breathing heavily, the backs of his fingers pressed into her cleavage as he held her trapped.

Evie, who rarely felt intimidated by men because of her height, was definitely intimidated now.

For once she felt dwarfed, his superior height making her feel small and insignificant and she swiftly re-evaluated her belief that it would be nice to meet a man taller than her.

Through the mist of panic, her brain finally latched on to something he'd said.

'Photographer?' Trying to breathe, she stared up at him blankly. 'What photographer?'

His eyes dropped to her mouth and that single look weakened her knees. For a moment she saw what other women saw. Raw sex appeal. She might have been attracted to him herself if she hadn't been so terrified. Wondering if she was the only one who was feeling suffocated, she gasped as he suddenly released her. Her hands shot out to balance herself and the silk throw slid to the ground.

With a squeak of embarrassment, Evie made a grab for it but not before she'd seen the sudden darkening in his eyes and heard the burly security man gulp. 'I need to get dressed!' She'd hung her wet clothes on the heated towel rail in the bathroom, but they ought to be dry by now.

With a contemptuous sound, Rio Zaccarelli turned away from her. 'It's a little late for modesty, don't you think? By tomorrow, that photograph will be all over the world.'

'What photograph?' She wrapped the throw around her as tightly as she could. 'I have no idea what you're talking about.'

Rio gave a growl of anger. 'The photograph of us kissing. I want the name of the photographer and the name of the person who put you up to this. Start giving me facts.'

Evie glanced back towards the bedroom, retracing the events of the past few minutes. 'I…someone took a picture of me?'

A muscle flickered in his jaw. 'Generally, I pride myself on my control but today I seem to be falling short of my usual high standards. If you don't want to see a first-hand demonstration of the meaning of the word angry, then don't play stupid.'

'I'm not playing stupid! I didn't see a photographer. You were in my line of vision, remember? All I saw was you.'

Deep colour highlighted his cheekbones and his eyes

burned. 'Are you seriously expecting me to believe that you didn't see the light or the man running out of the room?'

Evie thought back, but all she could think about was how amazing it had felt to be kissed by him. She remembered warmth, the most incredible excitement, flashing lights—*flashing lights?*

Appalled, she stared at him and his mouth twisted in cynical derision.

'Memory returning?' He was so arrogantly sure of himself that Evie bristled and decided that there was no way she was confessing she'd thought the lights were part of the firework display set off in her body by his incredible kiss. His monumentally overinflated ego obviously didn't need any help from her.

'I didn't see him. As I said, you were blocking my view of the room.'

'Unfortunately, I wasn't blocking his view of you. He now has a picture of us—' his expression was grim as he watched her '—together.'

As the implications of his words sank home, Evie felt her limbs weaken. 'Hold on a moment. Are you telling me that some stranger just took a picture of me, naked on the bed?' Panic and horror rushed up inside her. She hated having her picture taken, even when she was fully clothed, but naked—?

'I've already warned you—I'm not in the mood.' There was no mistaking the deadly warning in his tone or the tension in his body language. He was a man no one was likely to mess with and Evie felt her mouth dry as her gaze clashed with pitch-black eyes.

'I'm not in the mood, either,' she squeaked. 'And I'm not playing games. How did a photographer get in here? Why would he want to take a photograph of me? What's he going to do with it?' Anxiety set her tongue loose but he silenced her with a single searing glance.

'If you utter one more ingenuous question I just might drop you naked on the street outside. How much did he pay you?'

Struggling to keep up with his thought process, Evie opened her mouth and closed it again. 'You honestly think anyone would pay to take a picture of my body? Are you mad?' Her voice rose. 'Presumably, you've already noticed that I'm not exactly a supermodel! The only way anyone would be interested in looking at me naked is one of those hideous before and after photos. You know—*"and this is Evie before she went on the wonder diet and lost twenty kilos."*'

His eyes blazed dark with incredulity. 'Is that all you can think about? Whether the photographer took your good side?'

'No, because I don't have a good side! I look the same from every angle, which is why I never let anyone take my photo!' She'd never before met a man she wanted to kiss and slap at the same time and it was such a shockingly confusing sensation that her head spun. She wanted to defend herself. She wanted to protest that she wasn't superficial and that having a photograph taken of her naked was right up there with her worst nightmares. It was like being back in the playground.

Evie the elephant—

'Wh…what's he going to do with that photograph?' She tried to calm herself down with logic and reason. This wasn't the playground. 'No one is going to want to look at a picture of me naked. There is no reason anyone would want to publish a picture of me…' as she stared into his taut, handsome face, her voice faded to a horrified whisper '…but there's every reason why they'd publish a picture of *you*.' And she was in that picture. Suddenly, everything was clear. She thought of all the vile, degrading 'kiss and tell' stories she'd read. 'Oh, my God—'

Rio was watching her, his mouth tight. 'How much did he pay you?'

'Nothing! I don't know anything about this! I'm as innocent as you are.' But she could tell he didn't believe her and
what she saw in those glittering black eyes was so terrifying
that she wanted to confess everything on the spot. Because
his expression was so scary, she looked at his mouth instead
and suddenly all she was thinking about was that scorching
kiss. *Where had he learned to kiss like that?*

'Innocent girls don't lie in wait, naked, on a guy's bed.'

'I wasn't lying in wait! How could you even think that? I've
been kicked out of my flat and I had nowhere to go last night
and—' Evie thought about the sequence of events. Carlos
had offered her the use of the room. When she'd refused,
he'd insisted. It was Carlos who had encouraged her to take
a shower and dry her wet clothes on the radiator. Appalled,
she looked up at Rio Zaccarelli and saw his mouth tighten
as he read her mind.

'Your face is very revealing, so don't even think of telling
me you have no idea what's going on.' The menacing chill in
his voice confirmed just how much trouble she was in and
she felt the colour drain out of her cheeks as he turned up
the pressure.

'I've been set up.'

A dangerous glint shone in his eyes. 'I'm listening.'

He didn't believe her. 'Carlos gave me instructions to
sleep here tonight—' Evie clutched at the silk throw, her
mind racing forward with possible scenarios, all of which
sickened her. No matter what she said, Rio Zaccarelli wasn't
going to believe that she had nothing to do with this. 'I was
really, really stupid—what are they going to do with that
photograph?'

For a moment he didn't answer. He simply stared at her,
as if he were making a decision about something. A slight
frown touched his brows and he strolled around her, looking at her from the front, the back and the sides. When he
finally spoke, his voice was hard. 'They're going to publish

it. By tomorrow, that photograph will be plastered all over the Internet and the newspapers.'

The bodyguard cleared his throat. 'Boss—'

Rio turned on him and said something in Italian that silenced the other man immediately.

Evie felt faint with horror. *'What?'* That was by far the worst scenario on her list and she gave a low moan of horror as she contemplated exactly what that would mean. 'I thought maybe they'd just use it to blackmail you or something—'

'Is that what they told you?' His tone was dangerously soft. 'Is that what you agreed?'

'No! I didn't agree anything. I was thinking aloud—' Flustered, realising that she was digging herself deeper and deeper into a hole, Evie sank her hand into her hair, trying to think straight so that she could be more articulate. 'What I mean is, at least if it's blackmail they could be persuaded not to publish it. Of all the things they could do with that photo, publishing it would be the worst. Do you have any idea how embarrassing that would be? I'd never be able to go anywhere ever again.'

'Embarrassing? Do you think I care about being embarrassed?' The lethal cocktail of physical height and powerful personality left her shaking and intimidated but all those emotions were eclipsed by the prospect of being exposed physically to the mocking eyes of the world.

'No, you probably don't care—' Evie's voice rose '—because *you're* not the one who was lying there naked with your bottom on full view! And stop trying to scare me! This whole thing is bad enough without having to wonder whether you're going to explode any minute.' She covered her face with her free hand—the other was still clutching the throw, holding it in place. 'Oh, my God—if that photo goes in the papers—everyone I know will see it—Grandpa will see it—he'll be mortified—' Melting with embarrassment, she looked at him helplessly. 'You *have* to do something. You have to stop it.

You're completely loaded—can't you pay them or something? Do whatever it is they want you to do.' The thought of being seen naked in public was the most hideous thing that had ever happened to her. Worse than being demoted. Worse than losing her job. Worse than being dumped by Jeff.

Evie cringed with horror as she tried to work out what angle the flash had come from and remember exactly how she'd been lying.

It took her right back to the nightmare days of hiding in the corner of the girls' changing rooms trying to wriggle into her gym kit with no one noticing.

'If you genuinely care, then perhaps you should have thought of the consequences before you agreed to lie on the bed.'

Evie ground her teeth. 'I lay on the bed because I didn't have anywhere else to lie, OK? I told you—I lost my flat. I was in a fix and when Carlos made that offer—' she licked her lips '—it just seemed too good to be true. Turned out it *was* too good to be true. Look, it doesn't really matter whether you believe me or not. What's important is stopping that photograph. *Please* pay them off.'

His gaze was steady. 'They don't want money.'

'Then what do they want?'

He turned away from her but not before she'd seen the dark shadow flicker across his face. 'They want to make my life…difficult.'

'What about *my* life?'

'They're not interested in you. You've played your part. You're expendable. I'm sure you can find some lucrative way to use your five minutes of fame.'

'Do you honestly think I want to be famous for the size of my bottom?'

'If you are genuinely distressed about the idea of being pictured, why did you agree to this?'

'Are you thick or something? *I didn't agree to it!*'

There was a crashing sound as the door to the suite burst open behind him and three uniformed hotel security men pounded into the room, horribly out of breath.

Evie suddenly wished she could vanish into thin air.

Rio took a slow, deliberate look at the watch on his wrist. 'I have been in this hotel for seventeen minutes,' he said in an icy tone, 'and no one has challenged me. That is sixteen and a half minutes too long. The security code for the Penthouse hasn't been changed since the last time I stayed here as a guest, which is presumably how a complete stranger managed to access the suite. The security camera at the rear entrance is pointed away from the street. A journalist managed to get access to my suite. Is this how you protect the guests in your care?'

Evie watched as Arnold's forehead grew shiny with sweat. The security chief was one of the few people who had been kind to her since she'd arrived in London and she felt a tiny flame of anger warm her insides as she saw him squirm.

'We didn't know you were arriving in the middle of the night, sir. We were expecting you later this morning and—' His jaw dropped as he saw Evie. 'Evie? What are you doing in the Penthouse?'

Evie tightened her grip on the silk bedspread. 'I had nowhere to sleep last night, Arnold—'

Rio's eyes narrowed. 'You know this woman?'

'Of course. Her name is Evie Anderson.' Arnold's expression softened. 'She works here as a receptionist—I mean, a member of the housekeeping staff.'

Evie was just beginning to hope that Arnold might vouch for her integrity when the door to the Penthouse opened again and a portly woman in her fifties arrived, breathless and flustered. It was obvious that she'd dressed in a hurry and her skirt was on back to front and the buttons on her shirt unaligned. Clearly woken from sleep, one half of her hair was flattened to her head and the other was in wild disarray.

Evie groaned in horror. *No.* How had Tina found out?

'Mr Zaccarelli—we were expecting you much later to-day—I'm so sorry no one was here to greet you—' Oozing deference, the woman's discomfiture was almost painful to watch. 'I'm Tina Hunter, Director of Guest Relations. We're going to do anything in our power to make sure your stay here is memorable.'

Tina's eyes widened with horror as she turned her head and saw Evie.

'*Evelyn? What do you think you're doing?*' She turned back to Rio, squirming with mortification. 'I'm *so* sorry. She's given us nothing but trouble, that girl—thinks she's better than the rest of us. It's my fault for giving her a second chance, but that's me all over. I've always been a soft touch. Evelyn, I want you to collect your things and go.'

Shocked by the injustice, Evie stared at her. 'You haven't even asked for my side of the story.'

Tina's cheeks turned scarlet. 'You're naked in a guest's bedroom. That's enough for me. Let me just say that I find it incredibly tacky that you would try and force yourself on a billionaire.'

'Excuse me?' Almost speechless with outrage, Evie exploded. 'Look at the guy! Even if I wanted to, I'm hardly likely to be able to force myself on him, am I? He's built like a—' Her voice tailed off and colour poured into her cheeks.

Tina was shaking with anger. 'Get your things.'

'I don't have any things. Everything I owned was in a bag and I left it in the basement. Carlos was supposed to arrange for it to be brought up here so that I could change into dry clothes. Funnily enough, it never appeared.' Evie scraped a strand of hair behind her ear with a hand that shook, afraid that this was going to be the moment that she finally lost it.

She felt tears scald the back of her eyes as she made a last-ditch attempt to extricate herself. 'Carlos ordered me to sleep here last night, not that I expect any of you to believe me.'

'Of course we don't believe you!' Tina exploded. 'Why would the Manager of this hotel give a member of the house-keeping staff permission to spend the night in the Penthouse? A room that costs twelve thousand pounds a night.'

Evie paled. 'How much? That's outrageous.'

'What's outrageous is you standing there behaving like Lady Godiva. You need to find yourself another job, young lady. Since you're so free with your body, I'm sure there are no end of options open to you if you're seeking new employment,' Tina snapped. 'And don't look so shocked. You're standing there half naked, so this "I'm an innocent girl from the country" act is wearing a little thin. You may look wholesome, but I think we all know different. Why do you think I moved you off Reception? We had such a crowd around the desk, the hotel almost ground to a standstill.'

'I was being friendly! You told me I was the public face of the hotel and I assumed you'd want that face to be smiling, not miserable! You're *so* unfair—it's Christmas and there's not a single drop of Christmas spirit or compassion in any of you. And I'm naked because my clothes were wet, not because I want a career as a porn star.'

Tina pointed towards the door. 'You're fired. Get out.'

'What, dressed like this?' Evie gaped at her. 'No way! This is the throw from the bed and I'm not giving you reason to sue me for theft on top of everything else, not to mention indecent exposure as I trail along the corridors. I think you're all vile. None of this is my fault, but I'm going to be the one who suffers. I'll get dressed and then I'll leave and I hope you all have a really Happy Christmas!' Thinking of her grandfather's reaction when he saw the photograph of her naked and kissing a stranger, Evie gave a strangled moan and shot into the only room with a lock on the door.

* * *

Wholesome—

Rio stared at the locked door, his mind moving faster than the speed of sound as he swiftly formulated a plan that could turn this situation to his advantage.

Square-jawed, purple in the face, Tina turned to the security men with the purpose of an army commander preparing for a forward push. 'She's locked herself in. Open that door and escort her off the premises. We'll do what we can to keep this out of the papers.'

Rio roused himself. Fired by the challenge, always at his best under pressure, he took control.

'Out,' he ordered harshly, striding towards the door of the suite and holding it open. 'All of you. Now.'

They all looked at each other and Rio gave a smile that shifted the atmosphere from one of tension to one of terror.

'Organise a staff meeting for one o'clock this afternoon.' Like a laser-guided weapon locking on his target, he transferred his gaze to the security chief. 'At that meeting I want the name of the person responsible for the fact that the security cameras in the street were pointing the wrong way. I want a report on how security at the hotel can be upgraded so that I have a guarantee that any intruder entering this building will be challenged within thirty seconds of entering the premises—'

'But this is a hotel, sir; people come and go—'

'If you're not up to the job, just say so, and I'll replace you with someone who is. My personal security team will assist you in preparing the report, if you wish to stay.'

Arnold quailed under that icy stare and Rio continued.

'It's your job to differentiate between guest, gawker and criminal. That's the job I pay you to perform. And you—' Rio shifted his gaze to Tina. 'You're fired.'

Tina gaped at him, her jaw slack, her unmade-up face an unflattering shade of scarlet. 'You can't just fire me—'

'I own this hotel. I can do anything I like.'

'You have no grounds—'

'Bullying and staff intimidation are grounds enough in my book,' Rio said coldly, 'and that's just the beginning. I have a full report on my desk, which includes recommendations on staffing. Your name appears on almost every page. Do you want me to go on?'

Tina gulped and opened her mouth but no sound came out.

Without a flicker of expression on his face, Rio opened the door wider. 'That's it,' he said pleasantly. 'You can go now. And on your way out ask someone to come and remove this Christmas tree. While I'm staying here, I don't want to know it's Christmas. Am I understood? No baubles, no berries, no tree, no tinsel.'

One by one, they shot past him and Tina paused, clearly panicking about her future. 'What about Evelyn? She's the cause of all this. She should be removed from the premises.'

Rio, who had been rapidly formulating a backup strategy since 'whiter than white' had exploded into the ether, sent her a look that had her scurrying out of the door.

Strolling back to the bathroom, he stared with brooding concentration at the closed door.

Wholesome.

The problem might just turn out to be the solution, he mused.

'All right, Sleeping Beauty. I've slain your dragon. You can come out now.'

CHAPTER THREE

He'd fired Tina!

With her ear pressed to the smooth wood of the door, Evie listened with her mouth open, unable to believe what she was hearing.

Afraid to make a sound in case he realised she'd been eavesdropping, she tiptoed away from the door and leaned her burning cheek against the cool marble wall of the bathroom, her knees weak and shaking.

He'd seen right through Tina and fired her on the spot. Obviously, the rumours about him being super-bright were true. All right, so he was ruthless and wasn't afraid to axe jobs, but still—maybe he wasn't so bad…

Still in shock, Evie let out a long breath. She felt as though she should feel sorry for Tina, but it was hard to feel sorry for someone who created an atmosphere of intimidation. She remembered the threats, both spoken and unspoken, the way she transformed confident staff into doubting, apologetic wrecks. Since her demotion to housekeeping, Evie had mopped up more tears than she had floors.

Had he heard the rumours? Was that what he'd meant by seeing Tina's name on every page of his report?

Who else was on his list to be fired?

Realising that she had to be right at the top, Evie closed her eyes.

There was no doubt in her mind that she was going to be next and she didn't even care any more. All she cared about was that stupid, horrid photograph. Perhaps she ought to ring Cedar Court and ask the staff to make sure that her grandfather didn't see any newspapers or television.

But her grandfather loved his newspaper. He did the crossword every day.

If they banned it, he'd just want to know why.

Hyperventilating again, Evie clutched the edge of the washbasin and forced herself to breathe steadily.

She'd thought life couldn't get much worse, but suddenly it was a million times more disastrous.

Her grandfather would panic if he knew she'd lost her job and had nowhere to live, but it was nothing to what he'd do when he saw pictures of her naked and kissing a stranger. She could just imagine what Mrs Fitzwilliam would make of that. *I hear your precious little Evie has turned into a bit of a goer—*

'You have ten seconds to come out of that bathroom.'

The deep male voice held sufficient authority to confirm all Evie's darkest suspicions about his intentions. He was obviously dealing with his problems with the brutal efficiency for which he was famed, and she was the next problem on his list. *The worst was still to come.*

She looked round desperately, searching for an escape. Apart from flushing herself down the toilet or trying to squeeze down the plughole, there was no way out of this bathroom.

Why, oh, why, had she taken up creepy Carlos's suggestion of sleeping in the Penthouse? Why hadn't she followed her initial instinct that it was a bad idea? And why had Rio Zaccarelli decided to arrive at the hotel early when the rest of London was asleep? The man obviously was a machine.

'Two seconds—' The hard, cold voice made her jump and Evie stared helplessly at the door, trying to think what to do.

She needed a plan. She needed to think what she could say that might help her situation.

While she was in here, she was safe. What could he do? He was hardly going to break the door down, was he?

There was a tremendous crash, the sound of wood splintering and Evie screamed as the door crashed open, slamming against the sleek limestone wall of the luxurious bathroom.

Rio Zaccarelli stood in the doorway rubbing his shoulder. 'What is the matter with the staff in this place? When I give you an order,' he thundered, 'I expect you to follow it. And I *don't* expect to have to demolish my hotel so that I can hold a conversation with one of my employees.'

Stunned that the door was still on its hinges, Evie gulped. 'I—you—are you *OK*? I mean—I've seen people crash through doors in the movies but I always assumed the door is made out of cardboard or something. I've never seen anyone actually do it with a real door. That must have hurt.' She looked at his powerful shoulders doubtfully, wondering whether all that muscle would act as a barrier to pain.

'*Sì*, it hurt.' He rolled his shoulder experimentally, checking for damage. 'Which is why, next time, I'd appreciate it if you'd just do as I say and open the damn door.'

Evie gave a choked laugh, clutching the silk throw against her. 'Why? So that you can fire me in person?'

'Who says I'm going to fire you?'

'You fired the tyrannosaurus.'

'Tyrannosaurus?' Still rubbing his shoulder, he frowned, his expression dark and menacing. 'I presume you're talking about that officious woman with the unfortunate hair. That's what you all call her?'

Evie froze. 'No, of course not,' she lied. 'We call her Tina.' *Or meat-eater, because she feasted on hotel staff for breakfast.*

'She didn't seem too impressed with you.'

'No.' It was impossible to argue with that. Utterly defeated,

Evie felt the last dregs of spirit drain out of her. What was the point in defending herself? It was over. 'I think it's fair to say I don't have an enormous number of supporters in high places.' Tina had demoted her. Carlos had tried to grope her and, when she'd rejected him and humiliated him, he'd set her up.

Thinking of her grandfather, Evie wondered whether it was worth begging Rio Zaccarelli to give her another chance. Gazing into those unsympathetic black eyes, she decided that it was a waste of breath. She doubted there was a gram of compassion anywhere in his muscle-packed frame.

'I have a big problem.' His deep voice slid over her nerve-endings like treacle and Evie snatched in a breath, shocked by the sudden heat that shot through her. Underneath the dangerously slippery silk throw, she was suddenly horribly conscious that she was still naked.

If ever there was a more uneven confrontation, this had to be it.

Everything about him suggested raw masculine power, from the dusky shadow of his jaw to the tiny scar that flawed the skin above his right eye.

A vision of Jeff's baby-smooth face flew into her head but Evie realised that to make comparisons between the two men would be nothing short of ridiculous. They had nothing in common. Nothing at all.

Rio Zaccarelli might have been dressed for a formal dinner, but the external trappings of sophistication didn't fool her for a moment. This man wasn't tame or civilised. He was hard and unyielding and he'd do whatever he needed to do to achieve what he wanted.

A real man.

Suffocated by the heat in the air, her limbs suddenly felt heavy and her heart hammered against her ribs. Her instincts were telling her to run, but she couldn't move.

She tried to conjure up an image of Jeff's face again but

found that she couldn't. Instead, her mind was filled with a vision of burnished skin and eyes full of sexual promise.

To make matters worse, two walls of the opulent bathroom were mirrored, which meant that his iron-hard physique was reproduced several times over, dominating her vision.

Seriously unsettled, Evie clutched at the throw. 'If you'd give me five minutes privacy, I'll get dressed.'

'You own clothes?'

'Of course I own clothes! They're drying on the—' Evie turned her head and her eyes widened. 'I left them right there—on the radiator. They're gone.' Her mind explored possible explanations and came up with only one. Feeling the panic rise again, she looked at him and he lifted an eyebrow in weary mockery.

'They walked out of the room under their own steam?'

'Forget it.' Her voice choked, Evie lifted her hand like a stop sign. 'I've had enough of this! There's no point in me saying anything because you're not going to believe me anyway.'

'Strangely enough, you're wrong.' His tone was grim. 'I'm guessing that Carlos had something to do with the mysterious disappearance of your clothes. Am I right?'

Evie lowered her hand slowly. 'H-how do you know that?'

'Because he invited you to stay in the Penthouse and I doubt he did that out of generosity of spirit.'

Relief spurted through her veins. 'I didn't think you believed me—'

'I never thought you acted alone. Now it's all slotting together—' A muscle flickered in his cheek and he muttered something in Italian under his breath.

Evie was rigid with tension. 'I didn't know what was going on. I still don't, but it doesn't really matter. I just want to get out of here. If someone could lend me some clothes, I can go.'

'You're not going anywhere.'

Her heart rate increased. 'If that whole naked photograph thing was a set up then the best thing is surely for me to get as far away from here as possible. I'll go somewhere no one can find me.'

He started to laugh, but there was no trace of humour in the rich masculine sound. It was loaded with cynicism and derision. 'Are you really that naive? The press can find anyone.'

That news shook Evie. 'But why would they want to? I'm no one.'

'Perhaps you were "no one" before you chose to lie naked on my bed with me, but now you're a person of extreme interest.'

'I wasn't *with* you.'

'Yes, you were.'

'Well, that part was your fault. You were the one who kissed me and, quite frankly, I have no idea why you did that.' And she wished he hadn't because, in the midst of this crisis, those feelings kept rushing back to torture her.

His mouth, moving over hers with erotic purpose.

'None of this is my responsibility. You were the one lying there naked.' He issued that statement with such arrogance that Evie simply gaped at him, wondering how it was possible to be terrified of someone and turned on at the same time.

'And that means what? That you kiss every naked woman you see?'

'Normally, the woman gets naked *after* I kiss her,' he drawled. 'That's the usual order of things. Despite the lengths some women go to attract my attention, no one has ever gone quite as far as stripping naked and lying on my bed. That was a first.'

'I thought we'd established that I was set up!' Evie's voice rose. 'If I'd known you were going to arrive early, do you honestly think I would have been lying there?'

'Yes. That photograph will sell for a fortune.'

'Maybe it will, but it won't be me making the fortune,' Evie snapped, stalking out of the bathroom with the throw trailing behind her like a wedding gown.

'Where do you think you're going?'

'Out of here. I'm sick of seeing your reflection in the mirrors. One of you is bad enough. Ten is more than I can take. I'm going to ring Housekeeping and get them to send up a uniform and then I'm going to go and hide somewhere even the press can't find me.'

'Running is *not* the way to handle this.'

'Well, if you can think of a different plan, I'd love to hear it. This is easy for you. You have bodyguards and you own tall buildings with fancy security. All you have to do is lock yourself in your gilded palace until the fuss dies down, but I have to live with the fact that photograph is out there. Everyone who wants a laugh can look at it. They'll probably start a Facebook page for it—*The biggest bottom in the world.*' Evie tripped on the throw and stumbled. Steadying herself, she blinked back tears. 'I have to live with the fact that my eighty-six-year-old grandfather is going to see me with my naked bottom in the air, kissing a stranger! If he has another one of his turns it will be *all* your fault.'

'Which is going to shock him most? Seeing your naked bottom, or the fact that you're kissing a stranger?'

Evie snatched the phone up. 'You're not even funny.'

'Do I look as though I'm laughing? You have *no idea* how serious this is for me. For you, it's embarrassing; for me, it's—' He broke off, his voice unsteady and Evie paused with the handset in her hand, transfixed by the raw emotion she saw in his eyes.

'For you it's what? A deal you don't want to lose? Is this an ego thing? It has to be because you clearly don't care about the embarrassment and I can't honestly believe you'd be making this much fuss about money. I mean, it's not as if you don't already have plenty!' When he didn't answer, she gave a humourless laugh. 'Oh, forget it. I don't know why I'm expecting you to care any more than Carlos cared. Why does it matter to you that one more woman's reputation is shattered? I'm just another notch on your bedpost.'

'I do not make notches on my bedpost,' he said thickly. 'I am very choosy about my relationships.'

And he wouldn't be choosing a woman like her. Evie turned scarlet and stabbed the number for Housekeeping. 'Hello? Margaret? I'm really sorry to bother you, but could you possibly deliver a fresh housekeeping uniform to the Penthouse, please. I've…spilled something…sorry?' She blushed and turned her head away, lowering her voice. 'Size twelve…I said size twelve…I'm not whispering—' She gave a gasp as the phone was removed from her fingers.

'She said size twelve,' Rio drawled, 'and, while you're at it, send some underwear and shoes. She takes a—' his gaze slid to her cleavage '—thirty-four DD and her feet are—' He lifted an eyebrow in Evie's direction.

'Forty,' she said faintly and he delivered that information in the same commanding tone and ended the call. Then he answered his mobile, which was buzzing in his pocket and spoke at length in Italian, leaving Evie standing with a scarlet face, still trying to work out how he'd been able to guess her bra size so accurately.

He was still in mid-conversation when there was another buzzing sound and he drew his BlackBerry out of a different pocket without breaking conversation.

Evie watched in disbelief as he talked into one phone while emailing from the other.

'Sì—Sì—Ciao.' He ended the conversation and frowned at her. 'Why are you staring?'

'How many phones do you have?'

'Three. It makes me more efficient.'

'What happens if they ring at the same time? Most men aren't that good at multi-tasking.'

He gave a cool smile. 'I'm not most men. And I'm excellent at multi-tasking.' As if to test that theory, two of his three phones rang simultaneously and Evie moved to the window as he dealt swiftly with one call and then the other.

It was still dark outside, but the roads far beneath her were already busy as cars and taxis inched their way over snowy streets.

She leaned her cheek against the glass, watching people carrying on with their lives, wishing she could swap with them. Or put the clock back. She wished she'd never spent the night in the Penthouse.

Her eyes stung with tears and she blinked rapidly, determined not to cry. It was just because she was tired, she told herself fiercely.

What should she do? She couldn't decide whether it was better to ring her grandfather and warn him that he might see some very embarrassing pictures of her in the press, or say nothing and just hope that he didn't read that page in the paper.

But someone was bound to point it out, weren't they? She never ceased to be depressed by the enjoyment some people took from watching another's misfortune.

'Move away from the windows. Your clothes have arrived—you can change in the bedroom.'

Evie turned, wondering how her colleagues in Housekeeping had managed to produce underwear and shoes so quickly. Then she looked at the elegant packaging on the boxes and realised they'd simply used the expensive store in the hotel foyer.

'I can't afford to pay for those.'

He looked at her with ill-disguised impatience. 'The price tag on your bra is surely the least of our worries at the moment.'

'To you, maybe, but that's because you don't have to worry about money,' Evie said stubbornly. 'I do. Particularly as I appear to have just lost my job.'

The phone rang in his pocket again but this time he ignored it. 'Get dressed. Consider the clothes a gift.'

'I can't accept a gift of underwear from you. It wouldn't be right.'

'In that case, think of them as an essential part of our crisis management programme. The longer you continue to walk around naked, the more likely we are to find ourselves in even hotter water.'

He had a point.

Opening one of the boxes, Evie spotted a silky leopard-print bra and panties and crushed the lid back down, her face scarlet. 'I can't wear something like that.' Hardly daring to look, she prised the lid off the other box and her eyes widened when she saw the contents. 'I can't wear those, either—'

'Why not? They're shoes. I realize they're not strictly uniform, but they will do until we can get you something else.'

'But—' She stared down at the sexy shoe with the wicked heel. It was the most beautiful, extravagant, indulgent thing she'd ever seen. 'I don't wear heels. I can't.'

'You don't have to walk far in them.'

'It isn't the walking.' Her face was almost the same shade of scarlet as the sole of the famous shoes. 'You may not have noticed, but I'm already taller than the average woman. If I wear heels, I look like a freak. Everyone will stare.'

'After last night, they're going to be staring anyway. They'll stare harder and longer if you're barefoot. Put them on.' Without giving her the opportunity to argue, he turned back to the phone, leaving Evie to stare at him in exasperation, wondering what day it was. Had December nineteenth been designated Humiliate Evie Day and someone had forgotten to tell her?

Juggling the throw with the boxes, she struggled into the master bedroom and closed the doors. At least she wouldn't be naked.

Feeling relieved to finally ditch the throw, Evie slung it back on the bed and slithered into the underwear. It fitted perfectly. Then she pushed her feet into the shoes, almost losing her balance as she teetered precariously on the vertiginous heels. She felt like a circus performer practising on stilts.

Risking a look in the mirror, she gave a moan of horror.

She *looked* like a circus performer.

She looked like a giant.

She was about to take them off when the door to the bedroom opened.

Rio's gaze swept her from head to foot.

'*Maledizione*—' His eyes went dark with shock and Evie wanted to fall through the floor as she intercepted his look of stunned astonishment.

Embarrassment got her moving. 'Get out,' she shrieked, grabbing the throw again. 'I'm getting changed.'

'Does the phrase "shutting the stable door after the horse has bolted" mean anything to you? I've already seen you naked.' Displaying not the slightest consideration for her feelings, he allowed his gaze to travel slowly down every centimetre of her body. 'I've never seen a woman who looks like you.'

For Evie, already sensitive about her looks, his comment delivered the final blow to her crumbling self-esteem.

'It's your fault for getting me those stupid shoes when anyone with half a brain could have guessed they'd make me look ridiculous. And that's before I put on the uniform. I always wear flats, OK? Ballet pumps. Court shoes with no heel. Get out of here! I'm fed up with being a laughing stock, although I suppose I ought to get used to it because it's nothing to how I'm going to feel tomorrow when that photo is published—' Pushed to the limit, she flopped onto the bed, buried her face in the pillow and sobbed her heart out.

Everyone was going to see her naked and her grandfather was going to be horribly, hideously ashamed of her. She'd wanted to make him proud, but the truth was all he really wanted was to bounce a great-grandchild on his knee and that was never going to happen.

She was a big, fat disappointment.

Lost in the nightmare of the moment, she gasped in shock as strong hands closed over her shoulders and Rio flipped her onto her back.

'Stop crying!' He sounded exasperated. 'You'll make your eyes red and that could ruin everything.'

'Ruin what? Just go away. Stop mocking me.'

Astonishment lit his dark eyes. 'When have I ever mocked you?'

'You said you'd never seen anyone who l-looked like me,' Evie hiccuped, 'and I think it's horribly mean of you to poke fun at me, even if it is partly my fault we're in this mess. We're not all supermodels and wearing supermodel labels doesn't change that. I can push my feet into designer shoes just like Kate Moss but that doesn't give me Kate Moss's legs.'

'Which is a good thing,' he drawled, 'because Kate would find it extremely hard to strut her stuff on the runway if you had her legs. For the record, I wasn't mocking you. I was complimenting you.'

Evie, who had never been complimented on her looks in her life before, looked at him through eyelashes welded together with tears. 'Pardon?'

His jaw tensed. 'I find you attractive. Why the hell do you think I kissed you in the first place?'

'Because you have an abnormal sex drive and you can't resist anyone naked?'

'I have a healthy sex drive.' His dark gaze was unmistakably sexual. 'I *definitely* don't kiss women who try and pick me up. That's a first for me.'

'I wasn't trying to pick you up—' Still struggling to accept the unlikely fact that he actually did find her attractive, Evie sat up. 'You don't think I'm too tall?'

'Too tall for what?' That silky tone turned her insides into a quivering mass.

'For…a woman.' Evie licked her lips. 'I make most men feel small and insignificant. They usually don't want to stand next to me. But I guess you're pretty tall yourself.'

'Six four,' he breathed, his eyes scanning the length of her legs. 'And I've never had a problem with a woman's height.'

That was because he was unlikely to meet a woman taller than him, Evie thought weakly. 'Most people think I'm a freak.'

Without giving her a chance to argue, he scooped her off the bed and dumped her on her feet in front of the mirror. 'Look at yourself. Tell me what you see.'

Evie closed her eyes. 'I don't see anything.'

'*Look!*'

Evie flinched and opened one eye cautiously. 'Evie the elephant,' she said immediately and his brows met in an impatient frown.

'If that title is a throwback to your childhood, then you'd better let it go now. You're stunning and that gives us a major problem.'

Stunning?

Evie, who couldn't even for a single moment think why being considered stunning would present a major problem to anyone, looked at him dizzily. 'Even if that was true, which it isn't, I don't see how that could be a problem. How can being stunning be a problem? People judge by appearances. I've never been a member of the "oh, it's such a bore to be beautiful" camp.'

'It's a problem because you need to look wholesome.'

Evie was about to say that she'd been trying to escape from the 'wholesome' image for most of her life, when he took her hair in his hands and twisted it, assessing the effect with narrowed eyes. 'You have good skin.'

'And freckles.'

'Freckles are good. They suggest a healthy outdoor life. Wholesome.'

Why did he keep saying wholesome?

'I'm not with you—'

'Unfortunately, you *are* with me and that is why we have a problem.'

'We wouldn't have a problem if you hadn't kissed me.'

'I'm fully aware of that fact.' He paced over to the window, keeping his back to her. 'Get dressed.'

Wriggling into the housekeeper uniform, Evie stared at his broad shoulders. 'I don't understand why you're so stressed about this. You celebrities are always in the newspapers. You may be the reason they want that photo, but it's going to damage me far more than you.'

He turned, and the expression on his face was all it took to silence her. His eyes were haunted and there was a tension in his body that was unmistakably real.

'The damage to me could be incalculable,' he said coldly and Evie thought back to the exchange he'd had earlier with Carlos.

Whatever the 'deal' was, he was obviously prepared to stop at nothing to make sure it went through. It had to be about more than money, she thought. It had to be something to do with ego. Winning. The addictive quality of power.

'And creepy Carlos did this to you on purpose and I got caught in the middle, is that right?'

'So it would seem.'

She wondered what Carlos had against Rio Zaccarelli. What was he trying to achieve with that photograph? If it hadn't been her, would he have used someone else? 'If there is no way you can stop that photograph being published then I'd better make a phone call.'

His eyes narrowed. 'You're calling a lover?'

Evie gave a hysterical laugh. 'Oh, yes—I have loads of those—' Catching the dangerous gleam in his eyes, her laughter faded. 'Not a lover. I'm calling my grandfather, if you must know.'

Bold black eyebrows met in a fierce frown. 'How old are you?'

'Twenty-three, but, like most people of his generation, he doesn't believe in public displays of affection,' Evie said wearily, 'and he absolutely doesn't believe in one-night stands. Neither do I, for that matter.' She tried to sound casual, as if talking about sex was something she did all the time, rather than something she never did.

She stared at Rio Zaccarelli, the epitome of male sophistication, and felt her face grow scarlet.

Her grandfather definitely would have classed him as a real man.

It was the ultimate irony, she thought, to have been caught naked with him.

As if—

'So you don't have a lover at the moment.' His slumberous gaze rested on her mouth. 'That's good.'

'Well, that depends on where you're standing,' Evie muttered, wishing she wasn't standing quite so close to him. She was getting hotter and hotter. 'If you must know, I was supposed to be getting married yesterday but my fiancé dumped me. If that hadn't happened I'd be in Bali now, not London. I wouldn't have lost my job and my flat and generally had a completely awful six weeks and there might have been the smallest, remotest chance that my grandfather might be bouncing a baby on his knee next Christmas. As it is, there's no chance. None. I don't expect you to understand. You look like the sort of person whose life always goes according to plan.'

'My plan,' he said tightly, 'wasn't to find a strange woman lying naked in my bed. Fortunately, I've always considered adaptability to be an asset. I can turn this situation around.'

'You can?' Evie's gaze drifted to the neck of his shirt. Dark hairs tangled at the base of his throat and disappeared inside the snowy-white shirt. She imagined the hair hazing his chest and narrowing over his abdomen, which was no doubt as muscular as the rest of him. Shocked by her own thoughts, she lifted her eyes back to his and discovered that he was watching her with an unsettling degree of sexual interest.

'*Why* did he dump you?'

'Why does it matter?' *Was she supposed to read him a list?* Evie chewed the corner of her fingernail and then gave an embarrassed shrug. 'Because he met someone more exciting. Because I'm the girl next door and he's known me since I was three years old. Because I was taller than him and I made him feel less of a man—' She stared at him with exasperation, wondering why she was having to spell this out. 'Because I'm *me*. He sent me a text, dumping me.'

His lips thinned with disapproval. 'That's bad.'

'Hypocrite. Are you seriously trying to tell me you've never dumped a woman?'

'I wouldn't use the word "dumped". I've ended plenty of relationships, but always in person. I've never sent a text. That's cowardly.'

'I suppose it's human nature to avoid a difficult conversation.'

'Difficult conversations are part of my daily existence.'

Evie had no trouble believing that. 'Jeff is nothing like you.' A wimp, her grandfather had called him. 'Perhaps he was sensible. After all the lies he told, I would have blacked his eye if he'd told me in person.'

His eyes lingered on her hair. 'A true redhead with a temper to match.'

Reminded of the embarrassing fact that he knew she was a true redhead, Evie ploughed on. 'What this boils down to is that my grandfather isn't going to be impressed to see me naked with another man. He's very old-fashioned. I don't want him to think I'm like that. I'm *not* like that! I don't flit from one man to another.'

'Unless the other man was someone important to you.' Rio spoke under his breath and she had a feeling that he was thinking aloud.

That thought was confirmed when she muttered, 'Sorry?' and received no response.

'If it was someone you'd been secretly seeing. A rebound relationship that turned into something special—' He paced the length of the bedroom and then turned to look at her, his eyes burning dark. 'Wholesome.'

'You make me sound like a breakfast cereal,' she said irritably. 'Why do you keep saying that?'

'Never mind. How long ago did you start working here?'

'I don't know…I…'

'Think!'

'Don't shout at me! I can't concentrate when people shout!'

Rio sucked in a breath. 'I'm *not* shouting. I just want an answer. When?'

'About six weeks ago. I came down after Jeff dumped me. I started as a receptionist. I thought it was my big break.'

'Six weeks—' Before the words had left his lips, his BlackBerry was in his hand and he was checking something. 'I was staying in the Penthouse six weeks ago. I spent one night here on my way to New York. I need you to find out if you were working here then.'

'I know I was because I made a point of avoiding you. So

what? What difference does that make?' Failing to follow his train of thought, Evie looked at him blankly but he was already dialling a number and speaking into his phone in Italian.

He made call after call and each time Evie opened her mouth to ask him what was going on, he simply lifted his hand to silence her until she was ready to scream with exasperation.

'Hello, I'm here too!' After his seventh consecutive phone call, she waved at him. 'I need to ring my grandfather.'

'First, I want to get this announcement into the press and arrange a photo.'

'What announcement? What photo?' Worried, irritable, Evie snapped at him. 'Haven't we had enough photos for one day?'

He gave a lethal smile. 'This photograph will be different.'

'Different as in I get to wear clothes? Yippee.' She didn't know how she was still managing to joke because she'd never felt less like joking about anything in her life.

She knew enough about the press to understand that scandal and humiliation sold better than anything else. 'Can't you just stop them printing the photograph? Isn't there a privacy law or something?'

'That isn't going to help us. The best thing we can do is stop this whole thing looking sleazy.' Ruthlessly focused, he strode towards the door of the Penthouse. 'Stay out of sight. Whatever you do, don't emerge from the bedroom until I come and get you. I don't want anyone to see you.'

'Why? What are you going to do?'

'Find you some proper clothes and then show the world we didn't have a one-night stand.'

Bemused, Evie stared at him. 'How?'

'By proving that we share something special.' A triumphant gleam in his eyes, he yanked open the door and turned to look at her. 'I'm going to announce our engagement.'

CHAPTER FOUR

Rio gave his Director of Communications a volley of instructions over the phone and then updated his lawyers.

Listening to Pietro's dire predictions, he felt his stomach clench.

Whiter than white….

He should have anticipated this.

He should have known they'd do something to try and stop this deal going through. He'd been arrogant, allowing himself to relax and think that the whole thing was in the bag.

Sweat cooled his brow and he realised that his hand was shaking. Making a conscious effort to control his breathing, he hauled his emotions back and buried them deep. Emotions had no place in negotiation, he knew that. And this was the most complex, delicate negotiation he'd ever conducted.

'Whatever it takes,' he promised his lawyer. 'You wanted wholesome—I'm giving you wholesome.'

When the delivery arrived at the Penthouse, he dismissed the staff member and took the boxes through to the bedroom himself. He then handed them to the girl without breaking off his conversation and without risking another look at her luxuriant red hair.

Why the hell had he kissed her?

He was well aware that his own libido had catapulted him into this situation. If he'd taken one look at her and left the room, the photographer wouldn't have been able to get his shot.

As it was…

With a low growl, Rio focused his mind on the present.

Having hammered out the plan with his team in Rome, he was about to call his team in New York when he heard the bedroom door open.

The girl stood there, her eyes blazing with anger, her hair flowing like liquid fire down her back. 'Excuse me! In case you've forgotten, this affects me, too. Do you intend to discuss any of this with me or are you just going to do your own thing?'

'I don't problem solve by committee.' Congratulating himself on his brief to the stylist, Rio scanned the discreet, elegant dress with satisfaction. It was perfect. She managed to look wholesome and sexy at the same time. *This could just work.* 'I'm busy sorting out our problem right now.'

'No, Mr Zaccarelli, you're sorting out *your* problem—I'm incidental. You haven't once asked what I want to do about this mess which, by the way, is ultimately the fault of you and your stupid, slimy hotel manager, who can't keep his hands to himself.' She stalked across to him and shoved the redundant housekeeper uniform into his hands while Rio dissected that sentence into its relative parts.

'What do you mean, he "can't keep his hands to himself"? Are you saying he touched you?' Astonished by the sudden explosion of anger that was released by that unexpected revelation, Rio was suddenly glad he'd fired Carlos on the spot. His voice cold, he probed for the details. 'Did you report him for sexual harassment?'

'No. I broke his finger.'

'You *broke* his finger?'

'My grandfather taught unarmed combat during the war. He taught me self-defence.'

Distracted by that unexpected confession, Rio looked at her in a new light. 'I'll remember that.'

'You should. But, to repeat, you're not solving *our* problem, Mr Zaccarelli, you're solving *your* problem.'

'Call me Rio. I think we moved on to the first name stage about an hour ago. And, if it weren't for you, we wouldn't have a problem.' His observation appeared to act as fuel to her already happily burning temper.

'If creepy Carlos hadn't used me, then he would have used someone else and frankly I wish he had because then I wouldn't be in this mess.' She paced the room, trying to work off her stress.

Watching all that fabulous hair ripple down her back, Rio fought the urge to flatten her against the nearest hard surface and conduct in-depth research into the impact of extremely long legs on the enhancement of sexual pleasure.

He had no idea what her true role had been in what he now recognised as a final desperate attempt to stop this deal going through. Maybe she *was* innocent. Maybe she wasn't. Either way, she was the means by which he was going to extract himself from the catastrophic mess he now found himself in.

The upside of his plan was that he didn't need to struggle to keep his hands off her. In fact, the more hands the better.

He was slightly puzzled by her lack of confidence. Accustomed to women so narcissistic that they used every reflective surface to admire themselves, it came as a shock to discover one who didn't seem to spend her time in endless self-admiration. When she'd confessed that men found her too tall it had been on the tip of his tongue to point out that height was irrelevant when you were horizontal, but he'd managed not to voice that thought aloud. Rio wondered whether it would count as a charitable act to demonstrate just how well those endless legs of hers would wrap around his waist.

'You look perfect in that dress.'

'I look like a politician or something.' Keeping her back to him, she paced towards the window and Rio frowned.

'Don't go near the windows.' His clipped command earned him a challenging glance.

'Why? We're too high up for anyone to see.'

'In today's world of long lenses?' Watching her lose more colour from her face, he let the observation hang in the air. 'The next photograph they take of us will be when I'm ready and not before.'

'I don't want any more photographs taken!' But she moved away from the window, fiddling nervously with the fabric of her dress as she paced in the other direction. 'Look—this whole engagement thing is ridiculous. Can't you just stop that photo being printed?'

'No.' Rio recoiled from the sheen of tears he saw in her eyes. 'But I can stop it looking like a sleazy one-night stand. We're going to make people believe we're in a relationship— serious about each other.' Looking at her now, those high heels elongating her spectacular legs, he was even starting to believe it could work. No red-blooded male would question his interest.

'It's a really s-stupid plan.'

Rio, who had been congratulating himself on a truly genius idea, was insulted. 'It's an incredible plan.' His tone cooled. 'You're lucky I'm not currently involved with anyone.'

'Lucky?'

Rio dismissed thoughts of the Russian ballerina. 'It's unusual for me not to be in a relationship.'

'Well, I suppose that's one of the advantages of being filthy rich. Where there's money, there will always be women.'

Taken aback by that diminution of his qualities, Rio breathed deeply. 'Women are generally interested in more than my wallet.'

'How do you know? They're not going to tell you, are

they? And I don't suppose gold-diggers come with a warning hanging round their neck.'

'I can spot a gold-digger in the dark from a thousand paces.' He ignored the discordant image in his head that reminded him that on at least one occasion that statement had proven not to be true.

'Good for you.' Her slightly acidic tone matched her growing agitation. She explored the room, picking things up and putting them down again. First the vase on the table, then a notepad, then a remote control. She squinted down at it and pressed a button mindlessly and a gas fire flared to life behind a glass panel in the wall.

Swearing under his breath, Rio crossed the room and turned her to face him. 'I know you're anxious that they're going to print your photograph but, trust me, it will be fine providing people think we're together. This is the best way of dealing with it.'

'That's just your opinion.'

Rio, who had never before had his opinion dismissed, ground his teeth. 'If you have an alternative suggestion, then I'm listening.'

'No, you're not. You're pretending to listen while secretly thinking that you'll let me say my piece and then just do what you were planning to do all along, but it isn't going to work. I won't pretend to be engaged to you.'

Assuming that her reluctance was rooted in her insecurity, Rio sought to reassure her. 'By the time we've done something about your wardrobe, your nails and your hair, it will be easy to convince people that we are involved with each other.'

'Is that supposed to make me feel better?' She put the remote control down slowly and carefully, as if it were a potential murder weapon. *'You'll look fine, Evie, once I've turned you into something decent.* Is that what you're saying?'

Her tightly worded question triggered all the alarms in Rio's internal warning system.

'If this is going to be one of those, *Does my bottom look big in this?* conversations, then don't go there,' he warned, his tone thickened with frustration. The clock was ticking and her resistance was an obstacle he hadn't anticipated. Not for one moment had it entered his head that she'd be anything other than compliant. 'If you hadn't been lying naked on my bed, I would not have been tempted to kiss you,' Rio exploded with the tension that had been building since the photographer had chosen to elbow his way into his life. 'If you had worn clothes or at least slept under the covers—'

'If you had shown some self-control—'

Rio breathed deeply because that was a charge from which it was almost impossible to defend himself and that particular aspect of this whole seedy situation disturbed him far more than he was prepared to admit. He was always extremely careful with his liaisons and he never indulged in one-night stands. And yet where had his self-control been a few hours ago when he'd seen her lying on his bed? Not for the first time, he wondered what would have happened had the photographer paused before taking his photograph. *How much more revealing and incriminating would a later picture have been?*

'There is no point in dwelling on what is done,' he said tautly, 'and the truth is that a photograph of you naked in that bed was all that was needed. The rest would have been easily created from association and artistic use of Photoshop.'

'You mean they would have manufactured a photograph of the two of us together?'

'Photography software is increasingly sophisticated and you *were* in my bedroom. Stop throwing out obstacles when the solution I'm proposing is in both our interests. Your reputation stays intact. You mentioned that you have nowhere to live—I'm offering you somewhere to live. You get to stay here, in the most highly prized hotel suite in London. Anything you want, you can have. Most women in your position would be extremely excited at the prospect of an all expenses paid holiday complete with shopping.'

'Women are not a homogeneous breed, Mr Zaccarelli— we're individuals with individual tastes and needs. And why do you care so much about whether it looks like a one-night stand or something more? What is this deal you keep talking about?'

The question caught him off guard. For a brief moment he felt his control start to unravel. 'You don't need to know. Rest assured that I have a whole team of lawyers working night and day to make sure that it doesn't fall apart at the eleventh hour.'

'And if it does?'

A chill ran down his spine. 'It won't.'

'Providing I do as you say. I don't understand why this story could ruin it for you. Is this deal of yours with some old-fashioned guy who thinks you should have a blameless reputation or something?'

'Something like that.' Rio realised that his palms were sweating and he turned away from her, locking down his emotions with ruthless efficiency.

'So you'll do all this to win one deal? Money, money, money. Is that all that matters to you?' Increasingly agitated, she rubbed her hands down her arms. 'Well, I'm sorry if my decision loses you a few million, but I'm not prepared to do it.'

Back in control, Rio turned to look at her, sure that he must have misheard. 'Excuse me?'

'I won't do it. I'm just going to look more of a fool.' She covered her face with her hands and gave a moan of embarrassment. 'Every time I think about that photo being printed I just want to hide. Grandpa is never going to be able to hold his head up at senior poker ever again.'

Banking down his own frustration, Rio crossed the room. Gently, he pulled her hands away from her face. 'You are not going to hide. You are going to hold your head up high and look as though you are in love with me.' Appreciating the irony of his own words, he gave a faint smile and she instantly picked up on it.

'Don't tell me—usually you're telling women *not* to fall in love with you.'

'I'm not into serious relationships. They don't work for me. I'm not that kind of guy.' *Once, just once, and look where it had got him.*

'And I assume the public know that.'

'If you're worried that I won't be able to play my part, then don't be. I can be very convincing,' Rio assured her. 'The fact that I'm not usually serious about a woman will make this whole story all the more plausible.'

'And all the more embarrassing.'

Rio's jaw clenched and he spoke through his teeth, his patience severely tested. 'Are you saying it's embarrassing to be associated with me?'

'I'm saying it's going to be embarrassing when it ends. For all your so-called brilliant brain, you haven't thought this through. It's going to end—and then how will it look?'

'What does it matter?' Irritated to the point of explosion, Rio spread his hands in a gesture of exasperation. 'Relationships end all the time—it is a part of life. And that is surely a better option for you than having the world think you had a one night stand.'

'So basically I have two choices here—either I get to look like a big, fat slut or I get to be the only woman to be dumped twice in the space of months. Forgive me if I'm not jumping up and down with excitement at either option.'

'Relationships end. I still don't see the problem.'

Her eyes sparked. 'That's because you're only thinking

about yourself as usual. Not me. Have you ever been dumped, Mr Zaccarelli?'

'Rio.'

'Rio—' Using his name brought a flush to her cheeks. 'Has anyone ever told you they don't want to be with you any more?'

'No, of—' He caught himself and shrugged. 'No.'

'You were going to say *of course not*, weren't you?' She gave a disbelieving laugh. 'You are so monumentally arrogant and sure of yourself, but that explains why you can't understand my problem. You don't know what it's like to be rejected.'

'Given that this isn't a real relationship,' Rio said tightly, 'it wouldn't be a real rejection.'

'But if you're going to be as convincing as you say you are, then everyone is going to think it is! Six weeks ago my fiancé, a man I'd known since I was a child, called off our wedding—' She wrapped her arms around herself as if she were suddenly cold. 'Forgive me if I'm not rushing forward to embrace another public battering of my ego. It was bad enough the first time, having everyone feeling sorry for me. I couldn't even walk down the street without ten people saying they understood how hideously humiliated I must feel—this would be a thousand times worse. Only this time it wouldn't be just the village; it would be the whole world.'

'How would that be worse?' Genuinely baffled, struggling to understand, Rio stared at her. 'Why would you care what a bunch of strangers think?'

'I just would! I don't want loads of people I don't know discussing the fact that you dumped me. "Well, it's hardly surprising, is it?"' she parroted. '"I mean, what would a guy like him see in a girl like her?"'

'You'd rather they thought you'd had a sleazy one-night stand with me?'

She gulped. 'No. I'd rather they weren't talking about me at all. But I especially don't want them speculating on why I always get dumped.'

Aware that the clock was ticking and that they needed to get on with this if it was going to have any chance of working, Rio rubbed his hand over the back of his neck and applied his mind to a solution. 'I'll put out an announcement telling everyone you're a wonderful woman and that I have huge respect for you.'

She cringed. 'That would make people feel even *more* sorry for me.'

'I'll say that we will always be friends.'

'Which is basically like saying our relationship fizzled because you don't find me attractive.'

Trying to conceal his mounting exasperation, Rio inhaled deeply and offered up the only other solution that presented itself. 'If it's the dumping part that really worries you, then *you* can dump *me.*'

She stared at him. 'Sorry?'

'I'll allow you to dump me,' he said tightly. 'Problem solved.'

'That wouldn't work.'

'*Now* what? Why wouldn't it work?'

'Because you're rich and handsome. No one would believe it. Why would anyone in my position dump a man like you?'

'That's easy. I'm a total bastard,' Rio said immediately, relieved to be able to deal with that obstacle so simply. 'No one who knows me will have any trouble believing you kicked me out.' His confession drew a tiny smile from her.

'You're that bad?'

Transfixed by that smile, Rio couldn't look away from her mouth. 'I'm terrible. I'm dominating, I like everything my own way—basically I'm horribly selfish, inwardly focused,

I set myself a punishing schedule and frequently work an eighteen-hour day, which usually means that all I want to do when I'm with a woman is have sex.' *And he wanted to have sex with her, right here, right now.* It exasperated him to realise that, even in this most delicate of situations, he could barely keep his hands off her.

'You manage to fit sex into your punishing working day?' Her voice was faint. 'When?'

'Whenever I feel like it—' He was intrigued by the colour in her cheeks. 'So that's settled then. I'll do something awful—'

'You mean you'll behave the way you usually behave.'

'Something like that.' He acknowledged the barely veiled insult with a dismissive shrug. 'You'll dump me and, just to make sure it looks completely authentic, I'll go round looking moody for a few weeks.'

'So you admit to being selfish, inwardly focused and a total bastard, but no woman has ever dumped you. Why? What have you got going for you?'

Rio gave a slow, confident smile. 'If we're spending the foreseeable future together then you'll have time to discover the answer to that yourself.'

'If you're talking about sex, then you can forget it. Unlike you, I think sex should be part of a relationship.'

'So do I.'

She backed away. 'Yes, but the difference is that you don't want your relationships to go anywhere, and I do. Just so that there's no misunderstanding, I'm telling you now that I'll be sleeping in the second bedroom.'

Rio, who had his own ideas about where she'd be sleeping, decided to handle that issue later. 'So you'll do it? Good. And, when the time comes, you dump me.'

'I still don't see how we can convince them that we're together.'

'By being seen together,' he said smoothly, taking her

hand and hauling her against him. 'The first thing you need is a ring, so let's go. I'm about to buy you the biggest diamond you've ever seen.'

'I've never been in a chauffeur driven car. There's masses of room.' Evie stretched her legs out in front of her, aware that Rio was watching her with amusement.

'That's the general idea.'

'Why do you need so much room? You could have a party in here.'

'Not a party, but sometimes I do conduct business meetings in the car if I'm travelling short distances.'

'What happens for long distances?'

'I use my private jet.'

Evie gave a choked laugh. 'Private jet. Of course. This year's *must have* accessory. No serious tycoon should be seen without one.'

'Not an accessory,' he drawled, 'but a practical, money-saving tool.'

'Money-saving.' Evie nodded, struggling to keep her face straight as she slid her hand over the soft leather seat. 'Of course. I find the same thing. When I'm economizing, I turn down the heating and watch my food budget but I always make sure I leave the private jet well alone. As you say, it's such a practical, money-saving tool.'

'This may surprise you, but when you spend as many hours in the air as I do, that becomes a truth.'

As the gulf in their lifestyles opened up between them, Evie's smile faltered and she flopped back against the seat. 'This is ridiculous,' she muttered. 'It's never going to work. Give me one reason why a guy like you would ever be involved with a woman like me?'

'You have incredible legs.' He moved so quickly that she didn't anticipate it. Before she had time to respond, his hand was buried in her hair and his mouth descended on hers in a kiss that sent her brain spinning. 'I love the way you taste,' he murmured huskily and she gasped against his lips.

'OK, enough, you don't have to keep kissing me—' Seriously unsettled by the way he made her feel, Evie shoved at his chest, alarmed when he didn't budge. She'd always considered herself pretty strong for a woman but her violent push had no effect on him. 'It was kissing me that got us in this mess—'

'But now we're in this "mess", as you call it, we might as well enjoy it. They'll believe it, *tesoro,* once they see you.' He showed no inclination to stop what he was doing. 'You have amazing hair, fantastic breasts—'

Evie moaned as his mouth trailed along her jaw. 'Those are all physical things. That's just sex.'

'Never underestimate the power of sex. Sex is a very important part of a relationship.' One hand slid down her back to her bottom and Evie wriggled away, mortified.

'Don't do that—'

'Why not?'

'Well, for a start because someone might see you—'

His eyes gleamed into hers. 'And that would be a problem because—?'

Evie could hardly breathe. For a moment she'd forgotten that the whole objective of this charade was for people to see them. Confused, she wondered whether he was faking the attraction. But then she remembered the kiss that had started all this…

'Unless people have X-ray vision, they're not going to be able to see your hand on my bottom,' she croaked and he gave a wicked smile as he ran his fingers through her hair.

'Any red-blooded male glancing into this car will have a pretty accurate idea of the location of my missing hand.'

'You're not funny.' She'd barely thought about sex before she'd met him. Now she was finding it hard to think about anything else. Was he going to keep kissing her? Did he think she was made of stone? Embarrassed by the burning heat between her thighs, Evie pulled away from him and this time he released her, smiling slightly as he watched her shift to the furthest corner of her seat.

His whole attitude should have been enough to make her dislike him, but instead she found herself alarmingly turned on by the electric combination of smooth sophistication and command. It was humiliating, she thought, squirming in her seat, to find a man as basic as Rio so attractive. But evidently she wasn't the only one. After all, *he'd* never been dumped...

They were driving through the upmarket streets of Knightsbridge. The windows of Harrods, the world famous store, were decorated for Christmas and everywhere she looked there were rich-looking women wearing fur and dark glasses, stepping out of expensive-looking cars.

By the time Rio's driver pulled up outside an exclusive jewellers, Evie had lost all desire to be seen in public. Even in the smart outfit and sexy shoes, she didn't fit.

Two guards stood either side of the heavy glass door and, even from the protective cocoon of Rio's car, she could see that the few pieces on display in the window would have satisfied royalty.

Thoroughly intimidated, she thought about the tiny diamond that Jeff had given her when he'd proposed. At the time she'd thought it was small because they were saving for a deposit so that they could buy their own cottage. Now she realised it had been small because he'd been spending most of their shared savings on his other girlfriend.

She'd been a total idiot. But it was partly her fault, wasn't it? She and Jeff had grown up together. Everyone had assumed that one day they'd get married. Evie had told herself that the fact she felt no spark was because she wasn't a particularly passionate person. She'd assumed Jeff was the same.

And then she'd discovered what he'd been doing with Cindy, the librarian from the next village…

She stole a sideways glance at Rio, her gaze resting on his mouth, remembering the sizzling, steamy kiss. Sparks had been shooting all over the place.

And now she was expected to pretend they were in a relationship.

'You expect me to go in there? Why can't they come to us? In the movies you just pick up the phone and loads of jewellers come running to the hotel with a selection of rings.'

'In the movies, they're not trying to attract the interest of the paparazzi.' Rio leaned across her to undo her seat belt. 'If I'd ordered them to bring the rings to the hotel, it wouldn't have been anywhere near as loud a statement.'

Flattening herself to the seat, Evie stared at him, determined not to be impressed. 'I still don't understand how this is going to work. If the whole point of this is to get the paparazzi to take a photograph of us, shouldn't someone have called them and told them we're here?'

'No need. Wherever I go, you can find photographers.' Rio's tone was bored. 'It's part of my life, which means it's now part of your life. Get used to it.' As the driver opened the door Rio gestured for her to leave the car but Evie didn't budge.

'You mean there might be someone out there with a camera? Am I supposed to smile and wave?'

'You're not the Queen,' Rio said dryly. 'Just act normally.'

'But none of this is normal for me! I wouldn't find myself in front of rows of paparazzi,' Evie said irritably. 'I don't know what I'd do. Look over my shoulder, probably, to see who they were photographing because it certainly wouldn't be me. Unless they were taking snaps for a Miss Unbelievably Big Bottom contest.'

'If you mention your bottom again, I will be forced to strip you naked and examine it in detail,' Rio promised silkily and Evie exited the car faster than rum from a bottle.

Just as he'd predicted, a flashlight immediately exploded in her face and she would have stopped if he hadn't propelled her forwards through the doors that had been opened for him as soon as he'd stepped out of the car.

'I thought you wanted to be seen,' Evie hissed under her breath and he curved his hand around her waist and guided her into the exclusive store.

'I never talk to the press,' he purred. 'I never give interviews. I have no intention of altering that pattern. We want this to look as authentic as possible, remember?'

Exasperated, Evie stared up at him. 'How are they supposed to know we're engaged if you don't tell them?' Her face cleared. 'Oh—I get it. I'm supposed to strategically flash the ring on the way out.'

'We'll leave by the back entrance so that no one will see us. In the event that there is a photographer covering the rear of the building, you hide the ring. You put your left hand in your pocket so that no one can get the shot.'

'So we're buying a ring to convince them we're engaged, but we're not going to let them see it?'

'That's right.'

'Have you banged your head or something? You're not making sense.'

'I'm making perfect sense.'

'Not to me. If we go out of the back of the building it's going to look as though we don't want them to see us.'

'Exactly right.' He smiled at the manager who was hovering discreetly. 'Franco—'

'Signor Zaccarelli—' the man oozed deference '—it's good to see you again.'

'Again? How many women have you brought here?' Evie muttered under her breath, but the only indication that Rio had heard her was his vice-like grip on her hand. 'Squeeze any tighter and you'll break my fingers and then you won't get a ring over my knuckle.'

Rio released his grip and urged her forward. 'We need a diamond, Franco.' He glanced down at Evie, a smile on his lips. 'A very special diamond for a very special woman.'

Evie was about to tell him that his smooth talk wasn't the slightest bit convincing when he lowered his mouth and kissed her.

Somewhere in the distance, through the swirling clouds of desire that descended on her brain, she heard one of the sales assistants sigh with envy.

To her, it appeared completely staged but apparently Franco was convinced because he smiled, almost convulsing with delight as he led them through to a private room. 'A very special diamond. Of course. You've come to the right place.'

Evie sat there shell-shocked from the invasive pressure of his mouth, wishing they'd had a conversation about how they were going to play this. Had he said anything about kissing? And what was she supposed to do about the ring? Was she supposed to pick the least expensive one? Or maybe that didn't matter. Presumably a man who considered a private jet to be an 'economy' wouldn't care about the price of a diamond. Or maybe he was planning to ask for a refund when this was over.

She threw Rio an agonized look but he simply smiled. The fact that he was so relaxed simply added to her growing tension.

More aware than ever of the differences between them, Evie shifted uncomfortably and was about to say something when a slender girl entered the room carrying a box.

A hush fell over the room and Evie glanced around her, wondering what was going on. Why was everyone silent?

'It's the Apoletta diamond,' Franco told them in reverent

tones, taking the box from the girl and opening it himself. 'A thing of beauty and perfection, like your love.'

Evie was about to suggest that if the ring was supposed to be a manifestation of their relationship then a small lump of coal might be more appropriate, but one look at Rio's face stopped her. He was looking at her with such intensity that for a moment she stopped breathing and, during that one intimate glance, she made the unsettling discovery that she was as vulnerable to his particular brand of sexual magnetism as all the other women in the room. Even armed with his frank admission of his long list of deficiencies, she couldn't control the explosion of excitement that held her in its grip.

Rio ignored a question from Franco, his attention entirely on her. Then he slid his hand behind her neck and slowly but deliberately kissed her mouth, his lips lingering against hers for long enough to send her heart racing frantically out of control.

'Ti amo,' he said huskily and Evie, dazed by the look as much as the kiss, wondered what it would feel like if a man looked at you like that and meant it.

Without taking his eyes from hers, Rio removed the ring from its velvet nest and slid it onto her finger with cool, confident hands and an unmistakable sense of purpose.

Evie stared down at the incredible diamond, thinking about the sunny morning a few months earlier when Jeff had done the same thing. The ring Jeff had given her had been too big for her finger, whereas this one—'It's exactly the right size.'

'Like Cinderella,' one of the girls sighed and Evie frowned, wondering what was meant by that remark. Did she look as though she'd been cleaning the cellar in rags?

'She means that it's a perfect fit,' Rio said dryly, apparently developing a sudden ability to read her mind. 'And she's right. It's a perfect fit. We won't have to have it adjusted.'

Finding the fact that it fitted slightly spooky, Evie wondered whether it was a fluke or whether Rio was as skilled at guessing the size of her finger as he was her underwear and dress size.

Good guesswork or a man experienced with women?

Another girl entered the room. 'I just thought you should know that it's a media circus out the front.' She sounded apologetic. 'I have no idea how they discovered you were here. Someone must have tipped them off.'

Rio's jaw tightened and for a moment Evie genuinely believed he was annoyed.

'Do you have another entrance?'

'Yes, sir.'

He made a swift phone call and rose to his feet, drawing Evie close to him. 'My driver will meet us out the back. That way, no one should see us.'

Evie hurried alongside him, conscious of the strength of his fingers locked with hers as they were led towards the back of the store. 'Rio—' she hissed his name '—don't we have to pay or something? I don't want to set the alarms off and have to spend Christmas in custody, if it's all the same to you.'

He didn't slacken his stride. 'It's been dealt with.'

'How? Where?'

But he simply propelled her to the back of the store. Moments later, Rio's driver was speeding through the back streets of London's most exclusive area.

Evie flopped back against the seat, twisting the ring on her finger. She tilted her hand, admiring it from every angle, watching as it sparkled and glinted. 'I still don't understand why you went to all that trouble to buy a ring if you're not going to let anyone see it. You didn't even let them see you leave the shop.'

'They know I've left. The fact that I'm being secretive will make them more interested.'

'I hope you don't have an over-inflated idea of your own

importance. Otherwise, this whole idea is going to fall flat on its face.'

Rio's response to that was to hold out his phone. 'Call your grandfather.'

'What, now?' Evie had been putting off that moment and her stomach plummeted as she anticipated what her severe, principled grandfather would say about her current situation. 'What am I supposed to say? Hi, Grandpa, you may be seeing a picture of me naked in today's papers so I just wanted to tell you that I'm not starting a career as a glamour model—'

'It won't be in today's papers. It's too late for that. There's a strong chance it will make tomorrow's editions, but it may already be up on the Internet. Call.'

'My grandfather doesn't surf the Internet. He's eighty-six,' Evie squeaked but her observation merely earned her a lift of an eyebrow.

'What does his age have to do with anything?'

'You wouldn't be asking me that if you'd been to the Cedar Court Retirement Home. They celebrated when they got a decent TV picture. They probably think high speed broadband is another type of dressing for varicose veins.'

He didn't withdraw the phone. 'Call.'

'I can't.' Evie's voice was a whisper and she shrank back against the seat as she tried to delay the inevitable. 'This is the guy who took me on my first day at school. He taught me to ride a bike. He doesn't believe in holding hands or kissing in public. I'm all he has in the world and he thinks I'm a really decent, old-fashioned girl… In fact, I *am* a decent, old fashioned girl, or I was until I met you.'

'All the more reason to call him before he hears it from someone else.'

Running out of excuses, Evie took the phone reluctantly. Her hand shook as she keyed in the number. As she waited for him to answer, she pressed her fingers to the bridge of her nose and tried not to think about how disappointed her grandfather was going to be.

After all he'd done for her, after all his love and affection, he didn't deserve this...

'Grandpa? It's Evie...how are you doing?' Her voice sounded false to her and she wondered how long it would take her grandfather to pick up on the fact that something was wrong. 'Are you staying warm there in all this snow?' Maybe that was a good link, she thought desperately as she listened to his cheerful response—*I was a bit too warm, Grandpa, so I thought I'd take my clothes off...*

'No, nothing's wrong; I just thought I'd ring you for a chat.' Aware that Rio was watching her, Evie carried on making small talk about the weather and listening to her grandfather's observations about his friends. When he mentioned that he'd been boasting about her again to Mrs Fitzwilliam, two huge tears slipped from Evie's eyes and she covered her mouth with her hand.

With a sigh, Rio removed the phone from her. 'Mr Anderson? Rio Zaccarelli here—no, we haven't met, but I know your granddaughter—yes, I'm the same Zaccarelli that owns the hotel and spa chain—' he leaned back in his seat, not looking remotely discomfited by the prospect of dealing with what could only be described as a hideously awkward situation '—yes, it's still doing well, despite the economic climate—absolutely—' he smiled '—that's how I met Evie—'

Worried that Rio might actually say something that would make things even worse, Evie gulped down her tears and tried to grab the phone but he held it out of reach, laughing at something her grandfather had just said.

'I've already learned that to my cost—yes, she is—'

Evie frowned. 'I am what? What are you saying?'

Rio ignored her. 'I know about that. Yes, she told me. But his loss is my gain.'

Were they talking about her broken engagement? Evie covered her eyes with her hands, all too able to imagine what her grandfather was saying.

'Yes, a total loser—' Rio's voice became several shades cooler '—she's better off without him... No, not too badly—that's what we rang to tell you. We're engaged. I know it seems sudden but you can blame me for that—when I see something I want, I have to have it and I've never felt like this about a woman before.'

Evie peeped through her fingers and waited for Rio to pass the phone across so that she could receive a giant telling off from her strict grandfather. Instead, she heard laughter as Rio controlled the conversation.

'We wanted to warn you that there might be some revealing photographs in the press. My fault entirely—they follow me around, I'm afraid—' Rio's voice was smooth and he gave a slight smile in response to something her grandfather said. 'I agree—I've always said the same thing—that's right. No—no, she's fine—just a bit embarrassed because she's pretty shy about that sort of stuff... Yes, I know she's modest—' he shot her an ironic glance '—well, I have my lawyers onto it but if anyone mentions it to you, you can tell them the photographer was trespassing in a private room—yes, I'll hand you over—good to talk to you—look forward to meeting you in person—' Having moulded her rock-hard war veteran grandfather into the consistency of porridge, Rio handed her the phone, a smug expression on his face. 'He's delighted. He wants to congratulate you in person.'

Evie tentatively lifted the phone to her ear. 'Grandpa—?' She was unable to get a word in edgeways as her grandfather told her how delighted he was she'd finally met a real man and proceeded to spend the next five minutes extolling Rio's virtues, all of which appeared to centre around his ability to buck the market and grow his business, no matter what the economic challenges. The issue of the naked photograph appeared to have been absorbed along with all the other news.

Finally, her grandfather drew breath. 'Answer me one question—are you in love with him, Evie? That's all I want to know.'

Oh, dear God, how was she supposed to answer that? 'I—'

'It doesn't matter that a man is rich—what matters is whether there's strength and responsibility in his character. Rio Zaccarelli has all those qualities, but none of it matters if you don't love him.'

Talk about out of the frying pan into the fire. In order to stop her grandfather thinking she'd had a one-night stand, she'd gone along with Rio's idea but suddenly she was being sucked deeper and deeper into the charade.

Knowing her grandfather would worry, she gave the only answer she could. 'I love him, Grandpa.' She scowled as Rio raised his eyebrows, amusement shimmering in his black eyes. Doubtless he was so used to hearing besotted women say those words that he barely registered them.

Her grandfather sounded ecstatic. 'So it looks as though I might be bouncing that great-grandchild on my knee next Christmas after all.'

Great-grandchild?

Evie's mouth dropped in dismay. Somehow she'd gone from naked in bed, to engaged and then straight to pregnant!

How was she ever going to unravel this mess?

Hoping Rio hadn't overheard that particular part of the conversation, she lowered her head, allowing her hair to fall forward in a curtain, shielding her face. 'Well—let's just see how things go, Grandpa—no hurry—'

'Of course there's a hurry! I'm not getting any younger—'

'Don't say that. You know I hate it.' The thought of losing him horrified her and, when Evie finally ended the call, her hands were still shaking. Listening to her grandfather's animated voice had made her feel hideously guilty.

Oblivious to her mounting distress, Rio took the phone from her, smiling with satisfaction. 'That went well.'

She rounded on him, her eyes glistening with tears. '*That did not go well, Rio!* I just lied to my eighty-six-year-old grandfather. How do you think that makes me feel?'

'A great deal better than having to tell your eighty-six-year-old grandfather why you had a one-night stand with a man you'd never met before,' he said coldly. 'Calm down. If there happen to be any paparazzi around, I'd rather they didn't print the fact that we were having a row within ten minutes of putting the rock on your finger. Your grandfather was delighted to hear that we're together—a little surprised, perhaps, but basically pleased. I'm considered an incredible catch. You don't have anything to worry about.'

He reminded her of an armoured tank, forging forwards regardless of what was in his path. Her feelings were no more than blades of grass, easily squashed and ignored under the weight of his own driving sense of purpose.

When Rio Zaccarelli wanted something, he got it. And apparently he was willing to go to any lengths to secure this particular 'deal'.

'Why didn't I think this through? I've just raised his hopes and that's an awful thing to do.' Frantic, Evie reached for the phone again. 'I have to tell him the truth, now, before this whole thing escalates and he tells everyone I'm marrying a billionaire.'

'Leave it.'

'Rio, he thinks I'm going to get pregnant any moment! He wants to bounce his great-grandchild on his knee! I'm sorry, but I can't do this.'

But Rio had slipped the phone back into the inside pocket of his jacket. 'You agreed to the plan.'

'Because you railroaded me. I didn't have time to think it

through, but I can see now this is going to be really complicated and—'

'It's done. Too late.' With an infuriating lack of emotion,
he scanned the screen of his BlackBerry. 'The switchboard
at my corporate headquarters is jammed with journalists
seeking confirmation that I've just become engaged. The
story is out there.'

Her stomach lurched. 'And your people have confirmed
it?'

'They've said "no comment", which is as good as demanding that the press print an announcement. It's too late
to change your mind now. Stop panicking. Your grandfather
sounded fine about the whole thing. Tell me about Jeff.'

Evie tried to ignore the throbbing pain behind her eyes. 'I
don't want to talk about Jeff.'

'I'm not surprised.' Rio sprawled in his seat, texting with
astonishing speed and dexterity. 'He sounds like a total
loser.'

Evie stared at him in helpless disbelief. She wanted to
explain how worried she was about hurting her grandfather's
feelings, but she knew she was wasting her time. Rio Zaccarelli
didn't care about feelings, did he? All he cared about was
making sure his business proceeded unhindered.

'I really don't think I can go through with this.'

Rio watched her, a deadly gleam in his eyes. 'We made a
deal.'

'Yes.' Evie croaked the word, knowing that she was
trapped. If this was the only way to prevent that photograph
being published, then she had no choice.

Deals, deals, deals…

She'd made a deal with the devil. And now she was going
to pay.

CHAPTER FIVE

DRAGGING her aching limbs into the Penthouse suite, Evie toed off her shoes in relief and crumpled onto the rug. 'How does anyone walk in these things?' Staring up at the ceiling, she moved her toes gingerly. 'I feel as though both my legs have been chewed by a shark.'

'That is why you are lying on the floor?' Rio paused in mid-text, his eyes bright with incredulity. 'If you're tired, lie on the sofa.'

'I can't make it that far. I may never walk again.' Evie gave a long groan and flexed her sore feet. 'I bet you've never tried to squash your feet into a torture device before. Who invented heels? The Spanish Inquisition?'

Rio pocketed his phone, scooped her up and deposited her on the sofa.

'Oh—that's better.' Evie rolled on her side and closed her eyes, trying not to think about how his hands had felt on her skin. *How strong he was.*

'Most women find shopping a pleasurable pastime.'

'Yes, well, most women don't have to buy an entire wardrobe after just three hours sleep, and most women aren't shopping with *you*.' Yawning, Evie snuggled into the soft pile of cushions, twisting and turning to find a comfortable position. 'You said "no" so many times I thought that poor stylist person was going to throw herself out of the window.

I thought the objective was to have a high visibility shopping trip, not give some innocent woman a nervous breakdown.'

'I was trying to achieve a compromise between "wholesome" and "sexy", which proved to be something of a challenge.'

'Why do I have to look sexy?'

'Because it's important that you look like someone I'd date.'

Squashed flat by that comment, Evie curled up in a ball. 'Do you have any idea how insulting you are? Once in a while you could think about my feelings, otherwise I'm going to dump you long before this farce is supposed to end. And it doesn't really matter what the clothes look like, does it? It isn't as if we're going anywhere.' She glanced round the Penthouse, taking in the luxury. Something seemed different about the place, but she couldn't work out what. 'You won't even let me look out of the window in case someone takes my picture.'

'Astonishingly enough, I *am* thinking of you. It's precisely because we are going out that I expended all that time and effort in making sure you had an appropriate wardrobe,' he gritted. 'Tonight you're going to be walking down that red carpet with film stars and celebrities—I didn't want you to feel out of place.'

'Red carpet? What red carpet?' Evie shot upright. 'You didn't say anything about going out. I thought we were in hiding.'

'We were creating gossip and speculation which, by tonight, will have spread sufficiently to ensure that if that photograph appears it will be taken as confirmation that we are seriously involved.' Rio walked over to the desk and switched on his laptop. 'We have to be seen out together which, unfortunately, means that tonight we have to attend a film premiere and a charity ball.'

'Unfortunately? It's unfortunate that we have to attend a

film premiere and a charity ball?' Assuming he was joking, Evie started to laugh and then she saw the tension in his shoulders and the grim expression on his handsome face and realised that he was serious. He didn't want to go.

Her sudden excitement evaporated and she deflated like a balloon at a children's party. Her brain scanned all the possible reasons for his dark, forbidding scowl. 'You don't want to be seen with me.'

'*Obviously* I do,' he said tightly, 'given that it is the entire purpose of going.'

Evie sat with her back stiff, picking at her fingernails, telling herself that it was ridiculous to feel hurt by that comment. 'I understand that you feel you have to do it. But the reason you don't want to go is because you're embarrassed to be seen out with me.'

'I don't want to go because I'm incredibly busy at the moment.'

Something about the way he held himself told her that he was lying. Whatever was wrong, it had nothing to do with his workload. 'But we're going anyway?'

'Yes. We'll show our faces and then leave.' With a single tap of his finger, he brought a spreadsheet up on the screen. 'Wear the silver dress.'

Shimmering silver, Evie thought absently. *With swept-up hair.*

She should have felt thrilled but instead she felt the most crushing disappointment. 'What's the point of making a fuss if we're only going to stay five minutes?' The fact that he wasn't even looking at her increased her anger. 'It's hardly worth getting dressed, is it?'

'A brief visit is perfectly normal at these things. There is no point in wasting a whole evening when our purpose can be achieved in a short space of time.'

There was a tension in the room that she didn't understand. 'What if your purpose is to enjoy yourself?'

He was frowning at the screen. 'We're talking about a throng of people, none of whom have the slightest interest in anyone but themselves and their own self-advancement. As it happens, I have a very specific reason for going to this particular ball—I need to speak to Vladimir Yartsev.'

'Who is he?'

'Don't you read newspapers?'

Evie flushed. 'Sometimes. When I'm not working.'

'Vladimir Yartsev is a Russian oil oligarch. A very powerful man.'

'But not as powerful as you.'

A ghost of a smile touched his mouth. 'Different power.'

Evie curled her legs underneath her. 'Alternative energy. Like fossil fuels versus a wind farm.' Looking at the thin line of his mouth, she sighed. 'Sorry. I forgot you don't have a sense of humour. So this guy is going to be sitting at our table? I presume you want me to be extra-nice to him?'

'That won't be possible. He doesn't speak much English and I doubt his interpreter will be there.' Rio altered one of the figures on the spreadsheet. 'I'm sure if you smile at him it won't do any harm.'

His comment was so derogatory that she almost thumped him.

He made assumptions about people. Evie watched him, knowing that she was going to have the last laugh on this particular point. 'I won't need an interpreter. I'm good at communicating with people.' She was purposely vague. 'So you're hoping to meet up with this Vladimir guy—who else? Doesn't anyone just go to have fun?'

'They go to be seen. And at a charity ball they go to be seen spending money. It's a game. I go because there are a few contacts I need to make. I have no doubt it will be boring.'

'Thanks. So basically you're saying that not only do I

not look right, but I bore you. I can see we're in for a great evening.'

'I was talking about the other guests—' his tone was thickened with exasperation '—but carry on like this and I'll add you to the list. I've already told you—the reason I don't stay long is because I can't afford the time. I have work to do.'

All he did was work.

But he was taking her to a charity ball and a film premiere.

Evie felt a renewed flutter of excitement at the prospect of playing Cinderella for a night. 'So we're showing our faces at two events—but you have invites to loads more than that?'

'I have seven invitations for this evening. I've picked the two most high profile.' Showing no interest whatsoever in that fact, Rio focused on the screen. 'Normally, a hostess would do her utmost to avoid a clash, but this is Christmas so it's inevitable.'

Christmas.

Suddenly Evie realised what was different about the room. 'Someone's taken down all my decorations.' Horrified, she sprang to her feet and glanced around her. 'The tree has gone. And the holly—why would they have done that?'

'Because I gave instructions that all the decorations should be removed.'

Already bruised from his previous comments, it was hard to keep her voice steady. 'You didn't like the decorations?' 'No.'

She felt numb. 'I took *ages* getting them exactly right. I thought you'd be pleased—'

'I wasn't pleased.'

So she looked wrong, she was boring, and now he was saying she was useless at her job. It was the final straw.

Rio glanced up. 'While I'm staying here, I don't want to know it's Christmas.' His eyes were molten black and menacing. 'I don't want to see a single decoration. Is that clear?'

'Yes. It's perfectly clear.' Her voice high-pitched; deeply offended that he'd criticised her work, Evie stalked into the bedroom, yanking the doors closed behind her.

Her confidence in shreds, she leaned back against the doors.

Miserable, horrible, vile man.

Chemistry? Yes, there was chemistry—but she wished it was the sort that would result in some sort of explosive reaction that would blast him out of her life. He made her feel *small*. He made her feel useless and insignificant. Apparently she couldn't even decorate a Christmas tree to his satisfaction.

She stood for a moment, breathing deeply, horribly hurt by his dismissive comments. In a few sentences he'd shredded her fragile self-confidence.

With a sniff, she tried to tell herself that it didn't matter. Why should she care what he thought? So he hated her decorations. So what? The man was a cold hearted workaholic.

Fancy going to all this trouble just so that he didn't lose out on a stupid business deal.

He made Scrooge look like a cheerleader.

What sort of man would rather work than enjoy a night at a glittering Christmas ball? Did he think his entire business was going to fall apart or something?

Trying not to be hurt by the fact that he clearly wanted to spend as little time as possible in her company, Evie wrenched off the jacket that went with her 'wholesome' dress and flung it over the nearest chair.

Feeling miserable and unappreciated, she undressed and slipped under the covers, wanting to blot out her unhappiness with a much needed afternoon nap. As she closed her eyes she reminded herself that she was doing this so that her grandfather wouldn't be hurt and embarrassed. No other reason.

Once all the fuss had died down, she'd give Rio Zaccarelli the boot. Or should that be 'the stiletto'?

Either way, she was seriously looking forward to *that* day.

Rio fastened the sleeves of his dress shirt. Normally he relished the challenge of a difficult situation. On this occasion the stakes were too high to make the whole issue anything other than stressful. Adding an evening of Christmas celebrations into that mix simply increased the stress.

Get it over with.

There was no sound of activity from the bedroom and Rio wondered whether he should have checked on Evie. She'd been in there all day and they were supposed to be leaving in fifteen minutes. Was she still asleep?

Or was she still sulking over the Christmas decorations?

He was just walking towards the bedroom doors when they opened suddenly.

'Don't say a word. Not a word.' A dangerous glint in her blue eyes, she stalked barefoot across the carpet. A pair of silver shoes dangled from her fingers. 'Every time you open your mouth you say something nasty so, unless red eyes are the latest "must have" accessory on the celebrity circuit, then it's safer if you say nothing.'

Rio was pleased she'd instructed him to say nothing because, for once, the power of speech appeared to have deserted him. He'd been present when she'd tried on the dress—he'd approved it—but clearly he hadn't devoted his full attention to the task because he had no memory of it looking quite this good. Or maybe it was because he'd seen the dress in daylight and it was definitely designed to dazzle at night.

The fabric sparkled with every turn of her body and the effect was incredible—it was as if she were illuminated, each sensuous curve lit up and accentuated by the shimmering fabric. Her hair she'd scooped up and secured to the back of her head with silver clips, the slightly haphazard style both kooky and sexy.

'You look incredible.'

'Wholesome?'

He ignored the sarcasm in her tone. 'Sexy and wholesome. It's an intriguing combination. It would look even more effective if you could stop glaring at me.'

'I'll stop glaring at you when we're in public.' She was as prickly as a porcupine. 'Our deal doesn't include having to like each other, does it?'

Rio clenched his jaw. 'If I offended you, then I apologise.'

'*If?* There is no *if,* Rio. Of course you offended me! You criticised my work and then you criticised me. You're trying to turn me into a clone of the type of woman you date and then you get irritated when I'm not doing things right.'

'That isn't true, but—'

'No!' She lifted her hand like a policeman stopping traffic. 'Don't say anything else. You're incapable of speaking without being offensive.'

Unaccustomed to having to work so hard with a woman, Rio drew in a long, slow breath. 'It's snowing outside and that dress has no back to it. You'll need something to keep you warm—' He handed her a large flat box and she looked at him suspiciously before taking it with a frown.

'Now what? A cloak with a hood so that you can cover my face? A—oh—' she gasped, and then her face lost its colour and she dropped the box containing the snowy-white fur onto the carpet. 'I can't wear that. I won't wear fur.'

'It isn't real.' Wondering whether every interaction was going to result in confrontation, Rio stooped and retrieved it. 'It's fake.'

Evie stood with her hands behind her back. 'You're sure?'

'Positive.' He draped it around her shoulders. Her skin was warm and smooth against the backs of his fingers and he felt the immediate flash of chemistry. Her breathing was shallow and fast and for a moment she stood rigid, a faint bloom of colour lifting the pallor of her cheeks.

'Is that what you do when you offend someone? You buy them an extravagant gift rather than say sorry? Does it work?'

'You tell me. Your hair looks amazing against the white fur.' He saw the pulse beating in her throat and knew that she was feeling exactly what he was feeling.

'Don't think that just because I'm wearing this, I've forgiven you. I can't be bought.'

A woman who couldn't be bought.

Rio gave a faint smile at that concept.

'It does feel *gorgeous* against bare skin.' She wriggled her shoulders in an unconsciously seductive movement that sent his libido into overdrive.

Incredibly aroused, he drew her against him. 'You could remove the dress,' he suggested silkily, 'and just wear the fur.' Even without touching his fingers to her wrist, he knew her pulse was racing and Rio saw something in her eyes seconds before she looked away. *Desire.* Programmed to identify that look, he was about to suggest that the fur would be comfortable to lie on, when she shoved at his chest.

'You just can't help yourself, can you? We're supposed to be stopping the photo looking sleazy and all you want to do is stay in and make the whole situation even tackier. Or is this deal suddenly not important to you?'

Rio froze, horrified by the realisation that for a few precious seconds his mind had been wiped of every thought except for one and that was the erotic possibilities of fur against Evie's pale skin. 'You're right. Let's go.' Seriously disconcerted by the fact that she was so together while he was locked in the savage grip of rampaging hormones, he faced the lowering fact that, had she not stopped him, he would have tumbled her onto the rug in front of the fire and followed his instincts with no thought for anything except the demands of his own super-sized libido.

Exasperated with himself and seriously unsettled, Rio snagged his jacket from the back of the chair and urged her towards the elevator. 'The premiere starts in about fifteen minutes.'

'Great. So we'll be last.'

'That was the intention.' He pressed the button for the ground floor. 'We show ourselves in public when the crowd is at its maximum.'

'Why not? If I'm going to humiliate myself, it might as well be in a big way.'

Evie walked gingerly up the red carpet, relieved that the silver shoes were so much more comfortable than the red ones, her fingers gripping tightly to Rio's rock-hard biceps. Despite the falling snow, there was a huge crowd waiting in the hope of seeing the stars and Evie felt like a fraud as she heard the cheering.

'They're going to feel short-changed when they see me. What am I supposed to do?' She hissed the words between her teeth, her smile never faltering as what felt like a million camera lenses were pointed in her direction. 'Do I flash the ring? Do I look at you adoringly?'

'Just act normally.'

Evie felt a rush of exasperation that he had so little idea how she felt. 'I don't normally walk along red carpets in high heels pretending to be engaged to a very rich man I barely know. Some help here would be appreciated.'

'I'm by your side. That's all the help you need.' He paused to talk to a couple who seemed vaguely familiar. Relieved to see at least two friendly faces and trying to work out where she knew them from, Evie smiled and chatted, finding them surprisingly approachable. She *definitely* knew them from somewhere.

As Rio led her away into the foyer, she was still smiling. 'They were nice. I know I've met them before somewhere—I can't think where—I don't know that many people in London. Do they work at the hotel? What are their names?'

When he told her, she stared at him in mortified silence. 'Right. Both of them Hollywood stars. The reason I know their faces is because I've seen them both in the movies. *Now* I'm embarrassed. Oh, my God—they must have wondered why I was grinning at them like an idiot.'

'You were charming and not at all star-struck. And you didn't ask for their autograph, which is always refreshing.'

'That's because I didn't actually recognise them.' Evie tightened her grip on his arm. 'Do you think they realised? What if I offended them?'

'They enjoyed talking to you and the fact that you were so natural with them suggests that our relationship is an already accepted fact in some circles. You did well. There's no need to make holes in my arm.'

Evie slackened her grip. Determined not to make the same mistake again, she spent the next ten minutes glancing furtively around her, trying to put faces to names. The foyer was crammed with glamorous people, all of whom seemed completely comfortable in their equally glamorous surroundings. They looked like elegant swans, she thought gloomily, whereas she—she felt like an emu. Tall, conspicuous and horribly out of place amongst so many delicate, beautiful birds.

Watching her face, Rio sighed. 'You look as though you're about to visit the dentist. Try and relax.'

Finding the mingling in the foyer desperately stressful, Evie was relieved when they moved into the cinema for the showing of the film. Her spirits lifted still further when she discovered that it was a Christmas movie.

More comfortable in the dark, she slipped off her shoes and settled down in her seat, looking forward to a couple of hours of seasonal entertainment. Watching elves dance across the screen, she was just starting to feel Christmassy when she became aware that Rio was emailing someone on his BlackBerry.

'You're supposed to switch off your mobile.' The moment she said the words she realised how stupid she sounded. This wasn't a commercial showing. It hadn't escaped her notice that the other guests had been vying with each other in an attempt to exchange a few words with him. It was obvious that he was the most powerful, influential guest here. Who was going to tell him off?

Trying to block out the distracting sight of him ploughing through endless emails, Evie turned her attention back to the screen and soon she was lost in the film, sighing wistfully as Santa started putting presents in his sack. 'This is a lovely story,' she said dreamily, 'you really ought to watch it. It might help put you in the Christmas mood.'

The change in him was instantaneous.

Sliding his BlackBerry into the pocket of his dinner jacket, Rio rose to his feet in a purposeful movement, indifferent to the people around him trying to enjoy the film. 'Put your shoes back on. We're going.' Barely giving her time to slide her toes back into the silver shoes, Rio grabbed her hand and led her out of a door at the rear of the cinema.

'They're all looking at us—this is so embarrassing.' Breathless, Evie tried to keep up without twisting her ankle. 'Why are we leaving? I was enjoying myself.'

'I wasn't.' Talking into his phone again, he pushed open a fire door and Evie saw his limousine parked right outside.

'But I only watched about twenty minutes!'

'And that was twenty minutes too long. I can't stand sappy Christmas movies.'

'It hadn't even got going. Santa was about to be set upon by the bad guys determined to ruin Christmas,' Evie gasped, bending her head as he bundled her inside the car. 'Thanks to you, I won't ever find out how it ended.'

'How do you think it ended?' His handsome face was a mask of frustration and tension. 'Happily, of course. It's a Christmas movie. They only ever end happily.'

'I know it ended happily but I wanted to know *how* it ended happily. There's more than one route to a happy ending, you know. It's *how* they do the happy ending that makes it worth watching.'

He shot her a look of exasperation before turning his attention back to the screen of his BlackBerry. 'I would have thought you were too old to believe in happy endings—' he scanned, deleted, emailed '—especially after your recent experience.'

'Just because you haven't encountered a happy ending personally doesn't mean you stop believing in them.'

'If you go through life waiting for a happy ending then you're setting yourself up for permanent disappointment. If you're really that deluded then it's no wonder that you're currently single. No man could hope to live up to your ridiculously high levels of idealism. I almost feel sorry for Jeff.'

Digesting that cynical take on her approach to life, Evie stiffened. 'I gather you don't believe in happy endings. Just don't tell me that you don't believe in Santa or you'll completely ruin my evening.' Intercepting his incredulous glance, she gave him a mocking smile. 'You don't believe in Santa? Careful. If you don't believe, he won't come.'

Shaking his head in despair, Rio turned his head to look out of the window. 'How do you survive in the real world? I thought women like you were extinct.'

'There are some of us still flourishing in the wild.' Evie

leaned her head against the seat and closed her eyes. 'But we're an endangered species. We have to keep our distance from cynics like you who appear to have lost all hope, otherwise we become contaminated.'

'What are you hoping for?'

She kept her eyes firmly shut. There was no way he'd understand and he'd just laugh at her. 'Oh, this and that—the usual sort of stuff.'

'The usual sort of stuff being love, kids and marriage.'

'Go on—laugh. Just because I have my priorities right and all you think about is deals.'

'Trust me—there is *nothing* about love, marriage or kids that makes me want to laugh.'

'And half the world feels the same way as you.' Evie opened her eyes and turned her head to look at him. 'But I don't.'

'Why not? You were dumped six weeks ago.'

'I know.'

'You should be bitter and cynical.'

'How does that help?'

'It stops you having unrealistic expectations.'

'Or perhaps it stops you spotting love when you find it.' Evie adjusted her dress to stop it creasing. 'My grandparents were together for sixty years. I refuse to believe it isn't possible. Finding someone you can love and who loves you back might be rare, but it's not impossible.'

Rio's handsome face was devoid of expression.

Staring into his dark eyes, Evie felt the heat build in her body. 'It's probably different for you,' she said lamely. 'You're rich. Relationships must be even more complicated when you're incredibly wealthy.'

'You've already given me your opinion on the influence of wealth on personal relationships. Clearly you think no woman would entertain the idea of a relationship with me if I weren't wealthy.'

'I didn't say that. I'm sure there are women out there who like cynical men.' She told herself firmly that she wasn't one of them but, even as she gave herself a lecture, she was noticing the blue-black shadow of his hard jaw and the undeniably sexy curve of his mouth. Struggling hard not to think about sex, kissing or anything that required physical contact, Evie tried to lighten the atmosphere. 'If you haven't written your letter to Santa, how do you expect him to know what you'd like?'

'Are you intentionally winding me up?'

'Yes. Is it working?'

'Yes.' A glimmer of a smile pulled at the corners of his mouth and Evie's limbs weakened because he was even more gorgeous when he smiled and because she knew exactly what he could do with that mouth. And she couldn't stop thinking about it. She squirmed with awareness, furious with herself for being such a pushover. Rich, powerful guy—adoring girl. It was an embarrassing cliché.

As if—

'If I'm going along with this plan of yours,' she said quickly, 'there is one other thing I want at the end of it.'

'You can't renegotiate terms once they're agreed,' he said silkily, but Evie lifted her chin, refusing to let him intimidate her.

'I want a job when this is over. And, to be honest, that will look better for you, too. If I'm going to dump you and people find out I've lost my job they'll just assume you're petty and small-minded and you wouldn't want that.'

'Thanks for protecting my image.' His eyes gleamed with sardonic mockery. 'Do you have a particular job in mind? Santa's cheerleader?'

'I was employed to work on Reception,' Evie said firmly, 'and that's what I want to do. I was good at it.'

'So, if you were employed to work on Reception, why were

you working as a housekeeper when I arrived in the early hours this morning?'

'Because Tina demoted me. She said I talked too much.' Evie's eyes flashed defensively. 'But I don't see how you can talk too much as a receptionist. I was making people feel welcome. That's the job my grandfather thinks I'm doing, and that's the job I want when I finally dump you.'

'All right.'

Evie gulped. 'All right? You're saying yes? I can have my job as receptionist back?'

'I'm saying yes,' he drawled softly, 'although, if you're missing your grandfather that much, it strikes me you might be better taking a job closer to home.'

'There isn't anything. I tried that. No one needs my skills. What will happen to Carlos?'

'I have no idea.' Rio pressed a button by his seat and a panel opened. 'Do you drink champagne?'

Evie didn't want to admit she'd never tasted it. 'Of course.'

He withdrew a bottle from the fridge, popped the cork and poured the bubbling liquid into two tall slender-stemmed glasses. 'To our deal.'

Evie sipped from the glass he handed her and choked as the bubbles flew up her nose. 'Oh—that's—' she coughed '—yummy.' She took another mouthful. 'Happy Christmas. How long do we have to keep this up? When will you know if you've rescued your deal?'

He looked out of the window. 'We've arrived.'

And he hadn't answered her question.

Wondering once again what it was about this particular deal that was so important, Evie followed his gaze and gasped. 'We're at the Natural History Museum.' The famous building was illuminated against the winter night and thousands of tiny sparkling lights had been threaded through the branches of the trees. In front of the building was an ice rink and the whole place had been transformed into a winter paradise. 'I had no idea they held events here.'

'This is a very prestigious fund-raiser.'

'Can we ice skate?'

'Absolutely not.'

'But it's snowing.' Evie leaned forward, captivated by the atmosphere. 'It would be magical. Do you think we'll have a white Christmas?'

'I couldn't care less. Do you want an umbrella?'

'You don't like snow? Seriously?'

'It's useful when I'm skiing. The rest of the time it's an inconvenience.'

'When did you last make a snowman or throw a snowball?'

Rio frowned. 'We need to get out of the car, Evie.'

Evie didn't budge. 'You don't write to Santa, you hate decorations, you don't like snow, you won't ice skate—there must be *something* you like about Christmas. Turkey? Meeting up with friends? What's the best thing about Christmas for you?'

The door was opened by his security chief and a blast of cold air entered the car.

Rio stared at her for a long moment, his face unsmiling. 'The best thing about Christmas for me is when it's over,' he gritted. 'Now, get out of the car and smile.'

'So the rumours are true, Rio? You're engaged? You do realise you've just ruined every single woman's Christmas, and half the married ones, too?' Tabitha Fenton-Coyle stroked her long red fingernails over his sleeve. 'Tell me what it is about her that induced a hardened cynic like yourself into marriage.'

'You need to ask?'

'Well, she's pretty, of course, in a slightly unsophisticated way that a man might find appealing—' There was a flinty glint in Tabitha's eyes and Rio turned his head and noticed Evie laughing uninhibitedly with the two Russian billionaires, both known for their arrogant refusal to speak English at social events. They were taciturn, remote and notoriously unapproachable and yet both appeared to be listening to Evie with rapt attention.

How was she making herself understood?

From across the table, Rio tried to hear what she was saying. She was chatting non-stop, her hands moving as she illustrated her point. Occasionally she paused to sip champagne or listen to their response.

'Clever of you to find a woman who speaks Russian,' Tabitha said, 'given your business interests in that country. Is that how you met? Is she an interpreter or something?'

Evie spoke Russian?

Unable to hear her above the noise from the surrounding tables, Rio focused his gaze on her lips and realised that she was indeed speaking Russian.

His hostess was watching him. 'You didn't know, did you? Well, if she can persuade them to open their wallets when the charity auction begins, then she'll certainly get my vote.'

Where had Evie learned to speak Russian?

Why hadn't she mentioned it when he'd told her that Vladimir didn't speak good English and that she wouldn't be able to communicate without an interpreter? And then he remembered her responding that she wouldn't need an interpreter. At the time he'd assumed she'd meant that she'd be using sign language and lots of smiles—not once had it occurred to him that she spoke fluent Russian.

Coffee was served as the auction began and there was a sudden flurry of movement as people swapped seats.

Her cheeks pink with excitement, Evie swayed to her feet and found her way to the seat next to him. 'I'm having *such* a nice time. Those men are so sweet. You should have mentioned how funny they were.'

Rio tightened his grip on the glass. 'Just as you should possibly have mentioned the fact that you're fluent in Russian.'

'You were being arrogant and I thought it would be more fun to just surprise you. I thought it might teach you not to underestimate people.' Craning her neck, she looked over his shoulder towards the stage and the dance floor. 'What's happening now?'

Rio fingered the stem of his glass. 'I do *not* underestimate people.'

'Yes, you do. But you probably can't help it,' she said kindly. 'Is there going to be dancing?'

'It's the auction first. The bidding will raise money for the charity.' Rio was still watching her. 'Do you speak any other languages?'

'French, Spanish and Mandarin. So am I allowed to bid for something?'

'You speak *four* languages?'

'Five, if you count English. How much am I allowed to bid?'

'You don't speak Italian?'

'No.' She helped herself to a chocolate from the plate. 'That CD was always out of the library whenever I looked.'

Rio shot her an incredulous look. 'You taught yourself all those languages?'

'I'm good at languages. I taught myself the basics and then there was a teacher at school who helped me and I had a friend who spoke Mandarin and Russian.' She was looking across the room. 'Don't look now but there's a huge Christmas tree next to the stage—you'd better close your eyes or it will probably give you a nervous breakdown. I'm surprised you didn't phone ahead and ask them to remove it.'

Still absorbing the fact that she spoke five languages, Rio dragged his gaze to the stage and saw the Christmas tree. She was right; it was huge—a massive symbol of the unspeakable horrors of his childhood. There was a rushing sound in his ears and suddenly the voices around him seemed far away. Instead of staring at glittering baubles, he was staring into a deep, dark black hole. Memories formed pictures in his brain, taking on shapes he didn't want to see, like a grue-some kaleidoscope. That hideous morning. The discovery he'd made. The shock. And the emptiness.

Suddenly every sparkle in the room seemed to intensify the dark feelings swirling in his brain. Every silver star and rope of tinsel was a silent mockery.

Promising himself that they'd leave as soon as the auction was over, Rio sat still, ruthlessly wrestling his feelings back under control.

From inside a fog of unwelcome memories, he was dimly aware of Evie leaning across the table, coaxing the Russians into bidding enormous sums of money in the charity auction. Even Tabitha was looking impressed as Evie switched be-tween Russian and English, extracting more money from the billionaires than they'd sucked oil from the Caspian Sea.

If the circumstances had been different, Rio would have laughed. As it was, he just wanted to leave.

They'd been seen together. The ring had been photo-graphed. Rumours were spreading.

It was done.

Rio watched with a frown as Tabitha made sure that Evie's glass was kept topped up. She was drinking the champagne as if it were soda, and he realised that if he didn't remove her from this table quickly she was going to be drunk.

As the auction ended and a band started warming up on the stage, Rio drained his glass and turned to Evie.

'We're leaving.'

'No way! Not this time. I missed almost all of the film—I'm not missing the rest of the ball. The dancing hasn't started yet.' She started to sway in her seat in time to the music while Tabitha looked on with a mixture of condescension and amusement.

'If you can persuade Rio to dance with you, then I'm willing to believe he's in love. I've never known him to dance. If I didn't know better, I'd think he didn't have rhythm.' She gave Rio a knowing look and he saw Evie's happy smile falter as she digested the meaning behind those words.

Rio cursed silently.

She might be tipsy, but she wasn't so under the influence that she didn't recognise a barb when it was poked into her flesh.

Removing the champagne glass from her hand, he dragged her to her feet. 'You're right—we'll dance.' Without giving himself time to think about it, he led her onto the dance floor and slid his arm around her waist. 'Smile.'

'What is there to smile about? She's flaunting the fact she's had sex with you. She's *vile*. And you have no taste. No wonder you've never wanted to settle down with anyone if she's the sort of person you've been seeing.'

'I have *not* had sex with her,' Rio breathed, bending his head so that he spoke the words in her ear and couldn't be overheard. Immediately, her perfume wound itself round his senses. 'She was trying to cause trouble. Trying to hurt you. Don't let her. You're just over-emotional because you've had too much champagne. Now smile, because the whole purpose of tonight is to convince people our relationship is real.'

'Well, if this relationship were real, I would have punched her. And I'm not over-emotional, I'm justifiably emotional. That woman is a man-eater. She ought to be fenced in on a game reserve. Do you know that she's on her *fourth* husband? Evgeni and Vladimir told me that she only marries them for their money.'

Rio's tension levels rocketed up several more notches. 'You're on first name terms with the Russians?'

'I sat with them all evening, what did you expect? When I saw that awful Tabitha woman had separated us I almost had a heart attack. She put me there thinking I'd struggle, didn't she? She was trying to be unkind.'

Rio gave a faint smile. 'I think you won that round.'

'They told me that she takes men to the cleaners and lives off the settlement.'

'It's a popular career choice in certain circles.'

'Well, I think it's awful. No amount of money would make up for being married to someone I didn't love.' Evie slid her arms around his neck, her eyes slightly bleary. 'I mean, actually, when you think about it, that's not so far from prostitution, is it?'

Conscious of the shocked glances from those nearest to them, Rio smiled. 'Absolutely right,' he purred, vastly entertained by how outspoken she became when she'd had a few glasses of champagne. 'You might want to lower your voice before you cast any more aspersions on the character and profession of our illustrious hostess.'

Evie gulped. 'Oops. Do you think they heard me?'

'Definitely. They're doubtless all now engrossed in a fascinating debate as to whether our hostess is a prostitute or not.'

Evie leaned her forehead against his chest. 'Sorry. I may have drunk just a little bit too much champagne—I've never had it before and it's *delicious*.'

'You've never had champagne before?'

'Never. Last year, Grandpa and I treated ourselves to a bottle of Prosecco but it wasn't the same.'

Rio winced. 'No. It definitely isn't the same. Prosecco is excellent in a Bellini but it's not champagne.' He lifted his hand and removed a strand of fiery red hair that had somehow managed to tangle itself around his bow tie. 'I think I'd better take you home.'

'I don't want to go home. I want to dance. Anyway, I like it here and we're supposed to be seen.' Still clinging to him tightly, she swayed in time to the music and then looked up with a smile as everyone started singing *The Twelve Days of Christmas*.

'Oh, I *love* this. This used to be my party piece at school. I do all the actions. Wait till you see my Seven swans a-swimming—'

Rio inhaled deeply. 'Evie—' But she was already lifting her hands like a conductor, waving her arms and singing at the top of her voice along with everyone else.

'—partridge in a pear tree—'

'I'm taking you home.'

'No.' She dug her heels in like a stubborn horse. 'I'm not going anywhere. I've never been to a party as amazing as this one. I don't want it to end.'

Rio gritted his teeth. 'We have two more to attend tomorrow. And this time I won't make the mistake of giving you champagne beforehand.'

'I don't care about tomorrow. I want to live for today. I like *this* party.' She slid her arms around his neck and pressed herself against him, her breath warm against his neck. 'Please, Rio, dance with me. You know you want to.'

He locked his fingers around her wrists, intending to remove her arms, but then she smiled up at him and he found himself so captivated by that smile that instead of removing her arms, he slid his hands down her warm skin. Her back was bare, her skin warm and smooth and tempting and raw lust shot through him. Without thinking about what he was doing, Rio lowered his mouth towards hers.

'*Four calling birds, three French hens—*'

Rio froze as she started to sing again. 'Evie—'

'*Two turtle doves, and a—*'

'Evie!' Rio felt tension prickle down his spine.

'I like singing. If you want me to stop singing, you're going to have to gag me.'

'Good idea.' Rio closed the distance and captured her mouth with his. The chemistry was instantaneous and explosive. Because he had his hand on her bare back he could feel the tremors that shook her and he welded her closer to him, ignoring the curious looks of those around him.

After two of the most intoxicating, arousing, exciting minutes of his life, he lifted his head fractionally and tried to regain his balance. The kiss had done nothing except make him crave more. He wanted to touch and taste—he wanted to bury his face in her hair and feast on her body.

Around them, everyone was still singing but this time Evie wasn't joining in.

'When you kiss me, I don't ever want it to stop,' she murmured, her eyes slightly glazed. 'It feels incredible. Are you as good at everything else? If so, then it's no wonder every woman in the room is looking at me as if they hate me. They think we're having mad, crazy sex all the time. I wish. Maybe we should. It seems a shame to disappoint everyone.'

He cupped her face in his hands and stared down at her in exasperation. 'You're plastered. It's time I took you home.'

'I'm not plastered. And I don't want to go home. I'm having a really great time and I refuse to go home just so that you can weld yourself to your laptop again and ignore the fact it's Christmas. Kissing you, drinking champagne, dancing and singing—they're my favourite things. Honestly, Rio, you should sing too—it's fun—I'm feeling so *Christmassy*—' Her hips swayed and there was a huge smile on her face as she started to sing along again, joining in with the crowd, this time at double the volume—

When it came to *'Five gold rings'* she sang even louder, struck a dramatic pose and flashed her diamond in the air, beaming at Rio.

Before he could stop her, she flung herself towards the two Russians, kissed each of them on the cheek and then sprang onto a chair and from there onto the table.

Rio closed his eyes, cursing himself for not monitoring her champagne intake more closely. He contemplated removing her bodily but decided that she would probably make such a fuss that the best thing to do was to wait until the end of the song and hope she survived that long without falling off the table and doing herself serious injury.

Everyone was clapping and Evie was by now the centre of attention as she led the singing, her actions for *Seven swans a-swimming* causing such hilarity that Rio shook his head in disbelief.

'She's certainly the life and soul of the party,' Vladimir was suddenly beside him, speaking in slow, broken English, and beaming up at Evie, who was still mimicking a swan. 'That joint venture you wanted to explore in Moscow—we're willing to give it some consideration. Fly over in the New Year and meet with us. Evie can translate for you.'

Rio, who had given up on the usually taciturn Russians, was about to confirm the details when an overenthusiastic re-enactment of *'Three French hens'* almost sent Evie spinning off the table.

'*Scusi*—' Crossing to the table, he caught Evie as she lost her balance and she tumbled into his arms, the silver dress shimmering under the lights.

'—*Two purple doves*,' she hollered, *'and a partridge in a pear tree.'*

Wild applause surrounded them and Rio winced. 'That's your party piece?'

'One of them. I also tell a great joke about a wide mouth toad which has brilliant actions.' She eyed the microphone on the stage. 'I suppose I could—'

'No,' Rio said hastily. 'You most definitely could not.'

'I love champagne,' she said happily, leaning her head against his shoulder. 'It's the nicest, yummiest, fizziest, happiest drink I've ever tasted. Is there any more?'

'It's run out. You drank it all. Thanks to you, the global champagne market is now in meltdown.'

'Shame.' She buried her face in his neck and breathed

deeply. 'You smell so good. Why do you smell so good? Will you kiss me again? And this time don't stop. The only thing I hate about kissing you is when you stop. I just want it to go on and on and on—could you do that, do you think? You did say you were good at multi-tasking.'

Rio tensed. 'Evie—'

'You're an incredibly sexy man. If I wasn't so afraid of being rejected again, I'd try and seduce you—' she was snuggling and kissing his neck at the same time '—but I've never seduced anyone before so it's probably a bit overambitious to start with you. Like climbing a mountain and deciding to start with Everest. I ought to practice on someone small, ugly and unsuccessful first and see how I get on.'

Rio felt his entire body tighten. 'You won't be practising on anyone tonight. We're going home.'

'Not without a present from the Christmas tree,' she coaxed, lifting her head and focusing with difficulty. 'It's all in a good cause. You pay money and they give you a surprise present. The money goes to the kids. So it's sort of two presents in one. Three presents actually, because you get a warm fuzzy feeling from being generous.'

Deciding that it was going to be quicker to buy the present than argue, Rio strode towards the tree, Evie still in his arms. Around them, people were smiling indulgently.

His pulse rate doubled as he approached the tree. The smell of pine invaded his nostrils, awakening thoughts and memories long dormant.

'Which present?' he growled, adjusting the angle of his body so that she could see the tree and he couldn't. 'Tell me which one you want.' Quickly. So that he could make his escape. The past was rolling over him like a dark cloud, its creeping menace threatening to seep under the barriers of his self-control.

'The pink one with the silver bow.' Her arms tightened

around his neck and Rio felt the moist flicker of her tongue against his throat.

'That one—' His voice tight, he indicated with his head towards the pink box and one of the staff untied it from the tree and handed it to him while one of his own security team discreetly dealt with the financial aspect of the transaction.

'Thank you.' Her voice was husky, her mouth tantalizingly close to his and Rio tried to ignore the perfume that wafted from her skin.

'We're going home.'

'So that we can experiment with fur against naked flesh?'

Jaw clenched tight, he reminded himself that she dreamed of happy endings.

If there was one thing designed to kill his libido, it was a woman who dreamed of happy endings.

'So that you can sleep off the champagne.'

'Wait—' Slightly breathless, she pressed her lips against his throat. 'I want the tree. Will you buy me the tree?'

Rio stilled. 'You want me to buy every present on the tree?'

'No, I want you to buy me the *tree*. I don't think I can stand the thought of Christmas without a tree. It's like having chocolate cake with no chocolate.' Still clutching the pink box, she snuggled against him, her voice coaxing. 'That tree would look fantastic in the Penthouse. It's even bigger than the one I decorated.'

The one he'd had removed.

'I don't want a tree.'

'Why not? I know you prefer to work over Christmas, but it isn't going to stop you working just because there's a tree in the room. It cheers everything up.'

'It doesn't cheer me up.'

She frowned. 'So it wasn't my decorations in particular that you didn't like. It's Christmas trees in general. Why?

You're never too old to enjoy Christmas. Having a tree will give you happy memories.'

Rio put her down so suddenly she staggered. 'I don't have any happy memories of Christmas.'

It was the stricken look in her eyes that made him realise just how harshly he'd spoken. 'I...I'm sorry,' she stammered. 'I didn't mean—'

'Forget it. Let's get out of here.'

CHAPTER SIX

I don't have any happy memories of Christmas.

Evie sat in the middle of the enormous bed, those words reverberating around her head. She'd put her foot in it, but knowing that didn't stop her wondering and asking herself endless questions.

Why didn't he have happy memories of Christmas?

She turned her head and looked towards the double doors that lay between her and the sitting room. They remained firmly closed.

What was he doing? Had he gone to sleep in the second bedroom?

They'd driven home without speaking, Evie silenced by that one revealing phrase and Rio communicating nothing. For once, his BlackBerry was silent and he'd simply stared out of the window at the snowy streets, his handsome face an expressionless mask.

But he *was* feeling, she knew that.

Not just feeling—*hurting*.

Knowing that she was risking another rejection, Evie slid off the bed and opened the doors quietly, afraid to disturb him if he was sleeping.

The huge living room was in darkness. The flames of the fire had almost flickered to nothing and all the lights had been extinguished.

He wasn't there.

She was overreacting. He'd obviously chosen to sleep in the second bedroom.

Evie was about to turn and go back to bed when she noticed a ghostly green glow in the corner of the room and realised that it was the laptop screen.

As her eyes slowly adjusted to the darkness, she saw that Rio was seated at the table.

'It's four in the morning,' she murmured. 'You should get some sleep.'

'I'm not tired.' His voice was barely audible. 'Go back to bed, Evie. Sleep it off.'

Knowing that she was unwelcome, she was about to do just that but her feet froze to the spot as her eyes adjusted to the dim light and she managed to make out his profile. He looked like a man on the edge. A man struggling to contain an emotion bigger than him.

He was still looking at the screen, but somehow she knew that this time he wasn't reading the numbers. His eyes were bleak and empty and she knew instantly that this was about Christmas.

I don't have any happy memories of Christmas.

What sort of childhood had he had, that he hadn't retained a single happy memory of Christmas?

The sudden stillness of the room seemed loud in her ears.

Evie stood still, knowing that she was intruding on a private moment. She knew she ought to back away and return to the neutral sanctuary of the bedroom. She ought to close those big doors and leave him to his dark thoughts. She was never going to see him again once this charade was over. Why did it even matter that he wanted to shut himself away and pretend Christmas wasn't happening?

But there was something about the bleak set of his features that made it impossible for her to walk away. She never would have been able to walk away and leave another human being in so much pain, and she had no doubt that he was in pain.

She'd become intimately acquainted with the signs after her grandmother had died. Night after night, she'd seen the same look on her grandfather's face as he'd sat in her grandmother's favourite rocking chair, just staring at her photograph. She'd kept him company in the darkness, afraid to leave him alone with his grief.

What had Rio Zaccarelli lost?

What was he thinking about, as he stared sightlessly at that screen?

Evie walked across to him, knowing that she was taking a risk. She was approaching when she should have run away.

Rio lifted his head and inhaled deeply. 'I said, go back to bed.'

'My head spins when I lie down.'

'You drank too much champagne. That feeling will pass. Drink lots of water.'

'I'm not drunk.'

The barest flicker of a smile touched his mouth. 'You were dancing on the table.'

'That wasn't because I was drunk. It was because I'd lost some of my inhibitions. If I had the confidence, I would have done the same thing sober. The drink just made me less anxious.'

'In that case, remind me never to escort you when you're drunk.'

'Tell me why you hate Christmas.'

Anger flickered across his face and his swift glance was loaded with warning. 'I think you should go to bed.'

'Only if you come too.' She had no idea what had driven her to say those words. Immediately, she wanted to drag them back. *What if he said yes?* She'd never had a one-night stand in her life. Compared with his experience and sophistication, she was a complete novice.

For a moment he simply watched her, his eyes glittering in the darkness. She had the feeling that he was fighting some brutal internal battle.

'Leave,' he said thickly. 'Right now.'

'I'm not drunk.'

'That isn't why I want you to leave.'

'Then—'

'I'm fresh out of happy endings, Evie. You won't find one within a thousand kilometres of me.'

Her mouth dried and her heart was pounding in her chest. 'I know that. You could never be my happy ending. But that doesn't mean…I want to know…'

His eyes were hard and unsympathetic. He gave her no help at all. 'What do you want to know, Evie?'

She licked dry lips. 'I want to know what it would be like,' she whispered. 'If the rest of it would feel as good as the kissing part.'

'You want to know how it would feel?' He rose to his feet so suddenly that she actually took an involuntary step backwards and he registered her retreat with a sardonic smile. 'I'll tell you how it would feel, Evie. It would feel good. We've both felt the chemistry. It would be incredible. Hot and crazy. For a short time.' His voice was thickened by emotion. 'And then I'd break your heart. Like that—' He snapped his fingers in a cruel, casual gesture that made her flinch. 'Easy.'

The blood was pulsing in her ears and it was difficult to breathe. 'That's fine.'

His gaze mocked. 'You're saying it's fine for me to break your heart?'

'No. I'm saying you won't break it. To break it, I'd have to be in love with you and I'm not in love with you. I wouldn't be that stupid.'

His lids lowered, half concealing black eyes that glittered dark and dangerous. 'Perhaps I'm not in the mood for a gentle seduction.'

Evie felt a spasm of fear, intermingled with the most fierce excitement she'd ever experienced. It was like a drug, urging her on to be more and more daring. 'If you're trying to scare me, you're not succeeding.'

'Maybe you should be scared, Evie.' His voice was lethally soft and cold as the ice that had formed on the windows. 'I'm not the right man for you.'

'I know that.' They were alone in the room and yet she was whispering. 'That isn't what this is about.'

'So what is it about? What are you trying to prove to yourself? Or is this good girl seduces bad boy, just to see how it feels?'

'No! I—' Evie broke off, struggling to breathe. 'I don't know what this is. All I know is…I thought you wanted… earlier you said…'

'I know what I said. I know what I wanted.'

'So—'

'Earlier, I didn't know what I was dealing with.'

Evie flushed. 'Because I love Christmas and believe in happy endings? I said I didn't believe in happy endings with you.'

His eyes held hers. 'If you play with fire, you'll get burnt.'

'Will you tell me why you hate Christmas?'

'No. And you're making this personal. A basic female mistake.'

'All right. Nothing personal. No questions.' Part of her was shocked at herself. What was she doing?

'You think you can go to bed with a man and not make it personal?' There was a layer of humour in his voice. 'You think you can do that?'

'Yes.' *No.* She had no idea.

Rio stared at her for a long moment and then lifted his hand and took a strand of her hair in his fingers. 'You should be more careful with yourself, Evie Anderson. You could get seriously hurt.' The backs of his fingers brushed her cheek and Evie shivered, dazed by the spark of electricity that shot through her body.

Her heart pounding, she turned her head and ran her tongue along his fingers.

His response was instantaneous. With a growl, he cupped her face in his hands and brought his mouth down on hers in a punishing, possessive kiss. He'd kissed her before, but this kiss was different. This kiss demanded everything and Evie felt all her senses ignite with explosive force. Within an instant she was light-headed, her limbs weak and wobbly.

With a moan, she slid her hands up his chest, over his shoulders, feeling the firm swell of muscle beneath her hands. He'd discarded his bow tie and undone the first few buttons of his shirt and her fingers slid inside, seeking, touching, exploring. She felt the pulsing heat of his body beneath her fingertips and made a small, desperate sound deep in her throat and then he was kissing her again and his tongue was hot against hers, his relentless seduction so much more practised than her own desperate offering.

The kiss seemed to last for ever and she felt her entire body stir, as if it had been waiting for this exact moment to come alive. And the feelings were so intense that it was impossible to stay silent.

When he pressed his mouth to the hollow of her throat she moaned, and when he dragged his mouth lower and toyed with the straining peak of her breast she arched her back and gasped his name. She wanted more, much more, and when he closed his hand over the hem of her nightdress she didn't stop him. There was a tearing sound as he ripped it from neck to hem and then she was naked, her body visible in the warm glow of the firelight.

If she'd thought that the semi darkness might give her some protection, she was wrong. Rio drew away from her, his breathing audible as he scanned her body, his gaze lingering on the fiery red curls that nestled at the juncture of her thighs.

'You can still change your mind.'

'No.' Emotion clogged her throat and the only thing in her head was a desperate need for this man. 'I don't want to change my mind.'

His fingers speared her hair and tightened, drawing her head back. His eyes were fierce, black and focused—focused on her.

For a few suspended seconds she didn't breathe and then he seemed to make a decision. Without speaking, he clamped his hand behind her head and claimed her mouth with ravenous hunger. It was a full on assault, his tongue in her mouth, his kiss blatantly sexual and brutally erotic and Evie went from freezing to boiling in a microsecond, her body burning up under the heat of his. She ripped at his shirt, clawing, tearing in a desperate attempt to get to the sleek male flesh beneath. Finally his shirt dangled open at the front and her hands slid inside and up to his shoulders. His body was a work of art, his muscles pumped up and hard, the dark shading on his chest accentuating strength and masculinity. Desperate to taste, Evie pushed at his chest and they rolled. Now he was the one on his back, his eyes glittering dark in the firelight as he watched her. Then his hand moved behind her head and he brought her mouth down to his, kissing her hungrily as her hair tumbled between them. Evie kissed him back, matching his hunger with her own, her hands sliding over his body as she straddled him. For a moment she paused, her hair tumbling around them, her senses reaching overload. His eyes were dark, so dark, and she felt an overwhelming thrill of excitement as she felt him, hard and ready beneath her. In that single moment, her breath caught. It was like reaching the top of a roller coaster and realising that there was no turning back.

'You're shaking—' His voice was raw and thickened

with the same passion she was feeling. 'Do you want me to stop?'

'No,' she whispered. She leaned forward so that her mouth brushed his. 'I can't stop. I want this more than anything. I want *you.*'

'Why?'

She sensed his struggle to hold back. It was visible in his eyes and in the tension of his sleek, pumped muscles.

'Does it matter?' Her mouth was against his. 'It feels right. Can't that be enough?'

He didn't answer her question. Instead, he closed his hands over her hips and lifted her, flipping her gently onto her back, once more the aggressor as he came over her. The outside world melted away. Details blurred. Dimly, Evie registered that he was now naked and that brief glimpse was enough to send nerves licking along the edges of her excitement.

He devoured her mouth and she kissed him back, every bit as hungry for him as he very clearly was for her.

The heat was shocking, an inferno of dangerous desire and carnal craving and, when he dragged his mouth from her lips to her neck, Evie sucked in air and tried to focus. But there was nothing to hold on to except him. Her whole world was tumbling around her and he was the only solid thing remaining. When his hand slid between her thighs she moaned against his mouth and he murmured something in Italian, his clever fingers sliding skilfully against delicate flesh. He knew exactly where to touch her, *how to touch her,* and Evie felt the ache in her body intensify until it was almost agonizing. She shifted her hips on the rug, whimpered his name, but Rio simply watched her, his mouth only a breath away from hers as he tormented her with merciless skill.

'Please,' Evie begged, arching towards him, 'Please, Rio—'

As if something snapped inside him, he shifted onto her.

He stroked her hair away from her face and scanned her features with eyes that were dark with secrets.

She felt the hardness of him brush against her and tensed. 'Please—' In desperation, she ran her hands down his body and her heart gave a little lurch as she touched the power of him.

He leaned his forehead against hers, holding her gaze. 'I don't want to hurt you—'

'You won't.'

There was a brief pause while he protected her and then he was inside her, hard and hot. The size of him shocked her and Evie forced herself to relax as she learned to accommodate him.

'Breathe—' His voice was husky and he lowered his mouth to hers. 'Breathe, *tesoro*.'

'Can't—' Her body was on fire and he gently brushed her mouth with his, tracing her lower lip with his tongue as he eased deeper.

She felt an agonizing flash of pain, immediately followed by excitement as he moved against sensitive flesh and she dug her nails hard into his back, feeling the tension shimmering in his powerful frame.

He was holding back. *Holding back for her.*

Her heart was pounding, her cheeks were flushed and her blood raced with every agonizingly slow stroke. Pleasure streaked through her and she cried out his name, telling him how much she wanted him, how much she needed him and he answered with his body, driving into her with controlled force, attacking her senses with a savage sensuality.

The storm inside was fierce and furious, raging through her like a wild beast, ready to burn up everything it touched. What they shared was primitive and elemental and she knew deep down in the very fibre of her being that nothing was ever going to be the same again.

She felt his fingers dig hard into the soft flesh of her thigh and then faster, harder, he built the rhythm until there was nothing in her head but a thundering roar, until everything inside and around her shattered into a million tiny fragments and she fell, spinning and tumbling, into a different world.

When she woke, she was alone in the bed. At some point during the early hours he'd transferred her to the bedroom, tucking her under the soft duvet. She had a vague recollection of pleading with him to join her and an equally vague recollection that his response to her request had been to pull away and return to the living room, making good on his earlier warning that their intimacies would be physical, not emotional. He'd returned to his laptop—to his own silent world. A world that didn't include Christmas or people.

A world that didn't include her.

Dizzy with lack of sleep, her body aching in unusual places, Evie slid out of the bed, blushing as she realised her nightdress was probably still lying in pieces on the floor of the living room.

So this was how it felt to sleep with a man you weren't in love with.

Padding across the thickly carpeted floor, she gazed in the mirror at herself, trying to see the differences. Same blue eyes. Same freckles. Same crazy morning hair.

She looked the same. Outwardly, nothing had changed. Maybe she could live a life that included sex without happy endings. Other women did it all the time. Maybe she could too.

Hearing his voice from the living room, Evie quickly pulled on a robe and followed the sound. He was on the phone, talking to someone in a time zone more alive than theirs. He'd made love to her for most of the night, but that hadn't stopped him working. Nothing stopped him working. But now she was wondering whether work was a refuge rather than a goal. A place to escape rather than a strategy for global domination.

The first thing she saw when she entered the room were newspapers stacked on the low table between the sofas.

Her stomach lurched and she felt sick with apprehension.

This was it. This was the moment she'd been dreading. This was the reason for the charade.

Had they printed that horribly revealing photograph?

Was that why he was on the telephone?

Hardly daring to look, she sank onto the sofa and stared at the newspaper on top of the pile, forcing herself to breathe slowly. It was one of the tabloids. If anyone had printed the picture of her naked, surely it would be them. Her hand shaking, she reached out and lifted it onto her lap. The headlines blurred and suddenly she didn't want to look, as if postponing the moment could alter the outcome.

'*Calma, tesoro.* It's all right.' His voice was deep and firm. 'They printed a lovely picture of you with your arms around my neck. The caption is "Tycoon tumbles" or something equally unimaginative. I expect your grandfather will be satisfied with it.'

What did he mean by that? 'So you were right.' Even though he'd reassured her, her fingers were damp with sweat as she forced herself to turn the pages. 'Because we gave them another photo opportunity and a bigger story, they used that instead. Thank you.' The relief was almost painful. 'Thank you so much.' Her eyes glistened as she looked up at him. 'I don't know what I would have done if they'd used that photograph. I'm so grateful to you.'

A muscle flickered in his jaw. 'You have no reason to be grateful to me, Evie.'

'Yes, I have. It was your idea to give them a better story. I would have tried to pay them off and that never would have worked because I suppose they would have just kept coming back for more money.'

He drew his hand over the back of his neck and she saw the muscles in his forearm flex, revealing a tension she didn't understand. 'Evie—'

'You don't have to say anything,' she said hastily. 'I do realise that this is just one day and that they could use that photograph tomorrow, but I'm not going to think about that now. We'll take it a day at a time. Maybe we can make sure they take another photograph of us tonight. Keep giving them something else to print. I promise not to dance on the table again, no matter how Christmassy I feel. What are our plans?'

He didn't answer immediately and she turned her attention back to the newspaper, turning the pages until she found the photograph. 'It's big. I had no idea they'd be that interested.' And she saw instantly why he'd made that comment about her grandfather liking the photograph. She was in Rio's arms, smiling up at him, looking completely smitten. No one looking at that picture would have questioned the authenticity of their relationship. A strange feeling twisted in the pit of her stomach. Was that really the way she'd looked at him? Had he noticed? 'We look good. They were obviously convinced.'

'Champagne certainly brings out an interesting side to you,' he drawled softly and she glanced up to find his eyes on her face.

'I really wasn't drunk.'

'But you were a virgin.'

Fire rose in her cheeks and she sat in silence for a moment, trying to find the right response. 'So what?'

'Why didn't you tell me?'

Was that the reason for his tension? Was it simply the fact that he was so much less experienced than him? 'Well, it isn't exactly something that comes up in conversation,' she said lightly, 'and I don't see that it matters. You wanted someone wholesome. If the press choose to dig around in my past they won't find anything. Isn't that what you wanted?' She kept noticing small things about him—like the bold curve of his eyebrows and the cluster of dark hairs revealed by the open neck of his shirt. Knowing what she knew now, she could easily picture the rest of his body—his chest shadowed with the same dark hair, concealing well defined muscle and breathtaking power. Knowing what she knew, everything was different. More sharply defined, more acutely felt.

The unspoken sexual component to their relationship had been there from the first moment they'd met but it had been enhanced a thousand times by the intimacies they'd shared in the flickering glow of firelight.

'You told me you were engaged.'

'I was.'

'But you didn't have a physical relationship?' His tone was incredulous.

'If you saw the house where I grew up, you wouldn't find it so surprising.' Evie pushed her hair away from her face with a hand that wasn't quite steady. 'I was all set to go to university, but after my grandmother died I couldn't bear to leave my grandfather on his own. I got a job in the village and went to night school to study languages. Jeff and I started dating because we were the only two people under fifty in the village. There was no way I was going to have sex in Grandpa's house. Even if it had been possible, it wouldn't have felt right.'

'Presumably, you didn't conduct your entire relationship with your grandfather looking on. There must have been *some* moments when you were alone.'

'Yes, I suppose there were—' Evie hesitated. 'But neither of us…we didn't really… Honestly, I think we were just friends. We should never have been anything else but I think we were swept along by the expectations of everyone around us.'

'Friends?' His dark brows locked in a puzzled frown and she smiled, thinking how much she'd learned about him in such a short time.

'I bet you've never been friends with a woman in your life, have you?'

'If by "friends" you mean no sex, then the answer is no. So you were engaged, but you never had sex.'

'I don't think either of us was in any hurry.'

'You were in a hurry last night,' he said silkily. 'Or was the champagne to blame for your sudden transformation from virgin to vamp?'

She sucked in a breath, mortified at his blatant reminder of her own desperation. 'No,' she said softly. 'It was you.'

'Let's test that theory, shall we?' He drew her to her feet and a thrill of expectation shot through her.

'Now?'

'Was it the champagne, Evie?' He murmured the words against her mouth and her eyes closed, her heart racing crazily as she rose on her toes and slid her arms around his neck. He slid his hands down her back and pressed her into him, his kiss tasting of hunger and passion.

Evie opened her mouth under his, matching his erotic demands with her own. Dimly, she registered that she shouldn't be feeling this way. They'd made love for most of the night and yet the fierce hunger inside her was as acute as if they hadn't ever touched. She was greedy for more of what they'd shared.

Rio pushed the robe down her arms with confident hands and the silky fabric slid over her hips and pooled on the floor, leaving her naked.

'It's daylight—' Evie could feel her face burning and he gave a slow smile as he tightened his hands on her shoulders and moved her away from him slightly.

'I know.'

'Stop staring at me,' she muttered. 'You've been with so many seriously beautiful women—'

'And none have excited me the way you do,' he said huskily, sweeping her into his arms and carrying her into the bedroom. 'You have the most incredible body.'

'You only think that because you're tall—and strong, which is why you can carry me without putting your back out—'

'You are extremely slender—' he lowered her onto the mattress '—most of your weight is your breasts and your astonishingly long legs and I have no complaints about either so you have no reason to be shy.' He stripped off his shirt and came down beside her in a fluid movement. 'I've never been with a woman as inexperienced as you—'

'I think I prefer the word "wholesome".' Her confidence faltered. 'Is it a problem?'

'No. It's a complete turn-on. But I'm probably going to shock you.' His dark eyes held hers for a moment and then he gently brushed away a strand of hair from her forehead with the tips of his fingers. 'I'm going to teach you everything you don't know, *tesoro*.'

The brief flicker of trepidation was swiftly transformed into breathless excitement as he kissed his way across her jaw and down her body to her exposed breasts. When he fastened his mouth over one straining peak the pleasure shafted through her and when his skilled fingers toyed with the other the torment rose to screaming pitch.

By the time he eventually pushed her thighs apart she was writhing against the sheets, the excitement ripping through her body like a vicious storm.

With no concession to the bright rays of sun spotlighting the room, Rio parted her with gentle fingers, placed his mouth against her and proceeded to subject her to the most extreme degree of erotic torture. With infinite skill, he explored her with tongue and fingers until Evie was on fire, her whole body burning in the flames he'd created. Tortured by the heat, she tried to move her hips to relieve the unbearable ache but he pinned her flat with his free hand, channelling the whole erotic experience into that one molten part of her until there was nothing in her world but him and the feelings he created.

Overwhelmed, she writhed and sobbed. 'Please—oh— how can you do those things at the same time—?'

He gave a husky laugh. 'I told you I was good at multi-tasking—'

Out of her mind with desire, Evie barely registered the fact that he was now above her before he sank into her with a single possessive thrust that filled her completely. The force and power of him stretched her sensitive flesh and she imme-diately shot into a climax so intense, so exquisitely agonizing, that her nails dug hard into the sleek muscle of his shoulder as her body convulsed around his.

He captured her mouth, kissing her with erotic intent as he slowly built the rhythm again, driving them both back towards that same peak. And this time, when she tumbled, she took him with her and he kept his mouth on hers, shar-ing every cry and every gasp, their bodies locked together in a shimmering heat created by the intensity of their own passion.

CHAPTER SEVEN

'YOU'RE insatiable. It's been more than a week—you should be bored with me by now.' Laughing, Evie rolled onto her stomach and leaned on Rio's chest. 'Aren't you ever tired?'

He watched her from beneath lowered lids, his gaze slumberous and unmistakably sexual. 'No. I find sex with you incredibly energizing.'

'So that's how you manage to work such long hours—'

'You should be grateful for that,' he said huskily. 'Otherwise, you wouldn't be getting any sleep at all, *tesoro.*'

'It's only two days until Christmas. You shouldn't be working.' Sometimes, when she woke in the dark, she discovered that he wasn't in bed with her. On one occasion she'd tiptoed sleepily from the bed to find him and discovered him working on the laptop, his gaze fixed intently on the ghostly green glow of the screen.

'I don't need much sleep. I had a few hours.' He slid his hand into her hair, pulled her head down and kissed her. 'Ready for breakfast?'

Evie felt a flutter of nerves in her stomach. Breakfast and mornings meant one thing to her. 'Have the newspapers arrived yet?'

He frowned. 'I have no idea and I don't care.'

'*I* care—I keep thinking about that stupid, horrid photograph.' The mood punctured, she rolled onto her back and stared up at the ceiling.

'Forget it.' Rio shifted over her in a smooth movement, his weight pressing her into the mattress. 'Yesterday they took photographs of you in the front row of the charity fashion show—they'll use one of those. Not one of you naked.'

'But you don't know that for sure—' She felt the sudden tension emanating from his powerful frame.

'I do. You need to trust me.'

Reasoning that he knew a great deal more about the media than she did, Evie forced herself to relax. 'OK. I trust you. But you *do* care, you know you do. That's why we're doing all this. You're worried about your deal going through. Is that still all right? I mean—' Suddenly she felt awkward asking. He didn't talk about stuff, did he? 'I know you don't talk about it but you're always on the phone and I can tell you're stressed about it.'

'I'm not stressed.' Only moments before he'd been relaxed. Now he was frighteningly detached, his handsome face an expressionless mask. 'And everything is fine.'

She shouldn't have asked. 'Good. Whatever it is must be worth a lot for you to care about it so much.'

'Yes. It's worth a lot.' Without warning, he sprang from the bed and prowled towards the bathroom. 'I'm going to take a shower. Order yourself some breakfast.'

His casual dismissal chilled her and Evie pulled the duvet over her naked body, feeling vulnerable and exposed. One minute they were incredibly close—the next, he shut her out.

Listening to the sound of the shower, she wondered what it was about this particular deal that was so important to him. She wished again she'd never raised the subject. Why was he so touchy? Was he worrying about it, or was it just that he didn't like talking about it?

She used the second bathroom to shower and change and was relieved when he joined her for breakfast.

Watching him cautiously, gauging his mood, Evie helped herself to a bowl of fruit. 'I checked the papers. You were right—they printed the photo from the fashion show.'

He poured himself a coffee. 'And what was the head-line?'

Evie blushed. 'Something stupid.' She wondered if he minded the media preoccupation with his love life but Rio simply smiled.

'The world appears to be revelling in my rapid and ex-tremely public conversion from never to forever. We're obvi-ously very convincing, *tesoro*.'

Captivated by that smile, Evie felt her breath catch and her heart gave a dangerous lurch. They were so convincing that she was starting to believe it herself. If it weren't for his occasional moments of icy detachment, it would have been frighteningly easy to forget that this wasn't real. *That some day soon he was going to expect her to dump him.*

Reminding herself to live in the moment, she ate a spoon-ful of fruit. 'We'd better make sure we give them something even more interesting to photograph today then. What are we doing tonight?'

'We have been invited by the Russians to watch a per-formance of the Bolshoi Ballet at the Royal Opera House at Covent Garden.'

'Wow.' Evie licked her spoon. 'I've never been to the ballet. That's really exciting!'

'Is it? I confess that men in tights don't excite me one little bit.' Rio rose to his feet as his phone rang. 'But, given that you're their new best friend and you speak fluent Russian, I'm sure we can make some use of the evening. Excuse me—I need to take this.'

'Of course.' Basking in the heady knowledge that she was useful to him, Evie felt a rush of pleasure that lasted through the day and the evening. She adored the ballet, was in awe of the elegant grandeur of the world famous Opera House and enjoyed acting as interpreter.

Vladimir was as charming to her as ever, but it was Rio who drew her attention. Cocooned in the private box, under the protection of darkness, she found herself looking at him every other second, her eyes drawn to the perfect symmetry of his arrogant features, fatally fascinated by the breathtaking power and masculinity stamped in every angle of his body.

Once, he caught her looking and raised an eyebrow in silent question. Evie simply smiled, relieved to be able to hide her fascination behind the charade of their 'relationship'. That was what she was supposed to do, wasn't it? She was supposed to look.

Again, the photographers were out in force, stealing photographs at every opportunity, but Evie felt nothing but relief because she knew by now that, providing they managed to get an interesting shot, they were unlikely to use the one she dreaded appearing.

They went from the ballet to another ball and this time Rio needed no persuasion to dance with her. His hand was warm on her bare back as they moved together, the rhythm of their bodies perfectly in tune after so many hours spent locked in intimacy.

'You're not singing tonight?' He murmured the words against her lips and Evie reminded herself that it was essential to breathe or she'd fall over. But, when he held her like this, she felt as though everything inside her was suspended.

No wonder no woman had ever dumped him.

He was so insanely gorgeous, who in their right mind would not want to be with him?

'No singing. They've already had that picture.' Her arms were locked around his neck and she could feel the heat of his body against hers. 'Grandpa liked it, by the way—he said it reminded him of last year when I did the same thing at the village hall.'

'You danced on the table?'

'No—fortunately, they didn't have champagne.' She smiled up at him. 'I'd love to do something really Christmassy. Can we go ice skating? I really envied those people skating when we were at the ball. Or maybe we could go and sing Christmas carols. I noticed an invitation for a celebrity carol concert at St Paul's Cathedral—are we going to that? I know you see Christmas as nothing more than an interruption in your working day, but I love this time of year.'

He didn't answer. At first, she thought he hadn't heard her question and Evie was about to open her mouth and ask again when she saw his eyes. It was like staring into a dark pool, knowing that beneath the still, glassy surface lay nothing but danger.

She shivered.

They'd stopped dancing. Stopped moving. Among the streamers and balloons, the people laughing, dancing and singing, they alone stood still, locked in the small private bubble they'd formed for themselves. Evie felt frozen and she thought absently that there was no reason to be cold when the room was so warm, but then she realised that the chill came from him. His skin was cold to touch, his eyes reflecting not celebration but an acute and bitter pain.

'Rio?' She spoke his name softly. She had no idea what was wrong, but she wanted to help and not just because of what they'd shared. She would have felt the same way about anyone who was suffering as much as he clearly was. 'Are you—' She broke off, frustrated with herself. What was she planning to say? *Are you all right?* Well, obviously, the answer to that was a resounding *no,* but he was hardly likely to tell her that, was he? He was the most fiercely private man she'd ever met.

And yet they must be conspicuous, standing there locked

together but not moving, like some elaborate sculpture of lovers.

Evie placed her hand on his cheek, alarmed by how cold he was. 'Shall we go?'

Finally, he seemed to hear her and he stared down at her blankly, as if he'd forgotten she was there. 'Yes,' he said at last. 'I think that would be a good idea.'

Aware that their behaviour was starting to draw curious glances, Evie stood on tiptoe and kissed him gently on the mouth. *Tomorrow's photograph,* she thought as a camera flashed and a woman sighed with envy.

It was snowing again outside and Evie sat quietly in the limousine as it moved silently through the white streets. Normally snow soothed her, but tonight nothing could ease the tension in the car.

She wanted to know what was going on in his head, but she also knew that he wouldn't want to tell her.

After a moment's hesitation, she reached across and took his hand in hers, oddly pleased when he didn't immediately withdraw his.

Once, during the silent journey, she sneaked a glance at his taut profile but he stared sightlessly into the winter night, apparently oblivious to everything except his own thoughts.

After a silent ride in the elevator, they stepped into the Penthouse and immediately the phone calls started.

So that was it?

Whatever menace lurked beneath the surface had apparently been ruthlessly repressed once more.

Evie stood awkwardly, hovering, while he took one phone call and then another before eventually deciding that she might as well go to bed and wait for him there. She had no expectation that he'd join her this time, but he did—at three in the morning, long after she'd ended her silent vigil.

This time there was no gentle seduction, no talking—just wild, out of control sex that blew her mind.

It was only afterwards, when his side of the bed had long grown cold, that she wondered what he'd been trying to escape. Because he had been trying to escape, of that she was sure. The raw, ruthless passion they'd shared hadn't been energizing sex, it had been oblivion sex.

She had to talk to him.

No one who felt that bad should suffer alone.

Feeling distinctly strange, Evie moved quietly into the living room. How did you approach a man you had wild, crazy sex with but no relationship? What were you supposed to say? Technically, were they friends now?

He had his back to her and he was talking in a low voice, his long fingers toying with a sleek, expensive pen.

She was so busy working out what she was going to say when he finished on the phone that it was a moment or two before she actually paid attention to his conversation.

It was his tone that made her listen. The hardness was tempered by something she hadn't heard in his voice before. There was no hint of the ruthless businessman, or the primitive lover. He was infinitely gentle and it was obvious that the person on the other end of the phone meant a lot to him.

More than a lot.

'*Sì tesoro—ti amo.*'

Evie froze. *Ti amo.* She didn't speak much Italian but she knew that meant *I love you.* Unable to help herself, she listened to the rest of the conversation and picked up a few more words. This man, who claimed not to believe in happy endings, was telling someone that he loved her. That he hoped to see her soon.

The scent of him still clung to her skin, as did hers to him, no doubt, and yet he was already making plans to see another woman.

Her skin felt icy-cold.

She'd slept with another woman's man.

Was this the secret that simmered beneath the surface? Was this the reason for his pain?

Nausea rose in her stomach and her legs felt as though they'd been turned to water.

She'd had sex with a man who was deeply involved with someone else.

Angry with him but even more angry with herself, Evie was about to move when he turned his head and saw her.

'Evie?' His voice was deep and male, surprisingly normal after the emotional tightrope they'd walked the previous night. 'You're awake early. I didn't see you there.'

'Don't worry about it.' She stood stiff, shivering slightly, feeling slightly detached from her surroundings. 'I'm going to get dressed. Then I'm going.'

He frowned. 'Going where?'

'I don't know.' Her shocked mind was paralysed. It refused to provide her with the words and the thoughts she needed to move forward. 'Anywhere but here.'

His eyes hardened. 'We made a deal. It would be catastrophic if you left now. I need you to stay.'

'Why? What's the point of this charade when you're already involved with someone else?' Emotion thickened her voice and she hated herself for not being the cool, rational person she wanted to be. She wanted to be sophisticated enough to thank him for a perfect no-strings-attached relationship and walk away. Instead, she wanted to claw his flawless features and thump him. She wanted him to hurt the way she was hurting. 'Does she know? Does she know about me?'

A muscle flickered in his cheek and he put his pen down, the movement slow and deliberate. 'You were listening to my phone call.'

'Not intentionally. And if you're expecting me to apologise for eavesdropping on a private conversation then forget it. There are some things that shouldn't be private.'

'*Calma*. Calm down.'

'No, I will not *calma* or calm down! I don't speak much
Italian, Rio, but I speak enough to understand the gist of what
you just said to her! I'm really astonished you've never been
dumped if that's the way you treat women. You're right—
you are a complete and utter bastard. This whole week we…
you…' She broke off, trying to control herself. 'How could
you do that? How could you do those things when you're in
love with someone else? I thought you were a free agent—
single. You should have *told* me you were involved with
someone.'

'I'm not involved.'

Her breathing was shallow. 'When you warned me that
you'd break my heart, I didn't expect it to happen quite this
quickly.'

'Evie—'

'No! Just don't make pathetic excuses, OK? I don't want
to hear them. I heard you! I *heard* you talking to your
girlfriend.'

He swore softly in Italian and turned away from her.

For a moment, staring at the rigid tension in those broad
shoulders, she thought he wasn't even going to bother defending himself.

And then he turned, a savage look on his face. 'You did
not hear me talking to my girlfriend. It wasn't a woman.' His
voice was raw and Evie stood still, frozen to the spot by the
look in his eyes.

'But—'

'You heard me talking to a child. She's four years old. A
child, not a woman. My daughter.' He let out a long breath.
'You heard me talking to my daughter.'

'All right. Keep me informed.' Rio terminated the conversation with his lawyer and looked up to see Evie standing
there. She'd changed into a pair of jeans and a blue cashmere

jumper. Her hair, still damp from the shower, accentuated the extreme pallor of her face.

'Why didn't you tell me you have a child?' Her voice was flat. 'Why didn't you mention it?'

Programmed to keep women at a distance, Rio kept his response cool. 'It isn't any of your business.' Seeing the hurt in her eyes, he wished he hadn't been quite so blunt. 'I don't talk about my private life. To anyone.'

'I'm not some journalist, Rio!' She swept her hand through her hair, her confusion evident in every movement she made. 'We slept together, for God's sake. We shared—'

'Sex,' Rio drawled. 'We shared sex. A physical relationship, however satisfying, doesn't give you access to the rest of my life. Don't make the mistake of thinking that it does.'

Her head jerked as if he'd slapped her and for a moment he thought she was going to do exactly that to him. Instead, she lost still more colour from her cheeks and nodded stiffly. 'Of course it doesn't. My mistake. You have a child. Forgive me for thinking that's something you might have mentioned.' She turned away from him and stalked towards the table that had already been laid for breakfast. 'Are those today's papers?' Her hands shook as she lifted one and flicked through it. 'Have they used the photograph? Or haven't you bothered to check? I'm worried we didn't give them much of interest last night.'

She was rigidly polite and Rio watched her in silence, knowing that he was going to have to tell her the truth and wondering why that felt like a difficult conversation. He'd done what needed to be done. In the same circumstances, he'd make all the same decisions. *So why did he feel so uncomfortable?* 'They haven't used it. They have, however, printed the one they took when you kissed me.' He watched her face as she picked up a tabloid paper and scanned the headline.

Her face was expressionless as she scanned the photograph. *Truly a time for miracles—Rio in love.* Some of the tension left her. 'Well, it seems we're off the hook for another day.'

Rio's jaw tightened. 'Evie—'

'Sorry—it's just that I'm finding this whole thing quite stressful, in case you hadn't noticed. Every morning we go through the same thing. And the worst thing is, there is never going to come a point when it goes away—they have that photo for ever, don't they? They can use it this year or next year—it never ends.'

Wondering exactly when he'd developed a conscience, Rio forced a reluctant confession past his lips. 'Evie, they won't use that photo.'

She looked up from the newspaper. 'It's all very well to say that while you're giving them something more interesting to print, but sooner or later they're going to get bored with our "romance" and then they'll be on the lookout for something more juicy.'

'I can guarantee they're not going to print that photograph.'

'How? Has your security team managed to track the man down?' With a soft gasp, she dropped the newspaper on the table. 'They found him?'

He had to tell her now. 'Yes. We found him.'

Relief crossed her face, to be followed quickly by consternation. 'But that doesn't mean you can stop the photograph. I mean, he's had loads of time to have sent it all over the place. It's probably too late.'

'He hasn't sent it anywhere. My security team confiscated his camera.'

'But how—'

'They confiscated his camera less than fifteen seconds after he took the offending photograph,' Rio confessed in a raw tone, telling himself firmly that he'd do exactly the same thing again in the same circumstances. 'That's how I know for a fact that he didn't send it anywhere. Antonio was outside the door of the Penthouse. He apprehended the guy before he'd taken two steps.'

A heavy silence descended on the room. Evie stared at him, digesting the enormity of his confession and Rio felt the tension inside himself double.

'You're saying—' she swallowed hard '—you're telling me—oh, my God.' She sank down hard on the nearest sofa, her breathing rapid. 'There was never a risk that the photograph would be published. You told me…you let me think…' She lifted her head to look at him and her eyes were huge and shocked. 'How could you do that?'

'Because it was necessary. It was the right thing to do.'

'The right thing?' She lifted her hands to her face and then let them drop again, clearly struggling to find the words to express herself. 'I was almost out of my *mind* with worry! My grandfather is eighty-six years old and I thought…I thought…' Her face was contorted with pain. 'I thought it would crucify him to see that photo. I was *so* worried—'

'Which is why I assured you that they wouldn't use the pictures.'

'But you didn't tell me *why* you were so sure!' She stood up, shock giving way to anger. 'You arranged the photographer! You were in league with creepy Carlos!'

'No—' Rio interrupted her hastily '—that isn't true. It *was* a set-up.' He raked his fingers through his hair, wondering how, of all the difficult negotiations he'd ever made, this one seemed the most challenging. 'But I admit that I turned it to my advantage. I had no choice.'

'You *did* have a choice. There is always a choice. You could have told me the truth.'

'I didn't know if you were involved or not.'

'I *told* you I wasn't.'

He decided not to waste time pointing out that plenty of her sex lied for a living. In the short time he'd known her, he'd started to realise that Evie didn't seem to think the same way as other women. 'By the time I realised that you were telling the truth, we were already deeply involved in the pretence. I was afraid you'd walk out on me.'

'So you used me. Is that what you're trying to tell me?'

Unable to find an alternative take on the situation, Rio felt sweat prickle his brow. 'Yes.'

'But you…' She jabbed her fingers into her hair, an expression of shocked disbelief on her face. 'But we had sex—what was your justification for that? Were there cameras in the room?'

'You initiated the sex.'

She gave a painful laugh. 'Well, that's you off the hook, then.' Her eyes were glazed with tears. 'You warned me you were ruthless and you told me that I'd find it easy to dump you—well, you were right. I'm dumping you. We now have the shortest engagement on record.'

'I accept that I was wrong not to tell you,' Rio breathed, 'but *don't* walk out.'

'Why? Because you haven't closed your precious deal yet? What is *wrong* with you? You don't need more money but you're so desperate to win you're willing to do whatever it takes.' A toss of her head sent her hair flaming down her back and she stalked back into the bedroom without glancing in his direction, flinging words over her shoulder like missiles. 'There are some things in life that are more important than money, Rio. People's feelings are more important. Integrity. Honesty. And if you don't know what any of those words mean then use some of that money of yours to buy a dictionary.'

Rio searched his brain for slick words that would extricate him from this hole, but found none. His instinct was to leave her alone, but his legs had different ideas and, moments later, he found himself standing in the doorway of the bedroom, watching her.

'I understood that you were worried, which is why I

constantly reassured you that the photograph would not be published. You should have trusted me.'

'Trusted you!' She turned on him, her eyes flashing. 'Why would I trust you? You're impossibly arrogant. You think you're right about everything. How was I to know that in this case the reason you knew the photograph wouldn't be published was because you had it in your possession all the time? I don't believe this is happening—' Her breathing was shallow and rapid. 'You were so angry with Carlos. I thought you were going to finish him off—but why would he have arranged that photograph?'

'Because Carlos is the brother of a woman I once had a relationship with,' Rio said savagely. 'It was a difficult relationship. She wanted more—'

'Then she was looking in the wrong place, wasn't she?' Her tone acid, Evie scraped her make-up from the top of the dressing table into her bag. 'Didn't she read the newspapers? Didn't she know that you don't do "more"?'

Telling himself that her anger was only to be expected, Rio ploughed ahead. 'She wanted me to marry her.'

'She wanted to spend the rest of her life with you? Clearly she was deranged.'

Knowing that he deserved that, Rio took it on the chin. 'She stopped taking contraception.'

Evie paused, a tube of lipgloss in her hand. 'She became pregnant? On purpose?' The shock in her voice almost made him smile.

'Yes, on purpose. On purpose, Evie.' He said the word twice, each time with emphasis, knowing that she had absolutely no idea what people could be like. She was such a crazy idealist, wasn't she? 'Are you going to ask me why?'

'I'm not stupid. I presume she thought you'd marry her.' She stuffed the lipgloss into her bag. 'Which, of course, you wouldn't.'

'No, because it never would have worked.' Rio growled

the words angrily. 'I offered her everything but that. I offered to buy her a house near me—I offered her financial support. But all she wanted was marriage and I'd made the mistake of being honest about how much I wanted to see my child. She used that knowledge to carry on blackmailing me. Only this time, instead of "I'm pregnant, marry me", it was "if you want to see your child, marry me".'

Evie stood still. Some of the anger in her face was replaced by uncertainty.

'She used my child as currency,' Rio said thickly. 'An object to be bartered with. I gave her sufficient funds to live in luxury for the rest of her life but she frittered it away on unsuitable friends and people I would not have allowed anywhere near my daughter. Because she had my child, I carried on trying to help. I even gave her useless brother Carlos a job in my hotel, under close supervision. But I was working behind the scenes to get custody of my daughter.'

'Custody?' Her eyes widened in shock and he gave a bitter smile because he'd seen exactly that same look on the faces of others.

'Yes, custody. And, yes, I know I'm a single man. A single man with a self-confessed relationship phobia. I am no one's image of ideal father material. It was easy for her to build a case, making me look unsuitable. I work inhuman hours, I have no history of commitment—' he breathed deeply '—it's possible I would never even have had a chance if it weren't for the fact that Jeanette left Elyssa unattended.'

'She left her child *alone*?'

Rio wanted to tell her not to be so naive, but realised that would be unfair. It wasn't naivety that prevented her from understanding why another woman might leave a child alone; it was her nature. He'd seen the way she cared about her grandfather. She was warm and loving—a nurturer who believed that families stuck together and supported each other through thick and thin.

'Jeanette didn't ever want a child. All she wanted was a tool to manipulate me. She doesn't have a maternal bone in her body.' He watched Evie flinch as he took a hatchet to her illusions. 'I imagine someone like you would find that almost impossible to believe, so let me tell you just how unhappy my daughter's life has been so far and maybe then you'll understand that there are times when "ruthless" is justified.'

'Rio—'

'She was left on her own in the house because there was no way Jeanette was wasting any of the money I gave her caring for a child she never wanted. I sent her staff; she fired them. I interviewed eight nannies personally. None of them lasted a day. Jeanette said she'd care for Elyssa herself, but she didn't. I've been fighting for custody since before my daughter was born but it was only six months ago, after she had a nasty fall in the house while she was on her own, that the tide turned in my favour. The police were called. Elyssa was taken into foster care while they reviewed the case. It's been a long, hard slog but we were almost there.'

'Were?'

'Elyssa is Jeanette's meal ticket,' Rio said, struggling to keep the emotion out of his voice. 'She doesn't want me to have custody. She reinvented herself as a model mother. She's been volunteering at the church, visiting the sick and the elderly, generally behaving like a perfect citizen.'

'And at the same time she's been trying to destroy your reputation? Make you look like an unsuitable carer for a child?'

'Unfortunately, over the years, I've managed to do that for myself. I've made no apology for the fact that I don't want commitment, never realising that the time would come when I'd regret expressing those sentiments in such a public fashion.'

'So that's why Carlos wanted me to spend the night. That's why he arranged the photographer. That's what the deal is.'

Her breathing quickened and her eyes held his. 'This deal isn't about money, is it? It isn't business. It's your daughter. The reason you didn't want those photographs published was because of your daughter. They were trying to make you look bad.'

Rio stood still, watching her. So much was riding on this conversation and yet, for once, his slick way with words had abandoned him. 'I've worked for years to reach this point.'

'But if your security team caught the man immediately—if you knew there was no danger of that photograph being exposed—why go through with that farce?'

'Because I thought you could help my case.' He didn't flinch from the truth. 'My lawyer told me to stay whiter than white or find a wholesome-looking woman. Until Carlos intervened, I'd settled on the first option. Then I saw you lying on the bed.'

'I was naked,' she said dryly. 'Not exactly wholesome.'

'No one looking at you could ever believe you were anything other than a thoroughly decent person,' Rio said roughly. *And he'd used her.* 'I'm a man who has said I'd never settle down—to convince people I'd changed my mind, it would have to be with someone completely different from the usual women I date. You fitted that description.'

She stood for a moment. 'And it didn't occur to you to just tell me the truth? You could have just asked for my help. You could have trusted me.'

'No, I couldn't.'

'Have you ever trusted a woman?'

Rio didn't even hesitate. 'I've never had reason to.'

Pain flickered across her face and he knew she was thinking about everything they'd shared. 'So what happens now?'

He clenched his fists by his sides, wondering why it suddenly felt so hard to remain detached when that was his normal default mode. 'That's your decision,' he said flatly.

'If you want to go home to your grandfather for Christmas, then I can arrange that. And of course you have a job as receptionist. You're overqualified for the position, but if that's what you want then that's fine by me. The one thing I ask is that you dump me, as we agreed, rather than telling the media the truth.'

'How have you kept your daughter's name out of the press?'

'That was part of my deal with Jeanette. And I admit we've been lucky. I suppose because I'm the last man in the world to want a child, they didn't look.'

'So you want me to dump you—' She rubbed her fingers across her forehead. 'But you haven't won your case yet, have you? I could make things difficult for you.'

'Yes.' The thought brought a bitter taste to his mouth. 'But I'll have to take that chance.'

'What makes you think you're the right home for a little girl, Rio? What can you offer a child?'

He didn't hesitate. 'Security. The absolute certainty that I'll always be there for her.' He'd never felt the need to explain or defend his decision to anyone before, but suddenly he had a burning need to defend himself to Evie. 'I'm not planning to nominate myself for super-dad any time soon, but I can offer her a stability that has never been present in her life.'

'That's quite a promise, coming from a man who doesn't believe in commitment.'

'This is one commitment I'm prepared to make.' He didn't expect her to believe him. How could he when he was well aware he'd given her no reason on which to base that belief?

And already his mind was computing the options because he knew she was going to walk out. Why wouldn't she? He'd deceived her. He'd used her. He'd hurt her. *He'd had sex with her—*

And now she was going to make him pay.

He needed to ring the lawyers and warn them, although what they would be able to do, he had no idea.

Reaching into his pocket for his phone, his fingers encountered his wallet. He paused and then pulled it out and retrieved the photograph from behind a stack of dollars. Hesitating for only a fraction of a second, he handed it to her. 'This is Elyssa. It's not a brilliant one—I took it with my phone in the summer. Her hair is darker than it looks in the photograph.' He watched as she stared down at the photograph.

'Please leave me alone,' she said hoarsely. 'I need a minute to myself.'

Rio hesitated, and then turned and walked back into the living room. Conscious of how much he'd hurt her, he retrieved his BlackBerry from his jacket pocket. The only option open to him now was damage limitation.

He was in the process of dialling his lawyer when her voice came from behind him.

'Put the phone down.' She stood in the doorway, stiff and unsmiling, the photograph still in her hand. 'I'll stay and finish this charade if you think it will help you. Not because you shoved a photograph of a vulnerable little girl into my hand and made me feel guilty which, by the way, was yet another example of ruthless manipulation on your part, but because you took that photograph in the first place. It's the first time I've ever known you to use your BlackBerry for anything other than work. If you carry a picture of your daughter around, there must be some good in you somewhere. I have yet to see it, but I live in hope. Unlike you, I'm prepared to take some things on trust. Given that Elyssa seems to have drawn the short straw with her mother, she needs someone who is prepared to stand up and fight for her, *not* that I think that excuses your appalling behaviour.'

Stunned by her words, Rio inhaled deeply. 'Evie—'

'And you need to learn to take some things on trust, too.

You need to show some faith in people.' She walked across the room and placed the photograph carefully in his hand. 'A little girl's future is at stake—you should have known I'd do the right thing. I didn't need a guilt trip to set me on the right path. If you'd told me the truth in the first place—' there were tears in her eyes '—I just wish you had told me the truth, Rio.'

'My daughter's future was all that mattered to me.'

'If you'd told me, I would have helped you.' Her lashes sparkled with moisture. 'You need to stop being such a cynic because the last thing a little girl needs is a father who is a cynic. When you're reading her fairy stories, maybe it's right to adapt the ending—maybe it isn't right to tell children that they all lived happily ever after, I don't know—but neither is it right to bring her up believing that everyone is guilty until proven innocent. That there is no good in anyone. That all people are out to get what they can out of everyone else. If you're going to apply corporate principles to parenting, then it's never going to work.' Taking a deep breath, she squared her shoulders. 'Now, get your coat and phone that driver of yours. We're going shopping.'

Still braced for catastrophe, it took Rio a few moments to assimilate the fact that she wasn't leaving. She was offering to stay. Her generosity floored him. 'Of course I'll take you shopping.' His voice was husky with an emotion he didn't recognise and he lifted his hand and brushed a strand of hair away from her moist cheek. Gratitude, he thought. And admiration. He realised that he'd been wrong about her again. She was far, far stronger than she looked. 'I'll buy you the biggest diamond you've ever seen as long as you tell me I'm forgiven.'

'I didn't say anything about diamonds and I didn't say anything about forgiveness. We're going to a toy shop. If you truly intend to be a father to Elyssa, then you need to start learning what little girls like for Christmas.' Despite everything, there was humour in her gaze. 'I probably ought to warn you that I'm something of an expert. Fasten your seat belt because I have a feeling this is going to be a steep learning curve.'

CHAPTER EIGHT

'FAIRY wings?' RIO's tone was incredulous. 'You're sure?'

Evie reached for a pair of pink gossamer wings which hung from a metal hook. She felt devastated. Ripped to shreds by the revelation that he'd lied to her. 'Trust me, fairy wings are always a hit with four-year-olds. Better buy a spare pair, ready for when she breaks these.' It felt strange, having this conversation with this man. She had a sense that what she was saying was as alien to him as the Russian Vladimir spoke.

As if to confirm her suspicions, he looked at her blankly. 'Why will she break them? She's a little girl, not a Sumo wrestler—'

'Yes, but she'll want to sleep in them,' Evie explained patiently, 'because that's what little girls always do and sleeping in them will break them. When that happens you can either explain to her that they're gone for ever or you can spoil her rotten and get her another pair. Normally I'd suggest it's dangerous to spoil her but, given that she's obviously had a completely rubbish time lately, I think an extra pair is probably in order.'

Without hesitation, Rio cleared the shelves of pink fairy wings.

'I meant one spare pair,' Evie said faintly, 'not ten.'

'I'm not risking anything. As you say, she's had enough trauma for one lifetime.' Rio handed them to his stunned bodyguard. 'So we have fairy wings and spare fairy wings and spare spare fairy wings. What next?'

Thrown by the sight of the normally taciturn Antonio struggling to balance a mountain of fairy wings, Evie managed a smile. 'If you're attacked now, this will be interesting. You'll just have to bash them with your magic wand or something—'

Antonio's mouth twitched. 'I'll remember that.'

'Don't worry about Antonio,' Rio drawled. 'He probably trained in the same unarmed combat camp as your grandfather. If the chips were down, he'd find a way to turn fairy wings into an assault weapon.' His gaze met hers. 'It's good of you to do this for me.'

She felt frozen inside. 'I'm doing it for her, not you.' She ignored the tiny part of her that questioned that claim, just as she ignored the commotion in her nerve-endings that told her he was even more lethally attractive when he was vulnerable. 'Let's go. We need dolls.'

'I'm not sure about dolls. Last time I saw her, I took her a doll.' He scanned the rows of toys with something close to despair. 'I think I probably chose the wrong sort. There were millions. The one I picked had a very elaborate costume and she was very frustrated when it wouldn't come off.'

Evie's heart twisted at that image—the arrogant, self assured tycoon taking a serious knock to his self-esteem as he struggled to choose a doll. 'I expect she'd like a doll that can be dressed and undressed. They make one that cries and wets itself.'

His expression was comical. 'There is a market for that?'

'A huge market,' Evie told him, enjoying the look of shock on his face. 'You pour the milk in one end and it comes out the other, just like real life.'

Rio shuddered and he said something in Italian. 'That is *fun*?'

'It's role play. Didn't you ever play mummies and daddies—?' Evie took one look at his face and shook her head. 'Forget I said that. I don't suppose commitment games were ever your thing. Take it from me, most little girls are a sucker for caring for a baby. Put a real baby in a room and the girls are all over it in minutes. Whatever anyone says about feminism, most little girls love pretending dolls are babies.'

'Did you?' Suddenly his gaze became disturbingly acute and Evie felt the slow burn of colour in her cheeks.

'Yes.' She turned away from him and took the stairs two at a time. There were some things it didn't pay to think about. Especially not around this man. She just wanted to get this over with so that she could go into hiding and lick her wounds. 'Here—dolls. I'll grab a shopping trolley. I don't think poor Antonio can carry any more.'

'A whole floor of dolls?' Rio looked horrified. 'How do you know where to start?'

Evie tried to translate it into terms he'd understand. 'Like any product, you have to segment your market. There's a specific market for young children. Then they segment the market again—dolls that cry, dolls that—'

'OK, fine. I get the picture—' he interrupted her hastily '—so which is the market leader?'

'This one.' She pointed and Rio lifted it off the shelf gingerly.

'How many spares do we need?'

'At least one. It's very easy to leave a doll on a plane.' Suddenly realising what she'd said, Evie gave a wry smile. 'On the other hand, you do *own* the plane, so you'd be able to retrieve it without long and fruitless arguments with unhelpful airline staff. You could probably get away without spares.'

Clearly not prepared to take any risks, Rio added five identical dolls to the growing pile of toys in the trolley. 'I have five homes,' he said by way of explanation. 'It's probably best to have a spare in each.'

'Five?' Evie blinked. 'You have *five* homes?'

'You're thinking that it will confuse a small child?' He added a small stack of accessories to the pile. 'I've been thinking the same thing. In fact, I've been restructuring my business so that I can spend as much time as possible at my palazzo in Florence, to give her stability. My team have decorated a room exactly like the one she is in at the moment so that it seems familiar. It's right next to mine and I have already appointed a very experienced English nanny who is ready to move in at a moment's notice.'

Evie felt the hot sting of tears scald her eyes and turned away in horror, blinking rapidly. For crying out loud, what was the matter with her? Why did the thought of him studying a child's room and creating an identical version make her want to sob? Struggling for control, she picked up a doll from the shelf and pretended to examine it. Her insides were at war and, when she felt Rio's hand close over her shoulder, the tears formed a lump in her throat. 'This is a good one.' She thrust the doll at him and he studied it in silence.

'Are you sure? I'm no expert, but I don't think so.'

Dragging her gaze from the dark shadow of his jaw to the doll she'd handed him, Evie realised that he was right. The doll she'd selected was completely unsuitable for a young child. Apart from the fact that the clothing was covered in intricate beading, there was a clear warning that it wasn't intended for children under the age of eight. She wasn't concentrating. Her mind was all over the place.

His hand still on her shoulder, Rio returned the doll to the shelf. 'I've upset you again.' His voice was low and all Evie could do was shake her head, frightened by the intensity of her feelings.

'No.'

'You're trying not to cry. I know enough about women to recognise the signs.'

'I believe you. I'm sure you've made enough women cry in your time.'

'But normally they don't try and hold it back. As usual, you have to be different. If you want to sob, then sob. I know I deserve it. I really have been a bastard to you.' He smoothed her hair away from her face but she moved her head away sharply.

'Don't touch me. And don't use that word in a toy shop.' Evie almost wished she could cry. It would have been easier to hate him. The problem was, she didn't hate him. She didn't hate him at all. He'd used her, he'd lied to her, but she still didn't hate him.

Ignoring her warning not to touch, he closed his hands over her shoulders. 'Evie—'

'Let's just get this done. I'm tired. I haven't had much sleep in the last few days.' She tried to pull away from him but he held her, his physical strength evident in his firm grip.

'We were talking about where Elyssa would enjoy living most. Do you have an opinion on where a little girl would like to live? I assumed a child would rather live in one place as much as possible and Florence is a wonderful city, but if you think—'

'I honestly don't know.' Evie finally managed to pull away from him. 'Why would I know? I'm not a mother. I probably know less than you do.' All she knew was that her mind was a mess. She'd told herself that he was totally the wrong man for her because he wasn't the family sort. He'd emphasised that he wasn't interested in commitment. And now she discovered he had a daughter he clearly adored and every decision he made, even the one to use her so ruthlessly to achieve his own ends, demonstrated the level of his commitment to his child. The fact that he was clearly struggling so hard to do the right thing somehow made the whole thing all the more poignant. He hadn't chosen fatherhood, but he was determined to do it right. He was facing his responsibilities. Despite what everyone said, Rio Zaccarelli didn't have a problem with commitment. His problem was with his own relationships with women. And that was hardly surprising, was it, given the women he'd met in the past?

Thinking about Elyssa's mother, Evie's throat was thick with emotion. Who would do that to a man? Or to a child? A solid lump seemed to have formed behind the wall of her chest. She kept seeing him removing that photograph from his wallet. Kept seeing him piling up fairy wings so that his daughter didn't suffer any more trauma. Her arm brushed against his and an electric current shot through her body and, at that moment, the truth lit up in her brain.

She'd fallen in love with him. At some point during the glittering, glamorous charade, the pretence had turned to reality.

It was a thrilling, sickening feeling. A sudden whoosh of the heart and a sinking of the stomach. Dread and desire intermingled with a knowledge that the whole thing was hopeless.

How could that have happened?

In such a short time and with a man like him?

How could she have been so recklessly foolish?

Parading his faults through her brain, Evie turned sharply and walked towards the end of the store, hiding her panic. 'You need books. Reading together is a great way to bond.' She blocked out an image of Rio sprawled on a bedcover covered in pink dancing fairies, reading to a small, dark haired girl who adored him. This was hard enough without making it worse for herself.

Her hands shook as she selected books from the shelves, conscious of his steady scrutiny.

'What's going on, Evie? When we came into this store you were hell bent on punishing me—you dragged me round pink fairy wings, handed me dolls and stuffed toys bigger than I am—and suddenly you look like the one who is being punished. You look like someone who has had a terrible shock.'

'No,' she answered quickly. Too quickly. 'Not a shock.'

'I wish you'd tell me why you're upset. Or is this still because you're thinking about my daughter?' He sat down on a chair in the reading area. He should have looked ridiculous, stretching his powerful body and long legs amongst the small bean bags and tiny colouring tables, but he didn't look ridiculous. Evie doubted Rio could look ridiculous anywhere. He had that ability to blend with his surroundings that came with confidence and self-assurance.

'Of course I'm thinking of your daughter.' Picking another two books from the shelf, she flicked through them. 'That's what we're doing here, isn't it?' She wished he'd stop looking at her. Suddenly, she was afraid that everything she was feeling might show on her face. The feelings growing inside her were so new she hadn't got used to hiding them yet.

'So we've done fairy wings, dolls, stuffed toys, games—' he listed them one by one, a trace of irony in his voice '—is there anything else you think she would like? What does a little girl really want?'

What does a little girl really want?

Evie stared for a moment, the question opening a deep rift inside her. It was the one thing she was able to answer with complete confidence. 'All a little girl really wants is her daddy,' she said huskily. 'The rest is just icing on the cake.'

'You're sure?' Rio tucked the phone between his ear and his shoulder as he opened the email. 'Yes, I have it here…I'm reading it right now…I'll make all the arrangements.'

When he finally ended the call, he knew his life had altered irrevocably. It was done. The lawyers had finally confirmed it. Elyssa was going to come and live with him. The courts had awarded him custody.

His gaze slid to the small mountain of toys that had been neatly stacked in one corner of the Penthouse, a testament to Evie's dedication to her task. His little girl would want for nothing, not that he was kidding himself for one moment that the future was going to go as smoothly as that one shopping trip. For a start there was his own inexperience to take into account, and then there was the inescapable fact that Elyssa had spent the past few years with a woman so self-absorbed that the needs of her child had largely gone unnoticed. Whichever way you looked at it, there was a rocky road ahead. Staring at the toys, he suddenly wished Evie was there to guide him through more than just his choice of doll.

But that was a crazy thought, wasn't it? A selfish thought, because he had nothing to offer her. Not even a defence against her accusation that he'd used her.

He had.

He'd done what needed to be done, without a flicker of conscience. But he didn't need to use her a moment longer. Their charade could end. Evie could get on with her life— could concentrate on making her grandfather proud.

She could go home for Christmas.

He sat there for a long moment and for once his phones were silent.

Through the wraparound glass of the luxurious Penthouse, he could see that the snow was falling again and immediately he thought how pleased Evie would be.

She loved snow.

Rising to his feet, he decided he needed to tell her, but when he searched the Penthouse there was no sign of her. At some point during his endless phone calls, she'd gone out.

Antonio entered the suite in response to his urgent call. 'Miss Anderson has gone to the park, boss.'

'What do you mean, she's gone to the park? It's seven

degrees below freezing and it's still snowing—' Rio prowled across the thick carpet. The snow was floating past the window, thick flakes that landed on the ground and settled. The streets were virtually empty of people and traffic, everyone trapped indoors because of the weather. For the first time in over a decade the pond in the park had frozen over. A few ducks waddled sorrowfully across the ice. Staring through the window, he peered through the swirling flakes but failed to spot her. 'What the hell is she doing in the park?'

Antonio cleared his throat. 'She's building a snowman, boss.'

'She's—*what?*'

'A snowman.' Antonio was smiling. 'It's surprisingly good, actually. She's managed to—'

'Spare me a description of the snowman.' Rio spoke through his teeth. 'Did she leave a message for me?'

'Yes. She said to tell you that she needed fresh air and that she'd be back when she was finished.'

'Where exactly is she?'

'The far side of the pond, sir. Shall I call your driver?'

Rio strode across the room and snatched his coat from the back of the chair. 'No. I'll walk.'

'In that case, perhaps you would give this to Evie, sir, with my compliments.' Antonio dug his hand in his pocket and withdrew a carrot. 'I went down to the kitchens and found it for her. She might find it useful.'

Rio stared at it. 'Call me stupid,' he said slowly, 'but I can't for a moment imagine what possible use she will have for a single raw carrot.'

'Then you've obviously never made a snowman, boss. It's for his nose. I tried to get a slightly smaller one, but the kitchen—'

'All right—I get the picture.' Feeling out of touch with everyone around him, Rio pushed the carrot into his pocket and strode across the room to the private elevator. As he reached the doors, he paused, his mind exploring an idea. His instinct was to reject it instantly, but for once he fought that instinct.

Why not?

It would please her and he certainly owed her a small bite of happiness after the way he'd treated her.

Having delivered his instructions to a bemused Antonio, Rio left the hotel and crossed the snowy street, wondering what on earth he was doing chasing a girl across a park in the freezing cold.

He found her kneeling in the snow, scooping snow into balls and adding them to a snowman, who was now wearing her hat. Her hair spilled over the shoulders of her quilted jacket and her cheeks were pink from the cold. Her lips were moving and at first he thought she was talking to herself, and then he realised that she was singing.

'Five gold rings, four calling birds, three French hens—'

'—and a girl with double pneumonia,' Rio drawled as he walked over to her. He pulled the carrot out of his pocket and handed it to her. 'Here. Give the guy a nose so that you can come inside and warm up.'

'I'm fine. I'm happy here. Thanks for the carrot.' Without looking at him, she pressed it into the snowman's face and sat back on her heels. 'What do you think?'

Rio decided that this was probably one of those occasions when honesty was not required. 'Spectacular,' he said tactfully. 'A real gladiator of a snowman.' Why wasn't she looking at him? He changed his position so that he could get a better look at her face and saw that her eyes were red.

He'd made her cry.

Forced to confront the damage he'd caused, Rio gave a bitter smile. The fact that she'd still been prepared to help him despite her own personal agony made him feel about as small as the snowflake that landed on his hand.

She pulled off her gloves and blew on her hands to warm them. 'There's no need to go overboard. I know you think I'm crazy.'

He thought she was astonishing. As brave as she was beautiful.

'I'm no judge of snowmen.' He dug his hands in his pockets. 'I've never seen anyone make one before. But you clearly find it an absorbing occupation so I'm willing to be converted.'

'You've never made one yourself?'

'Never.'

'Then you're missing out.' She pushed two pebbles into the snow above the carrot and then sat back to admire her handiwork.

Rio fought the sudden desire to roll her in the snow and warm her up in the most basic way known to man. 'You need to move the pebble on the left up a bit—they're not even. He's squinting.'

Flakes of snow settled on her hair as she shifted the pebble. 'What are you doing out here, Rio? Shouldn't you be on the phone, brokering some deal or sorting out a crisis?'

'I left the phones in the Penthouse.'

She managed a smile. 'All three of them? Won't the business world crumble?'

Rio suddenly discovered that he couldn't care less. 'Come back inside with me.'

The smile vanished. 'I'm happy here.'

'You're soaked through and freezing.'

'I love the snow.' Lifting her face into the falling flakes, she closed her eyes. 'If I keep my eyes shut, I'm a child again.'

Rio felt the tension flash through his body. 'And that's a good thing?'

'Oh, yes.' Clear aquamarine eyes looked into his. 'One of my favourite childhood memories is going to the forest with my grandfather to choose a tree. I used to just stand there, breathing in the smell of pine. Have you ever stood in a forest and just smelt the air? It's the most perfect smell—sharp and pungent—it gets into your nose and then your brain and suddenly you just *feel* Christmas all the way through your body. Smells do that to me. Are you the same?'

He had no idea how to answer that question. 'No,' he said finally. 'I'm not the same.'

The happiness in her eyes dimmed. 'I don't suppose you stand still long enough to notice smells. You're always on the go, pushing another deal through. You don't even take Christmas off.'

Rio looked at her, torn between wanting to know more and wanting to change the subject. 'So what did you do when you and your grandfather had chosen the tree?'

'We took it home and decorated it. That was the best part. We couldn't afford fancy decorations so Grandma and I made stars out of flour and water, baked them in the oven and painted them silver.'

Rio remembered the way she'd stared at the elaborate decorations on the Christmas tree at the ball. He found it all too easy to imagine her sitting at the kitchen table, a huge smile on her face, her hair like a burning bush. 'How long have you lived with your grandparents?'

She reached for a twig and snapped it in half. 'Since I was four years old. My parents had gone away to celebrate their wedding anniversary and I was staying with my grandparents. I remember being really excited about sleeping in their spare bedroom. It's a tiny attic room with a sloping roof and views across the lake and the forest. It felt like the biggest adventure of my life and I couldn't wait to tell my parents every last detail.' She paused and there was a sudden hitch in her breathing. 'And then my grandfather came into my room one morning and told me that they wouldn't be coming to get me. Their car hit black ice. They didn't stand a chance.'

Rio stood still, feeling hopelessly inadequate. He watched in silence as the snow fluttered onto her shoulders. Her vibrant hair was the only warmth and colour in the place. Everything was cold, including him. Her revelation deserved a response, but he had no idea what that response should be. He wasn't used to emotional confessions. People didn't confide in him. They discussed stocks and bonds, mergers and acquisitions—not feelings.

He didn't do feelings.

Wondering what had happened to all the smooth words that were always at his disposal, Rio stumbled awkwardly through foreign territory. 'So you stayed with them?'

'My grandfather had just retired. They were looking forward to enjoying some time together. They'd even booked a world cruise—' her voice was soft '—they cancelled it. They gave me a home.' She breathed deeply. 'They became my parents.'

And the love she felt for her grandfather was a living, palpable thing. He saw it in her eyes and in her smile. In everything she did.

'You're lucky.' The moment he said the words, he braced himself for a sharp comeback. She was going to tell him that he was the lucky one. She was going to remind him that he was a billionaire with five houses and a private jet.

But she didn't say any of those things. Instead, she wiped snow from her cheeks with her gloved hand and nodded. 'I know I'm lucky. That's why I was so upset and worried about that photograph of me naked. After everything they did for me—all the sacrifices they made so that I could have a warm, loving home—I couldn't bear that my grandfather would think I'd let him down like that. All I've ever wanted is to make them proud of me.' She bit her lip. 'I'm still mad with you for not putting me out of my misery sooner, but I'm also just so relieved that Antonio intercepted the guy so quickly. It could have been worse.'

Her pragmatic approach intensified his feelings of guilt and Rio swore softly under his breath. 'I was wrong to do what I did.'

'No, you weren't. You did what you needed to do for your little girl.' She rocked back on her heels and studied her snowman. 'You were prepared to do anything to protect her. I like that. It's good. It's what families should do. They should stick together, no matter what. Family should be the one dependable thing in a person's life.'

'Why is your grandfather so desperate for you to be married?'

'I've told you—he's old-fashioned.' Picking up the other half of the twig, she pushed it into the other side of the snowman. 'He believes that as long as you have family, everything can be all right with the world.'

'All right, *now* I feel seriously guilty,' Rio said gruffly and she smiled up at him, a sparkling smile that warmed the freezing air because it was delivered with such bravery.

'If you're capable of feeling guilt, then there's hope for you, Mr Zaccarelli.'

Was there? He'd lived without that emotion for so long he wasn't even sure he knew how it felt.

'Come back to the hotel. It's absolutely freezing out here.'

'Are you telling me you're cold? Big tough guy like you?' Her voice was teasing and her eyes danced with mockery as she looked up at him. 'You're a wimp. My grandfather will be relieved when I give you the boot. He wants me to find a real man, not some shivering, pathetic creature who can't stand a shift in the weather.'

She squealed with shock and laughter as Rio moved swiftly and tumbled her backwards onto the snow.

'Are you calling me a wimp?' His mouth brushed her soft lips, tasting softness and laughter. He was about to turn the kiss into something less playful when she stuffed a handful of snow down the front of his sweater. Rio swore fluently as the ice froze his skin. 'Is that your test of a real man?'

'That's just one of them. I started with something gentle. I didn't want to be too hard on you.' She was still laughing but, because he had her body trapped under his, he felt the change in her. Looking into her eyes, he saw something that sucked the humour out of the situation—something he'd seen many times before in a woman's eyes.

For a second he couldn't move and he wondered if she even realised what she'd revealed, lying there under him with her hopes and dreams exposed.

And then he sprang to his feet, his withdrawal an instinctive reaction pre-programmed by life experience and a bone-deep cynicism about the durability of relationships. It would be cruel, wouldn't it, to hurt her more than he already had—this child-woman who still believed in happy endings.

'You're shivering.' Keeping his tone matter of fact, he hauled her to her feet and brushed the snow off her jacket. She was looking past him and for a moment he thought she was just avoiding eye contact, and then he saw her expression change. 'What's the matter?'

'Behind you,' she muttered. 'Another photographer. Why are people so interested in your life? Everywhere you go there is a bigger, longer camera lens. We'd better look as though we're in love.' The word tripped off her tongue as if it had no significance and Rio stared down into her sweet, honest face, wondering whether she'd tell him the truth.

But she didn't say anything and he felt something tug inside him.

'We don't have to do that. We can end this charade whenever we like. It's over.' He slid his hands into her hair, suddenly realising he no longer had a legitimate excuse to kiss her.

'What do you mean?' Her eyes widened and then shone as she grasped the implications of his words. 'Are you saying—?

Oh, Rio—you have custody? I'm so pleased! That's fantastic.'
She flung her arms round his neck and hugged him tightly,
whooping with joy and kissing him over and over again. Her
eyes glistened with tears of joy and he brushed them away
with his thumb, fascinated by the way she showed her emotions so freely; touched that her pleasure for his daughter
could transcend her own pain.

'There is still some red tape to play with, but my lawyers
think that Elyssa will come and live with me the week after
Christmas. For what it's worth, they think that seeing me
with you tipped the balance.'

'Well, I'm glad about that. So what does this mean?'

What did it mean? Rio had been searching for the answer
to that question.

When women had fallen in love with him before he'd
always considered it to be a question of 'buyer beware'. They
should have known better.

But Evie lived her life by a different rule book.

'Let's go back to the hotel. I have a surprise for you.'

It was over.

She no longer had a part to play in creating this happy
family.

Evie stood in the elevator, trying to keep the smile on her
face. It was selfish of her, wasn't it, to feel so devastated? The
whole reason this charade could now end was that someone
extremely sensible had decided that a little girl should live
with her daddy. As someone who had known that terrifying
feeling of loneliness and abandonment, she should be thrilled
that another little girl's dreams were going to come true. And
she was. She really was. But was she a wicked person to wish
that she could have had just a couple more days?

Forcing her own feelings aside, she smiled at Rio, determined not to make a fool of herself. *She didn't want his pity.*
The only thing she wanted from him was something quite

different. Something he wasn't able to give. 'You have plans to make. Just let me know what you want me to do.' She kept her voice brisk and practical. 'How you want me to handle things.'

He frowned. 'Handle what?'

'I'm going to dump you, remember? And, boy, am I going to enjoy that part.' Evie rubbed her hands together, wondering whether her voice sounded just a little forced.

'We'll discuss details later.' There was a tension in his shoulders that she attributed to his reaction to the momentous news. Either that or his ego was struggling with the notion of being publicly rejected.

It seemed incredible to her now that only weeks earlier she'd been about to marry another man. What she'd shared with Rio had taught her that what she'd shared with Jeff had been bland and colourless, like existing on a diet of bread and water and then suddenly discovering the variety of colour and texture of real food.

She wondered if she'd ever find anyone else who made her feel the way Rio did.

Blinking rapidly, Evie reinforced her smile as the elevator doors opened. 'Building snowmen is hungry work, so I certainly hope that—' She stopped, the words dissolving in her mouth as she saw the Penthouse.

It had been transformed from an elegant living space into a sparkling winter paradise.

Silver snowflakes were twisted through boughs of holly and an enormous Christmas tree, even bigger than the one she'd decorated, took pride of place next to the fire. It looked like a child's fantasy.

The only thing missing was Santa.

The moment the thought entered her head, Santa appeared from the second bedroom, complete with red robes and full white beard.

Evie blinked. And then she peered closer, through the

clouds of ridiculous white beard, and started to laugh. 'Antonio? Is that you in there?'

'Ho, ho, ho—'

Appalled to find tears in her eyes, Evie kept smiling. 'That doesn't quite work with an Italian accent. First fairy wings, now Santa—your job description seems to have shifted slightly over the past week.'

'I have a gift for you.' Overplaying his role like mad, Antonio reached into his sack with a flourish and pulled out a large square parcel. 'This has your name on it.'

Evie took it, wondering what all this meant. 'Am I supposed to keep it until Christmas?'

'No, you open it,' Rio said immediately as he urged her further into the room, away from Antonio who discreetly let himself out of the Penthouse.

Evie looked around her, unable to believe what she saw. 'But you don't...you hate...' She swallowed. 'You've done this for your little girl. I thought Elyssa couldn't be with you for Christmas.'

'I haven't done this for Elyssa.' His voice was rough and held a touch of uncertainty. 'I've done it for you.'

'For me?'

'Because you love Christmas and, this last week, I've deprived you of Christmas. I'm making up for it. Open the present. I hope you like it.' His eyes were wary and Evie wanted to say that the only present she wanted was him, but she couldn't, could she?

He didn't want that and it took two people to make a relationship work.

Dipping her head, she ripped the paper off the box and opened it. At first she thought there was nothing inside, and then she saw the envelope.

Puzzled, she discarded all the packaging and opened it. Inside was a printed ticket and it took a moment for her to understand what it meant. As the words sank into her brain, she gasped. 'I can spend Christmas Day with my grandfather?'

'Because the snow is so bad and your roads are pathetic, I am going to fly you by helicopter to this place where your grandfather lives—' Looking ridiculously pleased with himself, Rio outlined the plan. 'We will all spend the day together.'

Looking at Rio, with his sleek, expensive clothes and his taste for the best in everything, Evie gave a disbelieving laugh. 'Rio, you eat in hideously expensive restaurants—your chefs are the best in the world—I'm sorry, but I can't see you eating Christmas lunch in the Cedar Court Retirement Home.'

'*Sì,* I have thought the same thing myself,' Rio confessed, 'which is why two of my top chefs are currently preparing to cook lunch in more challenging surroundings than usual.'

'You're kidding.'

'It will be a true test of their talents, don't you agree?'

'But who is cooking lunch in your restaurants?'

'Someone. I don't know.' He spread his hands in a gesture that was pure Italian. 'I don't micro-manage every part of my business.'

'But if they don't do a good job, they're fired.'

'Very possibly. Are you pleased with your gift?'

Evie found it hard to speak. The fact that he'd done this made everything all the more mixed up in her head. Would it have been easier if he hadn't been so thoughtful? *Would it have been easier to walk away cursing him?* 'I'm *so* pleased,' she said huskily, standing on tiptoe and kissing him. 'Thank you. Can I phone him and tell him?'

'He might be rather busy. All the residents are currently with a stylist, choosing new outfits for Christmas Day.'

Overwhelmed by his generosity, Evie swallowed. 'Rio—you didn't have to do this—'

'I wanted to. As a thank you.' He slid his hands into her hair and brought his mouth down to hers and Evie immediately responded, wrapping her arms around his strong neck and pressing her body against his.

As a thank you. Of course. What else?

And she knew it was also a goodbye.

After tomorrow, it would be over. She wouldn't see him again.

He hadn't said what he wanted to do about ending their relationship in public, but presumably he'd chosen to wait until after Christmas Day so that her grandfather wasn't upset.

Rio pressed his mouth to her neck and gave a groan. 'We probably shouldn't be doing this—'

'I want to.' Evie spoke without hesitation, her eyes closing as he slowly unzipped her coat and trailed his mouth lower. 'I want to spend tonight with you.' If this was their last night together, then she wanted something she could remember for ever. She wanted memories to keep her warm.

She couldn't have him for ever, but she could have him for now.

'You're sure?' His voice was deep and husky and she nodded.

'Completely sure.'

It was only later, much later, when she was lying in the darkness, cocooned in his arms and sleepy from his loving, that she asked the question that had been hovering on her lips for days. 'Will you tell me why you hate Christmas? You don't have to if you don't want to, but—'

'It was never a good time of year for me.' He tightened his grip on her. 'Every Christmas was a nightmare. I'm the product of a long-term affair between my mother and a very senior politician who was married with his own family. Christmas Day was the one day he always spent with them. I was eight years old when he finally found the courage to tell her he was never going to leave his wife. I found her body lying under the Christmas tree when I got up in the morning.' He spoke the words in a flat monotone, the same voice he might have used when discussing the share price.

Evie lay immobile, shock seeping through her in icy rivulets, like melting snow. The vision played out in her brain in glorious Technicolor. An excited eight-year-old dashing downstairs to see if Santa had left presents under the tree and discovering death in all its brutal glory.

She wanted to say something—she wanted to find the perfect words that would soothe and heal—but she knew that such words didn't exist. She knew from experience that there weren't always words that could smooth the horrors of life, but she also knew that human comfort could sometimes warm when the temperature of life turned bitter cold. So she tightened her grip on him and pressed her lips against his warm skin, her muffled words intended to comfort, not cure.

'The doctor had given her tablets for depression.' Now that he'd started speaking, he seemed to want to continue. 'She'd swallowed them all, along with a bottle of champagne her lover had given her for Christmas. I called an ambulance but it was too late.'

Evie's eyes filled with tears. 'So what did you do? Where did you go?' She thought of her own loving grandparents and the tears streamed down her face and dampened his skin. 'Did you have family?'

'I gave the hospital the number of my father—' he wiped her tears with his fingers and gave a humourless laugh '—that must have been quite a Christmas lunch, don't you think? I believe it was his wife who answered the phone so he probably had some explaining to do.'

'Did he take you into his family?'

'Yes, on the surface. As a senior politician he had to be

seen to be doing the right thing and I was effectively an orphan. In practice, they sent me to boarding school and tried to pretend I didn't exist. His wife saw me as a reminder of her husband's lengthy infidelity, his daughter saw me as competition and my father saw me as nothing but a bomb ready to explode his career. He told me I'd never make anything of myself.'

'He should have been ashamed of himself—'

'His career disintegrated soon after that, so I don't think life was easy for him.'

Evie pressed her damp cheek against his chest. 'So now I understand why you were prepared to fight so hard for your little girl. Why you wanted to be a father to her.' And she understood why every Christmas tree slashed at the wound he'd buried so deep. And yet he'd put his own feelings aside in order to decorate the Penthouse for her. She wanted to ask why he'd done that—*why he'd put himself through that.* 'I love you, Rio.' Suddenly it seemed terribly important that she tell him, no matter what happened when the sun rose. No matter what he thought of her. 'I love you. I know you don't love me back—I can understand why you're so afraid to love after what you learned about relationships as a child, but that doesn't change the way I feel about you. I want you to know you're loved.'

He gave a low groan and pulled her onto him, wrapping his arms around her. 'I know you love me. I saw it in your eyes when you looked at me in the park.'

'Oh.' Embarrassed, she gave a tiny laugh. 'So much for hiding my feelings. Just don't ever invite me to play poker.'

'Evie—'

'Don't say anything.' She pressed her mouth to his. 'This has happened to you a load of times before. I know it has. It's fine. Don't let's think about tomorrow. Let's just enjoy right now. Right now is all that matters.'

She lay awake in the darkness, holding him, wishing she could hold the moment for ever and stop dawn breaking.

It was the end, she knew that.

For the first time in her life, she didn't want Christmas Day to come.

CHAPTER NINE

Rio was up with the dawn, all dark shadows of the night thrown off as he showered and changed and spoke into two of his three phones while making the arrangements for the day.

Moving more slowly, Evie dressed and collected together the presents she'd bought for her grandfather. A soft cashmere scarf for his walks in the gardens of the home, a reading lamp and some of his favourite chocolates.

As Rio made the final preparations, she wandered back into the sitting room and stared wistfully at the decorations. How much courage had it taken, she thought, to adorn the Penthouse with the flavour of Christmas when the taste must be so bitter to him. A great deal of courage. Obviously, he wasn't a wimp.

He was a real man.

'Are you ready?' He strode up to her and relieved her of the parcels and Evie took a breath.

No, she wasn't ready. But she was never going to be ready for him to walk out of her life.

'I've never been on a helicopter before,' she said brightly. 'Life with you has been one big new experience.'

He smiled and kissed her on the mouth with erotic purpose. 'We're not finished yet.'

No. They had today. One whole day.

Her heart skittered and jumped and she wanted to ask him what his plans were for the announcement, but he was already striding into the elevator, this time going up to the roof, to the helicopter pad.

And then they were flying across the snow-covered English countryside and Evie thought she'd never seen anything more beautiful in her life. Beautiful and poignant because the enforced silence made her mind focus on the fact that everything she did with him today would be for the last time.

By the time they finally landed in the gardens of the Cedar Court Retirement Home, she was barely holding herself together. Even the prospect of seeing her beloved grandfather couldn't lift her sagging spirits. What made the whole thing even harder was that Rio seemed completely energized.

'I am looking forward to finally meeting your grandfather, having spoken to him so many times on the phone.'

So many times? Evie frowned. She knew he'd called her grandfather twice, but she wasn't aware of any other occasions. Before she could question him, the doors opened and she saw all the residents lined up in their finery. She saw Mrs Fitzwilliam with her hair newly styled and then there was her grandfather, dressed in his best suit and smiling proudly at the head of the line.

Within a second she was in his arms and kissing him, her tears mingling with his as they hugged and talked at the same time and he felt solid and safe and such an important part of her life that she wondered why on earth she'd ever thought she could live happily in London. Maybe she'd be all right, Evie thought as she closed her eyes and hugged him. Maybe she'd survive.

They spent precious minutes catching up and it was a few moments before she realised that the entire retirement home had been transformed into a silver and white paradise, just like the Penthouse.

'Your Rio has done us proud, that's for sure. You found

yourself a real man, Evie. I can see how much you love him,' her grandfather said gruffly and Evie's control almost cracked as she wondered how on earth she was going to explain to him when the time came to break it off. She cast a helpless glance at Rio but he merely smiled and turned to say something in Italian to Antonio.

Rio's chefs had surpassed themselves but Evie barely touched her lunch, relieved when her grandfather finally rose to make a speech and she could give up the pretence of eating. He thanked the chefs, the styling team and most of all Rio. And then he looked at Evie, his eyes full of love.

'Sometimes,' he said quietly, 'life doesn't turn out the way you plan it. When Evie came into our lives, we became parents all over again and those years were the happiest I've known. Evie, I want you to know that, no matter what happens, I'll always be proud of you. Not because of what you do, but because of who you are.'

His words cut the final thread on her control. Evie felt tears scald her eyes and she had the most awful feeling that her grandfather knew that her life had tumbled apart in London. Had he somehow discovered that she'd lost her flat and her job? Had he guessed that this whole thing with Rio was a farce? She took a gulp of the champagne Rio had provided, blinking rapidly to stop the tears from falling. She was so choked that she was relieved when Rio stood up.

And then she saw the serious look on his handsome face and relief turned to alarm. Oh, no. Please don't let him decide that this was a good time to tell the truth. Not on Christmas Day.

She wanted her grandfather to have the very best day of his life—

Her anxious gaze met Rio's and she mouthed the word *don't!* but he simply smiled as he lifted his glass.

'I agree with every word that has been spoken. Life certainly doesn't turn out the way you plan.' His voice was smooth and confident and it was clear from the way he spoke and stood that he was comfortable addressing large groups of people. 'When I arrived in London twelve days ago, my plan was to sort out a complicated business issue and then spend the next few days blocking out the fact that it's Christmas, because that's what I do. Every year I try and forget it's Christmas.' A shocked silence greeted his words and Evie felt her mouth dry as she anticipated what he might say next.

'But this year—' he paused and a faint smile touched his hard mouth '—this year I met Evie and all my plans changed. Instead of doing deals, I was dancing. Instead of analyzing shares, I was building snowmen. When I arrived in London I had no plans to fall in love and certainly no plans to get married—' he let the words hang in the air and a stunned silence spread across the room '—but that's because I didn't know that people like Evie existed.'

Nobody moved.

Evie felt as though she was going to pass out. She saw her grandfather beaming at her and several of the elderly women fanning themselves as they watched Rio standing there, tall and impossibly handsome. She felt a burst of hope, followed by a cascade of incredible joy, immediately tempered by caution because she was so terribly afraid she might have misunderstood.

Was this still pretending? Had he decided to take their charade one step further before shattering it for ever?

She glanced around, wondering if the press had some-how gained access to this private event, thinking that only a long lens could have triggered that speech from him. But there were no fancy cameras. There were no journalists or paparazzi scrambling to record the moment.

So why was he saying these things?

'Evie—' He took her hand in his and drew her firmly to

her feet. 'I know how much you love me. What you don't know is how much I love you.'

Her knees felt weak and her body started to tremble. 'Rio—'

'It's real.' Reading her mind, he pressed his mouth to hers, his kiss a lingering promise of a lifetime of love. 'This isn't for the press, or for your grandfather. It's just for us. I want you to marry me.'

'But—'

'I live and work in such a hard, cynical world. I deal with hard, cynical people—and then I met you.' He stroked her hair away from her face, watching her expression as if he were trying to interpret every blink. 'Yesterday, when I finally heard that I had what I wanted, I couldn't work out why I didn't feel more elated. And I realised it was because gaining my daughter meant losing you and I didn't want it to be that way. I'm afraid that my biggest fault is that I want everything.'

Evie was laughing through her tears. 'Greedy.'

'Yes. And selfish, and ruthless—' Smiling, unapologetic, he leaned his forehead against hers. 'You already know that I'll do whatever it takes to get what I want, and I want you, for ever, so you might as well just surrender without a fight.'

For ever?

Happiness flooded through her. 'You don't have to fight.'

'Marry me,' he murmured softly. 'We need to give your grandfather a baby to bounce on his knee and in the meantime he can make a start with Elyssa. She's in desperate need of spare family. She has us, of course, but a wise person once told me that it's useful to have spares of everything so I thought it would be good to collect some more relatives for her.'

Evie buried her face in his neck, half laughing, half crying, thinking that if this was how love felt then from now on every day was going feel like Christmas. 'I—'

'I think the rest of this conversation should be conducted in private,' Rio breathed, sweeping her into his arms so that the toe of her shoe narrowly missed the Christmas pudding. 'Please enjoy the rest of your meal. This afternoon we have dancing. And singing. And Evie will be back to give a private performance of her much acclaimed version of *The Twelve Days of Christmas* but, as that requires dancing on the tables, it has to be after we've finished eating.'

'Rio, you can't just—' Mortified, Evie turned scarlet. 'They're all looking! What do you think you're doing?'

'What am I doing?' There was laughter in his voice. 'I'm behaving like a real man, *tesoro*. If you have any complaints about that, you can take it up with your grandfather.'

Twelve months later

'Can I hold her?'

'Of course you can,' Evie said immediately. 'She's your baby sister.'

Elyssa stepped closer and peered at the baby's face. 'She's very small.'

'Well, she's only three weeks old. You were this small once.'

'But I didn't live with you then.'

'No.' Evie reached out a hand and stroked Elyssa's dark hair. 'But you live with us now. We're a family. Always.'

'I liked being your bridesmaid. I'm pleased you married my Daddy.'

Evie swallowed. 'I'm pleased, too. Now, sit back in the chair and then I'll hand Lara to you. She needs to feel secure.'

The little girl wriggled to the back of the chair and held

out her arms and Evie sat down next to her and carefully gave her the baby, willing the infant not to wake up and cry.

From beyond the windows she heard the sound of a helicopter and moments later Rio appeared in the doorway. His exquisitely tailored suit moulded to his athletic physique and Evie felt her stomach drop. Even after a year together, she still found it hard to breathe when he was in the same room as her.

'I'm sorry I'm late,' he drawled, dropping his briefcase and walking across to them. 'There were a few things I had to arrange. Last minute Christmas shopping. What have I missed?'

'Daddy! Have you bought my present?' Elyssa wriggled with excitement and Rio dropped a kiss on the top of her head and dropped to his haunches.

'I might have done. You're holding Lara.' He shot a questioning look at Evie who smiled reassuringly.

'Isn't she doing brilliantly? She's so good with her sister.' As she spoke, the baby's eyes opened and Evie held her breath. *Don't cry.*

'She's looking at me.' Elyssa looked at her half-sister in fascination. 'Can she see me?'

'Oh, yes.' Watching the two of them together, Evie felt a lump in her throat. 'She loves you, Elyssa.'

'Grandpa and I hung her stocking on the fireplace and I wrote to Santa to tell him she's only a baby so he doesn't leave her unsuitable toys.'

'She's so lucky having you as a big sister.' It had taken months of patience but finally the nightmares had stopped and Elyssa had started to behave like a normal little girl. Far from unsettling her, Lara's birth appeared to have given her greater security—as if the arrival of the baby had somehow cemented their little family.

Elyssa kissed Lara's downy head. 'I can't wait for her to grow big enough to be able to play with me. Can you take her back now? She's really heavy for someone who only drinks milk.'

Rio expertly scooped up his baby daughter, holding her against his shoulder as he sat down on the sofa next to Elyssa. 'Did you decorate the Christmas tree while I was away?'

'Evie wanted to wait for you.'

Knowing how Rio felt about Christmas, Evie cast him an anxious look. It was enough for her that they were together and in England. She was still overwhelmed by his decision to buy the beautiful old Manor House close to the Cedar Court Retirement Home, meaning that she could have her grandfather to stay. He'd declared himself too old to be flying around the world to visit their other homes, so Rio had shifted his business operation to enable him to spend as much time in England as possible.

And her grandfather was delighted that his wish had been fulfilled twice over. He now had two great-grandchildren to hold on his knee.

Rio leaned across Elyssa and delivered a lingering kiss to Evie's lips. 'I missed you. No more work,' he promised, 'for the whole of Christmas. Anyone who phones me is fired.'

'I missed you, too.' She kissed him back, careful not to squash the baby. 'Are you serious? You're not working?'

'I have better things to do with my time. Put your coats on. We're going outside. I have a surprise for you both.'

'Outside?' Excited, Elyssa jumped to her feet. 'Can Lara come, too?'

'Not this time. We're leaving her with Grandpa for a moment.'

Evie's grandfather was obviously in on the surprise because he timed his entrance perfectly. 'Elyssa, there's someone at the front door for you.'

Elyssa shot out of the room and Rio took Evie's hand in his and followed. 'I hope you're not going to be mad with me—'

'That depends on what you've done.' Her eyes teased him and he kissed her again, unable to leave her alone.

'I may have gone a little overboard,' he confessed, 'but, after years of not celebrating Christmas, I'm determined to make up for it big time.'

Overwhelmed with love for him, Evie lifted her hand and stroked his hair. 'I wasn't sure how you'd feel this year—that's why we haven't decorated the tree. I thought you might rather we didn't.' Hesitant, she watched him. 'I know the whole thing has bad memories for you.'

'I'm making new memories—' he captured her hand in his, his voice husky '—with you.'

'Daddy, come on!' Elyssa was waiting impatiently and Rio released Evie and walked to the front door.

'Close your eyes and don't peep until I say so.'

Elyssa squeezed them shut. 'Can I look yet?'

Rio opened the door of the house. '*Now* you can look.'

Evie watched as the little girl opened her eyes. Wonder and happiness lit her whole face. Intrigued as to what had caused such a response, Evie turned her head and gasped as she saw the pretty white pony. He stood quietly, his breath clouding the air, a big red bow in his mane. Behind him was a sleigh piled high with presents.

'Daddy!' Elyssa could hardly speak. 'Oh, Daddy!'

Rio looked smug. 'You like him?'

'He's *mine*? Truly?'

'All yours.' Rio scooped her into his arms and carried her to the pony. 'His name is Snowflake and he's the latest member of our ever-growing family. It's a good job we have a large house.'

Elyssa had her arms around the pony, almost sobbing with excitement. 'He's so beautiful. Oh—oh—Mummy, have you seen him?'

Mummy.

Rio inhaled sharply and so did Evie because she'd waited

for this moment for so long. For almost a year she'd been encouraging the withdrawn, confused little girl to call her Mummy and finally now, on Christmas Eve, she'd said it. To hear her use the word so naturally felt like a miracle.

The best Christmas gift of all.

Warmth spread through her body and Evie walked across to Rio and took Elyssa from him, hugging her tightly, tears on her face.

'I see him, sweetheart, and I think he's completely perfect.'

Her grandfather appeared in the doorway, smiling his approval as he looked at Evie with her family.

Rio looked ridiculously pleased with himself. 'It's cold out here and neither of you are properly dressed. We'll go back inside and get wrapped up and then we can go round to the stables and see Snowflake and his friends.'

Evie glanced up at him. 'Friends?'

A smile transformed his face from handsome to breathtaking. 'I bought a few spares. I have a feeling we're going to be needing them before too long.'

Evie's heart stumbled. He wanted more children. A big family.

Her dream come true.

As she smiled up at him she felt something cold brush against her face and Elyssa gave a squeal of excitement that made the pony throw up his head in alarm.

'It's snowing! Mummy, Daddy, we're going to have snow for Christmas. Can we build a snowman? Do you know how?'

Rio brushed the snow from Evie's cheek. 'Yes, I know how. We need a carrot and some pebbles and a few twigs. And we need your mother because she's brilliant at building snowmen.'

'We also need enough snow,' Evie pointed out practically.

'We need to find something to do while we're waiting for it to settle.'

'I think I can solve that problem.' Rio pulled her back into his arms and held her tightly. 'How would you feel about decorating a Christmas tree?'

His Christmas Acquisition

Cathy Williams

Cathy Williams was born in the West Indies and has been writing Mills & Boon® romances for some fifteen years. She is a great believer in the power of perseverance, as she had never written anything before (apart from school essays a lifetime ago!), and from the starting point of zero has now fulfilled her ambition to pursue this most enjoyable of careers. She would encourage any would-be writer to have faith and go for it! She lives in the beautiful Warwickshire countryside with her husband and three children, Charlotte, Olivia and Emma. When not writing she is hard-pressed to find a moment's free time in between the millions of household chores, not to mention being a one-woman taxi service for her daughters' never-ending social lives. She derives inspiration from the hot, lazy, tropical island of Trinidad (where she was born), from the peaceful countryside of middle England and, of course, from her many friends, who are a rich source of plots and are particularly garrulous when it comes to describing Mills & Boon® Modern™ heroes. It would seem, from their complaints, that tall, dark and charismatic men are way too few and far between. Her hope is to continue writing romance fiction, providing those eternal tales of love for which, she feels, we all strive.

CHAPTER ONE

JAMIE was late. For the first time since she had started working for Ryan Sheppard she was running late due to an unfortunate series of events which had culminated in her waiting for her tube to arrive, along with six-thousand other short-tempered, frustrated, disgruntled commuters, so it seemed.

Wrapped up against the icy blast that raced along the platform—whipping her neatly combed hair into frantic disarray and reminding her that her smart grey suit and smart black pumps might work in an office, but were useless when faced with the grim reality of a soggy London winter—Jamie pointlessly looked at her watch every ten seconds.

Ryan Sheppard *hated* late. In fairness, he had been spoiled with her because for the past eighteen months she had been scrupulously early—which didn't mean that he would be sweetly forgiving.

By the time the tube train roared into view, Jamie had pretty much given up on getting into the office any time before nine-thirty. Because nothing would be gained from calling him, she had resolutely refused to even glance at the mobile phone hunkered down in the bowels of her bag.

Instead, she reluctantly focused her mind on the main reason why she had ended up leaving her house an hour later than she normally would have, and sure enough, all thoughts of her sister successfully obliterated everything else from her mind. She could feel the thin, poisonous thread of tension begin to creep through her body and, by the time she finally made it to the spectacular, cutting-edge glass building that housed RS Enterprises, her head was beginning to throb.

RS Enterprises was the headquarters of the massive conglomerate owned and run by her boss, and within its stately walls resided the beating pulse of all those various tentacles that made up the various arms of his many business concerns. An army of highly trained, highly motivated and highly paid employees kept everything afloat although, at quarter to ten in the morning, there were only a few to be glimpsed. The rest would be at their desks, doing whatever it took to make sure that the great wheels of his industry were running smoothly.

At quarter to ten in the morning, *she* would normally have been at her desk, doing her own bit.

But instead...

Jamie counted to ten in a feeble attempt to dislodge her sister's face from her head and took the lift up to the director's floor.

There was no need to gauge his mood when she pushed open the door to her office. On an average day, he would either be out of the office, having emailed her to fill her in on what she could be getting on with in his absence, or else he would be at his desk, mentally a thousand miles away as he plowed through his workload.

Today he was lounging back in his chair, arms folded behind his head, feet indolently propped on his desk.

Even after eighteen months, Jamie still had trouble reconciling the power house that was Ryan Sheppard with the unbearably sexy and disconcertingly unconventional guy who was such a far cry from anyone's idea of a business tycoon. Was it because the building blocks of his business

were rooted in computer software, where brains and creativity were everything, and a uniform of suits and highly
polished leather shoes were irrelevant? Or was it because
Ryan Sheppard was just one of those men who was so comfortable in his own skin that he really didn't care what he
wore or, for that matter, what the rest of the world thought
of him?

At any rate, sightings of him in a suit were rare, and only
occurred when he happened to be meeting financiers—although it had to be said that his legendary reputation preceded him. Very early on Jamie had come to the conclusion
that he could show up at a meeting in nothing but a pair of
swimming trunks and he would still have the rest of the
world bowing and scraping and asking for his opinion.

Jamie waited patiently while he made a production out of
looking at his watch and frowning before transferring his
sharp, penetrating black gaze to her now composed face.

'You're late.'

'I know. I'm really sorry.'

'You're never late.'

'Yes, well, blame the erratic public-transport system in
London, sir.'

'You know I hate you addressing me as *sir*. When I'm
knighted, we can have a rethink on that one, but in the meantime the name is Ryan. And I would be more than happy to
blame the erratic public-transport system, but you're not the
only one who uses it, and no one else seems to be running
behind schedule.'

Jamie hovered. She had taken time to dodge into the luxurious marble cloakroom at the end of the floor so she knew
that she no longer resembled the hassled, anxious figure that
had emerged twenty minutes earlier from the Underground
station. But inside she could feel her nerves fraying, unravel-

ling and scattering like useless detritus being blown around on a strong wind.

'Perhaps we could just get on with work and…and…I'll make up for lost time. I don't mind working through lunch.'

'So, if it wasn't the erratic public-transport system, then what kept you?' For the past year and a half, Ryan had tried to get behind that calm, impenetrable facade, to find the human being behind the highly efficient secretary. But Jamie Powell, aged twenty-eight, of the neat brown bob and the cool brown eyes, remained an enigma. He swung his feet off his desk and sat forward to stare at her with lively curiosity. 'Hard weekend? Late night? Hangover?'

'Of course I don't have a hangover!'

'No? Because there's absolutely nothing wrong with a little bit of over-indulgence now and again, you know. In fact, I happen to be of the opinion that a little over indulgence is very good for the soul.'

'I don't get drunk.' Jamie decided to put an immediate stop to any such notion. Gossip travelled at a rate of knots in RS Enterprises and there was no way that Jamie was going to let anyone think that she spent her weekends watching life whizz past from the bottom of a glass. In fact, there was no way that she was going to let anyone think anything at all about her. Experience had taught her well: join in with your colleagues, let your hair down now and again, build up a cosy relationship with your boss—and hey presto! You suddenly find yourself going down all sorts of unexpected and uncomfortable roads. She had been there and she wasn't about to pay a repeat visit.

'How virtuous of you!' Ryan congratulated her with the sort of false sincerity that made her teeth snap together in frustration. 'So we can eliminate the demon drink! Maybe your alarm failed to go off? Or maybe…'

He shot her a smile that reminded her just why the man

was such a killer when it came to the opposite sex. For any-one not on their guard, it was the sort of smile that could bring a person out in goose bumps. She had seen it happen any number of times, watching from the sidelines. 'Maybe,' he drawled, eyebrows raised speculatively, 'there was some-one in your bed who made getting up on a cold December morning just a little bit too much of a challenge…?'

'I would rather not discuss my private life with you, sir—sorry, *Ryan*.'

'And that's perfectly acceptable, just so long as it doesn't intrude on your working life, but strolling into the office at ten in the morning demands a little explanation. And fob-bing me off with promises to work through your lunch isn't good enough. I'm an exceptionally reasonable man,' Ryan went on, tapping his pen thoughtfully on his desk and run-ning his eyes over her tight, closed face. 'Whenever you've had an emergency, I've been more than happy to let you take time off. Remember the plumber incident?'

'That was once!'

'And what about last Christmas? Didn't I generously give you half a day off so that you could do your Christmas shop-ping?'

'You gave *everyone* half a day off.'

'Point proven! I'm a reasonable man. So I think I deserve a reasonable explanation for your lateness.'

Jamie took a deep breath and braced herself to reveal something of her private life. Even this small and insignif-icant confidence, something that could hardly be classed as a confidence at all, went against the grain. Like a time bomb nestling in the centre of her well-founded good in-tentions, she could hear it ticking, threatening to send her whole carefully orchestrated reserve into chaos. She would not let that happen. She would throw him a titbit of infor-

mation because, if she didn't, then the wretched man would
just keep at it like a bull terrier worrying a bone.

He was like that—determined to the point of insanity.
She figured it was how he had managed to take his father's
tiny, failing computer business and build it up into a multi-
national conglomerate. He just never gave up and he never
let go. His sexy, laid-back exterior concealed a strong and
powerful business instinct that laid down rules and watched
while the rest of the world fell into line.

She opened her mouth to give him an edited version of
events, filtered through her strict mental-censoring process, when the door to his office burst open. Or rather it
was flung open with the sort of drama that made both their
heads spin round simultaneously in surprise to the leggy,
blonde-haired, blue-eyed woman who literally flew into the
office. Her big, long hair trailed wildly behind her, a thick,
red cashmere coat hooked over her shoulder.

She threw the coat over the nearest chair. It was a gesture
that was so wildly theatrical that Jamie had to stare down
at her feet to stop herself from laughing out loud.

Ryan Sheppard had no qualms about bringing his women
into the workplace once he had signed off work for the day.
Jamie had always assumed that this was the arrogance of a
man who only had to incline his head slightly to have any
woman he wanted putting herself out to accommodate him.
Why go to the bother of traipsing over to a woman's house at
nine in the evening when *she* could traipse to his offices and
save him the hassle of the trip? When things had been particularly hectic, and his employees had been up and running
on pure adrenalin into the late hours of the night, she had
witnessed first-hand his deeply romantic gesture of sending
his staff home so that he could treat his date to a Chinese
takeaway in his office.

Not once had she ever heard any of these women complain. They smiled, they simpered, they followed him with adoring eyes and then, when he became bored with them, they were tactfully and expensively shuffled off to pastures new.

And such was the enduring charm of the guy that he still managed to keep in friendly touch with the majority of his exes.

But there had never been anything like this, at least that she could remember in her brief spell of working for him.

She couldn't help her snort of laughter at the unexpected sight of some poetic justice being dished out. She quickly tried to bury it under the guise of coughing, although when she caught his eye it was to find him glaring at her before transferring his attention back to the enraged beauty standing in front of his desk.

'Leanne…'

'Don't you *dare* "Leanne" *me*! I can't *believe* you would just break up with me over the *phone*!'

'Flying over to Tokyo to deliver the news face to face wasn't an option.' He glanced at Jamie, who immediately began standing up, because witnessing the other woman's anger and distress was something she would rather have avoided. But Ryan nodded at her to sit back down.

'You could have *waited* until I got back!'

Ryan sighed and rubbed his eyes before standing up and strolling round to perch on his desk. 'You need to calm down,' he said in a voice that was perfectly modulated and yet carried an icy threat. Leanne, picking it up, gulped in a few deep breaths.

'Cast your mind back the last two times we've met,' he continued with ferocious calm. 'And you might remember that I *have* warned you that our relationship had reached the end of its course.'

'You didn't mean that!' She tossed her head and her mane of blonde hair rippled down her back.

'I'm not in the habit of saying things I don't mean. You chose to ignore what I said and so you gave me no option but to spell it out word for word.'

'But I thought that we were *going* somewhere. I had plans! And what—' Leanne glared at Jamie, who was focusing on her black pumps '—is *she* doing here? I want to have this out with you in *private*! Not with your boring little secretary hanging on to our every word and taking notes so that she can report back to everyone in this building.'

Little? Yes. Five-foot-four could hardly be deemed tall by anyone's standards. But *boring*? It was an adjective that would have stung had it come from anyone other than Leanne. Like all the women Jamie had seen flit in and out of Ryan's life, Leanne was the sort of supermodel beauty who had a healthy disrespect for any woman who wasn't on the same eye-catching plane as she was.

Jamie looked at the towering blonde and met her bright-blue eyes with cool disdain.

'Jamie is here,' Ryan said in a hard voice, 'because, in case you hadn't noticed, this is my office and we're in the middle of working. I'm sure I made it perfectly clear to you that I don't tolerate my work life being disrupted. Ever. By anyone.'

'Yes, but…'

He walked across to where she had earlier flung the red coat and held it out. 'You're upset, and for that I apologise. But now I suggest that you exit both my offices and our relationship with pride and dignity. You're a beautiful woman. You'll have no trouble replacing me.'

Jamie watched, fascinated in spite of herself, by the transparency of Leanne's emotions. Pride and anger waged war with self-pity and a temptation to plead. But in the end she allowed herself to be helped into her coat; the click of the door as she left the room was, at least, a lot more controlled than when she had entered.

Jamie studiously stared in front of her and waited for Ryan to break the silence.

'Did you know that she was coming?' he asked abruptly and Jamie turned to him in surprise. 'Is that why you chose today, of all days, to get here two hours late?'

'Of course not! I wouldn't dream of getting involved in your private life.' Although she had in the past: trinkets bought for women; flowers chosen, ordered and sent; theatre tickets booked. On one memorable occasion he had actually taken her to a luxury sports-car garage and asked her to choose which colour Porsche he should buy for a certain woman who had lasted no longer than a handful of weeks. He was nothing if not an absurdly generous lover, even if his definition of a relationship never contained the notion of permanence. 'And I don't appreciate being accused of…of… ever being in cahoots with any of your bimb—girlfriends.'

Ryan's eyes narrowed on her flushed face. 'The reason I asked was because you seemed to derive a certain amount of satisfaction from Leanne and her display of histrionics. In fact, I could swear that I heard you laugh at one point.'

Jamie looked at him. He was once more perched on his desk, his long, jean-clad legs extended and lightly crossed at the ankles. In heels, Leanne would have been at least six foot tall and he had still towered over her.

Jamie felt a quiver of apprehension race down her spine but for once she was sorely tempted to say what was on her mind.

'I'm sorry. It was an inappropriate reaction.' Except she could feel a fit of the giggles threatening to overwhelm her again and she had to look down hurriedly at her tightly clasped fingers.

When she next looked up it was to find that he was standing over her and, before she could push back her chair, he was leaning down, his muscular hands on either side of her, his face so close to hers that she could see the wildly extravagant length of his eyelashes and the hint of tawny gold in his dark eyes. He was so close, in fact, that by simply raising her hand a couple of inches she would have been able to stroke the side of his face, touch the faint growth of stubble, feel its spikiness against her fingers.

Assaulted by this sudden wave of crazy speculation, Jamie fought down the sickening twist in her stomach and carried on looking at him squarely in the face although she could feel her heart beating inside her like a jack hammer.

'What *I'd* like to know,' he said softly, 'is what the hell you found so funny. What I'd really like is for you to share the joke with me.'

'Sometimes I laugh in tense situations. I'm sorry.'

'Pull the other one, Jamie. You've been in tense situations with me before when I'm trying to get a major deal closed. You've never burst out laughing.'

'That's different.'

'Explain.'

'Why? Why does it matter what I think?'

'Because I like to know a bit of what's going on in my personal assistant's head. Call me crazy, but I think it makes the working relationship go a lot smoother.' In truth, Ryan didn't think that it would be possible to find anyone with whom he could have worked more comfortably. Jamie seemed to possess an uncanny ability to predict his moves and her calm was a pleasing counterpoint to his volatility.

Before he had hired her, he had suffered three years of terrific-looking fairly incompetent secretaries who had all developed the annoying habit of becoming infatuated with him. His faithful middle-aged secretary who had served him well for nearly ten years had emigrated to Australia and he had followed her up with a series of ill-suited replacements.

Jamie Powell really worked for him and it had nothing to do with the mechanisms of her mind or what she thought about him. But suddenly the urge to shake her out of her cool detachment was overwhelming. It was as though that shadow of a snicker that had crossed her face earlier on had unleashed a curiosity in him, and it took him by surprise.

He pushed himself away from her and walked across to the low sofa that doubled as a bed for those times when he worked so late that sleeping in his office was the easiest option.

Reluctantly, Jamie swivelled her chair in his direction and wondered how many billionaire bosses would be sprawled indolently on a sofa in their office in a pair of jeans and a faded jumper, hands clasped behind their heads, work put on temporary hold while they asked questions that were really none of their business.

Again that finger of apprehension sent another shiver down her spine. After a succession of unsatisfactory but emotionally important temp jobs, would she have taken this one if she had known the nature of the beast?

'I'm not paid to have thoughts about your private life,' she ventured primly in a last-ditch attempt to change the subject.

'Don't worry about that. I give you full permission to say what was on your mind.'

Jamie licked her lips nervously. This was the first time he had ever pinned her down like this, the first time he hadn't backed off when his curiosity had failed to find fertile ground. Now, like a lazy predator, he was watching her, gauging her reaction, forming conclusions.

'Okay.' She looked at him evenly. 'I'm surprised that this is the first time one of your girlfriends has seen fit to storm into your office and give you a piece of her mind. I thought it was funny, so I laughed. But quietly. And I wouldn't have laughed if I had left your office when I had wanted to, but you gestured to me to stay put. So I did. So you can't blame me for reacting.'

Ryan sat up and looked at her intently. 'See? Now isn't it liberating to speak your mind?'

'I know you think it's funny to confuse me.'

'Am I confusing you?'

Jamie went bright red and tightened her lips. 'You don't seem to have any morals or ethics at all when it comes to women!' she snapped. 'I've worked with you for well over a year and you must have had a dozen women in that time. More! You play with people's feelings and it doesn't seem to bother you at all!'

'So there's a lurking tiger behind that placid face of yours,' he murmured.

'Don't be ridiculous. You asked me for my opinion, that's all.'

'You think I use women? Treat them badly?'

'I…' She opened her mouth to tell him that she had never thought anything whatsoever about the way he treated women, not until this very moment, but she would have been lying. She realised with some dismay that she had done plenty of thinking about Ryan Sheppard and his out-of-hours relationships. 'I'm sure you treat them really well, but most women want more than just expensive gifts and fun and frolics for a few weeks.'

'What makes you say that? Have you been chatting to any of my girlfriends? Or is that what *you* would want?'

'I haven't been chatting to your girlfriends, and we're not talking about me,' Jamie told him sharply.

Her colour was up and for the first time he noticed the sultry depths of her eyes and the fullness of her mouth. She was either blissfully unaware of her looks or else had made a concerted effort to sublimate them, at least during working hours. Then he wondered how he had never really *noticed* these little details about her before. It occurred to him that they had rarely, if ever, had the sort of lengthy conversation that required eye-to-eye contact. She had managed to avoid the very thing every single woman he met sought to instigate.

'I treat the women I date incredibly well and, more importantly, I never give them any illusions about their place in my life. They know from the start that I'm not into building a relationship or working towards a "happy family" scenario.'

'Why?'

'Come again?'

'Why,' Jamie repeated in a giddy rush, 'are you not into building relationships or doing the happy-family thing?'

Ryan looked at her incredulously. Yes, he always encouraged an outspoken approach, both within the working environment and outside it. He prided himself on always being able to take what was said to him. He might choose to totally ignore it, of course, and did a great majority of the time, but never let it be said that he wasn't open to alternative opinions.

Except who had ever asked him such an outlandishly personal question before?

'Not everyone is.' But he was keen to bring the conversation to an end now. 'And, now that the cabaret show's over, I think it's time we get back to work.'

Jamie gave a little shrug and instantly resumed her professionalism. 'Okay. I didn't manage to find the time to look at those reports about the software company you're thinking of investing in. Shall I go and do that now? I can have everything ready for you by this afternoon.'

So, to Ryan's vague dissatisfaction, the day kicked off the way it always did: with Jamie working wonders with her time, sitting outside his office in her own private cubicle, where she did what she was highly paid to do with such staggering efficiency that he wondered how he had ever managed without her around.

His phone rang constantly; she fielded calls. The creative bods who worked on some of the games software three floors down burst into his office with some new idea or other, became over-exuberant; she ushered them out like a head teacher whose job it was to keep order in the classroom. When he made the comparison, his keen eyes noted the way she blushed and smiled, and then he grinned when she told him that she wouldn't have to play head teacher if he was a bit better at playing it himself.

At three, he grabbed his coat; he was running late for a meeting with three investment bankers. She told him at the very least to take off the rugby shirt and handed him something a little more presentable from the concealed, fully stocked wardrobe in the suite opposite his office. Everything was back to normal and it was beginning to grate on him.

At five-thirty, he got back to his office after a successful meeting to find her gathering her things together and slipping on her coat. About to switch off her computer, Jamie felt her heart flutter uncomfortably. She hadn't been expecting him to be back before she left.

'You're leaving?' Ryan tossed his coat over his desk and began pulling off the unutterably dull grey woollen jumper which he had obligingly worn for the benefit of the bankers.

Underneath, the white tee-shirt barely concealed the hard muscularity of his body. Jamie averted her eyes, mentally slapping herself because she should be used to all this by now and she wasn't sure why she was suddenly reacting to him like a complete idiot. Maybe it had something to do with her sister being back on the scene. There would be a psychological connection there somewhere if she could be bothered to work it out.

'I…I *would* have stayed on, Ryan, but something's come up, so I have to dash.'

'Something's *come up*? What?' He headed straight to where she was still dithering in front of her computer terminal and lounged against the door frame.

'Nothing,' Jamie muttered.

'Nothing? Something? Which is it, Jamie?'

'Oh, just leave me alone!' she blurted out, and to her horror she could feel her eyes welling up at the sudden intrusion of stress that had presented itself in her previously uncomplicated life. She looked away abruptly and began fiddling with the paperwork on her desk, before turning all her attention to her computer in the desperate hope that the man still leaning against the door frame would take the hint and disappear. He didn't. Worse, he walked slowly towards her and she felt his finger on her chin, tilting her face up to his.

'What the hell is going on here?'

'Nothing's going on. I'm just…just a bit tired, that's all. Maybe I'm…coming down with something.' She shrugged his hand off but she could still feel it burning her skin as she quickly stuck on her thick black coat and braced herself for the biting cold outside.

'Is it to do with work?'

'I beg your pardon?'

'Has something happened here at work that you're not telling me about? Some of the guys can be a bit rowdy. Has someone said something to you? Made some kind of inappropriate remark?' He suddenly blanched at the possibility that one of them might have seriously overstepped the mark and done something a little more physical when it came to being inappropriate.

Jamie looked at him blankly and shook her head. 'Of course not. No, work's fine. You'll be relieved to hear that.'

'Some guy giving you grief?' He tried to sound sympathetic but his imagination had broken its leash and was filling his head with all sorts of images that were definitely in the 'inappropriate' category.

'What kind of grief?'

'Has someone made an unwanted pass at you?' Ryan said bluntly. 'You can tell me and I'll make damn sure that it never happens again.'

'Why do you think that I would need help in sorting out something like that?' she asked coolly. 'Do you think that I'm such a fool that I wouldn't know how to take care of myself if some guy decided to make a pass at me?'

'Did I say that?'

'You implied it.'

'Other women,' Ryan said, his big body tensing, 'are probably just a bit more experienced when it comes to men. You... I may be mistaken, but you strike me as an innocent.'

Jamie stared at him. She distantly wondered how they had reached this point in the conversation. How many wrong turnings did it take to get from discussing a software report to her sex life—or lack of it?

'I think it's time I head home now. I'll make sure that I'm in on time tomorrow.' She began moving towards the door. She was only aware of him shifting his stance when she felt the hot weight of his fingers curled around her wrist.

'You were upset. Can you blame me for wanting to know why?' He gave a little jerk and pulled her towards him.

'Yes, I can!' Her mouth was dry and she knew that she was flushed. In truth, she felt as though her body was on fire.

'I'm your boss. You work for me, and as such you're my responsibility.' His eyes drifted down to her full mouth and then lower, to the starched white shirt, the neat, tailored jacket. He was aware of her breasts heaving.

'I am my own responsibility,' Jamie said through tight lips. 'I'm sorry I brought my stress to work. It won't happen again and, for your information, it has nothing to do with anything or anyone in this office. No one's been saying anything to me and no one's made a pass at me. I haven't had to defend myself but I'm just going to say this for the record— if someone *had* done something that I found offensive, then I would be more than capable of looking out for myself. I don't need you to step in and defend me.'

'Most women appreciate a man jumping to their defence,' Ryan murmured and just like that the atmosphere changed between them. He slackened his grip on her wrist but, instead of pulling away her hand, Jamie found herself staring up at him, losing herself in the depths of his eyes, mesmerised. She blinked and thankfully was brought back down to planet Earth.

'I am *not* most women,' she breathed. 'And I'd really appreciate it if you could let me go.'

He did, stepping aside, watching as she stuck on her coat and wrapped the black scarf around her neck.

She couldn't look at him. She just couldn't. She didn't understand what had happened back there but she was shaking inside. Not even the thought of Jessica could distract her from the moment. And she was horribly aware that he was staring at her, thinking that she was over-reacting, behaving like a mad woman when all he had done was to try and understand why she had been acting out of character.

She worked for him, and as her boss he had seen it as his civic duty to protect her from possible discomfort in her working environment, and what had she done in response? Acted like an outraged spinster in the company of a lech. She was mortified.

And then she had *stared* at him. Had he noticed? He noticed everything when it came to women and the last thing she needed was for him to think that she saw him as anything other than her boss, a man whom she respected but would always keep at arm's length.

'I've left those reports you asked me to do on your desk in descending order of priority,' she said crisply. 'Your meeting at ten tomorrow's been cancelled. I've rearranged it and you should have the new date updated onto your phone. So...'

'So, you can run along and nurse your stress in private,' Ryan drawled.

'I will.'

But she spent the entire journey back to her house dwelling on the tone of his voice as he had said that. She wondered what he was thinking of her. She didn't want to, but she did.

The barrier she had imposed that clearly defined both their roles felt as though it was crumbling around her like a flimsy pack of cards, and all because he had happened to catch her in a vulnerable moment.

Thanks to Jessica.

It was pitch-black and bitterly cold as she walked from the Underground station to her house. London was in a grip of the worst winter weather for twelve years. Predictions were for a white Christmas, although it had yet to snow.

In her house, however, the lights were on. All of them. Jamie sighed and reflected that, on the bright side, at least Jessica had managed to locate the key in its secret hiding spot under the flower pot at the side of the house. At least she had made it down to London from Edinburgh safe and sound, even if she brought with her the promise of yet more stress.

CHAPTER TWO

'But you don't *understand*…'

Jamie took time out from loading the dishwasher to glance round at her sister, who was wandering in a sulky fashion around the kitchen, occasionally stopping to pick something up and inspect it with a mixture of boredom and disdain. Nothing in the house was to her taste; she had made that very clear within the first few minutes of Jamie pushing open the front door and walking in.

The place, she'd announced, was poky. 'Couldn't you have found something a little more comfortable? I mean, I know Mum didn't leave us with much, but honestly, Jamie!' The furnishings were drab. There was no healthy stuff in the fridge to eat and, 'What on earth do you do for alcohol in this place? Don't tell me that you while away your evenings with a cup of cocoa and a good book for company?'

Jamie was accustomed to the casual insults, although it had been so long since she had actually set eyes on her sister that she had forgotten just how grating they could be after a while.

Their father had died when Jamie was six and Jessica still a three-year-old toddler and they had been raised by their mother. Jamie had been a bookworm at school, always studying, always mentally moving forward, planning to go to university. She left Jessica to be the one who curled her hair and painted her fingernails and, even at the age of thirteen, develop the kind of wiles that would stand her in very good stead with the opposite sex.

Jamie had never made it to university. At barely nineteen she had found herself first caring for her mother—who, after a routine operation, had contracted MRSA and failed to recover—then, when Gloria had died, taking on the responsibility of looking after her sixteen-year-old sister. Without Jamie even noticing, Jessica had moved from a precocious pre-teen to a nightmare of a teenager. Where Jamie had inherited her father's dark looks and chosen to retreat into the world of literature and books, Jessica had been blessed with their mother's striking blonde looks. Far from retreating anywhere, she had shown a gritty determination to flaunt as much of herself as was humanly possible.

A still-grieving Jamie had suddenly been catapulted into the role of caretaker to a teenager who was almost completely out of control.

What else could she have done? Gloria had begged her to make sure to keep an eye on Jessica, to look after her, 'Because you *know* what she can be like—she needs a firm hand…'

Jamie often wondered how it was that she hadn't turned prematurely grey from the stress of it.

And now, after all that muddy water under the bridge, stuff she still could hardly bear to think about, here was Jessica, back on the scene again, as stunning as ever—more, if that was possible—and already making Jamie grit her teeth in pointless frustration.

'I understand that you have responsibilities, Jess, and they may be getting to you but you can't run away from them.' Jamie slammed shut the dishwasher door with undue force and wiped her hands on a tea towel.

Dinner had been a bowl of home-cooked pasta with

chicken and mushrooms. Jessica had made a face and flatly refused to eat any of the pasta because she was off carbs.

'It's all right for you!' Jessica snapped, scooping up her poker-straight blonde hair into a ponytail before releasing it so that it fell in a heavy, silky curtain halfway down her back. '*You* don't have to deal with a bloody husband who works all the hours God made and expects me to be sitting around with a smile pinned to my face, waiting for him to return for a nice hot meal and a back massage! Like some kind of creepy Stepford wife.'

'You *could* get a job.'

'I *got* a job. I got eight jobs! It's not my fault if none of them suited me. Besides, what's the point me going out to work for a pittance when Greg earns so much?'

Jamie didn't say anything. She didn't want to think about Greg. Thinking about Greg had always been a downhill road. Once upon a time he had been her boss. Once upon a time she had fancied herself in love with him—a secret, pleasurable yearning that had filled her days with sunlight and made the burden of looking out for her younger sister more bearable. Once upon a time she had actually been stupid enough to think that he would wake up one day and realise that he cared for her in the same way she cared for him. Unfortunately, he had met Jessica and it had been love at first sight.

'Have you thought about volunteer work?' she offered, fed up.

'Oh, purr…leese! Can you *really* see me doing anything like that, Jamie? Working in a soup kitchen in Edinburgh? Or arranging flowers in the local parish church and doing fund raisers with the old biddies?'

She had dragged one of the chairs over and was sitting with her long legs propped up on the chair in front of her so that she could inspect her toenails which were painted a vibrant shade of pink.

'I'm bored,' she said flatly. 'I'm bored and I'm fed up and I want a life. I'm too young to be buried in the outskirts of Edinburgh where it rains all the time, *when* it's not snowing, hanging around for Greg, who only cares about sick animals anyway. Did you know he's got a fan club? The dishiest vet in town—it's pathetic!'

Jamie turned away and briefly squeezed her eyes tightly shut. It had been years since she had last seen Greg but she remembered him as clearly as if it had been yesterday. His kind face, the way his grey eyes crinkled when he smiled, his floppy blond hair through which he constantly ran his fingers.

The thought of her sister being bored with him filled her with terror. In the end, Greg had been her salvation. He had taken over the business of worrying about Jessica. Jessica might not need him, but she, Jamie, most definitely did!

'He's crazy about you, Jess.'

'Loads of guys could be crazy about me.'

Jamie felt her body go cold. 'What does that mean? Have you? You're not doing anything stupid, are you?'

'Oh, don't be such a prude.' But she sighed and leaned back against the chair, letting her head flop over the back so that she was staring glassy-eyed up at the ceiling. 'No, I'm not doing anything *stupid*, if by that you're asking me whether I'm having an affair. But the way I feel...'

She allowed that possibility to take shape between them and it was all Jamie could do not to slap her sister. However, years of ingrained caretaking papered over the passing temptation. This, she felt, was a subject best left alone in the hope that it might just go away. She was busy wondering what topic she could choose that might be safer when the doorbell rang.

'Someone flogging something,' she muttered, relieved for the distraction. 'Please, Jess, just give Greg a call. He must be worried sick about you.'

She left the kitchen to a disgruntled Jessica informing her that she had no intention of doing any such thing, that he knew perfectly well where she was, just like he knew that she needed some space.

Jamie wondered how long Greg would carry on waiting while Jessica hunted around for this so-called space she was intent on finding, and she was still chewing it over in her head as she pulled open the front door.

The sight of Ryan standing on her doorstep was so shocking that for a few seconds her mind went completely blank.

He had never, ever been to her house before. Not even when they had happened to drive out of London to attend a meeting. He had never picked her up or dropped her off. She hadn't even thought that he knew where she lived.

Eventually, her brain caught up with what her eyes were telling her, and she stopped gaping at him open-mouthed and actually croaked, 'What are you doing here?'

'You were stressed out. I was worried about you. I thought I'd drop by, make sure you were all right.'

'Well, I'm fine, so I'll see you tomorrow at work.' Belatedly, she remembered her sister scowling in the kitchen and she stepped outside and pulled the door quietly closed behind her, taking care not to shut it completely.

'How did you find out where I live?' she hissed under her breath. Under the lamplight, his face was a contour of harsh shadows and his eyes glittered in the semi-darkness. He was still in his work clothes, the jeans, the faded sweater, the trainers and the coat, which she knew had cost the earth, but which he wore as casually as if he had got it from the local Oxfam shop.

'Personnel files. It really wasn't too difficult.'

'Well, you have to go.'

'You're shaking like a leaf. It's cold out here—let me in for a few minutes.'

'No!' She saw his eyebrows rise fractionally and added, stammering, 'I mean, it's late.'

'It's eight-forty-five.'

'I'm busy.'

'You're on edge. Why? Tell me what's going on.' Ryan laughed. 'You're my indispensable secretary. I can't have you storing up nasty secrets and then suddenly deciding to walk out on me, can I? What would I do without you?'

'I…I'm obliged to give a month's notice,' Jamie stammered. Ryan Sheppard on her doorstep suddenly seemed to throw that all-important distance between them into confusion and she didn't like it.

'So you *are* thinking of leaving me. Well, it's a damn good thing I turned up here to get the full story out of you, isn't it? At least this way I can defend my corner.' For some reason he felt disproportionately let down by the thought of her just dumping a letter of resignation on his desk without any forewarning and then jumping ship. 'So, why don't you invite me inside and we can discuss this like two adults? If it's more money you're after, then name the amount and it's yours.'

'This is crazy!'

'I know. And I hate dealing with crazy.' He reached out and pushed the door open just as Jessica's petulant voice wafted from the direction of the kitchen, carolling to ask where Jamie was, because she really needed something to eat—and was there anywhere they could go for a halfway decent salad? She didn't fancy being cooped up for the rest of the night.

And then there she was, long and beautiful and blonde, and all the things that Ryan looked for in a woman, standing by the banister as Jamie turned around with a sigh of resignation. Stunningly pretty, stunningly fair-haired and dangerously bored with her husband.

If Jamie could have reached out and pushed Ryan straight back out of the front door, then she would have done so, but he was already inside the tiny hall, removing his thick coat while his eyes never strayed from Jessica.

'Well, well, well,' he drawled in a lazy undertone. 'What have we here…?'

'My sister,' Jamie muttered.

The glitter in Jessica's eyes mirrored his lazy speculation and Jamie felt a chill run down her spine.

There was no need for her to make introductions. Not when her sister was sashaying forward, hand outstretched, introducing herself—with, Jamie noted, her left hand stuck firmly behind her back.

'You never told me that you had a sister,' Ryan said, turning his fabulous eyes to Jamie.

Standing to one side like an uninvited spectator in her own house, Jamie's voice was stiff when she answered, 'I didn't see the relevance. Jessica doesn't live in London.'

'Although, I might just be thinking of changing that.'

Jamie's head whipped round and she stared, horrified at her sister. 'You can't!'

'Why not? I told you. I'm bored in Scotland. And, from what I see here, London certainly has a hell of a lot more to offer. Why did you never mention that you had such a dishy boss, Jamie? Did you think that I might dash down here and try to steal him from you?'

Jamie held on to the banister, feeling faint, and Ryan, lounging only feet away from her, took the opportunity to gauge the electric atmosphere between the sisters. Arriving unannounced on his secretary's doorstep had been a spontaneous decision which he had begun to regret on the drive over, but now he was pleased that he had made the journey.

'How long are you in London?' He looked at Jessica but his mind was still on Jamie and on that ferocious wall of privacy she had erected around herself. Purpose, he thought, unknown.

'She's literally only here for a day or two before she returns to Scotland. She's married and her husband will be waiting for her.'

'Did you have to bring that up?'

'It's the truth, Jess. Greg's a good guy. He doesn't deserve this.' *And* you *certainly don't deserve* him, she thought.

'I'm having lots of marital problems,' Jessica insisted to Ryan. 'I *thought* that I could come down here and find some support from my sister, but it looks like I was wrong.'

'That's not fair, Jess! And, besides, I'm sure Mr Sheppard doesn't want to stand here and listen to our family history.'

'Please, feel free to go on. I'm all ears!'

'You need to go.' Jamie turned to him. Every muscle in her body felt like it had been stretched to snapping point and the ground under her feet was like quicksand. One minute she had been on solid ground and then, in the blink of an eye, her sister was on her doorstep, Ryan was in her house breaking down her fortifications just by being there, and she was struggling in quicksand. 'And you, Jess, need to go to bed.'

'I'm not a kid any longer!'

'You behave like one.' In terms of condemnation, it was the first time Jamie had ever taken such a dramatic step. She had been conditioned to look after Jessica, to treat her like a baby, to make sure that her needs were met because she, Jamie, was the stronger one, the older one, the one upon whom the responsibilities lay.

In the tense silence that followed her flat statement,

Jessica hesitated, confused, then her lips pursed and she glared sulkily at her sister.

'You can't make me go back up to Scotland, you know,' she muttered.

'We can discuss this in the morning, Jess,' Jamie said wearily. 'I think I've had enough stress today.'

'And she *is* stressed.' Ryan inserted himself into the conversation and Jessica sidled a little closer to him, her body language advertising her interest in a way no amount of words could have done. 'She arrived late for work this morning.'

Jessica giggled and looked at her sister slyly. 'If you'd told me that you were running late, I would have got off the phone sooner. I know you're a stickler for punctuality. Don't worry. I'll be good as gold while I'm here, and you can be the perfect little secretary again and get in to work on time. Mind you…' She looked at Ryan coyly. 'If I had a boss like this one, I'd be getting in to work at six and leaving at midnight. Or maybe not leaving at all…'

Jamie turned on her heels and stalked off towards the kitchen. She knew how these conversations with her sister went. The slightest whiff of criticism and she would react with jibes below the belt that were designed to wound. Jamie had long discovered that the fastest way of dealing with this was to walk away from the situation, to treat her sister like a child who was not responsible for her tantrums. They blew over as quickly as they materialised and making herself scarce removed her from the eye of the storm.

She half-expected Jessica to linger on the staircase, turning on the full-wattage smile and bringing all her feminine wiles to play in an effort to charm Ryan. But, in fact, barely had Jamie sat at the kitchen table than Ryan appeared in the doorway and looked at her quietly, his hands shoved into his pockets.

An uncomfortable silence gathered around them which she broke by reluctantly offering him a cup of coffee.

She would cheerfully have sent him on his way, but there were things that needed to be said, and, reluctant as she was to open up any kind of discussion on her private life, she had no idea how she could avoid the issue.

'Where's Jessica?' she asked, standing up and moving across to the kettle.

'I sent her on her way.'

'And she listened?'

'I have that way with women.'

Jamie snorted, no longer bothering with the niceties that would have been more appropriate given that he was the guy who paid her salary. He had invaded her territory, and as far as she was concerned niceties were temporarily suspended.

'Now you know why I got in late to work this morning. Jessica kept me on the phone for nearly an hour. She was a mess. I only knew that she had decided to sort herself out by coming down here when she phoned me from the train.'

'No big deal.' Ryan took the mug she was holding out to him and sat down. 'Family crises happen. Why didn't you just tell me the truth this morning?' He watched her and realised that she was barely seeing him as she walked towards the kitchen table, nursing the mug in her hands. For a man who was fully aware of the impact he had on the opposite sex, being rendered invisible was a new experience.

He, on the other hand, keenly noted this new casual dress-code of hers, the one she used when she wasn't wearing her work hat. Lazy eyes took in the way her jeans clung to a body that curved in all the right places and the way her long-sleeved tee-shirt skimmed a flat stomach and lovingly contoured pert, full breasts. Even her hair looked different—less neat and pristine, more tousled, as though she had spent time running her fingers through it. Which, judging from what he had picked up of the atmosphere in the house so far, she probably had.

'I suppose because I happen to think that what happens in my private life is no business of yours.'

'Oh, for God's sake, I didn't even know that you had a sister! How much of a state secret could that possibly be?'

Jamie flushed and fiddled with the mug before taking a sip of coffee. 'I...I'm not really the confiding type.'

'Really? I'd never have guessed.'

'I didn't tell you about Jessica because the chances of you ever running into her were non-existent. I live in London, she lives just outside Edinburgh. She isn't a part of my daily life.'

'And that was exactly the way you wanted it until she had the misfortune to need your support.'

'Please don't presume to have any insight at all into my family affairs!'

'If you don't want me to presume, then you're going to have to be a bit more forthcoming.'

'Why? What difference does it make? I do a very good job for you and that's all that matters.'

'Why are you so uncomfortable with this conversation?' He could have let it go. She was right; she delivered the goods when it came to her job and whatever happened outside it was absolutely none of his business. But Ryan decided that he didn't want to let it go. It was as though a door had been partially opened and what lay behind it promised to be so intriguing that he was compelled to try and push the door a little wider.

'You don't understand. You're my boss, for a start, and like I said I'm not into confiding. I prefer to keep my own counsel. Maybe it's a reaction to having a sister like Jess. She always made so much noise that it was just a lot easier to keep quiet and let her get on with it.'

'Easier, but maybe not better. Forget for a minute that I'm your boss. Pretend that I'm just anybody—your next-door neighbour who has come over to borrow a cup of sugar, co-incidentally just at a time when you need a shoulder to cry on…'

'I'm supposed to think of you as my next-door neighbour on the scrounge for a cup of sugar?' She was momentarily distracted enough by the image to feel her lips twitch. 'What would you be doing with the cup of sugar?'

'Baking a cake, because I happen to be a kindly and caring neighbour who enjoys baking. It's my favourite pastime. Next to flower arranging and cross stitch.' She was relaxing. She was even smiling and he felt a kick of gratification that he had been responsible for that. For some reason, he didn't care for the idea of her stressed out, tearful and unable to talk to anyone about it. His experience of women was that they couldn't wait to pour their hearts out and confide in whomsoever happened to be willing to listen. He was the youngest of four and the only boy in the family. He could remember many an instance of sitting out one of his sister's ridiculously long phone calls, waiting impatiently to use the telephone.

This level of reticence was new to him. 'So…?' he prompted encouragingly.

'So, look, I'm not sure how to say this but…' Jamie sighed and adopted a slightly different approach. 'Now that you've met my sister, what do you think of her?'

'After all of my five-second acquaintance, I'm only quali-fied to tell you that she's very attractive.'

Jamie felt a stab of disappointment but she nodded sagely at him. 'She's always been the prettier one.'

'Hang on a minute…'

'Spare me the kindness. I'm stating a fact, and it's not something that's ever bothered me anyway.' But for a fleeting second Jamie wondered what he had been about to say. Of course, it would have been a polite lie, but nevertheless… 'Jessica's beautiful and she knows it. She's also married and going through a bit of a bad patch which will blow over just so long as…'

'As she's not offered any distractions by someone like me?' He looked at her coolly.

'I know what type of girls you go for—tall, blonde, beautiful and pliable. Well, Jess is tall, blonde, beautiful and at the moment she happens to be very pliable. I know you probably think that I'm being totally out of order in saying this stuff, but you chose to come here, and now that you're here I'm afraid I have every right to say what's on my mind.' She licked her lips nervously. 'I hope I'm not jeopardising my job by telling you this.'

'Jeopardising your job? What kind of person do you think I am?' He was outraged to think that she could even consider him the type of man who would penalise her for speaking her mind. Was that what she thought of him? Under her cool, dutiful exterior, did she think that he was some sort of monster?

'Don't worry, your job is perfectly safe, and if you're so obsessive about your privacy then I'm happy to walk out that door right now and leave you to get on with hiding behind your walls. As for your sister, she might be the sort of woman I date, but I don't date married women, even married women who claim to be unhappily married.'

He stood up and the colour drained from Jamie's face. She had enjoyed the free and easy way he had always had with her. It was all part and parcel of his unconventional personality, that curious, alluring mix of creativity, intelligence and self-assurance. Did she want to lose that? Did she want a boss who stuck to the rules and never teased her, or over-stepped the boundaries in asking about her personal life? That thought left her cold and she hurriedly got to her feet and reached out to put a restraining hand on his arm.

'I'm sorry. I know how that sounded, but I have to look out for my sister. You see…' She hesitated a fraction of a second. 'Our dad died when I was six, and when Jess was sixteen Mum died after complications following an operation. It was horrible. I was left in charge. Mum made me promise that I would look after her. I was about to go to university, but I found myself having to get a job and look after Jess.'

'That was a lot of responsibility for someone so young,' Ryan murmured, sitting back down.

'It wasn't easy,' Jamie agreed. 'Jess was boy crazy and I nearly tore my hair out making sure she showed up at school every day and left with a handful of qualifications.'

'What were you doing for a job?' he asked curiously, and was even more curious when slow colour crept into her cheeks and she looked down.

'Oh, just working at a vet's. It wasn't what I had expected to be doing at the age of nineteen, but I enjoyed it. The thing is…'

'What had you expected to be doing?'

'Huh?'

'Your plans? Dreams? Ambitions? What were they before your life was derailed?'

'Well…' Jamie flushed and hesitated. 'I wanted to go to university and study law. Seems like a lifetime ago! Anyway, that's not important. The important thing is that I just wanted to warn you off her.'

'Tough, having to give up on your dreams. There must be a part of you that resents her.'

'Of course there isn't! No one can help what life throws at them.'

'Noble sentiment. Alas, not many of us are noble creatures.'

'As I was saying…' Jamie chose to ignore the invitation to elaborate. 'I just wanted to warn you off her.'

'Because she's going to dutifully return to her husband and they're both going to live happily ever after?'

'Yes!'

'Warning duly noted.'

'What warning?'

Jessica was standing in the doorway of the kitchen, and with a sinking heart Jamie realised that she hadn't vanished because she had been instructed to vanish—she had vanished so that she could have a shower and resurface in the least amount of clothing possible. She was kitted out in slinky lounging culottes and a tiny vest, worn bra-less, that left nothing to the imagination. She had a stupendous figure and every inch of it was available for inspection as she walked slowly into the kitchen, enjoying the attention.

Through the thin, grey vest, Jamie could see the outline of her sister's nipples. Ryan would similarly be taking that in. Yes, he had told her that he would keep away from Jessica, but how strong was any red-blooded man's will power when it came to a sexy woman who was overtly encouraging?

'Well?' Jessica paused and leaned against the counter, legs lightly crossed at the ankles, her back arched so that her breasts were provocatively thrust forward. 'What warning?'

'A warning,' Ryan drawled, 'that I'm not to interfere and try and persuade you to return to your husband.'

Jessica looked at her sister narrowly. 'That true, Jamie?'

'Why would he lie?'

'So you don't mind me staying with you for a while? Maybe until Christmas is over? I mean, it's only a couple of weeks away. I could help you decorate the tree and stuff and by then I might have got my head together.'

Boxed in, Jamie had no choice but to concede defeat.

'Hey, we could even have a party!' She looked sideways at Ryan and shot him a half-smile. 'I'm great at organising parties. What are *you* up to at Christmas, anyway?'

'Jessica!'

'Oh, don't be such a bore, Jamie.'

'I'm in the country,' Ryan murmured. 'Why?' He had already received so many invitations to join people for Christmas lunch that he was seriously considering ignoring them all and locking himself away in his apartment until the fuss was over.

'You could join us here.'

Adjacent to Jamie, he was aware of her look of pure horror at the suggestion. He nearly burst out laughing, but he managed to keep a straight face as he appeared to give the offer considerable thought.

'Well…' He hesitated. 'I am in the unique position of spending Christmas day without my family.'

'Where are they?' Jessica strolled towards him, her thumbs hooked lightly into the elasticated waistband of the culottes so that they were dragged slightly down, exposing a flat, brown belly and the twinkling glitter of her pierced navel.

No wonder Jamie worried about her sister, Ryan thought. The woman was clearly a walking, talking liability to anybody's peace of mind.

'They're in the Caribbean.'

Jessica's eyes rounded into impressed saucers and her mouth fell open. 'You're kidding.'

'I have a house there and this year they've all decided to spend Christmas and New Year in it.'

'I don't know why we're having this silly conversation,'

Jamie interrupted crisply. 'Ryan already has his own plans for Christmas.' She rose to her feet and pulled open the dishwasher, which was her way of announcing that it was time for the impromptu evening to come to an end. But Jessica was in full flow, quizzing Ryan about his house in the Caribbean, asking him what it looked like, while he answered with just the sort of indulgent amusement that she was accustomed to getting. It had never mattered what boundaries Jessica had over-stepped; the world had always smiled and allowed her to get away with it. Whoever said that beautiful people didn't lead charmed lives?

'I'm open to persuasion,' Ryan finished, leaning back and watching Jamie bang pans into cupboards, frustration stamped on her face, her mouth downturned and scowling. 'What were *you* going to do, Jamie? Bit boring if you had been planning to stay in on your own.'

'I would rather call it peaceful,' she snapped. 'And, besides, I had plans to go out for drinks on Christmas morning with some friends and I would probably have hung around for their alternative Christmas lunch.'

'I want traditional,' Jessica stated flatly.

'What's Greg going to do?' Jamie spun round to look at her sister. 'Does he know that you're planning on abandoning him for Christmas day?'

'He won't mind. He's on call, and anyway, his parents can't wait to have him all to themselves so that they can tell him what a rotten wife I am. So…' That technicality concluded, Jessica turned her attention back to Ryan, who looked as comfortable and settled in the kitchen as though he had been there a million times. 'Will you come? Jamie's never been into Christmas, but I'll make her stick up a tree, and it'll be festive with a turkey and all the trimmings!'

'I'm sure he'll think about it. Just stop nagging him, Jess!' Jamie was pretty sure that she could convince Ryan to ignore her sister's rantings. He was a guy who was in great demand. The last thing he would want to do would be to sit around a small pine table in a kitchen and dine on a turkey reluctantly cooked by his secretary. Just the thought of it made her shiver in nervous apprehension.

'It's wonderful the way you can answer on my behalf.' Ryan grinned at Jamie, who scowled back at him. 'It's probably why we work so well together. You know just when to read my mind.'

'Ha-ha. Very funny.'

'But she's right.' He stood up and glanced at Jessica. 'I'll think about it and let Jamie know.'

'Or you could let me know. I'll give you my mobile number and you can get in touch any time at all. No need to go through Jamie.'

He left five minutes later and Jamie sagged. The peace of having her sister upstairs safely in bed was greatly diminished by the nasty tangle of thoughts playing in her mind.

Not only had Ryan found out more about her in the space of an hour than he had in eighteen months, but she was now facing the alarming prospect that, having wedged his foot through the door, it would be impossible to get him to remove it.

Everything that had always been so straightforward had now been turned on its head.

And what if the man decided to descend on them for Christmas lunch?

Apprehension sizzled in her and, alongside that very natural apprehension, something else, something even more worrying, something that closely resembled…anticipation.

CHAPTER THREE

CHRISTMAS'S rapid approach brought a temporary lull in the usual relentless work-ethic. Ryan Sheppard made a very good Christmas boss. He entered into the spirit of things by personally supervising the decorations and cracking open champagne at six every evening for whoever happened to be around in the countdown to the big day. Extra-long lunch hours shopping were tactfully overlooked. On Christmas Eve, work was due to stop at twelve and the rest of the day given over to the Secret Santa gift exchanges and an elaborate buffet lunch which would be prepared by Ryan's caterers.

On the home front, Jamie was stoically putting up with a sister who had decided to throw herself into the party season with gay abandon. She tagged along to all the Christmas parties to which Jamie had been invited, flirted outrageously with every halfway decent-looking bachelor, and in the space of a week and a half collected more phone numbers than Jamie had in her address book. There was, ominously, no mention of Greg. If they were in contact, it certainly wasn't via the landline. Jamie had stopped asking because the response of tear-filled eyes, followed by an angry sermon about the valuable space for which she was still searching, was just too much of a headache.

A tree had been erected and Jessica had enthusiastically

begun helping with the lights, but like a child, had become bored after fifteen minutes, leaving Jamie to complete the task. Clothes were left strewn in unlikely places and were retrieved with an air of self-sacrifice whenever Jamie happened to mention the state of the house. The consequence of this was that Jamie's peaceful existence was now a round-the-clock chore of tidying up behind her sister and nagging.

Of course, Jamie knew that she would have to sit her sister down and insist on knowing when she intended to return to Scotland, but like a coward she hid behind the Christmas chaos and decided to shelve all delicate discussions until Boxing Day at the very least.

There was also the hurdle of Christmas day to get through. Ryan had, totally unexpectedly, accepted Jessica's foolish invitation to lunch and, with the prospect of three people cutting into a turkey that would be way too big, Jamie had invited several other members of staff to come along if they weren't doing anything.

Three guys from the software department had taken her up on the invitation, as well as a couple of her girlfriends whom she had met at the gym when she had first arrived in London.

Jamie anticipated an awkward lunch, but when she mentioned that to her sister, Jessica had smiled brightly and assured her that there was no need to worry.

'I'm a party animal!' she had announced. 'I can make any gathering go with a bang, and I've got loads of party hats and crackers and stuff. It'll be a blast! So much better than last year, which was a deadly meal round at the in-laws'. I can't wait to fill Greg in when the last guest leaves.'

'I'm surprised you even care what he thinks,' Jamie had said and was vaguely reassured when her sister had gone bright red.

Not that she had dwelled on that for any length of time.

Most of her mind for the past week had been taken up with the prospect of Ryan descending on her house for Christmas lunch.

And now the day had finally arrived. It came with dark, leaden skies and a general feeling of anticlimax; although some snow had been forecast, it appeared to be in the process of falling everywhere else but in London.

From downstairs came the thud of music, a compilation of songs which Jessica had prepared during her spare time. Peace seemed a distant dream. At eight-thirty, Jamie had thoroughly cleaned the bathroom, which had been taken over by her sister in a series of undercover assaults, so that each day slightly more appeared on the shelf and in the cabinet.

Now, sitting and staring at her reflection in the mirror, Jamie wondered how much longer she would be able to cope with a very hyper Jessica.

Then she thought about her outfit: a long-sleeved black dress that, she knew, would look drab against the peacock-blue of Jessica's mini skirt and her high wedges that would escalate her height to six feet.

By the time the first guest arrived, Jamie was already settling into her role of background assistant to her life-and-soul-of-the-party sister.

Every nerve in her body was tuned to the sound of the doorbell, but when Ryan eventually appeared, she was in the kitchen, as it happened, doing various things with the meal. Outside alcohol was steadily being consumed and Jessica was flirting, dancing and enjoying the limelight, even though the guys concerned were the sort of highly intelligent eccentrics she would ordinarily have dismissed as complete nerds.

The sound of his voice behind her, lazy and amused, zapped her like a bolt of live electricity and she leapt to her feet and spun around, having been peering worriedly into the oven.

'Well,' he drawled, walking into the kitchen and peering underneath lids at the food sitting on the counter, 'looks like the party's going with a swing.'

'You're here.'

'Did you think that I wasn't going to turn up?' Since the last time he had seen her in jeans and a tee-shirt, he had found himself doing quite a bit of thinking about her. As expected, she had mentioned nothing about her sister when she had been at work, which didn't mean that their working relationship had remained the same. It hadn't. Something subtle had altered, although he had a feeling that that just applied to him. She had been as efficient, as distant and as perfectly polite as ever.

'I'm nothing if not one-hundred-percent reliable.' He held out a carrier bag. 'Champagne.'

Flustered, she kept her eyes firmly on his face, deliberately avoiding the muscular legs encased in pair of black trousers and the way those top two undone buttons of his cream shirt exposed the shadow of fine, dark hair.

'Thanks.' She reached out for the carrier bag and was startled when from behind his back he produced a small gift-wrapped box. 'What's this?'

'A present.'

'I'm still working my way through the bottle of perfume you gave me last year.' She wiped her hands and then began opening the present.

Her mouth went dry. She had been privy to quite a few of his gifts to women. They ranged from extravagant bouquets of flowers to jewellery to trips to health spas. This, however, was nothing like that. In the small box was an antique butterfly brooch and she picked it up, held it up to the light and then set it back down in its bed of tissue paper before raising her eyes to his.

'You bought me a butterfly,' she whispered.

'I noticed that you had a few on your mantelpiece in the sitting room. I guessed you collect them. I found this one at an antique shop in Spitalfields.'

'It's beautiful, but I can't accept it.' She thrust it at him and turned away, her face burning.

'Why not?'

'Because…because…'

'Because you don't collect them?'

'I do, but…'

'But it's yet another of those secrets of yours that you'd rather I knew nothing about?'

'It just isn't appropriate,' Jamie told him stiffly. In her head, she pictured him roaming through a market, chancing upon the one thing he knew would appeal to her, handing over not a great deal of cash for it, but it never took much to win someone over. Except, she wasn't on the market to be won over. Nor was he on the market for doing anything but what came naturally to him—thinking outside the box. It was why he was such a tremendous success in his field.

'Okay, but you know that it's an insult to return a gift.' Ryan shrugged. 'I'm in your house. Consider it a small token of gratitude for rescuing a lonely soul from wandering the streets of London on Christmas day.'

'Oh, please.' Her breathing was shallow and she was pain-fully conscious of the fact that whilst outside the music was blaring, probably getting on the neighbours' nerves, inside the kitchen it was just the two of them locked in a strange intimacy that terrified her.

This was not what she wanted. She urgently reminded herself of Greg and her foolish love-sick infatuation with him before Jessica had arrived on the scene and stolen his heart.

But to insist on returning the brooch would risk making just too big a deal of it. It would alert him to the fact that for some reason his gesture bothered her.

'I haven't got anything for you,' she said uncomfortably.

'I'll live with that. Why butterflies?'

'My father was keen on them,' Jamie said awkwardly as another piece of information left her and travelled across to him. 'Mum told us a lot about him. He loved to travel. He particularly loved to travel to study insects, and out of all the insects butterflies interested him most. He liked the fact that there were so many different varieties of them and they came in so many different colours and shapes and sizes. Mum said that he figured they were a lot more interesting than the human species.'

Her voice and expression had softened as she lost herself in a memory that hadn't surfaced for years. 'So I started collecting them when I was a kid. I just keep the better ones on show, but I have a box upstairs full of silly plastic ones I had when I was growing up.' A sudden blast of music hit her as the kitchen door was pushed open and the moment of crazy reminiscing was lost with the appearance of Jessica, now wearing a shiny party hat and with her arm around one of the computer geeks, who looked thrilled to death with the leggy blonde clinging to him.

'Enjoy the attention, buddy.' Ryan grinned at his top software-specialist. 'But bear in mind the lady's married.'

Outside, the party of six guests had swelled to ten. Jessica had asked a couple of others 'to liven things up'. Bottles of wine were ranged on the sideboard in the living room and the chairs had been cleared away to create a dance floor of sorts.

Walking into the room was like walking into a disco, but

one where the decor was comprised of a Christmas tree in the corner and random decorations strung along the walls. In the centre of it all, Jessica was living up to her reputation as a party animal.

Swaying to the music with a drink in one hand and her eyes half-closed, she was the peacock, proud of her stupendous figure, which outranked even those of the gym queens at the side, and the cynosure of all male eyes.

When the beat went from fast to slow, Jamie looked away as Jessica draped herself over Ryan.

So what else had she expected? That he would actually be able to resist the allure of an available woman? A dull ache began in her head. She mingled and chatted and even half-heartedly danced with her colleague Robbie who charmed her with an enthusiastic conversation about something he was working on at the moment, something guaranteed to be bigger and better than anything else on the market.

While Ryan danced on with Jessica.

Several of the neighbours began popping in, drawn by the music. On either side, they were young, professional couples whom Jamie had glimpsed in passing. Now, she realised that they were people with whom she could easily become friendly, and the distraction was a blessing. It took her out of the living room and into the kitchen, where they congregated and compared notes on the neighbourhood.

She wasn't too sure how the matter of eating was going to be achieved. As expected, the bulk of the preparations had been left to her while her sister had stalked ineffectively around the kitchen with a glass of wine in her hand, sighing and making useless suggestions about what could be done to speed up the whole process. 'Dump the lot and order in a Chinese', had been one of her more ridiculous offerings, especially considering she had been the one to insist on the full turkey extravaganza.

Flushed from the heat in the kitchen, and nursing enough low-level resentment to sink a small ship, Jamie was fetching the wretched turkey out of the oven when Ryan's voice behind her nearly made her drop the hapless bird.

'You need a hand.'

Jamie carefully deposited the aluminium baking dish on the counter and glanced across to him.

'I'm fine. Thank you.'

'Just stating the obvious here, but martyrs aren't known to be the happiest people on the face of the earth.'

'I'm not being a martyr!' She turned to look at him, hacked off and grim. 'I was coerced into doing…*this*.' A sweeping gesture encompassed the kitchen, which looked as though it had been the target of a small explosion. 'So I'm doing it.'

'Exactly—you're being a martyr. If you didn't want to do all…*this*—' he mirrored her sweeping gesture '—then you shouldn't have.'

'Do you have any idea what my sister's like when she doesn't manage to get her own way?' Jamie cried with a hint of hysteria in her voice. 'Oh, no, of course you don't, because *you* haven't had years of her! Because *you* are only being shown the smiling, sexy side that leaves men breathless and panting.'

'My breathing's perfectly normal.' He rescued the potatoes and began searching around for other dishes, into which he began piling the food. 'Look, why don't you go and drag your sister in here and force her to give you a helping hand?'

Jamie opened her mouth to tell him just how silly his suggestion was—because Jessica never, but *never*, did anything she didn't want to do—and instead sighed wryly.

'That would come under the heading of "mission impossible".'

'In that case, I'm helping, whether you like it or not.'

'You're my boss. You're not supposed to be in here helping.'

'You're right, I am your boss—you are therefore obliged to do whatever I ask.'

Jamie couldn't help it. She went bright red at the unintended innuendo and was mortified when Ryan burst out laughing.

'Within reason, of course…' He raised his eyebrows in amusement. 'Although I gather from your sister that there wouldn't be any outraged boyfriend threatening to break my kneecaps if I decided to push the point…'

He was still grinning. *Laughing* at her. She turned away abruptly, knowing that the back of her neck was giveaway-red and that her hands were shaking as she poured gravy into the gravy boat and busied herself with the roast potatoes.

'Jessica shouldn't be talking about my private life!' she managed, on the verge of tears. Tears of pure frustration.

'She said that you didn't have a boyfriend,' Ryan said mildly. 'What's the big deal?'

'The *big deal* is that it's none of your business!'

'You know, it's dangerous to be so secretive. Makes other people even more intrigued.'

'There's nothing intriguing about my private life,' Jamie snapped. 'It's not nearly as glamorous or adventurous as *yours.*'

'If you really thought that my life was glamorous, exciting and adventurous, then you wouldn't be so disapproving—and don't deny that you disapprove. You admitted it yourself—you think I'm an unscrupulous womaniser with no morals.'

'I never said that!' She met his amused grin with a reluctant smile of her own. 'Okay, maybe I implied that you… Why are you being difficult, Ryan Sheppard?'

'What an outrageous accusation, Jamie Powell,' Ryan said piously. 'No one likes being accused of being exciting and adventurous.'

'I never said that. You're twisting my words.'

'You know, you may not be obvious in the way that your sister is, but when it comes to getting a man—and believe me, I know what I'm talking about—you have...'

'Stop! I don't want to hear what you're going to say.'

'Somehow, over the years, your sister has managed to destroy your self-confidence.'

'I have plenty of self-confidence. I work with you. You should know that.'

'Yes, you certainly do when it comes to the work front, but on an emotional level let's just say that I'm beginning to see you for the first time.' *And liking what I see*, he could have added.

Jamie didn't like the sound of that. She also didn't like the way his throwaway remarks were making her question herself. *Was* she lacking in self-confidence? Was he implying that she was emotionally stunted?

'You *were* going to help, or at least that's what you said. You never mentioned that you were going to play amateur psychologist. So can you get the plastic cups from the cupboard over here, and stop giving me lots of homespun advice? And I don't,' she burst out, unable to contain herself, 'have a boyfriend because I've never seen the need to grab anything that's available because it's better than nothing at all!'

She found that they were suddenly staring at each other with the music outside—a dull, steady throb—and the aromatic smells in the hot kitchen swirling around them like a seductive, heady incense.

'Good policy,' Ryan murmured, taking in the patches of heightened colour in her cheeks and the way her eyes glittered—nothing like the cool, composed woman he was so accustomed to working alongside.

'And if I *did* have a man in my life,' she heard herself continue, with horror, 'he certainly wouldn't be the sort of person who runs around breaking other people's kneecaps.'

'Because you can take care of yourself.'

'Exactly!'

'And you definitely wouldn't be drawn to a caveman.'

'No, I wouldn't.'

'So what *would* you be drawn to?'

'Thoughtful. Sensitive. Caring.' With sudden alarm, she realised that somewhere along the line she had breached her own defences and allowed emotion to take control over her careful reserve.

But she had just been so mad. After the nightmare challenge of having to cope with her sister landing on her doorstep with her uninvited emotional baggage, and the chaos of having to deal with a Christmas lunch that had been foisted upon her, the thought of Jessica getting drunk and gossiping about her behind her back to her boss had been too much.

'I'm sorry,' she apologised stiffly, turning away and gathering herself.

Not so fast, Ryan wanted to say, *not when you've set my mind whirring.*

'For what?' As in the office, they seemed to work well together in the kitchen, with Jamie dealing with the food while Ryan efficiently piled the dirty dishes into the sink. 'For happening to have feelings?'

'There's a time and a place for everything.' Her voice was definitely back in full working order; frankly, if he chose to snigger at her behind her back at her woefully single state, then that was his prerogative. 'My kitchen on Christmas day definitely isn't either.'

'We could always alter the time and the venue. Like I

said, it's important for a boss to know what's going on in his secretary's life.'

'No. It isn't.' But of course he was teasing her and she half smiled, pleased that the normal order was restored.

Watching her, Ryan felt a sudden kick of annoyance. Would he have taken her out, maybe for dinner, in an attempt to prise beneath that smooth exterior? He didn't know, but he did realise that she was quietly and efficiently re-erecting her barriers.

Oozing sympathy, he turned her to face him, his hands resting lightly on her shoulders. 'People tell me that I'm a terrific listener,' he murmured persuasively. 'And I pride myself on being able to read other people.'

Jamie opened her mouth to utter something polite but sarcastic, and instead found herself dry-mouthed and blinking owl-like as he stared down at her. He really was sinfully, shamefully beautiful, she thought, dazed.

'And I didn't mean to offend you by suggesting that your outgoing, in-your-face sister might have been ruinous on your levels of self-confidence. I'm just guessing that you've been messed up in the past.'

'What are you talking about?' she whispered.

'Some loser broke your heart and you haven't been able to move on.'

Jamie drew her breath in sharply and pulled away from him, breaking the mesmeric spell he had temporarily cast over her. She pressed herself against the kitchen counter, hands behind her back.

'What did my sister say to you?'

Ryan had been fishing in the dark. He had been curious—understandably curious, he thought. In his world, women were an open book. It was refreshing to be challenged with one who wasn't. Now, he felt like the angler who, against all odds, has managed to land a fish.

She was as white as a sheet, and although she was trying hard to maintain a semblance of composure he knew that it was a struggle.

So who the hell was the guy who had broken her heart?

'This is ridiculous!' Abruptly, Jamie turned away and began gathering a stack of plates in her hands. They were all disposable paper plates because there was no way that she would be left standing by the sink after the last guest had departed, washing dishes while her sister retired to bed for some well-deserved sleep after copious alcohol consumption.

'Trust me, he wasn't worth it.' Ryan was enraged on her behalf.

'I really don't want to talk about this.'

'Sometimes those caring, sharing types can prove to be the biggest bastards on the face of the earth.'

'How would *you* know?' She spun round to look at him with flashing eyes. 'For your information, the caring, sharing guy in question was the nicest man I've ever met.'

'Not that nice, if he trampled over you. What was it? Was he married? Stringing you along by pretending he was single and unattached? Or maybe promising to dump his wife who didn't understand him? Or was he seeing other women on the side? Underneath that caring, sharing exterior, was he living it up behind your back—was that it? Word of advice here—men who get a tear in their eye during sad movies and insist on cooking for you because they get home at five every evening don't necessarily have the monopoly on the moral high-ground. You've got to let it go, Jamie.'

'Let it go and start doing *what*?' she heard herself asking as she gripped the paper plates in her hand.

'Join the dating scene.'

'So that I can…?'

'Finish what you were going to say.' Ryan moved to block

her exit. 'Like I said, there's never any need for you to think that you can't speak freely to me. We're not in a work environment here. Say whatever you want to say.'

'Okay, here's what I want to say—whatever hang-ups I have, there's no way I would join any dating scene if there was a possibility of bumping into men like you, Ryan Sheppard!'

Ryan's lips thinned. She was skating dangerously close to thin ice but hadn't he invited her to be frank and open with him? Hadn't he insisted? On the other hand, he hadn't expected her to throw his kindness back in his face. He was giving her the benefit of his experience, warning her of the perils of the sort of smiley, happy jerk she claimed to like, providing her with a shoulder to cry on—and in return…?

'Men *like me*?' he enquired coldly.

'Sorry, but you did ask me to be honest.'

Ryan forced himself to offer her a smile. 'I don't lead women up the garden path and break their hearts,' he gritted.

'No one led me up a garden path!' But she had said too much. She was hot, bothered and flustered and regretting every mis-spoken word. 'We should get this food out there before it all goes stone cold,' she carried on.

'In other words, you want this conversation terminated.'

Jamie avoided his eyes and maintained a mute silence. 'I apologise if I said certain things that you might construe as insulting,' she eventually offered in a stilted voice, and he scowled. 'And I'd appreciate it if we could just leave it here and not mention this conversation again.'

'And what if I don't agree to that?'

Jamie looked at him calmly, composure regained, but at a very high cost to her treasured peace of mind. 'I don't think I could work happily alongside you otherwise. I'm a very private person and it would be impossible for me to function if I feared that you might start...' *Finding my life a subject for conjecture.*

'Start what?'

'Trying to get under my skin because you find it amusing.'

Her eyes weren't quite brown, Ryan caught himself thinking. There were flecks of green and gold there that he had never noticed before. But then again, why would he have noticed, when she kept her eyes studiously averted from his face most of the time?

He stood aside with ill humour and pushed open the door for her and immediately they were assailed with the sound of raised voices and laughter. While they had been in the kitchen, a cabaret had obviously been going on and, sure enough, Jessica had pulled one of the tables to the side of the room and was doing her best to hang some mistletoe from the light on the ceiling in the middle of the room, while surrounded by a circle of guests who were clearly enjoying the spectacle.

Food was greeted with clapping and cheering. The neighbours made a half-hearted attempt to head back to their houses, but were easily persuaded to stay. All hands hit the deck and more drink surfaced while, to one side, Jamie watched proceedings. And Ryan watched Jamie, out of the corner of his eye. Watched as she pretended to join in, although her smile was strained whenever she looked across to her flamboyant sister. Surrounded by an audience, Jessica was like one of the glittering baubles on the Christmas tree.

It was nearly five-thirty by the time the food had been depleted and Jamie began the laborious process of clearing.

Exhaustion felt like lead weights around her ankles and she knew that her tiredness had nothing to do with the task of making Christmas lunch. It was of the mental variety and that was a much more difficult prospect to shake off.

Talking to Ryan in the kitchen, exploding in front of him like an unpredictable hand grenade, had drained her and she knew why.

For the first time in her life, she had allowed herself to let go. The result had been terrifying and if she could only have taken it all back then she would have.

Sneaking a glance to her right, she looked at him. He had dutifully helped clear away dishes, along with everyone else minus her sister, and now he was laughing and joking with the guys from his office. Doubtless he had completely forgotten their conversation, while she…

She watched as, giggling and swaying her hips to the rhythm of the music, Jessica began beckoning him across to where she had positioned herself neatly underneath the precariously hanging bunch of mistletoe.

Ryan looked far from thrilled at the situation and for once Jamie was not going to rush in and try and save her sister from herself. If Jessica wanted to fool around in her quest to find herself, then so be it. Jamie had spent a lifetime standing behind her, desperately attempting to rescue her from her own waywardness.

Lord, in the process she had even forgotten how to take care of her own emotional needs! She had bottled everything up; how pathetic was it that the one time she actually managed to release the cork on that bottle it was with her boss, the least appropriate or suitable person when it came to shoulder-lending! He went through women like water and had probably never had a decent conversation of any depth with any of the bimbos who clung to him like superglue. Yet she had directed all her angst at him—in an unstoppable stream of admissions that she knew she would eternally live to regret.

She was turning away, heading for the sanctuary of the kitchen, when she happened to glance through the window.

No one had bothered to draw the curtains and there, stepping out of his car—the same old battered Land Rover which he had had ever since she had first started working for him—was her brother-in-law.

For a few seconds, Jamie could scarcely believe her eyes. She hadn't seen Greg for absolutely ages. She had fled with her pride and dignity intact, determined to keep her love for him firmly under wraps while he got on with the business of showering Jessica with his devotion. Since then, she hadn't trusted herself to be anywhere near him, because she would rather have died than to let her secret leap out of its box.

The years hadn't changed him. He was turning now to slot his key into the lock; everything about him was surprisingly the same. His fair hair still flopped over his eyes and he still carried himself with the same lanky awkwardness that Jamie had once found so incredibly endearing. She could make all that out even under the unsatisfactory street lighting.

She peeled her eyes away for a fraction of a second to see Jessica reaching out to put her hands on Ryan's shoulders. In a second, Jamie thought with a surge of panic two things would happen: Greg would turn around and look straight through the window, and Jessica would close her eyes and plant a very public kiss on Ryan's mouth.

Galvanised, she sprinted across the room. If she had had time to think about it, she wasn't sure whether she would have followed through, but as it was she acted purely on instinct, fired by a driving need to make sure that her sister didn't completely blow the one chance she had in life of true happiness—because Greg was as good as it would ever get for Jessica.

She pulled Ryan around and saw his surprise mingled with relief to have been spared the embarrassment of having to gently but firmly turn Jessica away. Janie reached up and curled her hand around his neck, and even at the height of her spontaneity she was stomach clenchingly aware of the muscularity of his body.

'Wha...?'

'Mistletoe!' Jamie stated. 'We're under it. So we'd better do what tradition demands.'

Ryan laughed softly under his breath and curved his hand around her waist.

As far as days went, this one was turning out to be full of unexpected twists and turns; he couldn't remember enjoying himself so much for a very long time indeed.

He didn't know what had brought about this change in Jamie but he liked it. He especially liked the feel of her body as it softened against his. He felt her breasts push against his chest. She smelled of something clean and slightly floral and her full mouth was parted, her eyes half-closed. It was the most seductive thing he had ever experienced in his life.

Who was he to resist? He gathered her to him and kissed her, a long, deep kiss that started soft and slow and increased tempo until he was losing himself in it, not caring if they were spectator sport.

He surfaced when she twisted out of his arms and turned around. Reluctantly, Ryan followed her gaze, as did everyone else in the room, to the blond-haired man standing in the doorway with an overnight bag in one hand and a bunch of straggling flowers in the other.

CHAPTER FOUR

RYAN looked at his watch and scowled. The offices were pretty bare of staff, just the skeleton lot who got more of a kick at work at their computers, creating programmes and testing games, than they did in their own homes.

Not the point.

The point was that it was now ten fifteen and Jamie should have been in one hour and fifteen minutes ago. Christmas day had come and gone. Boxing Day had come and gone. She hadn't booked any holiday time beyond that.

He swung his jean-clad legs off his desk, sending a pile of paperwork to the ground in the process, and stalked across the floor-to-ceiling window so that he could look outside and, bad-tempered, survey the grey, bleak London streets which were eerily quiet in this part of the city.

He was still reeling from the events of Christmas day, much to his enduring annoyance. He had gone to satisfy a simple and one-hundred-percent understandable curiosity and had got the equivalent of a full round in a boxing ring—starting with that little conversation in the kitchen with Jamie, followed by her kissing him and culminating in the appearance of the man at the door.

It had been a comedy in three acts, except Ryan couldn't be further from laughing.

He could still feel the warmth of her mouth against his.

The memory of it had eaten into his Boxing Day, turning him into an ill-tempered guest at the party given by his god-child's parents, a party which had become a tradition of sorts over the years and which he had always enjoyed.

Glancing at his watch again, he was beginning to wonder whether Jamie had decided to jettison work altogether. A week ago such an act of rebellion bordering on mutiny would have been unthinkable, but in the space of a heartbeat all preconceived ideas about his quiet, efficient, scrupulously reserved secretary had been blown to smithereens.

He was in the process of debating whether to call her when his office door was pushed open and there she was, unbuttoning her sensible black coat and tugging at the scarf around her neck.

'This is getting to be a habit,' Ryan grated, striding back to his desk and resuming his position with the chair pushed back and his long legs extended to the side. 'And don't bother to try and tell me stories about delays on the Underground.'

'Okay. I won't.'

Things had irreparably changed. Over a fraught day and a half, Jamie had resigned herself to that and come to the conclusion that the only way she could continue working for Ryan was if she put every single unfortunate personal conversation they had had behind her. Lock them away in a place from where they couldn't affect her working life. And the kiss...

The horror of that moment and the fact that it still clawed away in her mind was something that would have to be locked away as well.

All the same, she was having a hard time meeting his eyes as she relieved herself of her coat, gloves and scarf and deposited the bundle of post on his desk, along with her laptop computer, which she switched on in an increasingly tense silence.

'Look, I'm sorry I'm late,' she eventually said when it seemed like the silence would stretch to infinity. 'It's not going to be a habit, and you know that I'm more than happy to work late tonight to make up for the lost time.'

'I can't have unreliability in my employees—beside the point, whether you're happy to work late or not.'

'Yes, well, I hoped that you might understand given the fact that half the country is still on holiday.' She couldn't prevent the edge of rebelliousness from creeping into her voice, but the past day and a half had been beyond the pale and nothing seemed to be changing. Greg had appeared on the doorstep, putting a swift end to proceedings on Christmas day. Who on earth had been willing to listen to Jessica's histrionics—because her sister had had absolutely no qualms about letting the rest of the world into her problems. Apparently no one. There had been a half-hearted attempt on the part of some to try and clear the sitting room but within forty-five minutes they had all dispersed—including Ryan, although in his case Jamie had had to push him out of the door. In true intrusive style, he had been sharply curious and more than happy to stick around. Jamie was having none of it.

And since then her house, the bastion of her peace of mind, had become the arena for warfare.

Jamie now knew far too much about the state of her sister's marriage for her liking.

With nowhere else to stay, and determined to put things right, Greg had now taken up residence in the sitting room, much to Jessica's disgust. Everything was chaotic and, although Jamie had sat them both down and gently advised them that perhaps sorting out their marriage problems was something that could be better done in their own home, there seemed to be no glimmer of light on the horizon.

Jessica was standing firm about needing her space and

Greg was quietly persistent that he wasn't going to give up on them because she was having a temporary blip.

And now Ryan was sitting stony-faced in front of her and she wasn't sure that she could bear much more.

'Can we get on with some work?' she half pleaded. 'There are a few contracts that you need to look at. I've emailed them to you, and I think Bob Dill has finally completed that software package he's been working on.'

Ryan discovered that he had been waiting to see how things would play out when she showed up for work. Now, it dawned on him that she intended to bury the whole Christmas episode, pretend none of it had ever happened.

He steepled his fingers under his chin and looked at her thoughtfully. 'Yes,' he agreed, tilting his head to one side. 'We certainly could have a look at those contracts, but that's not imperative. Like you said, half the country's still recovering from Christmas.' It was interesting to see the way she flushed at the mention of Christmas. 'Which brings me to the subject of Christmas day.'

'I'd rather we didn't talk about that,' Jamie told him quickly.

'Why not?'

'Because…'

'You find it uncomfortable?'

'Because…' Flustered, Jamie raised her eyes to his and found herself consumed with embarrassing, graphic recall of that kiss they had shared. She had never, in the end, even shared a kiss with Greg. All through that time she had dreamed about him, the closest she had come to actually touching him was on the odd occasion when his hand had accidentally brushed hers or when he had given her a brotherly peck on the cheek.

So why had she spent her every waking hour thinking about Ryan Sheppard, when she had happily worked alongside him for ages and always managed to keep him at a healthy distance? Was she so emotionally stunted that she had just switched infatuation? Did she have some kind of insane inclination to fancy the men she worked for? *No!* Jamie refused to concede any such thing. 'Because we have a perfectly good working relationship and I don't want my private life to start intruding on that.'

'Too bad. It already has.'

He abruptly leaned forward and Jamie automatically pressed herself back into her chair.

'And,' he continued remorselessly, 'it's already affecting your working life. That guy who appeared on your doorstep…'

'Greg,' Jamie conceded with reluctance. 'Jessica's husband.'

'Right. Greg. He's staying with you, is he?'

Jamie flushed and nodded. She looked wistfully at her computer.

'And you have no objections to having your house turned into a marriage counselling centre?'

'Of course I object to it! It's an absolute nightmare.'

'But they're still under your roof.'

'I don't see the point of discussing any of this.'

'The point is it's affecting your life and you can't separate the strands of your private life from your working life. You look exhausted.'

'Thank you very much.'

'So what are you going to do about it?'

Jamie sighed with frustration and shot him a simmering, mutinous look from under her lashes. Ryan Sheppard had a restless, curious mind. He could see things and approach them from different angles with a tenacity that always seemed to pay dividends. Where one person might look at a failing company and walk away, he looked and then looked a bit harder, and mentally began picking it apart until he could work out how to put it back together in a way that benefited him. Right now he was curious and, whilst she could hardly blame him, she had no intention of becoming his pet project.

But she grudgingly had to concede that he had a point when he said that the strands of her life were interwoven. She had shown up late for work because she had slept through her alarm, and she had slept through her alarm because Greg and Jessica had been engaged in one of their furious, long-winded arguments until the early hours of the morning. The muffled sound of their voices had wafted up the stairs and into her bedroom and she just hadn't been able to get to sleep.

Something in her stirred. She had never been a person to share her problems. Deep ingrained into her psyche was the notion that her problems belonged to her and no one else. It seemed suddenly tempting to offload a little.

'What *can* I do about it?' she muttered, fiddling with her pen.

'I can immediately think of one solution—kick them both out.'

'That's not an option. I'm not about to kick my sister out when she's come to me for help and support. Believe me, I know all of Jessica's failings. She can be childish and badly behaved and irresponsible, but in times of crisis she needs to know that she can turn to me.'

'She's a grown adult. She's fully capable of helping and supporting herself.' He was beating his head against a brick wall; he could see that. Lazily, he allowed his eyes to rove over her body, finally coming to rest of that full, downturned mouth. Out of the blue, he felt himself begin to harden and he abruptly looked away. Good God. It was as though his body was suddenly possessed of a mind of its own.

'You've met my sister. You can't really believe that.' Jamie smiled to lighten the mood, but Ryan's eyes remained grimly serious on her.

'Because you took her on as your responsibility at a young age doesn't mean that you're condemned to stick to the program till the day you die, Jamie.'

'My mother made me promise that I'd be there for her. I... You don't understand. I think of my mother asking me to make sure that I looked after Jessica, and my hands are tied. I couldn't let her down. And I couldn't let Greg down.'

Ryan stared at her and noticed the way she glanced away from him, offering him her delicate profile, noticed the way her skin coloured.

He thought back to that kiss, the way she had pulled him towards her and curved her small, supple body against his, offering her lips to him. And then Greg's appearance at the door, like an apparition stepping out of the wintry depths. His brain was mentally doing the maths.

'Why would that be?' he asked casually. Her eyes weren't on him as he strolled towards the coffee machine, which was just one of the many appliances he kept in his vast office to make life a bit easier when he was working through the night. He handed her a mug of coffee and Jamie absent-mindedly took it. It was her first cup of coffee of the morning and it tasted delicious.

'It's pretty hard on him,' she confessed, watching as Ryan rolled his chair towards her and took up position uncomfortably close. In fact, their knees were almost touching.

'Explain.'

'He's doing his best with my sister. She isn't the easiest person in the world. He's very calm and gentle but she more than makes up for it.'

'Calm and gentle,' Ryan mused thoughtfully.

'He's a vet. He has to be.'

'You worked for him, didn't you?'

Jamie shrugged and said defensively, 'I did, a million years ago. The point is, he likes talking to me. I think it helps.'

'He likes talking to you because you're a trained marriage counsellor?' Ryan found himself stiffening with instant dislike for the man. He had known types like him—the kind, caring, calm, gentle types who thought nothing of taking advantage of any poor sap with a tendency to mother.

'No, Ryan. I'm not a *trained marriage counsellor*, but I listen to what he says and I try to be constructive.'

'And yet you haven't constructively told the pair of them to clear off because they're wrecking your life. My guess is that your mother wouldn't like to think that you're sacrificing the quality of your life for the sake of your sister.'

'Not all of us are selfish!'

'I'd call it practical. Why did you leave?'

'I beg your pardon?'

'Why did you leave your job working for the gentle vet?'

'Oh.' Jamie could feel herself going bright red as she fished around for a suitable reply.

'Was it the weather?' Ryan asked helpfully as he drew his own conclusions.

'I... Um, I guess the weather did have something to do with my decision. And also...' Coherent thought returned to her at long last. 'Jessica was old enough to stand on her own two feet and I thought it was a good time to start exploring pastures new, so to speak...'

'And, I guess, with your sister marrying the caring, sharing vet.'

'Yes. There was someone to look after her.'

'But I suppose you must have built up some sort of empathetic relationship with our knight in shining armour who rescued you from your sister,' Ryan encouraged speculatively. His eyes were sharp and focused, noting every change of expression on her face. She had a remarkably expressive face. He wondered how he could ever have missed that, but then again this was new territory for both of them.

'Could you please stop being derogatory about Greg?'

Ryan glanced down. There was no need for him to ask her why. He already knew. Had she actually been in love with the guy? Of course she had. It was written all over her face. And that, naturally, would have been why she had fled the scene of the crime, so to speak. Had they slept together?

Ryan found that that was a thought he didn't like, not at all. Nor did he care for the fact that his conclusions were leading him inexorably in one direction.

That kiss she had given him, the kiss that had been playing on his mind for the past two days, had had its roots in something a lot more unsavoury than just a woman with a little too much wine in her system behaving out of character for the first time in her life.

She had seen Greg, and Greg had seen her, and she had succumbed to the oldest need in the world. The need to make another man jealous.

Had she been reminding Mr Vet of what he had missed? The sour taste of being used rose in Ryan's throat. It was a sensation he had never experienced. She had wanted to bury the incident between them. As far as he was concerned, he would fetch the shovels and help her.

'He doesn't have anyone else to talk to,' Jamie was saying now. 'He's an only child and I don't think his parents really ever approved of the marriage. At least, not from what Jessica's told me over the years. So he can't go to them for advice, and I suppose I'm the obvious choice to confide in because she's my sister and I know her.'

'And what pearls of wisdom have you thrown his way?' Ryan couldn't help the heavy sarcasm in his voice but Jamie barely seemed to notice. She was, he thought, too wrapped up in thoughts of her erstwhile lover.

She might complain about her house being invaded but chances were that she was loving every second of it.

'I've told him that he's just got to persevere.' She smiled drily. 'Who else is going to take Jessica off my hands?'

'Who else indeed?' Ryan murmured. 'So there's no end to this in sight?'

'Not at the moment. Not unless I change the locks on the front door.' Making light of the situation was about the only way Jamie felt she could deal with it, but her smile was strained. 'Things will sort themselves out when Christmas is done and dusted. I mean, Greg will have to return to work. He said that he's got cover at the moment but I think his animals will start missing him!'

Ryan stood up and began prowling through the office. Usually as easy-going and as liberal minded as the next man, he was outraged at the nagging, persistent notion that he had been manipulated to make another man jealous. He was also infuriatingly niggled at the thought that Jamie might have slept with the vet. Naturally, people were entitled to live their lives the way they saw fit, but nevertheless...

Could he have been that mistaken about her?

'And what if things don't sort themselves out over Christmas?'

'I prefer to be optimistic.'

'Maybe,' Ryan said slowly, 'what they both need is time on their own.'

'Do you think I haven't suggested that?' Jamie asked him sharply. 'Jessica has dug her heels in. She doesn't want to return to Scotland and Greg doesn't want to leave without her.'

'Wise man.' Ryan's voice was shrewd. 'She's an unexploded time bomb.'

'I don't see how this is helping anything,' Jamie inserted briskly. 'Course it's nice to talk, and thank you very much for listening, but...'

'Maybe they need time on their own away from Scotland. Being in the home environment might just pollute the situation.' He had absolutely zero knowledge when it came to psychoanalysis but he was more than happy to make it up as he went along.

A plan of action was coming to him and he liked it. More to the point, it was a plan that would benefit them both. He sat on the edge of his desk and looked at her.

'Pollute the situation?'

'You know what I'm getting at.'

'Where else are they going to go? I can't think that Greg has enough money to move them into a hotel indefinitely. Besides, that would only make things worse, being cooped up in a room twenty-four-seven. There would be a double homicide. Actually, it wouldn't get that far. Jessica would refuse to go along with the plan.'

Ryan made an indistinct but sympathetic noise and gave her time to consider the horror of housing a bickering couple for the indefinite future, because the caring vet might just prioritise his marriage over the animals pining for him in his absence.

'What a hellish prospect for you.' He egged the mixture as he scooted his chair back to his desk. 'I'll bet your sister doesn't exercise a lot of restraint when it comes to airing her opinions either.'

'That's why I was late,' Jamie glumly confessed. 'They were arguing into the early hours of the morning and I could hear them from my bedroom so I couldn't fall asleep. I was so tired this morning that I slept through the alarm.'

'I'm going to be joining my family in the Caribbean day

after tomorrow. Stunning house in the Bahamas, if I say so myself,' he murmured and Jamie nodded.

'Yes. I know—I booked the tickets, remember? Lucky you. I know what I should be covering while you're away but there are a couple of things you'll need to look at before you go. I'll make sure that I bring them in for you by the end of the day. Also, if your visit over runs, shall I get Graham to chair the shareholders' meeting on the eighth?'

Ryan had no intention of becoming bogged down in pointless detail. He frowned pensively up at the ceiling, his hands linked behind his head, then startled her by sitting forward suddenly and placing his hands squarely on his desk.

'Just an idea, but I think you should accompany me on my trip.'

For a few seconds Jamie wasn't sure that she had heard him correctly. Her mind was still half taken up with the technicalities of rearranging his schedule should he remain out of the country for longer than anticipated. There were a number of prickly clients who liked to deal with Ryan and Ryan alone, as the mover and shaker of the company. They would have to be coaxed into a replacement.

'Jamie!' Like a magician summoning someone out of a trance, Ryan snapped his fingers and she started and surfaced to slowly consider the suggestion he had posed.

'Accompany you?' she repeated in confusion.

'Why not? From where I'm sitting it sure beats the hell out of having to duck for cover from verbal missiles in your own house.' He stood up, began pacing through his office. He peered down at the stack of papers he had inadvertently sent flying to the ground earlier, decided to tidy it all up later and stepped over them to make his way to his coffee machine so that he could help himself to another mug of coffee.

'Also,' he offered, 'your sister and the vet might benefit from not having you around. I know you probably feel obliged to offer free advice, but sometimes the last thing people need in a time of crisis is a do-gooder trying to sort things out on their behalf.'

'I am not a *do-gooder* trying to sort anything out!' Jamie denied heatedly and Ryan shrugged.

'Okay, maybe the vet would be better off fighting his own battles without relying on his trusty ex-assistant to join in the fray.'

Looked at from every angle, that was an insulting observation, but before Jamie could splutter into more heated defence he was continuing in a thoughtful voice,

'And if they both prefer to hang out their dirty laundry in neutral territory, and a hotel room is out of the equation, then your place is as good as any—without you in it. You'd be doing them a favour and you'd be doing yourself a favour. No more sleepless nights. No more war zones to be avoided. No more playing piggy-in-the-middle. Chances are that by the time you get back they will have resolved their differences and cleared off and your life can return to normal.'

The promise of normality dangled in front of Jamie's eyes like a pot of gold at the end of a rainbow. She was in danger of forgetting what it was like.

'I couldn't possibly intrude on your family holiday.' She turned him down politely. 'But,' she said slowly, 'it *might* be a good idea if I weren't around. Perhaps—and I know this is very last-minute—I could book a few days' holiday?'

'Out of the question.' Ryan swallowed a mouthful of coffee and eyed her over the rim of the mug.

'But if I can leave here to go to the Caribbean, then surely I could leave to go somewhere else?' The weather was immaterial. It was the prospect of putting distance between Jessica, Greg and herself that was so tantalising. The Far East sounded just about right, never mind the jet lag.

'You can come to the Caribbean because I could use you over there. As you know, I'm combining my holiday with the business trip to Florida to give that series of presentations on trying to get our computer technology into greener cars.'

He glanced at the papers lying on the ground and strolled over to roughly gather them up and dump them on his desk. 'Still, sadly, in a state of semi-preparation.' He indicated the papers with a sweeping gesture while Jamie looked at him, unconvinced. Ryan rarely gave speeches that were fully prepared. He was clever enough and confident enough to earn a standing ovation by simply thinking on his feet. His grasp of the minutest details to do with the very latest cutting-edge technology was legendary.

'You could consider it something of a working holiday. I could get up to speed with these presentations before I fly to Florida. And,' he added for good measure, 'it's not as though you haven't travelled with me on business before...'

Which was a very valid reason for having her there— business. Of course, he was the first to acknowledge that it wasn't *exactly* the only reason for having her there. He genuinely thought that her presence in the house with her warring, uninvited guests was doing her no good whatsoever and there was also the small question of his curiosity; that was a little less easy to justify. But those recent revealing glimpses of her had roused his interest; why not combine his concern for her welfare with his semi-pressing need to get his presentations done and wrap them both up in a neat solution? Made sense.

He uneasily registered that there was a third reason. His mother and his sisters were relentlessly concerned with his moral welfare. His sisters had an annoying habit of bustling around him, trying to impose their opinions, and his mother specialised in meaningful chats about people who worked too hard.

Jamie would be a very useful buffer. There would be considerably less chance of being cornered if he made sure that she was floating somewhere in the vicinity whenever the going looked as though it might get dicey. Were he to be on his own, any attempt to excuse himself on the pretext of having to work would be thoroughly disregarded. With Jamie around, however, even his sisters would reluctantly be forced to keep a low profile in the name of simple courtesy.

'It's not the same.'

'Huh? What's not the same?'

'You're going to be with your family,' Jamie said patiently. 'Doing family stuff.' She wasn't entirely sure what that entailed. Family stuff, for her, had long meant stretches of tension and uncomfortable confrontations simmering just below the surface.

'Oh, they will already have done the family stuff over their turkey on Christmas day. They'll be desperate to see a new face and my mother won't stop thanking you for showing up. When my sisters get together, they revert to childhood. They giggle and swap clothes and waste hours applying make-up on each other while their men take over babysitting duties and countdown to when they can start on the rum cocktails. My mother says that it's impossible to get a serious word out of them when they're together. She'll love you.'

'Because I'm serious and boring?'

'Serious? Boring?' His dark eyes lingered on her and Jamie flushed and looked away. 'Hardly. In fact, having seen you over—'

'Who would cover for me in my absence?' she interrupted hastily just in case he decided to travel down

Memory Lane and dredge up her un-secretary-like behaviour on Christmas day.

Ryan dismissed that concern with a casual wave of his hand before giving her a satisfied smile.

'I haven't agreed to anything,' Jamie informed him. 'If you really think that you might need me there to help with the presentations…'

'Absolutely. You would be vital. You know I can't manage without you.'

'I don't want you to think that I'm in need of rescuing.' Sometimes that dark, velvety voice literally sent a shiver through her, even though she knew that it was in his nature to flirt. 'I don't. I might be in an awkward position just at the moment, but it's nothing that I wouldn't be able to handle.'

'I don't doubt that for a second,' Ryan dutifully agreed. 'You'd be doing *me* a favour.'

'Won't your family think it a bit strange for you to be dragging a perfect stranger along to their family celebrations?'

'Nothing fazes my family, believe me. Besides, what's one more to the tally?' He lowered his eyes. 'You have no excuse for refusing unless, of course, you can't bear to lose your role of personal adviser to the vet.'

'His name is Greg.' It was weird but Greg's effect on her was not what she had expected. She had always imagined that seeing him again would catapult her back to that time when she had been firmly in his power and used to weave innocent fantasies about him. She always thought that she would be reduced to blushing, stammering and possibly making a fool of herself but she hadn't. His allure had disappeared over the years. Now she just felt sorry for him and the situation in which her sister had placed him.

Watching her, Ryan felt a spurt of irritation that she had ignored the better part of his remark.

'Well?' he prodded. 'Do you think that you're too invaluable as unpaid counsellor to take a few days away from them? We'll be there for roughly five days. My sisters and their various other halves and children will leave at the beginning of the New Year. We will stay for a further three days until my conferences are due to begin and you can fly back to London when I fly to Florida. It's a lot to pass on, for the sake of being the vet's sounding board. Are you worried that he might not be able to survive this crisis without your input?'

'Of course I'm not!'

'Then why the hesitation?'

'I told you, I don't want to intrude.'

'And *I* told *you* you won't be intruding.'

'And I don't,' she belatedly pointed out, 'think that I'm invaluable to Greg. Like I said, I'm the only one he feels comfortable discussing all of this with.' Once upon a time, she might have been flattered, but now she was just impatient. 'But you're right—you're my boss. If I'm needed in a work capacity, then I'm more than happy to oblige. I'm very committed to my job, as you know.'

'I'm not a slave driver, Jamie. I won't be standing over you wielding a whip and making sure that I get my money's worth. Yes, we will do some work, but you'll have ample time to relax and de-stress. It'll be worth it to have you back in one piece when we resume work in January.'

Jamie nodded briskly. Whichever way it was wrapped up, Ryan was doing this for his own benefit. She had been inconsistent recently and he didn't like that. She was his efficient, well-run, well-oiled secretary and that was what he wanted back. It was why she was paid so handsomely. He could easily do whatever work he needed to do without her, but he had decided that her home life was interfering with her work life and, since her work life was the only thing that mattered to him, he was prepared to take her with him, away from the chaotic environment in which she now found herself.

'I'll see to the ticket, shall I?'

'First-class, with me. And sort out your replacement for while you're away. It's a quiet time. There shouldn't be anything that can't be handled by someone else for a short while.'

'Is there anything in particular you'd like me to read up on before we get out there? I wouldn't want to come unprepared.'

Ryan narrowed his eyes but her face was bland, helpful and utterly unreadable.

But that, he thought with a kick of satisfaction, was just an illusion, wasn't it? Strip away the mask and she was a hotbed of undiscovered fire.

'Nope. No reading to be done. But you might want to think about packing a few swimsuits. I'm going to insist that you enjoy yourself, like a good boss, and the house comes with an amazing pool. And don't look so appalled. When this is over, you're going to thank me.'

CHAPTER FIVE

So far she *had* thanked him; on at least four separate occasions she had thanked him. She had thanked him variously for giving her the opportunity to enjoy 'such a wonderful place', for allowing her to relax in 'such amazing surroundings', it was a 'guilty pleasure'. She had thanked him the day before when he had shooed her off to explore the tiny nearby town with his sisters. She had thanked him when he had insisted that there was no need for her to wake at the crack of dawn with her laptop at the ready, just because he happened to need very little sleep and enjoyed working first thing in the mornings.

Her copious gratitude was getting on his nerves. He had been hoping to reacquaint himself with the intriguing new face he had glimpsed behind her polite, efficient mask but so far nothing. Although, to be fair, his plans for her to be a buffer between himself and any awkward conversations with his family members had been spectacularly successful and he was rarely in her company without some member of the troupe tagging along, unless they were specifically working.

They had established one of the downstairs rooms as a makeshift office but its air-conditioned splendour, whilst practical, felt sterile when through the windows they could see the stretching gardens, fragrant and colourful with tropical flowers which spilled their vibrancy under the palm trees. So they had migrated to one of the many shady areas of the wide veranda that circled the house. Which, in turn, meant that they were open to interruption, sometimes from one of the four kids belonging to two of his sisters who used outside as their playground. Sometimes from one of his sisters or—and he would have to fling his arms up and concede defeat when this happened—all three. And sometimes from his mother, who would appear with a tray of cold drinks and proceed to embark on a meandering conversation with Jamie to whom she seemed to have taken a keen liking. This was partly because Jamie was such a good listener and partly because his mother was, by nature, a sociable woman.

But when they were alone together, Jamie was not to be distracted from what she considered the primary purpose of her all-expenses-paid winter break. The very second they were together, their conversation focused entirely on work and on progressing a series of elaborate flip charts in which Ryan had no interest and probably wouldn't use anyway. She asked him innumerable questions about various technicalities to do with car manufacture, displaying an admirable breadth of knowledge, but, the minute he attempted to manoeuvre the conversation to something a little more interesting and a little more personal, she smiled, clammed up and he was obliged to return to the subject in hand.

Right now, the evening meal was finished. Two of his sisters were settling their children, who ranged in ages from three to six. They would be chivvying their husbands, Tom and Patrick, into performing a variety of duties and neither would be released until those duties were satisfactorily completed. His sisters were nothing if not bossy. Susie—older than him by two years, and seven months pregnant—had disappeared back to England with her husband. The house was at least becoming quieter. It would be quieter still in a day's time when his other sisters headed back to their various homes.

Enjoying the peace of the gardens and lost in his thoughts, Ryan was only aware of Jamie's presence nearby by the low murmur of her voice.

His ears instantly pricked up. He had assumed that she had retreated to the conservatory with a cup of coffee.

Naturally, he knew that it was beyond rude not to announce his presence by making some obvious noise—rustling a few leaves or launching into a coughing fit, perhaps.

Instead, he endeavoured to make as little noise as possible. Of course, if she looked around carefully, she would be able to spot him, although it was dark and this part of the extensive gardens was a lattice-work of trees and shrubbery leading to the infinity pool, which overlooked the sea from the cliff on which the house was majestically perched.

The breeze was warm and salty and ruffled the fronds of the palm trees, leaves and flowers like a very gentle caress. In the distance the sea stretched, flat and black, towards the horizon.

And down the small flight of stone steps Ryan spotted her, sitting by the pool in darkness, talking softly into her mobile phone.

If she needed to make a call, she could have used the landline; he had told her this at the very start. Instead, she had chosen to sneak off to the pool so that she could...*what*? Conduct a clandestine conversation? And with whom? The vet, of course.

His lips thinned and he sprinted down the steps, appearing in front of her so suddenly that she gave a little shriek and dropped the phone.

'Oh, dear. Did I startle you?' He bent to retrieve the mobile which lay in various pieces on the ground.

Jamie, half standing, scrabbled to get the phone from

him as he clicked various bits back together, put it to his ear, shook it and then shrugged. 'You got cut off. Sorry. And I think the phone might be broken.'

'What are you doing here?' Over the past three days she had contrived not to be alone in his presence at all. Away from the safety net of the office, she had felt vulnerable and threatened in this island paradise. There was just too much of him for her liking. Too much of him wearing shorts, going barefoot, bare chested, getting slowly bronzed. Too much of him lazing around, teasing his sisters, letting them boss him around and then rolling his eyes heavenwards so that one of them laughed and playfully smacked him. Too much of him being silly with the children who clearly adored him. Too much of him being a *man* instead of being her boss. It unnerved her.

'What are *you* doing here?' He threw the question back at her, then sat down on one of the wooden deck chairs and patted the one next to him so that she reluctantly joined him. 'If you needed to make a call, you know that you could have used the landline. I did tell you that.'

'Yes, well…' She could barely make him out. He was all shadows and angles, and rakish in his low-slung khaki shorts and an old tee-shirt. To see him, no one would have guessed that he was a multi-millionaire.

'Personal call, was it?' Ryan prompted, undeterred by her reluctance to talk. 'How are they back home? Still alive and kicking, or has you sister put the vet out of his misery? I'm thinking that if they had sorted out their differences and re-turned to Scotland in the throes of rekindled love you would have reported it back to me.'

The darkness enfolding them in its embrace lent an air of intimacy that Jamie found disturbing. In fact, her heart was beating like a hammer inside her and her mouth felt horribly, treacherously dry. She physically longed for it to be daylight, with Claire, Hannah and Susie lurking nearby, and a flip chart behind which she could conveniently hide.

'Nothing's been sorted as yet,' Jamie conceded grudgingly. She felt very visible in her shorts and small striped vest, but it had been the first thing to hand after she had had a shower half an hour earlier. She hadn't expected to run into Ryan lurking like an intruder in the shadows.

'Oh, dear,' Ryan murmured sympathetically. 'Was that the vet on the phone?'

'Will you *please* stop calling him the vet?'

'Sorry, but I thought that's what he did for a living—tended to all those wounded animals who pined for him in his absence.'

Jamie glanced across at him but he was a picture of innocence. The light breeze ruffled his hair and he looked perfectly relaxed, a man at home in his surroundings.

'Yes, it was Greg, as a matter of fact.'

'Making a secretive call behind his wife's back? Hmm...'

'It wasn't a secretive call!'

'Then what was it? Obviously not a call you felt comfortable taking in front of the family.'

'You're impossible!'

'So what did the vet have to say?'

Jamie gritted her teeth together. Ryan was provocative by nature; it was nothing personal. They had both also strayed so far from their boundaries that the lines between them were getting blurred. She had met his family, seen him relaxed in his own home territory. She, in turn, had confided things she wouldn't have dreamt possible. But he was accustomed to breaking down boundaries and getting into the heads of other people; it was part and parcel of what made him a success. And if *she* found it impossible to deal with then it was a reflection on her, and to start huffing and puffing now and trying to evade his natural curiosity would seem strange. Strange was the one thing she knew was dangerous. It was an instinctive realisation. So what was the big deal in telling him what was going on with Greg and Jessica? It wasn't as though he was out of the loop. He was firmly embedded in it, thanks to a sequence of circumstances which she might not have invited but which had happened nevertheless.

'Jessica told me that the reason she felt that she needed more space was because she felt bored and isolated where they live. It's at least forty minutes into Edinburgh, and Jessica has always liked to be in the thick of things.'

'Odd match, in that case.'

'What do you mean?'

'I mean that the vet didn't strike me as the sort of man who prides himself on having a wild social life. I can't see him being the life and soul of any party.'

'You met him for five minutes! You don't know him at all.'

'Oh, yes, I'm forgetting that you two shared a special bond.'

'We didn't share a *special bond*.' But she could feel herself flushing, thinking about her youthful, romantic dreams.

Ryan ignored her heated protest. He didn't have to see her face to be able to take stock of the fact that she was flustered by what he had said—but then she would be, he thought edgily. He was beginning to loathe the caring vet with his menagerie of loyal animals.

'So what did your flamboyant sister see in him?' he persisted.

'He's absolutely one-hundred-percent devoted to her.'

'Ah, but is it mutual? One-way devotion could become trying after a while, I should imagine.'

'Won't your family be wondering where we are?'

'We're adults. I don't suppose they'll be worried in case

we miss our footing and fall in the pool by accident. Besides, Claire and Hannah are doing their nightly battle with the children, and my mother was feeling tired and took herself off to bed with a book and a cup of hot chocolate. So you can put that concern of yours to rest!'

'You have a fantastic family.' Jamie sighed wistfully, and for a moment Ryan was sufficiently distracted to silently wait until she expanded. Women always enjoyed talking about themselves. In fact, from his experience, they would hold court until the break of dawn given half a chance, but generally speaking their conversations were usually targeted to sexually attract. They flirted and pouted and always portrayed themselves in the best possible light. In the case of the women he dated—supermodels and actresses—their anecdotes were usually fond recollections of their achievements on stage or on the runway, often involving getting the better of their competition.

'A bit different from yours, I expect,' he murmured encouragingly when his lengthy silence didn't appear to be working.

'Totally different. You never talk about them.'

'And you've only now started talking about yours.'

'Yes, well, my situation is nothing like yours. When I think of Jessica, I start getting stressed. But *your* sisters… they're very easy-going.'

Ryan grinned. 'I have vague recollections of the three of them trying out their make-up on me when I was younger. Not so easy-going for me, I can tell you.'

Jamie laughed. She couldn't help herself.

'Still, it was tougher on you, raising a teenager when you weren't even out of your teens yourself.'

Lost in her thoughts, she was seduced by the warm interest in his voice, by the soft, warm breeze and the gentle, rhythmic sound of waves breaking against the cliff face.

She felt inclined to share, especially after her conversation with Greg.

'Even before Mum died, Jessica was a handful. I just did my own thing, but she was always demanding, even as a child. She was just so beautiful and she could twist Mum round her little finger. When I look at your sisters and see the way they share everything… Anyway.' She pulled herself together. 'I always think that there's no point weeping and wailing over stuff you can't change.'

'Quite. You were telling me about your conversation with the vet. You thought that your sister was bored because she was a party animal and the vet only enjoyed the company of his sick animals.'

'I never said any such thing!'

'I'm reading between the lines. Have you got an update on the real situation?'

Of course, Jamie thought, brought down to earth, he was keen to find out whether matters were being sorted. He needed her back and functioning in one piece, and the sooner Greg and Jessica sorted themselves out and cleared off the better for him. She would do well to remind herself that his interest was mostly self-motivated. She would also do well to realise that allowing herself to slip into a state of familiarity with him just because he happened to know a little bit more about her private life than he ever had would be madness. There was no chance that she could ever be interested in him in the way that she had been interested in Greg, because Greg represented just the sort of gentle, caring person she found attractive. But still…

'I think we might be seeing the true cause of everything that's been happening between Greg and my sister,' she told him crisply. 'Apparently Greg wants children and he thinks that it's a good time for them to start trying. That seems to have caused everything to explode.'

'Your sister isn't interested?'

'She hasn't mentioned a word of it to me,' Jamie said with a shrug. 'I'm guessing that she might have been feeling a bit bored, but the minute Greg mentioned kids she took fright and started feeling trapped. The only thing she could think of doing was to escape, hence her appearance on my doorstep. At least there's something tangible now to deal with, so you can relax. I'm sure they'll both get to the bottom of their problems by the time I return to England, and once they've disappeared back to Scotland everything will return to normal. I won't be arriving late to work and I'll be as focused as I've always been.'

She stood up and brushed the backs of her thighs where tiny specks of sand had stuck from the chair. She did her best to ignore his dark eyes thoughtfully watching her.

'So what are our plans for tomorrow? I know that your sisters leave with Tom and Patrick and the kids. I have no objection to working in the evening. You've been more than kind in letting me take so much time off to relax.'

'Let's not get back on that gratitude bandwagon,' Ryan said irritably. His eyes skimmed over her, taking in her slender legs, slim waist and pert breasts barely contained underneath the vest. Her work suits did nothing to flatter her figure. The memory of her full mouth pressed against his flashed through his head and ignited a series of images that made him catch his breath sharply. 'I haven't seen you at the pool,' he continued, standing up and swamping her with his potently masculine presence. Jamie instinctively took a small step backwards.

'I… I've sat there with my book a bit.'

'But not been tempted to get in the water. Don't you swim?'

'Yes.' She *had* stuck on her black bikini on one occasion, but the thought of parading in a pool in a bikini with

Ryan—her boss—splashing around, having fun with the family, had been too much. She had promptly taken it off and replaced it with her summer shift. Much safer.

'Then why the reticence? Did you feel shy with my noisy family all around?'

'No. Of course not!'

'Well, they'll be gone by tomorrow evening, and things will be a lot quieter here. You can start enjoying the pool in peace and quiet.'

'Maybe. I really should be getting in now.'

'Wild imagination here, but I get the feeling you don't like being alone with me. A guy could get offended.'

Jamie tensed. His lazy teasing was dangerously unsettling.

'Correct me if I'm wrong, but I spent three hours alone with you today.'

'Ah, but in the company of a flip chart, two computers and a range of stationery.'

'I'm just doing my job! It's what I'm paid to do and I'm going to head back now.'

Up the stone steps leading down to the pool, the path skirted the house, taking them across the sprawling gardens where palm trees fringed the edges, leaning towards the sea. Underneath, a huge variety of plants and shrubs were landscaped to provide a wild, untamed feel to the garden.

Jamie's feet seemed to have wings. She was acutely conscious of Ryan behind her. She had never been very self-confident about her body. With Jessica as a sister, she had been too aware growing up of the physical differences between them. She was shorter, her figure so much less eye-catching. And she was wearing shorts!

Of their own accord, her thoughts flew back to the parade of models who had flitted in and out of Ryan's life: blondes with legs to their armpits and hair to their waists.

Unconscious comparisons sprang to mind, addling her, and maybe that was why she stumbled over the root of a tree projecting above-ground, walking so quickly, rigid as a plank of wood, arms protectively folded and her mind all over the place. It was a recipe for disaster on a dark night in unfamiliar surroundings.

She gave a soft gasp as her body made painful contact with the ground but before she could stagger to her feet she was being lifted up as though she weighed nothing.

Jamie shrieked. 'Put me down! What are you doing?'

'Calm down.'

The feel of his muscular arms around her and the touch of his hard chest set up a series of tingling reactions in her body that made her writhe in his arms until she realised that her writhing was having just the opposite effect; he tightened his hold, pulling her more firmly against him. Instantly, she fell limp and allowed herself to be carried up to the veranda where he gently deposited her on one of the wicker chairs which were strewn at various intervals around the house.

'I'm absolutely fine,' she muttered through gritted teeth and was ignored as Ryan stooped down and removed her espadrilles.

His long fingers gently felt her foot and her ankle, which he ordered her to try and move.

'I haven't twisted anything!' she exclaimed, trying to pull her foot out of his grasp while her treacherous body was tempted to go with the flow and succumb to the wonderful sensation of what his hands were doing.

'No. If you had, you wouldn't be able to move it.'

'Exactly. So if you don't mind...'

'But you're bruised.' He was peering at her knee and then doing it again, sweeping her up and informing her that it was just as well to put no strain on it but that she needed cleaning up.

'That's something I can do myself.' Her breasts were pushing against his chest and, good lord, her nipples were hardening as they scraped against the fabric of her bra, and between her legs felt damp. Every bit of her body was responding to him and she hated it. It terrified the life out of her. She just wanted him to put her down so that she could scuttle back to the safety of her bedroom, but instead he was carrying her through the house, up the short staircase that led to the wing of the house where he was staying and then—when it couldn't get any worse as far as she was concerned—into his bedroom. Jamie closed her eyes and stifled a weak groan of despair.

She hadn't been here yet. His room was huge and dominated by an impressive bed fashioned out of bamboo. The linen was a colourful medley of bold reds and blacks and looked positively threatening.

Beneath the window was a long sofa and he took her to it and sat her down.

'Don't move a muscle. I have a first-aid kit in the bathroom—hangover from my Boy Scout days.'

'This is ridiculous—and you were never a Boy Scout!'

'Of course I was!' He disappeared into the adjoining bathroom and through the open door Jamie glimpsed him rifling through a cupboard, searching out the first-aid kit. 'I may even have earned a few badges.' He reappeared with a small tin and knelt at her feet. 'If you ever need a tent erecting, or a fire to be lit using only two pieces of wood, then I'm your man. Tsk, tsk—do you see those bruises on your knees? If you hadn't been rushing off like a bat out of hell this would never have happened.'

Jamie clamped her teeth together and refrained from telling him that if he hadn't appeared in front of her, broken her phone and then insisted on having a long, personal conversation with her she wouldn't have felt inclined to rush off and wouldn't be sitting here now in his bedroom while he...

She squeezed her eyes tightly shut, intending to block out the image of his down-bent head as he tended to her bruises, applying alcohol wipes to the surfaces, then antiseptic cream which he gently rubbed into her skin.

'No good applying any plasters,' he informed her. 'You want the sun to dry out these cuts and scratches.'

'Yep, okay. Thank you. I'll leave now, if you don't mind.'

'Shall I carry you?'

Her eyes flew open and she saw that he was grinning at her.

'Don't be ridiculous!'

'And to continue our conversation...'

'To continue our conversation about *what*?'

'About tomorrow, of course.'

She caught his eyes. He looked as innocent as the pure driven snow.

'What about tomorrow?' she stammered, walking towards the door.

'Well, you were telling me about what you wanted to do. Work wise.'

Had she? She couldn't think. Every nerve ending in her body was on fire. She was tingling all over and it was ludicrous. Having an insane crush on Greg had been bad enough but at least she could see the sense there. With Ryan Sheppard? She didn't even respect the sort of guy who dated a string of models, who never seemed to see beyond the long legs and the perfect figure! Ergo, she couldn't possibly have a crush on him. The soaring tropical heat was getting to her. She wasn't used to it.

'Yes!' The place was going to be empty, aside from his mother. Suddenly, the thought of even a tiny window when they would be together without the possibility of interruption was scary beyond belief. 'There are still loads of things to do and I have lots of ideas about your presentations—like, you really need to give a strong argument for implementing your system in their cars. New technology can do so much for the environment.'

She had reached the door without even realizing. Now her back was against the door frame and he was looking at her with his head to one side, the picture-perfect image of someone one-hundred-percent interested in what she had to say.

So why the heck was she feeling so nervous?

She quailed when he took a few steps towards her.

'Are you entirely sure that you're all right?'

He loomed over her, a darkly, wickedly sexy guy who was sending her mind into crazy disarray.

'Because you've gone pale.' He leant against the door frame and looked at her with concern. 'Nothing broken, but you could still be in a bit of shock at losing your footing like that. Happens, you know—you have a minor accident and you think you're fine but really...'

'I don't *think* I'm fine. I *am* fine.'

'I think we can afford to give work a miss tomorrow. Those harridans known as my sisters will be leaving, and as soon as they've gone the house is going to feel very empty. It might be an idea to do something with my mother, occupy her...'

'I'm more than happy to do that.'

'I think I might like to be included in the exercise,' Ryan murmured drily, looking down at her. She noticed the fine lines around his eyes that spoke of a man who lived life to the full, the thick sweep of his dark lashes, the deep bitter-chocolate of his irises flecked with tinges of gold. He was beautiful but not in a detached, frozen way. He was beautiful in a devastatingly sexy way and her pulses raced in easy, treacherous recognition of that.

'Of course! Actually, I think it might be a good idea if you and your mother had some, um, time together. You've hardly had a one to one with her since we got here.'

'Oh, there's no need for a one to one. Can I let you in on a little secret?' he murmured huskily, leaning towards her.

Jamie nodded because quite honestly she didn't trust herself to speak. She didn't think her voice would sound normal because her tongue appeared to be glued to the roof of her mouth.

'One to ones with my mother can sometimes be a little dangerous.'

'What are you talking about?' Locked into this intimate atmosphere, she found it impossible to tear herself away from his mesmeric dark gaze.

'She's developed an unnerving habit of cornering me about my private life.' In actual fact, Ryan hadn't meant to mention this at all. Underneath the confident, self-assured charm he was a lot more watchful and contained than people suspected, but he wanted to get under her skin. With each passing day, the desire had grown more urgent. He was frustrated by the way she blocked him, and frustrated with himself for a curiosity he couldn't understand. On a basic level, he realised that the confidences she had shared with him—which would hardly be termed earth shattering by most people's standards—were hugely significant for her. Possibly she regretted them. Scratch that—she *did* regret them but she was now unable to retreat.

However, that didn't mean that she was now on a new, no-holds-barred, sharing level with him. And he wanted her there. He actively wanted her to invite him into her thoughts—which would entail some confidence sharing of his own.

So, when she looked at him in silent curiosity, he heard himself say with utmost seriousness, 'I'm not sure that my mother is a firm believer in the virtues of playing the field. Nor, for that matter, are the harridans.'

'I don't think that there's any mother who would be thrilled to have a son who takes the fastest exit the second there's the threat of commitment with a woman.'

'Is that what you think I do?'

'Isn't it?' The silence that greeted her question was thick and heavy with a peculiar, thrilling undercurrent. Jamie desperately wanted to repeat her mantra about going to bed, but a weird and powerful sense of anticipation held her to the spot. When after a few seconds he didn't answer, she shrugged lightly and began turning away.

'Well, it's none of my business anyway. Although I resent the fact that you feel it permissible to ask whatever questions you like about my private life, even though you know that I don't want to answer them, and yet you can't be bothered to answer any that are directed at you. Not,' she added for good measure, her hand on the door frame, 'that I care one way or another.'

'I could be hurt by that,' Ryan murmured softly. 'You're my irreplaceable secretary. You're supposed to care.' It wasn't his imagination; when it came to women, he had the instincts of a born predator. He knew when they were reacting to him and Jamie was reacting to him right now. It was there in the slight flare of her nostrils, the faint flush that spread across her cheeks and the way her pupils dilated. Her mouth was half-open, as though she was on the verge of saying something, and her full, parted lips allowed a glimpse of her pearl-white teeth.

The urge to press her against the door frame and kiss her senseless was as overpowering as a blow to the stomach. He wanted to slide his hand underneath that tiny vest

of hers and feel the weight of her breast against the palm of
his hand. He wanted to taste her, right here, right now on
his bed.

Interest and curiosity were one thing, being torn apart by
inexplicable sexual desire was another. Jamie Powell might
have suddenly become dangerously intriguing but it would
be lunacy to follow it through simply to see where it led.
For a start, she was the best secretary he had ever had. For
another, she was no bimbo ready and willing for a romp in
the hay, no strings attached.

'You're right. It's none of your business.'

'Good night, Ryan. Thanks for taking care of my cuts
and bruises.'

He reached out and his long fingers circled her arm. 'My
father took his eye off the ball,' Ryan told her softly. 'He got
married, had four children… Like I said, he took his eye off
the ball. While he was busy being domesticated, his finance
director was helping himself to company funds. By the time
my father noticed, the company was virtually on its knees.
In my view, he worked himself into an early grave trying to
get it back in order but by then it was too late. I inherited a
mess, and I got it where it should be, and I have no intention
of taking my own eye off the ball. Thanks to my efforts, my
mother has the lifestyle she deserves and my sisters have
the financial security they deserve. So, you see, I have no
time for the demands of a committed relationship. I don't
need the distraction.'

Jamie found that she was holding her breath.

'So you're never going to get married? Have kids?
Become a grandfather?'

'If I do, it will be on my terms to someone who is willing
to take second place to the fact that my primary concern is
being one-hundred-and-ten-percent hands-on with my company. There's nothing that goes on at RS Enterprises that I

don't know about. That situation exists because I make sure that I never let my attention slip.'

'Lucky lady, whoever snaps you up,' Jamie murmured with sarcasm and Ryan released her and laughed softly and appreciatively.

'I date women who understand where I'm coming from.'

'Was Leanne the exception?'

'Leanne knew the score the minute she became involved with me. I'm honest to a fault.' He couldn't read a thing in the cool, brown eyes assessing him. He continued, irritated by what he took to be silent criticism from Jamie. 'I never make promises I can't fulfil and I never encourage a woman to think that she's got her feet in the door. I don't ask them to share my space. I discourage items of clothing from being left overnight at my apartment. I warn them that I'm unpredictable with my time.'

Jamie marvelled that he could still think that just because he laid down ground rules hearts would never be broken.

'Maybe you should tell your mother that.' Jamie snapped out of her trance and broke eye contact with him. 'Then perhaps she would stop cornering you with awkward questions.'

The shutters were back down. Ryan wondered whether he had imagined that response he had seen in her. Had he? Disconcerted, he frowned and half turned away.

'Maybe I'll do that.' He smiled at her with equal politeness. 'Honesty, after all, is always the best policy...'

CHAPTER SIX

CLAIRE and Hannah, their husbands and children left in a flurry of forgotten stuffed toys that needed to be fetched, a thousand things that had to be ticked off their check list and lots of hugs and kisses and promises to meet up just as soon as life returned to normal. And then they were gone and the house felt suddenly very quiet and very empty.

In two days' time, Ryan would take one plane to Florida while she took another back to England and Vivian, his mother, would stay on for a further week, joined by several of her friends for their annual bridge holiday.

With Vivian excusing herself for an afternoon nap and Ryan announcing that he intended to work, waving her down when she immediately started to talk about what they would be doing, Jamie found herself at a loose end. For the first time, she realised that it was a relief to have been deprived of her mobile phone. Normally, she would have been following the crisis between Greg and her sister in a state of barely suppressed stress, but without the means of contacting them unless she used the landline, which she didn't intend to, she felt guiltily liberated from the problem—at least temporarily.

For the first time since she had arrived, she decided to take advantage of the empty swimming pool, and was there in her bikini with her towel, her sun block and a book within forty minutes.

It felt like a holiday. The pool offered spectacular views of the sea and was surrounded by palm trees and foliage, ripe with butterflies and the sound of birds. Jamie lay down on her sun lounger and let her mind wander, and every one of its meanderings returned to Ryan. His image seemed to have been stamped on her brain and she wasn't sure whether that had always been the case or whether it was something that had occurred ever since some of the barriers between them had been eroded. Had she been sucked into his charming, witty, intelligent personality without even realising? Or had all that charm, wit and intelligence only begun working on her once he had uncovered some of those private details that she had striven so hard to keep from him?

She had been determined never to repeat the folly of getting personally involved with the boss. Falling for Greg had been a youthful indiscretion and she could now look back on that younger self with a certain amount of wry amusement, because her crush had been so *harmless*.

This situation with Ryan was altogether more dangerous because Ryan was just a more dangerous man. There were times when she physically reacted to him with something that was unconscious and almost primitive in its intensity, and when she thought about that she wanted to close her eyes and faint with the horror of it.

In comparison, her silly infatuation with Greg was exposed for what it had really been: something harmless that had occurred at just the time she had needed it. An innocent distraction from the stress and trauma of her home life. She had taken refuge in her pleasant daydreams, and her working life, which had involved spending hours in Greg's company, had been a soothing panacea against the harsh reality that had been waiting to greet her the second she had walked back through the front door at the end of the evening.

Greg had been kind, thoughtful and gentle and he had been a buffer between herself and the disappointment of having to give up on her dreams of going to university.

Ryan, however...

Yes, he was kind and thoughtful and gentle. She had seen it in a thousand ways in his interaction with his sisters, his mother, his nephews and nieces. But he was no Greg. There was a core of steel running through him that made her shiver with a kind of dangerous excitement that enthralled and scared her at the same time. When his dark eyes rested on her, she didn't feel a pleasurable flutter, she felt a wild rush of adrenalin that left her breathless and exposed.

It would be a relief to return to England. She hoped that Greg and Jessica would have sorted out their differences by then, but even if they hadn't she would still be returning to the protection of the office, her colleagues and the self-imposed distance between boss and secretary. Out here, a million miles away from her home territory, it was too easy for the lines between them to be eroded.

She flipped over onto her stomach, but even after half an hour, and with her sun protection liberally applied, Jamie was beginning to feel burnt. The sun out here was like nothing she had felt before. It was fierce and unrelenting, especially at this hour of the day. When she tried to read her book, her eyes felt tired from the white glare and after a while she dragged the wooden lounger under the partial shade afforded by an overhanging tree.

Then, when she began feeling uncomfortable even in the shade, she dived into the pool. Pure bliss: the water was like cool silk around her. She began swimming, revisiting a pleasurable activity which she had indulged only occasionally in London, because her working hours were long and she just never seemed to find the time.

Like a fish, she ducked below the surface of the water, mentally challenging herself to swim the length of the pool without surfacing for air.

Uncomfortable thoughts began to gel in her head as she swam, reaching one end, gulping in air and then setting off again.

She had given up going to the swimming baths because of her work. She had given up going to the gym three times a week because of her work. She made arrangements to see friends in the evening but had often cancelled at a moment's notice because Ryan had needed her to do overtime. She had thought nothing of it.

She had assumed herself to be a goal-focused person. She had patted herself on the back for being someone who was prepared to go the distance because she was ambitious and worth every penny of the three pay rises she had been given in the space of eighteen months. She had never thought that maybe she had gone that extra mile because she had enjoyed the opportunity of being with Ryan. Had she been the ever-obliging secretary because, without even realising it, she had wanted to feed a secret craving? Had she been smugly pleased with herself for having learnt a lesson from her experience with Greg, only to be ambushed by repeating her mistake without even realising it?

That thought was so disturbing that she was unaware of the wall of the pool rushing towards her as she skimmed underneath the water. She bumped her head and was instantly shocked into spluttering up to the surface.

When she opened her eyes, blinking the water out of them, it was to find Ryan leaning over the side of the pool like a vision conjured up from her feverish imagination, larger than life.

He was in his swimming trunks, some loose khaki-coloured shorts with a drawstring, and his short-sleeved shirt was unbuttoned.

Jamie was confronted with a view of his muscled, bronzed torso, which was even more disconcerting than the bump on her forehead.

'What are *you* doing here?' she gasped, in the flimsy hope that her fuddled brain was playing tricks on her.

'Rescuing you again. I had no idea that you were so accident prone.' He reached out his hands to help her out. Jamie ignored him, choosing to swim to the steps in the shallow end and sit there, half immersed in the water.

'What were you thinking, swimming like greased lightning and not bothering to judge how far away the wall was?' Ryan shrugged off his shirt and settled into the water next to her. 'Here, let me have a look at that bump.'

'Let's not do this again,' Jamie snapped, touching the tender spot on her head and wincing. 'My head is fine, just as my feet were fine when I fell yesterday.'

'Bumps to the head can be far more serious. Tell me how many fingers I'm holding up.'

'I thought you were working,' she responded in an accusing voice, watching out of the corner of her eye as Ryan lounged back against the step behind him, resting on his elbows. His eyes were closed, his face tilted up to the sun and, like an addict, Jamie found herself watching him, taking in his powerful, masculine beauty. When he opened his eyes suddenly and glanced at her, she flushed and looked away.

'I *was* working, but I couldn't resist the thought of coming out here and having a dip. I didn't realise that you were such a strong swimmer.'

'Were you *watching* me?'

'Guilty as charged.' But he wouldn't let on for just how long. Nor would he let on that he had felt compelled to follow her out to the pool. For once in his life, he hadn't been able to concentrate on work. Watching her from above as she had whipped like a fish through the water had mesmerised him. Her bikini was a modest affair in black, the least obviously sexy swimsuit he had ever seen on a woman, and yet on her it was an erotic work of art. Sliding his eyes across, he took in the generous cleavage and the full swell of her ripe breasts—more than a generous, *very generous*, handful.

Just looking at her like this, with sexual hunger, was playing with fire. Ryan was getting dangerously close to the point of no longer caring whether she was his perfect secretary or not or whether going to bed with her would be crazy or not.

'Have you been in touch with your sister?'

'Have you forgotten that you broke my phone?'

'You'll be amply compensated for that the very second I get back to England. In fact, you're authorised to use company funds to get yourself the best mobile phone on the market as soon as *you* get back to England. No stinting!'

'That's very generous of you.'

'Well, it was my fault that you dropped your phone and broke it, although strictly speaking you should have listened to me in the first place and used the landline.'

'Funny the way you cause me to drop my phone and break it and yet it's still my fault.'

Ryan gave a rich chuckle. 'My mother says that you're the only woman she's ever met who can keep me in line. I think it was the way you accused me of cheating at Scrabble last night and insisted I remove my word and take a hefty penalty. And, hearing that acerbic tone of voice now, I'm inclined to agree.'

'And *I'm* sure that all those other women you dated would be inclined to disagree!'

'Have I ruffled your feathers? It was meant as a compliment. And just for the record, all those other women I dated were perfectly happy to let me take the lead. I can't think of any of them keeping me in line.'

'You haven't *ruffled my feathers*! And if any of them had worked for you…'

'Worked *with* me. We're a team, Jamie.'

'Well, whatever. If any of them had worked *with* you, then they'd find out soon enough that the only way to survive would be to try and…'

'Take control? I never thought that I would enjoy a woman who took control, bearing in mind my own disposition, but spending time with you here is certainly—'

'Useful!' Jamie interrupted hurriedly. 'I really hope that you're managing to accomplish all the work you set out to do.'

'It gets on my nerves when you do that.'

'When I do what?'

'And don't try that butter-wouldn't-melt-in-your-mouth routine. You know exactly what I'm talking about. The second the conversation veers off work, you frantically start trying to change the subject.'

'That's not true! I've chatted about all sorts of things with your family.'

'But not with me.'

'I'm not paid to chat about all sorts of things with you.' Jamie desperately tried to shove the genie back into the bottle.

'Are you scared of me? Is that it? Do I make you nervous?'

Jamie suddenly bristled. 'No, you don't make me nervous. But I know what's going on here—you're not accustomed to lazing around for days on end. I haven't known you take more than a weekend off work in all the time I've known you.'

'You've actually noticed?'

'Stop grinning! You're out here and maybe a little bored, so you're indulging yourself by…by confusing me.'

'Am I? I thought I was trying to get to know you.'

'You *already* know me.'

'Yes. I do, don't I?' Ryan murmured softly for, thinking about it, he did. Not the details; he had only just discovered that she had a sister. But he knew *her* in a weird sort of way. Working so closely with her, he had somehow tuned in to her personality. He knew how she responded to certain things, her mannerisms, her thoughts on a whole range of subjects from remarks she had made and which he had clearly absorbed over time. All this had built a picture lacking only in the detail. Like an itch he couldn't scratch, the thought of the vet being the privileged recipient of those details niggled at the back of his mind like a nasty irritant.

'As much as you must know me, my conscientious little secretary, which means that you must know that I don't want you holding off on contacting your sister because you feel awkward using the telephone here. Unless, of course, you don't want your conversations with the vet overheard by anyone. Or maybe you're embarrassed to be caught playing long-distance counsellor with a married man.'

'That's totally uncalled for!'

'Every time I mention the guy, you look guilty and embarrassed. Why is that?'

'You don't know what you're talking about.'

'I have eyes in my head. I'm telling you what I see.'

'You have absolutely no right to make suggestions like that!'

'I take it that's the guilt talking, because you sure as hell aren't answering my question. Was there something between the two of you? *Is* there still something between the two of you?'

'That's an insult!' Jamie pushed off from the step and began swimming furiously towards the other end of the pool, her one instinct just to get away from him.

She knew that he was right behind her when she reached the other end and heard the sound of him slicing through the water, but she refused to look around.

'Greg is married to my sister!' She fixed angry eyes on him as soon as he was next to her. 'There is *nothing* going on between us.'

'But he wasn't always married to your sister, was he? In fact, *you* knew him before your sister did. I saw the way you looked at him when he came through your front door on Christmas day...'

'That's ridiculous. I didn't look at him in any way.' Had she? Yes, of course she had. She had seen him for the first time in ages and at that point she hadn't even been sure that she had put her silly infatuation to rest. Slow colour crept into her face.

'Out of sight,' Ryan murmured, 'doesn't necessarily mean out of mind.'

Flustered, Jamie looked away but she could feel a nervous pulse racing at the base of her neck just as she was aware of his watchful eyes taking in every shadow of emotion she was desperately trying to conceal.

'Is that why you rushed down to London?'

'I came to London because...because I knew that it would be easier to find a job down here. Also, when Jessica got married, I sold our childhood home and split the proceeds with her. It gave me enough to put aside some savings for a place of my own, and sufficient for me to find somewhere to rent while I looked for work. It was just a...a matter of timing.'

'Why am I not buying that?'

'Because you have a suspicious mind.'

'Did you sleep with him?'

'That's outrageous!'

'Good.' So she hadn't. He gave her a slow, satisfied smile. 'Although I sense that any competition in that area wouldn't be worth worrying about.'

'What are you saying?'

'Read between the lines. What do you think I'm saying?' Ryan didn't know when he had made the decision to over-step the mark. He just knew that he wanted her. The control that he had always been able to access when it came to women had disappeared under the force of a craving that seemed to have crept up on him only to pounce, taking him by surprise and demolishing every scrap of common sense in its voracious path.

He didn't give himself time to think. He also didn't give *her* time to think. In one smooth motion, he circled her, trapping her to the side of the pool by the effective measure of placing his hands on either side of her. He leant into her, felt her breath against his face, read the panic in her eyes that couldn't quite extinguish the simmering excitement. He had been right all along when he had sensed her forbidden interest in him and the knowledge gave him a rock-hard erection even before his lips touched hers.

Nothing had ever felt this good. That brief, public kiss they had shared at Christmas had been just a taster. Her mouth parted on a moan and, while her hands scrabbled against his chest in protest, the feel of her tongue against his was telling a different story.

He pushed her back against the wall so that his big body was pressed firmly against hers. The bottom of the pool sloped slightly upwards at this end and, standing at a little over six-two, Ryan was steady and balanced on his feet. For Jamie to keep her balance, however, she had to hook both her arms up on the wooden planks, which threw her breasts into tempting prominence. She attempted to say something and he killed the words forming on her tongue by deepening his kiss. Her eyes were half-closed. When she broke free to tilt her head back, he trailed his tongue against the slender column of her neck and Jamie shuddered in instant reaction.

More than anything else, she wanted to push him away but her will power had self-imploded and her body was as limp as a rag doll's as she soaked up the amazing feelings zipping through her as if a million shooting stars had been released inside her body.

She was dimly aware of him reaching down to hook her legs around his waist, and the nudge of his erection between her spread legs brought her close to swooning.

Water sloshed over the side of the pool as they moved frantically against each other. When he pulled down the straps of her bikini, she was self-conscious but only for a brief moment, then that, like her inhibitions, disappeared completely. With her body arched back and angled half out of the water, the touch of his mouth on her nipple was exquisite as the hot sun blazed down on them.

She could have stayed like this for ever, with him suckling on her breasts, massaging them with his big hands, rolling her nipples between his fingers and then teasing them with his tongue into hard, sensitised peaks.

It was only when he began to tug down her bikini bottom so that he could slide his fingers into her that Jamie's eyes flew open and she took horrified stock of the reality of what she was doing.

How on earth had this happened?

Of course, she knew. Why kid herself? She had been lusting after him for months—indeed, it felt like for ever. This was nothing at all like what she had felt for Greg. Not only had Ryan ignited something in her that had never been ignited before, but it was all the more powerful because it was wrapped up in a package that was more than just physical attraction. The whole complex, three-dimensional person had swept her off her feet. She hadn't even known that she had been carried away until now.

She wriggled, pushing him away from her, and then ducked under his hands so that she could swim away with frantic, urgent speed towards the far end of the pool.

Ryan easily caught up with her.

'What the hell is the matter?'

Jamie couldn't meet his eyes but she had to when she felt his fingers on her chin and was roughly made to look at him.

'I...I don't know what happened,' she whispered.

'That's fine because *I* know what happened and I'm more than happy to explain it to you. We're attracted to one another. I touched you and you went up in flames.'

'I didn't!'

'Stop pretending, Jamie. Why did you stop?'

'Because it's...it's wrong.'

She wasn't saying anything that took him by surprise. Only twenty-four hours ago he had thought about her and dismissed any notion of getting her into his bed as flat-out crazy. Yet here he was, and it didn't feel crazy.

'We're adults,' he growled. 'We're permitted to be turned on by each other.'

'You're my boss. I work for you!'

'I want more than your diligence. I want you in my bed where I can touch you wherever I want. I'm betting that that's what you want too, whether you think it's right or wrong. In fact, I'm betting that if I touch you right now, right here...' Ryan trailed his finger along her cleavage and watched as she fought to catch her breath '...you're not going to be able to tell me that you don't want me too.'

'I don't want you.'

'Liar!' He kissed her again and her lies were revealed in

the way she clutched at him, not wanting to but utterly unable to resist.

Jamie felt her weakness tearing her apart. Her mouth blindly responded and she missed his lips when he pulled back to look at her.

'*Now* tell me that you just don't know what came over you.'

'Okay. Okay. Maybe I'm attracted to you, but I'm not proud of it.' The words felt agonisingly painful and she twisted away from his piercing gaze. 'I… You're right, okay? I felt things for Greg. That's why it was important to leave, to live somewhere else, somewhere far away.' This felt like the final confession. She was now waving goodbye to her privacy for ever, but what was her option? She had to dig deep and find the strength to turn away from him with a good excuse because if she didn't he would devour her. She knew that.

Ryan had stilled. For a minute, his stomach twisted into a sickening knot. So she might not have slept with the vet, but she had felt something for him, maybe even loved him. He was shaken by the impact that her admission had on him.

'I made a mistake with Greg and I've learnt from it. I haven't come this far to make a second mistake. I won't climb into bed with you just for the hell of it. I'm going to go and I want you to promise me that you'll never mention this again.'

'What a lot of things I'm now under orders never to mention,' Ryan rasped in a savage undertone. 'And who ever said that sex between us would be a mistake?'

'I did.' This time she met his eyes squarely. 'I'm not like you. I'm not willing to fall in and out with bed with someone just because I fancy them. If you don't think that you can put this behind us, then I'm telling you right now that

I'll have my resignation waiting for you on your desk when you return to England from Florida.'

This wasn't a veiled threat, she meant every word of it; Ryan mentally cursed to himself. He had always accepted his ability to win women over. Jamie felt like the first woman he had ever really wanted and she was turning him down. Frustration ripped through him and he clenched his fists but there was nothing to say.

She was waiting for confirmation and he nodded curtly and in silence.

'Good.' Her body was still burning, but she had rescued what she could of her dignity. It felt like a very small victory. 'I'll head inside now.' She stepped out of the water and tried not to think of his hands all over her and his mouth lingering on her breasts. It had happened and it wasn't going to happen again. Just for good measure, and to show him that she meant business, she shot him one final look over her shoulder. 'Is there anything you'd like me to be getting on with?'

'Why don't you use your initiative?' Ryan said coolly. 'I would suggest something suitably engrossing that can help you forget this sordid little business of sexual attraction.'

On the tip of his tongue was the temptation to tell her that perhaps the vet *had* ended up with the wrong sister. Jamie didn't want a real man. She didn't want to be sexually challenged. No wonder she had fallen in love with a guy whose top priority was his sick animals with everything else taking second place. How demanding would a relationship with him be? Not very. Which would have suited his prim, efficient secretary right down to the ground.

And that closing thought should have made him feel a lot better as he watched her walk away with her towel firmly secured around her waist, but it didn't.

In fact, he felt a distinct urge to bash something very hard.

Instead, he made do with the pool. He swam with intensity, not looking up, until the muscles in his arms began to burn and the sun began its descent. He had no idea how long he did it. He was a prodigiously strong swimmer but even for him over two hours without rest began to take its toll.

Nevertheless, he might have continued swimming, slackening his pace, if he wasn't distracted by the sound of footsteps—running footsteps.

In the tropics, night fell quickly, preceded only by a window of blazing orange when the sun dipped below the horizon. The sky was orange now. Soon, it would be replaced by deep, velvety charcoal-black, but in the fading light he made out Jamie's slight figure as she paused at the top of the steps and then began running down them.

No wonder the woman had so many accidents!

Ryan heaved himself out of the water and without bothering to dry himself slung on the shirt which he had earlier discarded.

'Urgent work problem?' he asked sarcastically, and then paused when his eyes focused on her face and he took in her expression. She was panicked and her panic was contagious. He felt a sudden cold chill of apprehension. 'What is it? What's the matter?'

'It's your mother, Ryan. Something's wrong with her.'

'What are you talking about?' But he was already heading away from the pool, half running and half turning so that Jamie could talk to him.

'I had a shower, and when I couldn't find her anywhere I thought I'd check her bedroom to find out whether she wanted a cup of tea. When I went in, she was lying on the bed, white as a sheet. She said that she's had some tingling in her arms, Ryan, and her breathing's erratic. I rushed down here as fast as I could…'

They were at the house and Ryan was taking the stairs

two at a time, while Jamie raced behind him, out of breath in her haste to keep up. She must have been gone all of five minutes, if that, and she hoped, as she nearly catapulted Ryan in the doorway to the bedroom, that his mother had had a miraculous recovery. That all those little signs were no more than a bout of extreme exhaustion.

Vivian Sheppard was awake but obviously unwell and extremely frightened.

Within seconds, Ryan was on the phone to the hospital. The strings he was capable of pulling were not limited to his homeland; Jamie listened as he urgently asked for a specific consultant, watched as he nodded, satisfied with whatever reply he received.

'The ambulance will be here in five minutes.' He knelt by the bed and took his mother's hand in his own. Vivian, usually sprightly and full of laughter, was drawn but still managing to smile weakly at her son.

'I'm sure there's nothing to worry about,' she murmured and tut-tutted when he told her not to speak.

Behind him, Jamie hovered uncertainly, feeling like an intruder at a very private moment. She longed to see his face and desperately wanted to comfort him, but she kept her hands stiffly behind her back. As soon as she picked up the sound of the approaching ambulance, she ran downstairs and directed them to Vivian's bedroom.

To remain behind or to accompany them in the ambulance? Rather than impose an awkward situation on Ryan, who was grey with worry, she quietly informed him that she would stay at the house but would remain up until he returned.

'I can't tell you when that will be,' Ryan said, barely looking at her as he shoved on a tee-shirt and stuck his feet in his loafers.

'It's okay.'

'Thank God you went in to check in on her.'

Jamie placed her hand on his arm and felt the heat of his body through the dry tee-shirt. It took a lot to keep her hand there and not whip it away as though it had been burnt.

'I know you must be worried sick, but try not to be. Worry is contagious. You don't want your mother thinking the worst.'

'You're right,' Ryan agreed heavily. 'Look, I have to go. I'll phone the landline as soon as I can. Or better still…' he flicked out his mobile phone and handed it to her '…take this. I'll use my mother's phone to call you.'

Then he was gone, and in a heartbeat the sound of the ambulance siren was fading in the distance until the only sounds she could hear, once again, were the crickets and other night-time insects and the soft breeze sifting through the trees and shrubs.

Over the next three hours, she sat on the sofa in the living room with the windows open and a gentle breeze blowing back the white muslin curtains. His mobile was right there, on the small rattan table next to her, but it didn't ring. She must have dozed off; she was awakened by the sound of the front door slamming, then the sound of footsteps, and then Ryan was standing at the door to the room before she had much of a chance to gather herself.

'I thought you were going to call,' she said sleepily, shoving herself into an upright position on the sofa. 'I was worried. How is your mother doing? Is she going to be all right? What is the prognosis?'

Ryan walked towards her and sat on the sofa, depressing it with his weight and bringing her fractionally closer to him in the process.

'A minor stroke. The consultant says that there's nothing to worry about.'

'But you're still looking worried.'

'Can you blame me?' He leant forward and rested his head in his hands for a few moments, letting the silence settle between them. Then he looked at her and her heartbeat quickened because every instinct in her wanted to reach out and draw him to her so that she could smooth away the lines of worry on his face.

'Anyway, they did a number of tests on her, and they're going to keep her in for a couple of days so that they can do some more, but it's all very reassuring.'

'Did they say what caused it?'

'One of those things.' That was what had been said to him. Personally, he put it down to stress, and here things got a little difficult because what was there for his mother to stress about? She lived a relaxed and comfortable life. The only one she had ever been known to worry about had been her children, and with Claire, Hannah and Susie all settled and happy with their respective broods *he* was the only one left for her to be concerned about.

Over the past few hours, while he had sat on a hard chair in the hospital waiting for doctors to return with results of tests, Ryan had had time to think.

His mother had been worrying more and more over the past couple of years about his singleton status, the women he dated and the hours he worked. Had she been more anxious about it than she had let on? While he had been travelling the world, working all the hours God made and fitting in his no-strings attached relationships with sexy airheads, had she been fretting to the point that her health had suffered? He was assailed by guilt.

'Have you been in touch with your sisters?' He didn't want to talk. His silence was leaden and he was obviously a million miles away in his head. For some reason, that was painfully disappointing. Jamie wanted him to turn to her and she had to mentally slap herself on the wrist for her foolish weakness. It was as if a door in her mind had been unlocked and flung open and now that it had been she was besieged by frightening and unwelcome revelations about herself and the way she felt about him.

When she was beginning to think that she should go to bed, because she was clearly an inconvenience when he just wanted to be by himself, he looked up at her.

'I phoned Hannah and explained the situation. Of course she wanted to get straight back on a plane over, but I managed to persuade her that there would be no point. I will stay here until my mother is fit to travel and then I will return to the UK with her.' He hesitated and for the first time he focused fully on the woman sitting next to him.

'You'll have to cancel my trip to Florida. Get in touch with the office. Either Evans or George Law can handle it. Email them whatever information they need.'

Jamie nodded. He was still looking at her as though there was more to be said but he wasn't quite sure how to say it. Maybe, she thought, he was embarrassed to have her there when this family crisis was happening. Maybe he wanted her to leave immediately but was uncertain how to frame the request, considering it had been his idea to have her tag along with him in the first place.

'Of-of course,' she stammered, chewing on her lower lip. 'And...just to tell you that you shouldn't be, you know, embarrassed because you want me to leave. I absolutely and fully understand. What's happened is completely unexpected and the last thing you need is for me to be here. This isn't a time for your secretary to be hanging around getting in the way.' She tried a reassuring smile on for size. 'I'd probably feel exactly the same if the roles were reversed and you were *my* secretary.'

Her attempt to lighten the strained atmosphere fell flat-

ter than a lead balloon but after a few seconds he did manage to give her a crooked smile.

'I think you've got hold of the wrong end of the stick,' he
said eventually. 'I'm not sure how to tell you this…'

'Tell me what?' For the first time, Jamie felt a stab of
real apprehension. The incident by the pool resurfaced in
her mind and she cringed at the memory: that was the reason for his hesitation. He had had the chance to reflect on
their inappropriate behaviour and now had come the moment
of reckoning. Tears of bitter regret pushed their way to the
back of her eyes as she envisaged her wonderful, well paid,
satisfying job disappearing like a puff of smoke in the air.

CHAPTER SEVEN

RYAN continued to look at her. She had obviously fallen asleep on the chair; her cheeks were flushed and her hair was tousled. She looked young and innocent and nothing at all like the businesslike, crisp, efficient secretary he had become accustomed to. But then hadn't he seen the living, breathing, exciting woman behind the professional persona?

He reined back his imagination which would break free and gallop away. Right now, he needed to focus, because the conversation that lay ahead was probably going to be difficult.

'I honestly don't know how to say this...'

'I can't imagine you're ever stuck for words.' This was sounding worse by the second.

'My mother saw us. By the pool. Earlier today.'

'Oh, no.' Jamie put her hand to her mouth in dismay. Hot colour spread across her cheeks. 'How do you know? Did she tell you?'

'Of course she told me. I didn't use my imagination to work out a possible scenario. She decided to go for a little stroll around the gardens to see if some fresh air would give her more energy and she heard us. She followed the sound of our voices and I think she got a bit more than she bargained for.'

'I'm sorry. This is all my fault!' Suddenly there was no

part of her that could keep still and Jamie stood up to wander agitatedly around the room. She had to clasp her hands together to stop them from trembling and the wave of shameful discomfort was like a thousand painful burrs underneath her skin.

'I'll leave immediately.' She went to stand in front of him and drew in her breath to fortify herself against the mortification of meeting his eyes. 'It'll take me half an hour to pack.'

'Oh, for God's sake, don't be absurd!'

'I can't stay here. I don't think I'd be able to look your mother in the face. What we did was terrible. A mistake. She must have been appalled. Is that why…? Did we cause…?'

'No! Now sit *down*!' He waited until she was seated, although she still looked as though she would have liked to flee through the open door. 'What she saw didn't cause her to go into some kind of meltdown. My mother is pretty liberated when it comes to her children and what they get up to, believe me. In fact…'

'In fact *what*? I wish you'd just say what you have to say, Ryan. I'm a big girl. I can take bad news.'

'In fact, my mother was overjoyed at what she witnessed before she walked back to the house, no doubt with a smile on her face.'

'I'm sorry, but I don't know what you're saying.'

'I'm saying, Jamie, that my mother, as I've told you, has been, shall we say, anxious about my lifestyle for quite some time. I have no idea why, but there you go. The harridans have assured me that it's because I'm her only son and the baby of the family. At any rate, she saw us and she's jumped to certain conclusions.'

'What conclusions?' Jamie asked, totally bewildered by this point.

'That we're somehow involved.'

'We are. I work for you.'

'Strangely, seeing me all over you at the side of the pool didn't point to that particular conclusion. I've always maintained a healthy distance from the women who have worked for me in the past.'

'Involved?' Jamie squeaked, horrified.

'As in, an item. As in, romantically connected. As in...'

'I get the picture!'

'I'm not sure that you do, actually. My mother is under the impression that I've been too sheepish to say anything because I've always made a big deal of keeping my work life separate from my private life. In her wild and inventive imagination, we've only managed to keep our hands off one another while my sisters and their brood were around, but the second they all left we just couldn't help ourselves, it would seem.'

Jamie put her hands to her cheeks, which were burning hot. 'And did you tell her the truth?'

'Well, now here comes the tricky part...'

Ryan allowed a few moments of silence, during which he hoped she would join the dots and read what he was trying to say without him having to spell it out in black and white, but for once it seemed like her fine mind had deserted her.

'I couldn't,' he finally said bluntly.

'What do you mean *you couldn't*?'

'My mother has taken a shine to you. She's met a few of my girlfriends in the past and they haven't come up to her exacting standards.'

Distracted, Jamie couldn't resist the temptation to mutter under her breath that some of the girlfriends *she* had met would have fallen short of most mothers' standards, even if the standards weren't particularly exacting.

'She seems to think that we're involved in a serious relationship. I couldn't disillusion her because she's just had a stroke, albeit a mild one, and the last thing I want is for her to be subjected to any unnecessary stress. Not to put too fine a point on it, her last words before they wheeled her off for the first series of tests were that she was overjoyed that I had finally come to my senses and found myself a woman who could keep up with me.'

'This is awful!' Suddenly Jamie was really, really angry. Not only had she made a horrendous mistake—thrown away her precious privacy, engaged in wildly inappropriate behaviour and, worse, allowed herself feelings for a man who had no feelings for her—but now she was effectively being told that she wouldn't be able to put the whole sorry episode behind her because his mother had jumped to all the wrong conclusions and Ryan had made no effort to enlighten her.

'I appreciate that your mother doesn't need additional stress, Ryan, but it's going to be even more stressful for her if you deceive her over this and then have to tell her the truth when she's back on her feet. She'll never trust you again!'

'So you think that I should take the risk of damaging her health to be honest, do you? Do you imagine that you're the only person with a sense of family responsibility? My father died and my mother became the lynchpin of the family. She's been through a hell of a lot! She's had to cope with the shock of realising that the family finances had become a joke. She's had to suffer through tough times when so-called friends dropped by the wayside because she was no longer living in a big house and driving a big car.'

'And you had to witness all of that. How awful for you. I'm so sorry, Ryan. Truly I am.'

'We all have our stories to tell. Jamie! I was there to pick up the pieces, and when it comes to my mother's health and her peace of mind I'm not going anywhere. I'm still going to be here to pick up the pieces.'

It was shocking to see the lines of pain and worry etched

on his face. The Ryan who could take on the world and win was letting down his guard. Behind the dominant, powerful male, she had a glimpse of the confused boy who was forced to grow up fast. As she had.

'So I let my mother have the luxury of believing what she wanted to believe.'

'I...'

'You know what, Jamie? Perhaps you're right. Perhaps it would be better for you to leave. I'm sure I'll be able to explain your absence to my mother.'

In possession of what she thought she had wanted, Jamie found that she was now reluctant to leave. Ryan adored his family; he didn't have to verbalise it. Right now, he looked drained and so unlike the vibrant man she knew that her heart felt as though it was tearing in two. She knew that he wouldn't try to stop her if she decided to take him up on his offer and walk away, but their relationship would be irrevocably changed for ever. Would she even be able to continue working for him?

And why was she so angry at the thought of giving in to what he wanted? His mother was ill, and if a piece of harmless fiction would allow her to recover more quickly then where was the crime in that? They would return to London and in due course Ryan would gently break the news that they had broken up, amicably of course, and his mother would probably be sorry to hear it but her health certainly wouldn't suffer. Whereas now, still vulnerable, what if she *did* react badly? She was old and old people could be strangely fragile when it came to certain things, when it came to the well-being of their loved ones.

With a sickening jolt of self-awareness, Jamie knew why she was angry. Her anger stemmed from fear, whatever excuse she chose to hide behind, and her fear stemmed from the fact that Ryan had become far more than a boss to her.

She had feelings for him, and she might just as well have dug a hole for herself, jumped in and begun shovelling the earth over her head. She didn't want the pretence of being involved with Ryan because she was scared that the lines between fact and fiction might become blurred, scared that she would be left damaged, that the fiction would not be harmless after all, at least not to her.

Stuck between a rock and a hard place, Jamie navigated her way through a series of grim scenarios and, like a drowning person finally breaking the surface of the water, found the one and only way she could justify going along with his crazy idea and breathed a sigh of heady relief. She would treat it as a business proposition. He wanted her to play a pretend game, having no idea how dangerous for her the game could be, and she would box the pretence into a neat, controllable package and coolly look at it as just another part of her job.

'What exactly would this pretence entail?'

'Are you saying that you're willing to go along with me? It's a big ask, Jamie. I know that and, believe me, I would be very grateful indeed. But if you decide to jump in feet first then you can't decide halfway through that you'd really prefer the moral high-ground.'

'I'm taking it that this charade would only be appropriate while we're out here with your mother?'

'Naturally.'

'Which would be how long, exactly?'

'At least another week. I'm pretty confident that she will be able to travel back to the UK by then. She might even be able to travel back before, but I'm not into taking risks when it comes to my family.' He gave her a crooked smile, and Jamie tried to maintain a professional distance by not smiling back at him, although she could feel the hairs on the back of her neck stand on end. 'I've always saved my risk taking for the work arena.'

'Another week.' Jamie stared off into the distance and tried to break down the week into smaller, more manageable segments. Seven days during which there would be long periods of time in which there would be no need to pretend anything because his mother would probably be asleep or resting. 'Right,' she said crisply. 'I'll agree, on the condition that we get one thing perfectly straight.'

'And what might that be?'

'What happened out there by the pool was a terrible mistake.' Jamie looked at him squarely and directly. 'The sun, these exotic surroundings… Well, it was a moment of madness in unfamiliar surroundings and, yes, of course you're an attractive man. Things happened that shouldn't have happened. But I need your word that, if we're to pretend to be something we aren't for the sake of your mother, nothing physical must happen again. In other words, there must be very clear boundaries between us.'

A lull of silence greeted this remark, as thick and as heavy as treacle. Ryan's dark, inscrutable eyes resting lazily on her face made it difficult to hold on to her composure and she could feel tension coiling inside her, trickling through every part of her nerve-wracked body. Only a lifetime's habit of keeping her emotions to herself allowed her to maintain his gaze without flinching.

'Is that speech directed at yourself as well?'

'What do you mean?'

'I'm not some kind of arch seducer, lurking behind walls, waiting to pounce on an innocent victim. Sexual attraction is a funny thing in my experience. It hardly ever responds to the calm voice of reason.'

'Perhaps in your case, but certainly not in mine.'

'Maybe,' Ryan murmured, 'if you had ditched the virtue

and flung yourself at the vet he might have married a different sister.'

And just like that, he had changed the tenor of the conversation. With a single flick of the finger, he had overturned the pedestal on which she had valiantly sought to place herself, safely out of reach. Jamie's skin burned as she contemplated the awkward question that he had dragged out into the open.

How was it that she had never, not once, been really tempted to put her attraction to Greg to the test? How had it been so easy to restrain herself around him when with Ryan, a far more unsuitable and inappropriate candidate for her affections, she had gone up in flames, had found it impossible to rein back her frantic, screaming urge to touch him and to let him touch her? Was he now wondering the same thing? Would she be condemned now to always play the role of the woman who couldn't resist him? When they returned to England, and he resumed his life with the blonde bimbos and the airhead catwalk queens, would he still be smirking to himself that his quiet little secretary was lusting after him as she ducked behind her computer? Galling thought!

'Maybe I respond to you,' Jamie returned sharply. 'But I was thinking of Greg! Maybe it was all just a piece of weird, delayed emotional transference.'

'You used me as a substitute, in other words? Is that what you're saying?'

'I'm saying that there's no point analysing anything. What happened happened, but it's not going to happen again, and I need your word on that or else I won't agree to any charade. You needn't worry about me and those ideas you have about sexual attraction. I can handle myself.'

So, Ryan thought with slow-building murderous rage the likes of which he had never felt before, when she had arched back and succumbed to the sensation of his tongue gently caressing her nipple while the water lapped warmly around them had she actually been seeing the vet's face in her mind's eye? Ryan had never had much time for psychobabble but he could grudgingly see that the sudden appearance of the vet might have kick started something in her that had culminated in the temporary breaking down of her inhibitions with him. And he didn't like it.

'You have my word.' He smiled grimly and stood up. 'We should both get some sleep now. It's late. I'll be leaving for the hospital first thing in the morning.'

'Would…would it be okay if I came along with you? I've grown very fond of your mother in the short time I've known her. I'd like to see how she's doing for myself.'

Ryan began heading for the door. There was no point dwelling on the unsavoury possibility that he had been used as a substitute for someone else, that he had been the wrong boss, in the wrong place at the wrong time. He resisted the unnatural urge to worry the remark to death until he succeeded in extracting some alternative, more favourable explanation for the way she had responded to him. Instead, he locked the door on those unsettling thoughts and half-turned to find her right behind him.

Switching off the light, the room was suddenly plunged into semi-darkness but he could still make out the anxious glitter in her eyes. Whatever murky water happened to be flowing underneath their respective bridges at the moment, there was no doubt that she cared about his mother.

'There's no point, really. I'll tell her that you wanted to visit, but she'll be back here within a day or so and you can tell her for yourself. Your time would be better spent here, seeing to all the rearrangements that will have to be put in motion for the meetings in Florida. You'll need to make sure that all the relevant information gets emailed to George

Law. He would be a better bet to cover for me than Evans, I think. He might even find all those graphs and flip charts you prepared a handy tool.'

Jamie felt tears prick the corners of her eyes. She had to look away quickly and was grateful for the relative darkness. This was the Ryan she found so sweetly irresistible—the teasing, laid-back Ryan—and when that side of him went into retreat it was as if a dark cloud had settled over her world.

'You were never going to use any of them, were you?' she queried lightly, knowing that they were both attempting to find some of the familiar ground they had lost.

'I would have taken them all with me. As for using them, well, my speeches tend to be of the "winging it" variety, although that chart with all the different colours was very appealing.'

'I'll make sure that everything is sorted out,' Jamie promised, stepping into the hall and closing the door behind her.

'I'm sure you will. I have every faith in you.'

There was no need to dwell any longer on the dos and dont's of the strange game upon which she had agreed to embark.

As it turned out, she had less time to worry over it because Vivian was released the following day.

Jamie, having put through the final call to one of the senior conference organisers in Florida, was leaving the office at a little after five in the afternoon when she heard the sound of Ryan's car drawing up on the drive outside.

He had been out of the house since eight-thirty, calling only to tell her that he intended to stay in the town and use his time meeting with one of the head honchos of the tourist board so that he could throw around a few ideas he had had about the possibility of opening a boutique hotel on the island. Jamie knew that he had been playing around with the notion of extending the boundaries of his empire over the past few months, and she wasn't surprised that he would choose the island which he knew intimately.

She had no idea how the rest of the evening would evolve, and her stomach clenched into nervous knots as she headed towards the front door. But when it was pushed open she saw Vivian, pale but looking much healthier than before, preceding her son into the airy, flagstone open area.

'Darling girl, I'm so pleased to see you.'

Jamie walked into a warm embrace and managed to catch Ryan's eye over his mother's shoulder.

'How are you feeling, Vivian?'

'Like an old woman.' She dismissed it with a smile, linking her arm through Jamie's and walking towards the sitting room, which was one of the coolest rooms in the house thanks to the expanse of French doors which could be flung open to admit the balmy breezes, and the overhead ceiling fan. 'I thought that I was as healthy as a horse,' she confided, settling herself on the striped sofa where she suddenly looked much more frail. 'But don't we all, until something comes along to remind us that we aren't? Thankfully, my stroke was very, very mild. A warning, the doctor told me. I need to start slowing down.' She closed her eyes briefly and then opened them to smile at her son who had taken up position behind Jamie.

His hand was curved lightly on the nape of her neck and she was acutely conscious of the gentle stroking of his thumb on her skin. So this was what the charade felt like—a casual intimacy which his mother would expect of two people who were an item, and which was devastating on her senses.

Vivian was a smaller, softer, rounder version of her son. The same dark hair, the same dark eyes. These dark eyes were now happily taking them both in.

'My darling,' she said warmly. 'I can't tell you how thrilled I was when Ryan explained the situation.'

Jamie edged away from those disturbing fingers to sit on one of the upright chairs, leaving Ryan to sink onto the sofa next to his mother, conveniently no longer within touching distance. She tentatively touched the back of her neck where it still tingled, and pinned an engaging smile on her face.

'He's been a naughty boy. There was no need for the cloak-and-dagger routine. Of course, we all know how firm he's always been about keeping his love life—'

'Mother! I'm right here!'

Vivian patted his knee fondly but her eyes remained on Jamie. 'I know, and that's why I refrained from saying your *sex* life.'

Ryan groaned and flushed darkly. It was a pinprick of the comic in an awkward situation, if only Vivian knew.

'Away from the office, but I couldn't be more delighted. He must have told you that I've been worrying for some time now that he needs to find himself a good woman and settle down.'

'It's been mentioned,' Jamie murmured when she realised that an answer was expected of her, and Vivian greeted that acknowledgement with a beam of satisfied approval.

'Knowing that he has has made all the difference. I'm certain I'm back on my feet so quickly simply because I'm just so happy!'

Over the course of the next hour and a half, Vivian swatted aside enquiries about her nutrition regime, exercise plan and plans for when she returned to England in favour of the more absorbing topic of her son's good fortune in finding Jamie. She asked questions which brought a rush of embarrassed colour and tongue-tied silence to Jamie but which Ryan, Oscar-winning actor that he seemed to be, answered with aplomb.

She wondered aloud at her amazing ability to read a situation, exclaiming that she had just guessed from the *very start* that something was up by the way her son looked at Jamie. She blushed delicately when she referred to that moment when her suspicions had been confirmed, having accidentally spied them kissing at the side of the pool. She hastened to add that she had not lingered and so had witnessed nothing beyond 'a passionate kiss that said it all', while Jamie wished for the ground to open and swallow her up, hopefully to disgorge her into a world where the events of the past few weeks had never happened.

Vivian retired to bed with a light supper of tea and toast, leaving Jamie to glumly contemplate the mess into which they had both managed to get themselves.

'This,' she announced, as soon as Ryan was back in the sitting room, 'is a nightmare.'

'We'll discuss this outside. I no longer trust my mother not to pop up in unexpected places, and she doesn't need to have her high hopes dashed by a few careless words from you.'

He turned on his heel and she dashed behind him out onto the veranda, and then away completely from the house as they manoeuvred down the hill via a series of twisting wooden steps until they emerged onto the white, sandy beach below.

It was dark, but out here, under a full moon, the sea glinted and glittered like a placid lake of slick, black oil.

It was only the third time Jamie had actually been on the beach, and the first time at night, and she marvelled at its spectacular isolation. The house was very cleverly situated atop a natural, protected cove which could only be accessed by boat or via the grounds of the house, which were private property. Thus, it was perfectly peaceful. Bits of driftwood were scattered here and there, and the husks of fallen coconuts had been a never-ending source of fun and play for the little ones when they had been at the house. Ryan stooped to pick one up now and absently threw it out to sea in a long, wide arc before moving to sit on the sand, out of the reach of the sea gently lapping on the shore.

'I had no idea your mother was so...'

'Taken with the idea of you and I?'

'I was going to say desperate to see you settled down.'

'Are you saying that only a desperate man would choose you to settle down with?' He lay back on the sand with his hands folded behind his head and Jamie flounced down next to him, although sitting up so that she could glare at his face.

'That's not what I'm saying,' she denied in frustration. 'What on earth are we going to do?'

'We've already been over this.'

'I hadn't thought it through. I hadn't realised that we would have to build a great detailed story of how we...we...'

'Fell into each other's arms? Were drawn to one another over the coffee machine and the filing cabinets?'

'How can you think that it's funny? Your mother really believes that we're on the verge of announcing our engagement!'

'Now you're beginning to realise the position I was in when I found myself having to humour her. In her fragile condition, the last thing I could have done would have been to announce that we were involved in a little light-hearted hanky panky. I'm afraid she sees you as someone far too decent and moral and responsible to get carried away by lust, which would have left her thinking that I had seduced you for a bit of passing fun, only to toss you aside the second I was through with you.'

'You mean the way you usually treat the women you've been out with?'

'I refuse to be baited into an argument. This is the reality we're dealing with. I explained the situation to you and you signed up to the deal.'

'Yes, but I didn't sign up to any physical contact. You know that.'

He continued staring up, and to get his attention before her frustration ran away with her Jamie gathered some sand in her fist and slapped it down on his chest.

Quick as a flash, and before she could even think of taking avoidance tactics, his hand was curled round her wrist and he half sat up, propping himself up by his elbow.

'We're lovers, remember? My mother might be old but she's not away with the fairies. Keeping a healthy distance and smiling politely is going to set the alarm bells going in her head.'

'Yes, but—'

'But *what*? I touched you for three seconds on the nape of your neck. I wasn't plunging my hands down your tee-shirt!'

Jamie squirmed. His fingers were like a steel vice around her wrist, burning a hole in her skin.

'Why don't you pretend that I'm the vet?' he gritted savagely. 'Then you might start enjoying the occasional passing touch.'

She squeezed her eyes shut. She should never have implied that she had used him, should never have implied that she had been fired up by thoughts of Greg when Ryan had been touching her in the pool. That had been an outright lie, and afterwards she had felt like a coward who was happy to shunt the blame for her behaviour onto someone else because it was easier than having to accept responsibility for her own actions—misguided, stupid or otherwise.

She would not have liked it if a man had touched her intimately and she had responded to his touch, only to be told that she had been nothing but a fill-in for the woman he really wanted but couldn't have.

'That wouldn't work,' she confessed in a tight voice. 'Now, please let me go.'

Ryan released her immediately. He didn't know what the hell had prompted him to drag the vet into the conversation. He had determined to put that unpleasant conversation of earlier behind him and move on. Evidently, it had continued to prey on his mind.

'What's that supposed to mean?' He sat up and watched her narrowly as she massaged her wrist.

'I shouldn't have said what I said about... Sorry, I shouldn't have implied that you were a substitute for Greg. I've discovered that I put Greg behind me a lot longer ago than I thought.'

'Go on.'

'To what? There's nothing else to say. If I gave the wrong impression to you, then I apologise.'

'Let me get this straight.' Ryan only became aware of his black mood now that it was in the process of vanishing. 'You don't get turned on at the thought of the vet?'

'It would seem not.'

'So by the pool, that hot response really *was* all for me?'

'That still doesn't mean that it was right! What we did...'

'And you don't want any physical contact because I turn you on and you don't like that.'

'Something along those lines,' Jamie muttered, hot all over and agonisingly conscious of his glittering dark eyes fixed like laser beams on her face. 'I should tell you what I managed to sort out on the work front. I haven't had a chance, what with everything this evening.'

But, while her head was telling her that that was the best route away from this uncomfortable topic, her addled brain was refusing to go along for the ride.

Ryan tilted his head obligingly to one side. God, he suddenly felt on top of the world. He must have an ego as tough as an egg shell, he thought wryly, if a few insinuations and ill-chosen words from a woman who wasn't even his lover could reduce him to an ill-tempered bore. And if a retraction could reverse the effect in a heartbeat.

'You spoke to Law?' he prompted.

'And emailed all the info over. And…um…' Jamie licked her lips. 'I also contacted all the relevant people in, um, Florida.'

'And? Um? Ah, um…'

'You're making fun of me!'

'I'm intrigued by your sudden attack of nerves.'

'Can you blame me?'

Ryan didn't pretend to misunderstand her. 'No. No, I can't. You owned up to something you found difficult and I admire you for that. It was a brave thing to do. I'll keep all physical contact to the minimum, of course. If that's what you want.'

'It is.' Even to her own ears, she could hear the telltale waver in her voice.

'Okay, I won't touch you, but feel free to touch *me*,' he said in a husky undertone. 'Any time you like and anywhere you like because I'm happy to admit that you make me feel like a randy teenager. In fact, right now I'm hot for you, and I won't run screaming like an outraged virgin if you decide to touch me and feel for yourself.'

He hadn't just thrown down the challenge, he had hurled it like a javelin, and it lay between them now, waiting for her to decide what to do with it.

'Why do you have to make me laugh? It's not fair.' Jamie's breathing was shallow and painful and she leaned forward, resting on her outstretched hands, already knowing what she would do with that hurled challenge.

'Life seldom is. If you want me, you have to reach out and touch me.'

'Just while we're here,' she said on a soft moan. Of its own accord, her hand reached out to curl into the opening of his shirt, between two buttons, so that her knuckles were brushing his chest. 'Just for this week. If we can pretend to be something we're not for the sake of your mother, let's just pretend to be different people to one another. I won't be your secretary. You won't be my boss. Just for a few days, can we simply be two people, strangers who happened to meet on a very beautiful island in the Caribbean? Can we?'

'We'll pretend whatever you want,' Ryan growled. 'Now, take off your tee-shirt. Very, very slowly. And then your bra, also very slowly. I want to look at every intimate inch of your glorious body before I begin to touch it.'

A shiver of wicked, exquisite anticipation ripped through her. She should have been back-pedalling; she wasn't. Being here was a step out of time and why shouldn't she just give in to this thing? She had always lived a life of responsibility. She had always toed the line, trundling along in the slow lane, while her sister had lived life to the full in the fast lane. She had spent so much time picking up the pieces of Jessica's misadventures that she was in serious danger of forgetting what being young and carefree was all about.

So why shouldn't she spend a few days out here remembering? She had a sudden craving for some misspent time before it was too late.

With a smile and then a gurgle of laughter, she hooked her fingers under her tee-shirt and did as he asked. She pulled it over her head very, very slowly. Then she reached back to unclasp her bra, which she also removed very, very slowly.

Then she gave Ryan a gentle push back and when he was lying on the sand she straddled him, her breasts like ripe fruit waiting to be handled.

Between her legs, his erection was a rod of steel pushing against her.

And the look in his eyes! The hunger and the appreciation.

'What else,' she asked wickedly, 'would you like me to do?'

CHAPTER EIGHT

RAMPANT appreciation flared in Jamie's eyes. She couldn't help it and, after days of blissfully throwing caution to the wind she no longer bothered trying to keep her guard up. Why should she? Ryan was nakedly, enthrallingly turned on by her. In their moments of wild passion, he would whisper how much into her ear, and every husky syllable represented yet another wrecking ball aimed at her defences.

And it wasn't just about the sex. They took time out, shooed out of the house by Vivian who claimed she needed peace and insisted that the only way she could get it was if they weren't making a racket in the house. Not that they did, but Ryan was happy to go with the flow. The island was stunningly beautiful and he had seen precious little of it. He hadn't realised how much of his work he took with him wherever he went, and for the first time he sidelined it in favour of showing Jamie around.

He took her to the Blue Hole where they swam in crystal clear waters. They took boats to the various islands. She forced him to traipse through bush so that they could experience some of the wildlife and laughed when he confessed to a fear of all things creepy-crawly.

'I think you'll find that *real* men, like me, are proud to admit to things like that,' he informed her haughtily, keeping a healthy distance as she allowed a praying mantis to scramble over her hand.

She had never had overseas holidays as a child. Losing her dad at such a young age had imposed financial restrictions on their lives. In the still, dark hours with just the sound of the sea lapping on the beach below the house, it seemed easy to shed her natural reserve and observe her childhood from a distance, with Ryan sitting next to her, an encouraging listener.

And of course they still worked together. Their mornings were still spent in the office in the house, but working had taken on a whole new perspective. They never touched one another, but sometimes he would lean over her, reading something over her shoulder on her computer, and his proximity was tantalising and electric. She would look at him and their eyes would tangle with full-blown lust even though they would be conversing perfectly normally about something mundane and technical.

Right now, Jamie was primly logging off her computer, but under her tee-shirt she was bra-less and under the small stretchy skirt the dampness between her legs announced the urgency her body felt at the prospect of being touched there.

Ryan was on the telephone, sprawled back in the leather swivel chair, his eyes broodingly following her movements as she stood up, smoothed down her skirt, caught his eyes and held them in a bold, inviting gaze.

'We got the contract.' He pushed back the chair, stuck his feet on the desk in a manner that was so typically him that it brought a half smile to her lips and beckoned her to him with his finger. 'George was eternally grateful for your exquisite attention to detail in the reports you emailed to him before the meetings began.'

'Good.' Jamie allowed herself a smile of professional satisfaction.

'Is that all you have to say by way of congratulations?' Ryan murmured, his eyes darkening as he took in the gentle sway of her breasts under the tight tee-shirt.

He was finding that he could barely look at her without his body slamming into immediate response. Where was the man with the formidable control when it came to women? He seemed to have been hijacked by a guy with a semi-permanent erection and a head full of erotic images that only went away when he was in deep sleep. Even then he had woken up on a couple of occasions to find himself thinking of her, needing an immediate cold shower, because despite his attempts at persuasion she had refused to share his bed for the duration of the night.

'What else would you like me to say?'

'I'm someone who believes that actions speak louder than words.'

'How would you like me to act?' Jamie blushed when he raised his eyebrows fractionally and let his eyes travel with slow, lazy insolence over the length of her body. 'We can't.' Her voice was breathless. 'Your mother will be waiting on the veranda for us to join her for lunch.'

'Forgot to tell you. She got Junior to drive her into town for a check-up with the consultant and she said that she's going to meet one of her friends for a bite out while she's there. I have yet, to see someone recover more quickly from a health scare,' he continued drily. 'In fact, I haven't seen her so relaxed in a long time.' Now that he and Jamie were open in their relationship, whatever that relationship might be, his mother was as chipper as a cricket, lapping it all up, planning who only knew what in that head of hers.

Ryan closed his mind to what lay round an otherwise unexplored corner in the future. Instead, he focused on the sexy, sexy woman standing inches away from him in a skirt that revealed newly brown, slender legs and a top that was begging to be ripped off.

'So you have all the time in the world to demonstrate how thrilled you are that we've managed to hook this new, lucrative contract. On second thoughts, I think that *I* should be the one to show *you* how impressed I am for your invaluable contribution to us closing the deal.'

He sat forward and ran his hands along the sides of her thighs, stroking their soft, silky length until he felt her begin to melt. Then he slid his hands higher, hooked his fingers over the lacy elastic of her underwear and tugged. Jamie trembled. She propped herself against the edge of his desk and closed her eyes, losing herself in the glorious sensation of skirt and panties both being pulled down. She was burning up even though the air-conditioning was on, circulating cold air through the room.

Their love-making was usually at night, after his mother had retired for the evening. The stars and the moon had borne witness countless times to them on the beach, lying on a giant rug on the sand, lost in each other. Twice they had cooled off in the sea only to fall right back into each other's arms the second they were out. They had made love in his bedroom. In her bedroom. Once, memorably, in the kitchen, late at night and with the kitchen door shut just in case, which had involved certain mouth-watering delights that Ryan had enjoyed licking off her.

But the office had been a designated work area so that now there was something deliciously wicked about being in it half-undressed.

'We should go upstairs,' she whispered. Her fingers sifted through his thick, dark hair. She looked down as he stared up at her for a few seconds.

'Oh, I don't know,' Ryan drawled. 'It seems only appropriate that I should show my deep and undying gratitude for your hard work in a working environment.'

'What if one of the gardeners sees us through the window?'

'Good point. I'll dip the shutters while you stay right where you are and don't move a muscle.'

She did and when he resumed his position on the chair she yielded to his devastating fingers and tongue until she was on the point of collapse. He tasted her until she thought that her whole body was going to explode, until she was begging him to take her. Her breasts ached under the tee-shirt and she was driven to roll her fingers over her sore, tender nipples in a bid to assuage their painful sensitivity. Every time she glanced down to that dark head buried between her thighs, she felt weaker than a rag doll. There was something intensely erotic about the fact that he was still fully clothed while she was dishevelled and half-dressed.

'I can't stand this any longer,' she groaned shakily, and she knew that he was smiling as he continued to tease her throbbing clitoris with his tongue.

'I love it when you say that.' Ryan finally released her screaming body from the onslaught of his attention and carried her, cave-man style, to the long sofa where she lay and watched as he stripped off his clothes. She never tired of feasting on the hard muscularity of his body.

Of course, he worked out. In London, he was a member of a gym, where twice a week he treated himself to gruelling games of squash with a couple of guys from the office. He also seemed to play every other sport imaginable. Here, he ran—at five in the morning, he had told her a few days ago. She hadn't believed him until this morning, on the way to the bathroom, she had glanced out of her window to see him disappearing down the drive. They had only gone their

separate ways a few hours before. He was a man who needed
next to no sleep.

When he lightly touched himself, an involuntary groan
escaped her lips and he grinned. Her arm was resting lightly
across her forehead and she looked like a very beautiful
Victorian maiden caught in the act of swooning. Which, now
that he thought about it, was an image that was intensely
appealing.

'I'm glad you're satisfied with my level of appreciation,
milady,' he told her huskily.

He positioned himself directly over her, her legs between
his, and he pulled her tee-shirt over her head. She was already arching back, inviting his mouth to her breasts, offering the twin peaks of her nipples for his pleasure. Irresistible.
Making love to her was a constant struggle to keep himself
under control. The challenge of breathing in the dampness
between her legs had been struggle enough when it came
to self-restraint, and it was no easier as he dipped his head
so that he could suckle on her nipples, one at a time, loving
the way they engorged in his mouth.

He entered her with one single thrust when they could no
longer bear to go so far but not far enough. Her body shuddered as within seconds she was climbing that peak, tumbling into an orgasm that rocked her body, taking him with
her, their slick, slippery bodies fused as if one.

It was bliss to lie with him, squashed on the sofa, as they
gradually came back down to earth. It was just as well that
his mother was out, Jamie thought, because she knew that
there was no way she could have sauntered out onto the
veranda for lunch without betraying the tell-tale signs of a
woman who has been branded thoroughly by her man.

She stretched, settled down more comfortably against his
body. He cupped her breast absently, as though it was impossible for him to be this close to her without him touching

her intimately. She loved it. She loved that feeling of possession. Sometimes he would cup between her legs or else just distractedly stroke her nipple with his finger, circling its outline and then teasing her as he waited for her to react to his feathery touch.

Jamie could have stayed like this for ever.

She said, reluctantly raising the subject, 'Now that the deal is done and dusted and your mother is pretty much back on her feet...'

Ryan stilled because he knew that this was a conversation they had to have. He was needed back in London. He could delegate, but only to a certain extent. Decisions had to be taken about crucial deals and those decisions could not be made out here where the tropical sun and gratifying, relaxing sex on tap—not to mention their daily jaunts out where thoughts of work disappeared—were combining to erode his appetite for ferocious concentration.

Jamie waited for him to pick up the threads of the conversation, but he didn't and she stifled a sigh.

'We should be thinking of returning to the UK.'

'Yes,' Ryan said slowly. 'We need to.' Until this moment, he had really not considered the matter in a truly concrete way. He did now. It took seconds. The truth, laid bare in front of him, was that he couldn't walk away from what they had begun. Had he envisaged this outcome when he had casually enrolled her in his clever plan to placate his mother's nervous concerns?

'I'll need to make reservations.'

'You know how to ruin an atmosphere, Jamie.'

'I'm not trying to. I'm just...being realistic.'

'We'll leave on the weekend. That's the day after tomorrow.' He rolled onto his back and stared up at the ceiling where the sun filtering through the half-open shutters played on the woodwork in an ever-changing kaleidoscopic pattern.

'And then we go back to being the people we were before we came here.'

'How easy is that going to be?' He inclined his head to look at her, but her face was giving nothing away. 'Do you really imagine that we're going to be able to return to the soulless working relationship we had before all of this?'

'It wasn't a soulless relationship!'

'You know exactly what I mean. We can't tell the past to go away because it's inconvenient.'

'What are you trying to say?'

'I'm saying that this stopped being a game of charades the second we climbed into bed, and if you think that we can pretend that none of it ever happened, then you're living in cloud cuckoo land. It happened, and it will still happen even when we're back in London and you're sitting at your desk and I'm at mine. When we look at one another, we're going to remember, and you can't wish that simple fact away.'

'We should never have started this.' There was always a price to be paid at the end of the day, and for so much plea- sure the price was going to be steep. Jamie was now real- ising that she had got far more than she had bargained for. She had thrown off her old, careful, cautious self and let in a sentiment she now knew had been hovering on the sidelines, barely kept at bay, waiting to devour her. She had fallen in love with him and now she was drowning.

'Tell me I'm not going to get a long sermon loosely based on the notion of regret,' Ryan said curtly. 'I really thought that we had moved past all of that.'

'To what? Moved past it to what, exactly? You're right. It's going to be impossible to look at one another and pre- tend that none of this ever happened.'

'So we do the logical thing.' He smiled slowly and re- laxed.

'Which is?'

'We continue seeing one another when we get back to London. What we have isn't going to go away because we tell it to, so why bother to try? If anyone had told me two months ago—less—that we would end up in bed together, and loving every second of the experience, I would have thought they were crazy. But here we are and I'm not willing to put this thing to sleep, not yet, not when I still burn for you and you're on my mind every second of the day.'

Not yet. Those two words stuck in Jamie's head and in between the glorious temptation to greedily take what was on offer the reality of its inevitable ending dripped through the fantasy like poison.

This was a moment in time, a moment which he wanted to extend because he was enjoying himself. He had broken through his self-imposed taboo of sleeping with someone he worked with, and now that he had done that it was all systems go as far as he was concerned.

He wouldn't be lying there, getting himself twisted into little knots, as he mentally journeyed into the future and found all the flaws in his plan. He wouldn't be stressing because at some indeterminate time their relationship would end and he would be left hurt and ripped to shreds. None of that would occur to him, because for him she was a casual fling, something that had defied belief in taking shape and, having taken shape, had further defied belief by being enjoyable. And Ryan Sheppard was a man with a very healthy capacity for enjoyment.

Looking at him now, he was the picture of a man satisfied with what he saw as a perfectly reasonable solution to a situation.

'I can't believe I'm saying this,' he confided, 'but you're the sexiest woman I've ever taken to my bed.' He folded her in his arms and covered her leg with his thigh. 'And, as an added bonus, you make me laugh.'

Jamie would have given anything to just close her eyes and carry on living for the moment, just as she had spent the past days doing. She had slept with him and loved every minute of it, but now they were about to head back to London, and she could no longer pretend that she was the kind of girl who could live indefinitely in the present without a thought of the future. She was cursed with the burden of responsibility and too well-trained in the many ways of dumping it on her shoulders.

'When I touch you,' he admitted roughly, 'I forget what the concept of stress is. I've never played truant until now— all those trips when the thought of work never crossed my mind. And my mother is overjoyed with this situation.' He kissed her eyelids, which fluttered shut. 'Let's not put a spanner in the works by talking about regret. We agreed to put on an act. We didn't have to, as it turns out. Let's see where this thing takes us, Jamie, and when it's over I won't have to concoct a lie to my mother.'

When it's over. She wondered how he could build so many negatives into something he was trying to persuade her was a positive step forward, but of course he wouldn't even be aware of that. He was so accustomed to the short-term nature of his relationships that he wasn't even capable of thinking of them in any other way. Every adjective he used reminded her that, for him, this was a sexually satisfying but temporary situation. How long would it take, once they had returned to London, before the sexiest woman he had ever taken to his bed became yesterday's news?

Here, on the island, there was no competition. In London, there would be competition lurking round every corner, waiting to ambush him from behind every door, phoning him and texting him and emailing him. Where would *she* stand then? He would no longer be playing truant and she wouldn't be the person making him laugh.

She pushed herself up into a sitting position, feeling suddenly very exposed without a stitch of clothing on.

'We should get up. Get dressed. I'm hungry, and your mother will be back soon. I'm sure she won't want to stay out for too long in this sun, not after what she's been through.'

'I doubt she would turn a hair if she discovered that we were doing more than filing reports in here.'

'That's not the point,' Jamie told him sharply. She began levering herself off the sofa, only to be pulled back down so that she half fell on top of him, her breasts squashing against his chest.

'This conversation isn't over,' he grated. 'You opened it, and neither of us is going anywhere until it's been closed.'

'I don't know what you want me to say.'

'You damn well do, Jamie.'

'Okay. You want me to tell you that I'll continue sleeping with you until you decide that you're sick of me and chuck me over for your usual blonde-haired, legs-up-to-armpits bimbo!'

'Where did *that* come from?' He pinned her to the sofa and stared at her fiercely, although underneath his bristling brows she could see his bewilderment. He hadn't a clue what had prompted that outburst and that, in itself, was hurtful. She had a brief, searing fantasy in which he soothed away her fears and insecurities by telling her that there would never be another blonde-haired, legs-up-to-armpits bimbo, that she was the only woman for him, that he worshipped the ground she walked on and loved her to death. The fantasy vanished virtually as soon as it materialised.

'I've really…enjoyed *this*, but when we get back to London, things between us are going to get back to what they were. I know it's going to be difficult, but it won't be impossible. You'll be busy and distracted with other deals in the pipeline. I'll be busy trying to get rid of my sister who is still at my house. Your mother will probably want to see you a bit more often than she has in the past. In no time at all, we'll both look back on this as if it was a dream, something that never really happened.'

Ryan couldn't quite believe that she was effectively dumping him. He knew that she had been a reluctant bed-partner. He knew that she had principles which, once upon a time, he would have derided as positively archaic but which he had come to respect. But once she had slept with him, he had assumed a straightforward path leading towards a mutually agreed-upon outcome. Hell, people embarked upon marriage with fewer scruples and less psychoanalysis! The thought of no longer being able to touch her—or, worse, of seeing her on a daily basis and no longer being able to touch her—made his blood run cold, but Ryan suddenly felt as though he had gone the extra mile in the seduction stakes. He wasn't going to beg.

'Besides, it would be awkward. Sooner or later, people would find out. You know how that office buzzes with gossip. Both of us would lose respect.'

'Do yourself a favour and don't worry on my behalf. Gossip has never bothered me.'

'Well, it would bother *me*,' Jamie told him coolly. 'I've never liked the thought of people talking about me behind my back. Anyway, let's be honest, this isn't a relationship that's going anywhere.' She was disgusted with herself for the tiny thread of hope that continued to blossom inside her, the hope that he would leap into instant denial or at least pretend to give the matter some serious thought.

But he just said with an impatient shrug, 'Why does a relationship have to go somewhere? We're happy with this. That's all that matters.'

'Not to me!'

'Are you telling me that you want me to ask you to marry

me?' Ryan said slowly, fixing her with those fabulous eyes that gave the illusion of being able to see right down deep into her innermost soul.

'No! Of course not!' Jamie gave a shaky laugh. In her head, she could imagine his incredulity at such a preposterous idea: the secretary who after a few days romping in the sack suddenly got thoughts above her station, encouraged by his mother. 'But I don't want to spend time with someone in a relationship that's not going anywhere. I guess I've learnt some lessons from Greg.' Within reason, she was determined to be as truthful as possible.

'Right.' Ryan stood up and strolled towards the bundles of discarded clothes on the floor, his back to her, offering her a rejection that made her eyes sting. 'So it's back to business as usual,' he remarked, pulling on his clothes while she continued to watch him helplessly. He found himself thinking of creative ways he could use to get her to change her mind and scowled at his own weakness. He had had the rug pulled from under his feet and that, he decided, was why he now felt like hitting something very hard.

She had managed to scuttle back into her tee-shirt and knickers by the time he eventually turned around.

'We could continue to enjoy ourselves for the little time here we have left...' Jamie was ashamed of the desperation behind this suggestion.

The fact that she was as cool as a cucumber enraged Ryan even more. She had been nothing if not a star pupil, he thought savagely. From shrinking violet, she was now brazen enough to offer her body to him for a day and a half, with their cut-off point doubtless to be when Junior was carrying their cases to the car.

'A few more sex sessions for the road?' he asked with thick sarcasm and Jamie flinched. 'How many do you think we can fit in before the car is revving in the drive to take us to the airport?' This was supposed to have been fun. Once they returned to London, they would be working alongside one another and there would be no room for misplaced emotion.

Ryan shook his head, frustrated at his own inability to put things into perspective. Had it been a mistake to start this in the first place? Jamie was nothing like the women he had slept with in the past. At her core, she was intensely serious. She wasn't into the clubs, the parties and the expensive trinkets, and he had been challenged and seduced by the novelty of someone so different from what he was accustomed to. Add to the mixture the fact that she was intelligent and humorous, and then throw in the ease with which she had engaged his notoriously picky family members—was it any surprise that he had chosen to overlook the simple reality that she would not be satisfied with the sort of relationship he preferred?

'Get dressed.' He couldn't have a conversation with her when her body was still on tempting display.

Jamie went bright red and gathered up the rest of her clothing, taking his command for what it was. Now that they were over, he was already relegating her to his past. He was a guy who specialised in moving on when it came to women and he was already moving on, no longer interested in her body, possibly even turned off by the physical reminder of what they had shared.

She would take her cue from him. It had been a mistake to suggest that they enjoy themselves for the brief time they had left on the island, and she knew that that sign of weakness would return to haunt her at a later date.

'We'll have to maintain this fiction while we're still here,' Ryan told her with a shuttered expression and Jamie nodded, thankful for her hair swinging across her face as she looked down, hiding her giddy confusion.

She composed herself before raising her eyes to meet his. 'Of course.'

Her calm smile got on his nerves. He gritted his teeth together and shoved his hands into his pockets, where they bunched into fists.

'Look, I'm really sorry,' Jamie said awkwardly, trying to elicit a response, but the Ryan she had known over the past few days had disappeared from view. In his place was a cold-eyed stranger that chilled her to the bone and made her wonder whether they would ever be able to rescue their working relationship and return it to the uncomplicated place it had once inhabited.

'Sorry? For what?' He shrugged casually, walked towards the door and held it open for her to precede him out of the office, straight into the balmy tropical air that suddenly made him feel as though he was trapped in a greenhouse. 'I asked you to come here. You were quite happy to remain in London and play nursemaid to your sister.'

Jamie bit her lip and stifled the urge to argue with him on that point. He was now her boss once again and she seemed to have lost the right to speak her mind. Besides, he was barely aware of her presence, walking briskly towards the French doors and out onto the breezy veranda. She lagged behind and chose to hover by the door with her arms folded.

Ryan sprawled on one of the wicker chairs and stretched out his legs. 'I also persuaded you to play a role because it suited me, so I have no idea what you're sorry for, unless it's for climbing into bed with me—but, hell, we're both adults. We knew what we were signing up for.' He glanced over his shoulder to where she was dithering slightly behind him. 'Why don't you go and see to the arrangements for our flights back? And then you might as well use the rest of the day to get your things together.'

Jamie left him staring out at the distance. Effectively dismissed, she miserably obeyed orders. She managed to get them flights for the following day, which was a relief. In front of his mother, they made a passable show of togetherness but she retired very early for bed.

Landing in London was like reconnecting with a place she no longer recognised. After the sharp, bright technicolor of the island, and the slow, tranquil pace of life, the hustle and bustle of the grey streets and even greyer skies was a mournful reminder of what she had lost.

She felt like a different person—the person who had lived life in the slow lane, imagining herself to still have feelings for Greg, had disappeared. Ryan had awakened her and, for better or worse, she was no longer going to be the careful person in the background she had spent years cultivating.

For that, she was thankful. On every other score, the bright smile she kept pinned to her face bore no relation to the misery and confusion she was feeling inside—especially when, as they delivered Vivian to Claire and Hannah, both of whom had made the trip to the airport to collect their mother, she saw Ryan pick up a mobile on his cell phone.

She knew him so well that when he turned away, lowered his voice, gave that throaty chuckle, she realised that he was on the phone to a woman.

'Please tell me that I won't start back tomorrow with the usual delivery of flowers for the new woman in your life?' Her voice threatened to break when she said this, but it didn't, and in fact she was rather proud of her composure. The sun had turned him into a bronzed god and her breath caught in her throat as memories flooded her head, making her feel a little dizzy, but she kept smiling and smiling, even when he raised his eyebrows in a question.

'No idea what you're talking about.'

'Okay!' she said brightly, sticking out one hand to hail a cab.

'But if it did,' Ryan drawled, 'would it bother you?'

Jamie tugged her coat protectively around her. 'Honestly?'

Ryan felt an uninvited leap of interest. After the dance they had been doing around one another for the past day and a half, the thought of cutting through the facade was irresistible. A little honesty? Who could resist? He tilted his head to one side in a semi-nod.

'It wouldn't feel good.' Jamie kept her voice low, even and well-modulated. 'But I would do it, so please don't think that you would have to tiptoe around me. The working relationship we have is much more important to me than a brief fling. In fact...' She paused and glanced around her to where Ryan's driver was patiently waiting. He would be going straight to the office. She, on the other hand, would be returning to see what damage her sister had inflicted on her house in her absence.

'In fact...?' Ryan prompted.

'In fact, all said and done, you've done me a huge favour.'

'What are you talking about?'

'You've taken me out of cold storage. I think I had spent far too long kidding myself that I still had feelings for Greg. You made me see what a big mistake it was to bury myself in the past.' There was a strong element of truth in that but, more importantly, Jamie liked the control she could impose on her fractured life by rationalising her behaviour. She could almost kid herself that everything had happened for the best and, if she could convince herself of that, then she would be able to cope with Ryan whispering sweet nothings down the end of a phone to another woman. It made sense, and Jamie had to be sensible again. Her life depended on it.

'I'm a different person now. I'm going to really start enjoying London. I can see that I wasted a long time hibernat-

ing. Not consciously, of course, but I took a back seat and I
shouldn't have. So, that's all I wanted to say. Except, well,
your mother still thinks that we're about to tie the knot any
second now… Can I ask you when you intend to tell her the
truth?'

'Does it matter? After all, you're out of the equation now,'
Ryan told her politely.

'Yes, but *what* will you tell her? I'm very fond of Vivian
and the more I've got to know her the less I've liked what
we did.'

'Don't worry. I won't blacken your name, Jamie.'

'Thank you, because I would quite like to see your family. Some time.'

'That won't be appropriate.'

'Right. I understand.' She felt a lump in her throat and
looked away quickly.

'My mother is given to fond flights of fancy,' Ryan continued. 'And I don't want her to be encouraged into thinking that we're still an item. It won't work. As soon as she's
settled back, I'll break the news to her that we've parted
company, on perfectly amicable terms that allow us to carry
on working harmoniously together. Rest assured that if my
mother apportions blame to anyone, it'll be to me.'

'She'll be upset.' Jamie knew what it was like to live in a
bubble and how painful it could be when that bubble burst.

'In which case, I shall have to make sure that I give her
something else to think about and look forward to,' Ryan
murmured, leaning down so that Jamie felt his warm breath
against her ear, tickling her and doing all sorts of familiar
things to her body.

'What do you mean?'

'Well.' He straightened up and shot her a devilish grin
that made her toes curl. 'Maybe this has been a learning
curve for both of us!'

'Really?'

'Of course! You haven't got the monopoly on life lessons, Jamie. Whilst you're busy getting out there and discovering London, let's just say that *I* might finally start my search for the perfect partner. My mother wants me to settle down. The harridans keep nagging me. Yes, maybe it's time for me to think about tying the knot!'

CHAPTER NINE

RYAN looked at the blonde perched on the sofa in his office and she looked expectantly back at him. She was in search of an evening of fun, involving a very expensive meal, a very expensive club and possibly a very expensive trinket to wear around that slender, white neck of hers, something that would complement the tumble of vanilla curls that fell to her waist in artful disarray.

It was Friday night and he couldn't think of a single reason why he shouldn't shove the work to one side and look forward to the prospect of what was prominently an offer.

Instead, he found himself thinking of excuses to back out of his evening of fun and he scowled at his own idiocy.

Where was Jamie? Ever since they had returned to London two weeks ago, she had turned into an annoying clock watcher. Only now did he realise how accustomed he had become to her willingness to work long hours at his beck and call, and only now did he realise how much of his time had been spent in her company. A Friday evening had often seen them brainstorming something, occasionally with some of his computer whizz-kids who could be relied upon to sacrifice entire weekends in the pursuit of tweaking computer programs, very often on their own, calling in a takeaway and enjoying it with files and papers spread between them on his desk.

Gone; all of it. She was still the super-efficient secretary, always polite and unfailingly professional, but now she left when she should leave and didn't arrive a second before she was due.

Clearly she was pursuing that fabulous single life she had mentioned when they had parted company at the airport. He wouldn't know. She never mentioned a word of it and there was no way that he was going to play the loser and actually show an interest.

Abigail, whom he had now seen a couple of times and of whom he was already beginning to tire, leaned forward, flashed him a coy smile and stood up.

'Are we actually going to go out, Ryan, baby? Please don't tell me that we're going to spend Friday night in this office!'

'I've spent many an enjoyable Friday night here,' Ryan grated, but standing up and moving to help her with her coat.

'Well.' She pouted and then stretched up to briefly peck him on the lips. 'That's not *my* sort of thing. And good luck finding any woman who would enjoy that!'

Which brought him right back to Jamie. Pretty much everything seemed to bring him right back to Jamie these days. He didn't want to feel driven to watch her, but he did. He absorbed the way she moved, the way she leaned forward when she was studying something in front of her, tucking her hair behind her ear and frowning. He absorbed the way she nestled the telephone against her shoulder when she spoke so that she could do something else at the same time and then the way she lightly massaged her neck afterwards. He noticed how she shifted her eyes away from him when he spoke to her, and the faint colour that stole into her cheeks, which was the only giveaway that under the polite surface all was not as evenly balanced as she would have him believe.

Or was it?

Ryan didn't know and he hated that. Having always found it easy to walk away from relationships once they had begun to out-stay their welcome, he was finding it impossible to do the same with this one. Why? He could only think that it was because what they had had been terminated before it had had time to run its course. It was unfinished business. How could he be expected to treat it with a sanguine shrug of the shoulders?

Also, *he* hadn't generated the break-up. Ryan knew that that was nothing but wounded male pride, but it went into the mix, didn't it? And the whole mix, for him, was adding up to a very unpleasant fixation which he was finding hellishly difficult to shift.

It would help if he could generate more of an interest in her replacement.

It was after ten by the time they entered the exclusive club in Knightsbridge. They had dined in one of the most expensive restaurants in London, where Abigail had made gentle digs about his choice of dress. He had ordered more wine to get him over his growing irritation. She had spent far too long trying to engage his attention on various titbits of gossip concerning friends he didn't know and could not care less about. She bored him with anecdotes about the world of acting, which made him recognise the folly of dating yet another woman who thought that everyone was interested in a bunch of people egotistic enough to imagine that what they did for a living really was of immense interest to the rest of the human race. Abigail tittered, trilled, pouted and flaunted a body that he considered far too thin, really.

The trip to the club would probably mark the death knell of the relationship, if relationship it could be called, and that was the only reason he entered with something approaching a spring in his step.

It took him a few seconds for his eyes to adjust to the dim lighting. The club was intimate, with a number of tables for anyone wanting to dine or just sit and enjoy the spectacle of people on the dance floor. The bar area, sleek and very modern, was busy and waiters were doing the rounds, taking orders and pocketing the very generous tips given by the patrons. A live jazz band ensured that the atmosphere remained up market and sophisticated.

Ryan had been to this club a number of times before but this time he was less than impressed by the subdued lighting and eye candy. Maybe he was getting too old for this sort of thing. He was in his thirties now and there was a fine line between trendy and sad. He hadn't seriously intended to start hunting for the perfect marriage partner, as he had nonchalantly told Jamie two weeks previously, but now he wondered whether the time really had come to settle down. After all, he didn't want still to be coming to this place in five years' time, with another Abigail clone hanging on to his arm.

On the verge of telling his date that if she wanted to stay she would be staying on her own, he spotted Jamie, and the shock of seeing his secretary in a *club* was almost enough to make him think that his eyes were playing tricks on him.

Since when did Jamie frequent clubs? Ryan was rocked by the upsurge of rage that filled him. Was this what she had been busily doing on all those evenings since they had returned to London, when she had tripped over herself to join the throng of people leaving the building on the dot of five-thirty? Was this her bid to throw herself into living life in the fast lane?

Abigail had spotted some of her friends and he absently nodded as she disappeared into the crowd by the bar. He was keen to see who Jamie had come with. Her sister, maybe? She hadn't told him the outcome of Jessica's situation. Obviously, that had been just too personal a conversation for her to endure, and pride had stopped him from asking.

However, Jessica must still be on the scene, perhaps having ditched the caring, sharing vet, and was now introducing Jamie to what she had been missing: a sleazy, over-priced night club in the heart of Knightsbridge.

Ryan almost laughed out loud. Had she come to him for advice on where to go, he would willingly have told her, and would have steered her away from the dubious pleasures of seedy joints where middle-aged men tried to pick up young girls.

He had three bottles of the finest champagne sent over to Abigail and her crowd of giggling friends and received a beaming smile of appreciation in return. Then he got himself a whisky and edged over to wait for Jamie. She had disappeared in the direction of the cloakroom, on her own. Several heads—he noticed grimly, several *male* heads—had followed her progress across the crowded room and he could understand why. Gone were the flat shoes, the hair neatly tied up, the sober suit. In fact, gone was everything he associated with his secretary. She had been at pains over the past couple of weeks to revert to projecting the hands-off image, a daily reminder of her position within his company and in his life. She worked for him. She obeyed orders. She carried out her duties. And she locked him out of everything else.

Ryan swallowed a generous slug of whisky and scowled. She had vanished temporarily but her image was still seared into his head: the high stilettos, the tight, outrageously short red dress, the poker-straight hair parted to one side so that it swept across her face, giving her a come-hither look that frankly set his teeth on edge.

He couldn't spot Jessica anywhere or else he would have been tempted to personally congratulate her on the miraculous transformation of her sister.

He had worked his way towards the door through which Jamie would return and was on his second whisky by the time she emerged. He was in just the right position to reach out and grab her by the arm.

It gave her the fright of her life.

Jamie was bitterly regretting the crazy impulse that had brought her to the club with Richard, one of Greg's friends to whom she had been introduced just three days previously. Clubs just weren't her thing. The music seemed very loud, too loud to permit any sort of decent conversation, and it was really dark—especially when wearing very high heels. One wrong move and she would embarrass herself by crashing to the floor, so she had spent the past two hours taking very small steps and only reluctantly allowing herself to be dragged to the dance floor for a couple of upbeat tunes that she recognised.

And Richard… Well, he was a nice enough guy, fashioned in the same mould as Greg. Both of them had been to university together and both had studied to be vets, with Richard opting to work in London while Greg had moved north. He should have made the ideal date and Jamie was sure that, had she met Richard a year before, she would have warmed to his gentle personality and perhaps even embarked on a relationship that might have gone somewhere.

But she had been ruined by Ryan. Her ideal man no longer seemed to be the kind, placid sort. Compared to Ryan, with his vibrant, explosive, overpowering personality, Richard was a shadow of a man and they had established early on that there was no attraction. Which made this excursion to the club slightly more bearable; at least she didn't have to ward off unwanted attention from her date.

But she had dressed to kill and she knew that other men had been looking at her.

She was half-expecting one of them to sidle over and really throw her into a tizzy by asking her to dance, and the sudden tug on her arm as she emerged from the cloakroom where she had been taking cover for as long as had been humanly possible made her jackknife in startled horror.

Jamie turned, mouth open, to give whoever had had the nerve to grab her a piece of her mind. She was also poised to run. The club seemed full of lecherous old men with suspiciously young and beautiful girls dangling like trophies on their arms.

She was so taken aback at seeing Ryan that her mouth literally fell open in startled shock.

'What are *you* doing here?'

'Snap! I was about to ask *you* the same thing. Are you here with your sister? Painting the town red?'

'No, I'm not. And, in fact, I'd better get back to my table. My date will be wondering where I am.'

'Date? Date? What date? Are you telling me that you're here with a *man*?'

Jamie bristled at the tone of his voice. Did he imagine that she was incapable of having a life outside work? She had made it perfectly clear that she did. She had been at pains over the past fortnight to make sure that she left on time and arrived on time, the implication being that she had lots of other exciting things to do with her life aside from devoting all her time to him.

'That would be most people's definition of a date!'

'You came here with him or did you pick him up here? Because if you picked him up here then I would have to warn you to lower your expectations. Most of these guys come here to scout and see what they can pick up.'

Jamie started moving away and Ryan followed her. She had come here with a man. He was outraged at the thought of that. It felt suddenly imperative that he meet this guy. How had she managed to achieve that in the space of two weeks? Of course, he knew how. She had the body of a siren and she had obviously been determined to flaunt it.

His jaw tightened, and he was further disgruntled to discover that the man rising to greet her looked like a decent sort of guy: short brown hair, pleasant smile, wire-rimmed spectacles. Just the sort of man she had once professed to go for. Ryan tried not to scowl as introductions were grudgingly made. She hadn't been aware of him following her but, having turned around to see him towering behind her, she had had no option but to introduce the men to each other.

Next to Ryan, Richard looked flimsy and insubstantial, which further annoyed her.

'Can I be terribly rude, old man—' Ryan stepped in before she could dismiss him, which was what she clearly had in mind '—and ask your date for a dance? She left work ridiculously early today.'

'I left on time!'

'And there were one or two things I needed to discuss with her. I don't normally drag my work out with me, but…'

'Aren't you here with someone?' Jamie asked tartly, then she lowered her voice to hiss into his hear. 'Or are you one of those men who come here scouting to see what they can pick up?'

'Not my style.' He slipped his arm around her waist, already taking it as a given that the neat little guy she had come with would give his permission to have his date whipped away for a few minutes. He didn't look like the sort to put up much of a fight. Indeed, the man was happy to let his hot, sexy date get on the dance floor with someone else's arms wrapped around her, even though the hot, sexy date was making all sorts of noises about feeling tired and needing to sit it out.

'Tired?' Ryan murmured in a low, velvety drawl that had her skin breaking out in goose bumps. 'Surely not? How are you going to paint any town red if you're yawning at eleven on a Friday evening?'

The music had obligingly shifted from fast to slow, and Jamie stiffened as he pulled her towards him in a clinch that was far too intimate for her liking. She tried to pull back and he tugged her closer, resting his hand on the small of her back, reminding her of what it felt like to be touched by him. It was not a memory she wanted to linger over.

'I'm sure your date wouldn't approve of us dancing,' she said primly, following his lead and trying to hold herself as rigidly as possible. 'Where is she, anyway?'

'Behind you—a quarter to ten. Bright blue dress. Blue shoes.' He swung her around so that Jamie had a perfect view of a tall blonde with lots of long, tousled blonde hair and long, long legs. The pull of jealousy was so overpowering that she felt momentarily giddy.

Ryan had kept this one quiet. There had been no emails popping up on his computer, the password for which Jamie had, no breathy phone calls, no mention of anything having to be rearranged so that he could fit in his latest woman.

She didn't want to think about it, but she did. Was this one the serious one?

'She's very pretty,' Jamie said crisply. 'Have you introduced her to your mother as yet?'

'My mother,' he said into her ear, dipping her which made her feel very exposed in her too revealing dress, 'has yet to learn that you and I have broken up.'

'You mean you haven't told her?'

'No opportunity. Who's the guy, Jamie? Now that you've quizzed me about my date.'

'I haven't quizzed you!'

'Are you trying to avoid my question?' Her breasts against his chest were turning him on and he drew back slightly rather than risk having her feel his erection pushing against his zip.

'I don't see that it's any of your business.'

'I'm concerned about you. We *were* almost married, don't forget.'

'We were *never* almost married!'

'My mother would probably disagree. So I don't feel it's out of place to tell you that it's a big, bad world out there and you don't have much experience of it. In the space of a couple of weeks, you've managed to get yourself a man. He could be anybody.'

'How dare you?' Jamie gritted. 'I don't believe I'm hearing this!'

'You should be flattered that I continue to take an interest in your welfare. That guy may have a neat haircut and wear deodorant but it doesn't necessarily make him one of the good guys.'

Jamie almost snorted in disgust. Did Ryan Sheppard consider *himself* one of the good guys? Good guys didn't string women along! She bit back the temptation to ask him whether his date for the night—the one who had been abandoned in favour of his secretary for no other reason than he was incurably *nosy*—would categorise him as a 'good guy' when she was probably after love, marriage and the whole fairy-tale story. Chances were slim that he would deliver.

In fact, she wanted to ask him just how serious he was about the blonde. But there was no way that she was going to do that. The past two weeks had been agonising. Every day had been a challenge to not look at him, not react to him, desperately try to pretend that she was over whatever passing fling they had enjoyed. She wasn't going to encourage any kind of personal conversation now, and it infuriated her that just being here with him, seething at everything he had just said, still made her feel more alive than she had felt ever since she had returned to London.

'You read the papers. You watch the news. Low lifes are everywhere and some of them do a good job of passing for normal.'

'Well, thank you very much for you concern and your wise words, Ryan, but you can relax. Richard comes with personal recommendations.'

'Really? Spill the beans.'

'Greg introduced me to him, if you must know. He and Greg went to university together and Richard works in London.'

'Another vet? Didn't you get your fill of guys who miss their sickly animals whenever they're away from them for too long?'

'I'm not going to stand here and listen to this.'

'You're not standing. You're dancing.' He twirled her around and watched as the colour mounted in her cheeks and her hair became tangled and dishevelled. 'And is vet-number-one here with his erstwhile wife?'

The music stopped but when Jamie would have walked off he kept her firmly anchored by virtue of his fingers curled around her wrist. Out of the corner of his eye, he could see Abigail looking at them with scowling displeasure, and he knew that he should go across to her, at least make a show of wanting to spend some time in her company.

Without releasing Jamie, he beckoned across a waiter, who magically materialised, and whispered something into his ear. A few more bottles of champagne, he reasoned, to be delivered to the tall blonde in the blue dress—and his most sincere apologies, but he had business to discuss with his secretary. The thought of abandoning his conversation with Jamie was out of the question.

'I'm sure your date won't mind if we trip the light fantastic for a bit longer. And you were going to tell me about Vet One and your sister.'

Jamie gave an exasperated sigh. She didn't want this. She didn't want to be dancing with him, to feel his hand resting on her waist and the heat from his body scorching her. She was aware of the guilty thrill spreading through her body and she didn't want that either. She reasoned that it would do no good to storm off in a petulant strop. She was only dancing with him, for heaven's sake! And, besides, Ryan could be as tenacious as a dog with a bone. Did she really want him following her to her table? Joining them? Calling across his girlfriend to share the fun and laughter? No! One more dance and he would be gone and she would be able to breathe properly, she told herself fiercely.

'They've patched things up,' she said reluctantly and Ryan held her back so that he could look at her with interest.

'Why haven't you told me this before?'

'I didn't think that you would be that interested.'

'I'm cut to the quick, Jamie.' His voice was light, but he was surprised to discover that he didn't like being kept out of the loop with this information. Hell, she had retreated back into her impenetrable fortress and slammed the door firmly in his face. 'What happened?'

'Long story.'

'I'm happy to keep dancing until you've got it off your chest.'

'I had a heart-to-heart with Jessica when I got back to London.' Jamie was distracted enough not to notice the way he had pulled her closer to him. She thought back to that fateful conversation with her sister. It had been the best thing she had ever done and for that, she knew, she owed a great deal of thanks to Ryan and his family. She had seen, first hand, how relationships between family members should operate. She had witnessed how important it was to be open and honest.

She had also not been in the best of moods, back in her house, when she had been confronted with a sister who had not budged in her stance that marriage was a bore and she was due a life of fun and excitement. Greg was still there trying to play the persuasive card and so, it seemed, were all the ensuing arguments.

For the first time in both their lives, Jamie had sat her sister down and really given her a piece of her mind.

'I told her that it wasn't acceptable for her to descend on me and not really give a hoot whether she was disrupting my life or not. I told her that she was thoughtless and inconsiderate and that she was old enough to sort out her problems. I also said that she was being an utter fool, that Greg was crazy about her, that he was a treasure, and that if she decided to end the relationship then she should do it and stop dithering. Most of all I told her that she would have to sort things out somewhere else because I was fed up with both of them in the house.'

'A red-letter day for you, in other words,' Ryan murmured. Wisps of her hair brushed his lips and he stifled a shudder of pure craving. When she looked up at him with an open, genuine smile, the first he had glimpsed since they had returned to London, he was overwhelmed with the crazy sensation of just not feeling right in his own skin.

'It all came out then. Jessica told me that she was terrified of getting pregnant and losing her figure. I suppose I always envied her. She did what she wanted to do, and she always pulled it off because she was so beautiful, while I stayed in the slow lane, always being responsible, always there to pick up the pieces.'

Talking to him, Jamie realised how much she had missed it. It was unbelievable that in such a short period of time she had become accustomed to sharing her thoughts with him and appreciating his always humorous, always intelligent take on whatever she had had to say.

She felt a suspicious lump at the back of her throat and looked away quickly. It was very important not to give in to all those waves of nostalgia and regret that had a nasty habit of sneaking up on her when she wasn't looking. She had to remember that they had moved on from that place of lovers. He had a new girlfriend—probably a model or an actress, by the looks of her—thereby proving that he would always run true to form, that *she* had been nothing but a novelty to be enjoyed on the run. And she, in turn, had been making a huge effort to get out there. Well, she had accepted a date, which was a promising start.

'So there you have it!' she told him brightly. 'Not a particularly interesting story.'

'Let me be the judge of that. So where was hubby when all this soul-searching was taking place?'

'Out meeting Richard for a drink.'

'How very thoughtful of him to introduce the two of you.'

Jamie was finding it hard to recall exactly what Richard looked like. As usual, Ryan's image superimposed itself on everything and she felt angry and helpless at the same time at his way of just taking over her thoughts.

'Yes. We hit if off instantly.'

'Did you, now?' Ryan said through gritted teeth.

'Maybe I have a thing for vets!' she trilled gaily. 'Just like you have a thing for actresses and models.' Jamie hadn't wanted to say that, but the words popped out of her mouth, and her heart sank a little when he didn't utter a blanket denial to her sweeping generalisation.

'Maybe you do. Well, make sure that you give me ample warning if you decide to get married and start having a brood of children.'

'I don't think that marriage is something to be rushed into. Besides, I've only been out with Richard…' *once* '…a couple of times.' She smiled politely and drew away from him as the song came to an end. 'And, yes, I'll make sure that I tell you well in advance if and when I decide to tie the knot.'

'Hell, Jamie, have you ever heard of playing the field?' Ryan raked his fingers through his hair and glowered at her. A couple of dates and she wasn't denying the possibility that this might be the real thing! He wanted to root her to the spot, involve her in another dance, take the opportunity to tell her that throwing herself into the first relationship that came her way so shortly after they had broken up wasn't the right thing to do, but she was already walking away, threading a path through the crowds.

'You know that's not the way I am!' she told him over her shoulder, her voice bright and casual. 'And please don't follow me back to the table or I shall begin to feel really guilty about your poor girlfriend having to amuse herself.'

'Abigail's perfectly fine.'

'Really? Because she seems to be seething.'

'Question.'

Jamie stopped and looked at him. Even in this crowded place, he dominated his surroundings. His physical beauty leapt out and made a nonsense of all the other men in the cavernous room. No wonder his girlfriend looked put out. The competition in the club was stiff, lots of airhead blondes with long legs and short skirts, and a fair amount of them were openly sizing up the biggest fish in their midst.

'What is it?'

'Have you slept with him yet?'

His light-hearted, bantering tone said it all and an angry flush spread across her cheeks. Was he laughing at her? Was he thinking that she cut a ridiculous figure here, out of her comfort zone, dressed like a bird of paradise but without the streaming long hair and the endless legs? She wanted to hit him, and she balled her hands into fists and narrowed her eyes coldly.

'I really think it's time we ended this conversation, Ryan. I'll see you at work on Monday. Have a good weekend.' She turned away abruptly and walked with quickened strides towards the table, where Richard was waiting for her.

Why, she agonised, couldn't she have fallen for a man like Richard Dent? On paper, he was everything she had always reckoned she would want in a prospective partner. He was pleasant to look at, he was friendly, considerate and thoughtful. He had brought her flowers and had ruefully but manfully accepted it when she had told him that she liked him as a friend but that she wasn't interested in promoting a relationship with him. They had talked and, when she might have expected him to make his excuses and leave as soon as he could, he had insisted that they go out to the club, because why shouldn't friends have fun together?

She tried very hard to focus on what he was saying but her eyes kept straying, searching out Ryan, watching his body language with his girlfriend, torturing herself with thoughts of what they would be getting up to later.

Jamie spotted them leaving when Richard dragged her up to the dance floor for one last dance. Ryan's girlfriend seemed to be doing a great deal of excited gesticulating. He appeared to be ignoring her. Before she could look away, he caught her gaze, held it and then gave a slight inclination of his head. To her it seemed like a mocking salute, and in response she unconsciously and defensively allowed herself to relax in Richard's arms.

Of course it was a foolish, hollow gesture. Whilst he would be heading back to his place to fall into bed with yet another pouting blonde, she would be giving Richard a light embrace, exchanging mobile numbers and promising to meet up for a drink when their diaries permitted.

Her house, when she returned an hour later, seemed eerily empty. Jessica had taken everything with her and once Jamie had cleaned the place it was as though her sister had never been there. They had parted on good terms, and for the first time she wished she had her sister with her, someone to talk to instead of wandering alone into the kitchen where she made herself a cup of coffee and settled down to consider her options.

The reality of seeing Ryan with another woman had come as a brutal shock. Ahead of her stretched an endless future of seeing him with other women, waiting for him to fall in love with one of them. Out there, there would surely be a leggy blonde who had the personality to suck him in. How would she feel when that happened? Would she still be able to plaster a professional smile on her face and pretend that everything was all right? And, if she honestly couldn't see that happening, then surely the only course of action left would be to hand in her resignation?

It seemed like the next step forward and she was doodling on a piece of paper, working out what she would write, how she would explain her defection from a highly paid job which she had always loved, when the doorbell rang.

Jamie could only think that it might be Richard, at nearly one-thirty in the morning.

Still in her small red dress, but with her shoes kicked off in favour of some fluffy bedroom slippers, she wearily pulled open the door to find Ryan lounging outside, hands in his pockets.

'Do you usually open your door at this hour of the morning to anyone who comes calling?' He looked past her, compelled to see whether there was evidence of her date lurking around. 'It's dangerous.' He placed the flat of his hand on the door. 'You're going to ask me what I'm doing here and then you're going to tell me to leave. I'm not leaving. I want to talk to you. No—I *need* to talk to you. Where is your date?'

'He dropped me home and then left.' She hesitated, then took a deep breath. 'Which is just as well, because I need to talk to you too.' In that moment, Jamie made her mind up. She would have to hand in her resignation. She couldn't have Ryan taking time out from his hectic love life to deliver unwanted, uninvited advice to her. She didn't want him preaching to her about things she should or shouldn't do because they had been lovers and therefore he felt a misplaced sense of obligation. She certainly didn't want him thinking that he had a right to show up at her house whenever he felt like it to sermonise about her choices.

She led the way towards the kitchen and made him a mug of black coffee. Then she swivelled the draft copy of her resignation letter towards him.

Ryan stared down at it for a few seconds, during which his brain seemed to grind to a standstill. He picked up the piece of paper and reread her few polite lines but nothing appeared to be sinking in. 'What's this?'

'What does it look like, Ryan? It's my letter of resignation.' She wrapped her hands around the mug and stared at him, her heart racing like someone caught up in a panic attack. 'It's just a draft. I intend to type it out properly and it'll be on your desk first thing on Monday morning.'

'Over my dead body.' He crumpled the letter and tossed it on the table. 'Resignation not accepted!' He stood up, walked across to her, leaned down and shot her a look of savage fury. 'You're not resigning, and you're definitely not going to waste your time with that loser you're dating.'

CHAPTER TEN

'Don't you dare tell me what to do, Ryan Sheppard!' Jamie cringed back in the chair.

'Somebody's got to. For your own good.'

'Is that why you dashed over here? To give me a long lecture on being careful, because I'm obviously too naive and simple-minded to actually know how to live my own life?'

'You can't be serious about that guy after a couple of dates.' He pushed himself away from her and prowled angrily through the small kitchen, his movements jerky and restless. 'Did you tell him about us? Did he ask you to leave your job because of it? Because if that's the case then I'm warning you that the man is no good for you. Can you really see yourself in a position of subservience for the rest of your life?'

Jamie looked at him in complete bewilderment.

'Have you been drinking?' she asked eventually, which earned her a glowering look.

'You would drive any sane man to drink,' Ryan muttered under his breath. 'You told me that marriage wasn't on the cards!'

'Are you *jealous*?'

'Should I be?'

The silence stretched between them. 'Have you done anything that I should be jealous about?' Ryan shook his head and dealt her an accusing look. 'I don't do jealousy. I never have.' Suddenly those standard words which had once been true were exposed for the lie that they were. He was jealous as hell. Wasn't that why he had rushed over to her house? The thought of her being touched by anyone else had galvanised him into frantic action. She was still in her clubbing clothes. Had her date touched her underneath the skimpy little red dress?

Had he just missed the man by a whisker? Suddenly Ryan felt as though he needed something a lot stronger than a mug of black coffee.

'You can't resign,' he said finally. 'I won't let you.'

'Is that because I'm so indispensable? No one's indispensable. I think I'm quoting you when I say that. I can work out my month's notice and I'll make sure that I find someone equally dedicated to replace me.'

'You're irreplaceable.'

Jamie ignored the flush of pleasure those words gave her. Of course, Ryan would think her irreplaceable. Not only was he accustomed to the way she worked, but now that he had slept with her he must truly have entered his comfort zone. The physical side of their relationship might be over, but at the back of his mind he would always have how submissive and responsive she had been with him. It would have been easy for him to assume that that responsiveness would have been lasting, that she would have been even more obliging when it came to working overtime and putting herself out to suit him. Hence his horror now, faced with her resignation.

'Oh, please,' Jamie retorted with biting sarcasm.

'I didn't like seeing you with that guy.'

Jamie was so busy stoking herself into self-righteous anger, that Ryan had had the nerve to invade her privacy so that he could lecture her, that it took a few seconds for those words to sink in.

'What do you mean?'

'It seems that I do get jealous after all,' Ryan muttered in such a low voice that Jamie had to strain her ears to hear what he had said.

He returned to sit at the kitchen table, where he proceeded to frown at the floor before leaning forward, elbows on his thighs, rubbing his eyes with his fingers then looking up at her.

'You're jealous…' Jamie's heart sang.

'You've disappeared every evening on the dot of five-thirty ever since we got back to London.' Ryan glared at her accusingly. 'And then suddenly I discover the reason why. You've been going to clubs and seeing men behind my back.'

'I haven't been *seeing men*, and anyway you've been see-ing women as well,' Jamie countered, without letting on that she had been torn apart with her own little green monsters. And had he told her anything about his latest blonde? No, he had been spectacularly silent on that matter, so how dare he start criticising her for trying to have a life?

'Abigail was a mistake. I have no idea what I was think-ing.'

'Did you…did you sleep with her? Not that I care. I'm just curious.'

'You *should* care. You should care about everything I say and do and think because that's how I feel about you. And, no, I didn't sleep with her. I wasn't even tempted.'

Jamie breathed in sharply, almost not wanting to exhale just in case she broke the spell. Had he just said what she thought he had, or was she just imagining it?

'You didn't even tell me about your sister.'

'I…I was scared to carry on confiding in you, Ryan. I felt that we had been down that road and that if we were to continue working together then things would have to go back to where they had once been. I would have to start learning how to keep my private life to myself.'

'I was cut out of the loop and I didn't like it,' Ryan told her heavily.

Jamie felt giddy when their eyes met. Her mouth was dry and suddenly the kitchen just wasn't the right place to be having this kind of conversation. Her thoughts were in a muddle and she was beginning to ache from the hard kitchen chair. She needed to sink into something soft and yielding that would mould her trembling body.

'Perhaps we should go into the sitting room,' she suggested in a shaky voice. 'And if you're finished with that coffee I can make you another.'

'Because you think I need to sober up? I've had a bit to drink, but I'm by no means drunk.'

Jamie didn't say anything. She walked into the sitting room, very conscious of him following behind her. She had no idea what to make of what he had said to her. He was jealous; he *cared* about what she thought. He stridently, aggressively and possessively wanted her to care about what he thought. And he hadn't slept with the blonde bombshell.

Every instinct in her was nourishing the fragile shoot of hope that had begun to grow, but experience was still holding fast. She had made mistakes in the past. She forced herself to remember Greg. In retrospect, he had been nothing, but at the time she had happily built castles in the air and started hoping.

And then, with Ryan, she had fallen for him and had kidded herself that hopping into bed with him had been a moment of complete recklessness that she had long deserved. She had blinded herself to the obvious, which was that she had more than wanted him. She had needed him, was dependent and addicted to him. Then, once they had slept together, she had immersed herself in the pretence of being involved for Vivian's benefit, and those important lines between reality and fantasy had become blurred. She had started hoping for things. She seemed to make a habit of it.

So now, although she was badly tempted to take everything he said at face value and put the best possible interpretation on it, she resisted. Where would it get her? Was he just after a few more weeks or months with her because the leggy blondes were not quite doing it for him at this point in time? Or was he interested in having her around because he had chickened out of telling his mother the truth and he wanted to buy a little more time before he broke the news to her?

'I don't understand why you're telling me all of this now,' she said as soon as she was on the sofa. 'If you cared so much about being out of the loop, then it's funny that you didn't show any interest for the past couple of weeks.' She looked at him levelly. He had taken up position on one of the squashy chairs. It allowed her important breathing space. Still, she knew that her body was alive with emotion. Like an illness, the symptoms of which were branded in her brain, she could recognise all the familiar responses he evoked in her.

'You dumped me, Jamie.'

'I had to.' She looked away quickly, her face colouring. 'I'm not casual enough for a prolonged fling. I told you that at the time and I meant it.'

'Which brings us back to the date. Has he made you promises you think he'll keep?'

Jamie sighed and shook her head. 'It was nothing serious,' she confessed. 'Richard is a really nice guy, but...' *But he's not you.* 'But maybe I don't go for vets after all.'

'And I don't go for leggy blondes, now that we're on the confession bandwagon. It doesn't matter what glossy magazine they've stepped out of.'

Jamie held her breath, then exhaled slowly. 'What do you mean?' She watched cautiously as he stood up and walked towards her, hesitating before sitting down on the sofa.

'I used to, once. A hundred years ago. I thought it was what I wanted—a rich, rewarding work life and fun on the side with women who didn't make demands. I don't know when things started to change,' Ryan admitted with painful honesty. 'You came to work for me, Jamie, and you spoilt everything I had always taken for granted.'

'What do you mean?' But the open vulnerability on his face made her heart swell. When he reached out to stroke her wrist, she didn't pull her hand away.

'I got accustomed to having a relationship with a woman on my own level.'

'We didn't *have* a relationship.'

'I'm not talking about a sexual relationship. I'm talking about an emotional and intellectual relationship. Those are the strongest building blocks on the face of the earth, only I didn't realise it at the time. I just knew that I was increasingly frustrated with the women I dated. They were empty and shallow and they bored me. And then we went away, and we didn't just sleep together. We…we talked.

'For the first time this week, it finally dawned on me just how much time we spent together, how much I enjoyed that and just how far down the road I'd gone when it came to really having a conversation with a woman. When it was gone, it was like something I should have appreciated and valued had disappeared from my life and I didn't know how to reclaim it. We got back to London and you were never around. I missed you. I miss you.'

'You miss me?' Jamie stretched those three words out for as long as she could, so that she could savour every syllable.

'When you kissed me at that Christmas party, it was as if a light had suddenly started shining from nowhere. I told myself that you had only kissed me to make the vet jealous. I figured that you were still emotionally wrapped up with him.'

'I stopped being wrapped up with Greg a long time ago. He started going out with my sister, and I can't even remember being terribly upset about it, although I thought that I *should* be.' That episode was like a dream she had had a million years ago. It was something that was no longer relevant in her life at all. 'I kissed you because my sister was going to. She'd had too much to drink. I wasn't about to let Greg see his wife kissing some other guy under a sprig of mistletoe. That would have been the end of their marriage and there was no way I was going to allow that to happen.'

'And that's the only reason why?'

Jamie went bright red.

'I've bared my soul,' Ryan murmured. 'Are you going to shoot me down in flames now by not being truthful with me? I can take it.'

'I kissed you because I wanted to.' She met his eyes, held them. 'I didn't think so at the time but, looking back on it afterwards, yes, I wanted to kiss you because I'd been attracted to you practically from the first time I set eyes on you, Ryan Sheppard.'

'But you once told me that attraction wasn't enough.'

Her breath caught in her throat. They had both said a lot to each other, but the word 'love' had never entered the conversation. She had never allowed herself to wear her heart on her sleeve and even now it floated unspoken around them, challenging either one to pluck it out of the silence and give it a name. When Jamie thought about doing that, her throat went dry and she felt as though she suddenly had cotton wool stuffed in her mouth.

'I remember,' she croaked shakily.

'You were right.' He fiddled with her fingers but Jamie

could hardly concentrate on that. 'I fell in love with you and I don't even know when it happened. When we finally made love, I never stopped to ask myself why it just felt so damned *right*.'

'You fell in love with me?'

'You look shocked,' he said wryly. 'I'm surprised you haven't put two and two together already. I said goodbye to Abigail and couldn't wait to get over here. I was going mad wondering what you were getting up to with your date. He looked like the kind of sensitive, tree-hugging guy who wouldn't hesitate to pour out his feelings after five seconds. I felt like I'd left things too late.'

'I can't believe you love me.' Jamie reached out one tremulous hand to stroke his cheek. 'I love you too. I feel like I've waited all my life for you. When we made love and got involved in that pretend relationship for your mother, I knew that I couldn't carry on with it when we got back here because I would want much more. I knew you were into flings, and I knew that if you tossed me aside I would never recover. I thought that I had to be proactive.'

Ryan pulled her into him. After two weeks, the feel of her body against his was like a taste of coming home.

They fell back onto the sofa and she wriggled on top of him. It was unbelievably good. When he began kissing her, she was completely lost.

Later, she struggled to remember how they had made it up to her bedroom. She had a fuzzy recollection of clothes being discarded along the way.

She gave herself to him with a blissful sense of completion. There was no other way of describing it—Ryan Sheppard *completed* her. Without him, she was lacking.

Afterwards, with his arms around her, he murmured softly into her hair, 'Now, my darling, I never want to go through the torture I've been through over the past few

weeks. I'm afraid your brief taste of clubbing is at an end,
unless I'm there, keeping a watchful eye on you. And the
only way I can think of doing that is to marry you. So...will
you marry me, Jamie?'

'Yes!'

'As soon as possible?'

'Absolutely!'

'I'm a happy man.' He lay back, one arm flung over the
side of the bed, and smiled with contentment as Jamie covered him with little kisses.

Left to his own devices, Ryan would have married Jamie
within the week. His mother, however, was having nothing
of the sort. She wanted a full-blown affair, and in spite of
his low-level grumbling—for he couldn't understand why
on earth she hadn't already had her fill of full-blown weddings with his three sisters—Jamie was thrilled to accommodate her.

She was even more thrilled when Jessica offered to come
down to London for a week so that they could go bridal shopping together.

'But no clubs and drinking,' Jamie felt compelled to warn
her sister the week before she was due to arrive, and her
warning was met with a burst of laughter.

'You have my word,' Jessica readily agreed. 'I'm pregnant! I was going to wait and surprise you with a picture of
the scan, but I might just as well tell you over the phone. So
when we're not looking for the perfect ivory wedding dress
you might find yourself checking out prams and cots.'

Jessica had changed in more ways than one. Having confessed to feelings of deep insecurity at the thought of losing
her figure should she get pregnant, she had finally surfaced
to realise that Greg loved her for the person she was and not

for the perfect figure she happened to have had imprinted in her genetic code.

And, as Jessica always did, she was now throwing herself into her pregnancy, even travelling with her baby books which she insisted Jamie read.

'Because you'll be next…'

It proved to be an accurate prediction.

One year and two months later, Jamie would sit in Ryan's apartment with a dark-haired, gloriously chubby-faced Isobella gurgling in her basket next to her and with details of country properties spread out on the table.

'London,' Ryan had announced, 'is no place to bring up a baby. At least, not central London.'

So they were moving out to Richmond. Not too far, but far enough from the traffic and chaos. As was Ryan's style, once the decision had been made he moved into immediate action, sourcing houses and submerging himself so well into the role of the domesticated man that Jamie could only sit back and smile.

Loving her, he had told her, had changed him. The birth of his first child had changed him even more. Gone was the workaholic and in its place was a man who enjoyed immersing himself in all the small things that made life go round.

Now Jamie joined him in the kitchen, where he was pouring them both a glass of wine, and she dangled a brochure in front of her.

'Not too big,' she said, 'not too small and in the perfect location…'

'I knew that one would get to you.' He dropped a kiss on her head and grinned. 'Clambering roses, beams, view of the park… We'll have to wait and see, though. As we both know, size matters.'

Jamie giggled and warmed at the teasing hunger in his eyes.

'But…' he murmured, stepping towards her so that she could feel the size and girth of his erection. 'I actually wasn't talking about that. I was talking about the house. It has to be big enough for, let's just say, all future additions.'

Ryan couldn't imagine greater contentment. He cupped her head with his hand and kissed her tenderly on her lips. 'And,' he said, moving to hold her tighter and deepening his kiss, 'the sooner we get started on those additions, the better.…'

* * * * *

Caroselli's Christmas Baby

Michelle Celmer

For Steve, who truly is my hero.

Michelle Celmer is a bestselling author of more than thirty books. When she's not writing, she likes to spend time with her husband, kids, grandchildren and a menagerie of animals.

Michelle loves to hear from readers. Visit her website, www.michellecelmer.com, like her on Facebook or write to her at PO Box 300, Clawson, MI 48017, USA.

Prologue

"As your attorney, and your friend, I have to say, Giuseppe, that I think this is a really bad idea."

Giuseppe Caroselli sat in his wingback leather chair—the one his wife, Angelica, God rest her saintly soul, had surprised him with for his eighty-fifth birthday—while Marcus Russo eyed him furtively from the sofa. And he was was right. This scheme Giuseppe had concocted had the potential to blow up in his face, and create another rift in a family that already had its share of quarrels. But he was an old man and time was running low. He could sit back and do nothing, but the potential outcome was too heartbreaking to imagine. He had to do *something*.

"It must be done," he told Marcus. "I've waited long enough."

"I can't decide which would be worse," Marcus said, rising from the sofa and walking to the window that boasted a picturesque view of the park across the street, though most of the leaves had already fallen. "If they say no, or they actually say yes."

"They've left me no choice. For the good of the family, it must be done." Carrying on the Caroselli legacy had always been his number one priority. It was the reason he had fled Italy at the height of the Second World War, speaking not a word of English, with a only few dollars in the pocket of his trousers and his *nonni*'s secret family chocolate recipe emblazoned in his memory. He knew the Caroselli name was destined for great things.

He'd worked scrimped and saved until he had the money to start the first Caroselli Chocolate shop in downtown Chicago. In the next sixty years the Caroselli name grew to be recognized throughout the world, yet now it was in danger of dying out forever. Of his eight grandchildren and six great-grandchildren, there wasn't a single heir to carry on the family name. Though his three sons each had a son, they were all still single and seemed to have no desire whatsoever to marry and start families of their own.

Giuseppe had no choice but to take matters into his own hands, and make them an offer they simply could not refuse.

There was a soft rap on the study door, and the butler appeared, tall and wiry and nearly as old as his charge. "They're here, sir."

Right on time, Giuseppe thought with a smile. If there was one thing that could be said about his grandsons, they were unfailingly reliable. They were also as ambitious as Giuseppe had been at their age, which is why he believed this might work. "Thank you, William. Send them in."

The butler nodded and slipped from the room. A few seconds later his grandsons filed in. First Nicolas, charming and affable, with a smile that had been known to get him out of trouble with authority, and into trouble with the ladies. Following him was Nick's cousin Robert, serious, focused and unflinchingly loyal. And last but not least, the oldest of all his grandchildren, ambitious, dependable Antonio Junior.

His joints protesting the movement, Giuseppe rose from his chair. "Thank you for coming, boys." He gestured to the couch. "Please, have a seat."

They did as he asked, all three looking apprehensive.

"You are obviously curious as to why you're here," Giuseppe said, easing back into his chair.

"I'd like to know why we had to keep it a secret," Nick said, his brow furrowed with worry. "And why is Marcus here? Is something wrong?"

"Are you ill?" Tony asked.

"Fit as a fiddle," Giuseppe said. Or as fit as an arthritic man of ninety-two could be. "There is a matter of great importance we must discuss."

"Is the business in trouble?" Rob asked. For him, the company always came first, which was both a blessing and a curse. Had he not been so career-focused, he could be married with children by now. They all could.

"This isn't about the business," he told them. "At least, not directly. This is about the Caroselli family name, which will die unless the three of you marry and have sons."

That earned him a collective eye roll from all three boys.

"*Nonno,* we've been through this before," Nick said. "I for one am not ready to settle down. And I think I speak for all of us when I say that another lecture isn't going to change that."

"I know, that's why this time I've decided to offer an incentive."

That got their attention. Tony leaned forward slightly and asked, "What sort of incentive?"

"In a trust I have placed the sum of thirty million dollars to be split three ways when each of you marries and produces a male heir."

Three jaws dropped in unison.

Nick was the first to recover. "You're seriously going to give us each ten *million* dollars to get hitched and have a kid?"

"A *son*. And there are conditions."

"If you're going to try to force us into arranged marriages with nice Italian girls from the homeland, forget it," Rob said.

If only he could be so lucky. And while he would love to see each of them marry a nice Italian girl, he was in no position to be picky. "You're free to marry whomever you please."

"So what's the catch?" Tony asked.

"First, you cannot tell a soul about the arrangement. Not your parents or your siblings, not even your intended. If you do, you forfeit your third of the trust and it will be split between the other two."

"And?" Nick said.

"If I should join your *nonni,* God rest her saintly soul, by the end of the second year and before a male heir is born to any one of you, the trust will be rolled back into my estate."

"So the clock is ticking," Nick said.

"Maybe. Of course, I could live to be one hundred. My doctor tells me that I'm in excellent health. But is that a chance any of you is willing to take? If you agree to my terms, that is."

"What about Jessica?" Nick asked. "She has four children, yet I suspect you've not given her a dime."

"I love your sister, Nick, and all my granddaughters, but their children will never carry the Caroselli name. I owe it to my parents, and my grandparents, and those who lived before them to keep the family name alive for future generations. But I also don't want to see my granddaughters hurt, which is why this must always remain a secret."

"Do you intend to have us sign some sort of contract?" Tony asked, turning to Marcus.

"That was my suggestion," Marcus told him, "but your grandfather refuses."

"No one will be signing anything," Giuseppe said. "You'll just have to trust that my word is good."

"Of course we trust your word, *Nonno,*" Nick said, shooting the others a look. "You've never given us any reason not to."

"I feel the same way about the three of you. Which is why I trust you to keep our arrangement private."

Tony frowned. "What if you die? Won't the family learn about it then?"

"They won't suspect a thing. The money is already put aside, separate from the rest of my fortune, and as my attorney and executor to my will, Marcus and Marcus alone will have access to it. He will see that the money is distributed accordingly."

"What if we aren't ready to start families?" Rob asked.

Giuseppe shrugged. "Then you lose out on ten million dollars, and your third will go to your cousins."

All three boys glanced at each other. Knowing how proud and independent they were, there was still the very real possibility that they might deny his request.

"Do you expect an answer today?" Nick asked.

"No, but I would at least like your word that each of you will give my offer serious thought."

Another look was exchanged, then all three nodded.

"Of course we will, *Nonno,*" Rob said.

Had he been standing, Giuseppe may have crumpled with relief, and if not for gravity holding him to the earth, the heavy weight lifted from his stooped shoulders surely would have set him aloft. It wasn't a guarantee, but they hadn't outright rejected the idea, either, and that was a start. And given their competitive natures, he was quite positive that if one agreed, the other two would eventually follow suit.

After several minutes of talk about the business and family, Nick, Rob and Tony left.

"So," Marcus asked, as the study door snapped closed behind them, "how do you suppose they'll react when they learn there is no thirty million dollars set aside?"

Giuseppe shrugged. "I think they will be so blissfully happy, and so grateful for my timely intervention, that the money will mean nothing to them."

"You have the money, Giuseppe. Have you considered actually giving it to them if they meet your terms?"

"And alienate my other grandchildren?" he scoffed. "What sort of man do you think I am?"

Marcus shook his head with exasperation. "And if you're wrong? If they do want the money? If they're angry that you lied to them?"

"They won't be." Besides, to carry on the Caroselli name—his legacy—that was a risk he was willing to take.

One

Late again.

Terri Phillips watched with a mix of irritation and amusement as her best friend, Nick Caroselli, walked briskly through the dining room of the bistro to their favorite booth near the bar, where they met every Thursday night for dinner.

With his jet-black hair, smoldering brown eyes, warm olive complexion and lean physique, heads swiveled and forks halted halfway to mouths as he passed. But Nick being Nick, he didn't seem to notice. Not that he was unaware of his effect on women, nor was he innocent of using his charm to get his way when the need arose.

Not that it worked on her anymore.

"Sorry I'm late," he said with that crooked grin he flashed when he was trying to get out of trouble. Fat snowflakes peppered the shoulders of his wool coat and dotted his hair, and his cheeks were rosy from the cold, meaning he'd walked the two blocks from the world head-quarters of Caroselli Chocolate. "Work was crazy today."

"I've only been here a few minutes," she said, even though it had actually been more like twenty. Long enough to have downed two glasses of the champagne they were supposed to be toasting with.

He leaned in to brush a kiss across her cheek, the rasp of his evening stubble rough against her skin. She breathed in the whisper of his sandalwood soap—a birth-day gift from her—combined with the sweet scent of chocolate that clung to him every time he spent the day in the company test kitchen.

"Still snowing?" she asked.

"It's practically a blizzard out there." Nick shrugged out of his coat, then stuck his scarf and leather gloves in the sleeve—a habit he'd developed when they were kids, after misplacing endless sets of mittens and scarves—then hung it on the hook behind their booth. "At this rate, we may actually get a white Christmas this year."

"That would be nice." Having spent the first nine years of her life in New Mexico, she'd never even seen snow until she'd moved to Chicago. To this day, she still loved it. Of course, having a home business meant no snowy commute, so she was biased.

"I ordered our usual," she said as Nick slid into his seat.

He loosened his tie, and gestured to the champagne bottle. "Are we celebrating something?"

"You could say that."

He plucked his napkin from the table and draped it across his lap. "What's up?"

"First," she said, "you'll be happy to know that I broke up with Blake."

Nick beamed. "Well, damn, that is a reason to cel-ebrate!"

Nick had never liked her most recent boyfriend—the latest in a long and depressing string of failed relationships. He didn't think Blake had what it took to make Terri happy. Turned out he was right. Even if it did take her four months to see it.

But last week Blake had mentioned offhandedly that his lease was almost up, and it seemed silly that they should both be paying rent when he spent most of his time at her place, anyway. Despite being more than ready to get married and start a family, when she imagined doing it with him, she'd felt…well, not much of anything, actually. Which was definitely not a good way to feel about a potential husband and father of her children. It was proof that, as Nick had warned her, she was settling again.

Nick poured himself a glass of champagne and took a sip. "So, what did he say when you dumped him?"

"That I'll never find anyone else like him."

Nick laughed. "Well, yeah, isn't that the point? He was about as interesting as a paper clip. With half the personality."

She wouldn't deny that he'd been a little, well…bland. His idea of a good time was sitting at the computer, with it's twenty-seven-inch high-def monitor, for hours on end playing *World of Warcraft* while she watched television or read. The truth is, he would probably miss her computer more than her.

"He's an okay guy. He just isn't the guy for me," she told Nick. One day he would meet the game addict of his dreams and they would live a long happy life in cyberspace together.

Their waitress appeared to deliver their meal. A double pepperoni deep-dish pizza and cheesy bread. When she was gone, Nick said, "He's out there, you know. The one for you. You'll find him."

She used to think so, too. But here she was almost thirty with not a single prospect anywhere in her near future. Her life plan had her married with a couple kids already. Which is why she had decided to take matters into her own hands.

"There's something else we're celebrating," she told Nick. "I'm going to have a baby."

He bolted upright and set down his glass so hard she was surprised it didn't shatter against the tiled tabletop. "What? When? Is it Blake's?"

"God, no!" She could just imagine that. The kid would probably be born with a game remote fused to its hands.

Nick leaned forward and hissed under his breath, "Whoever it is, he damn well better be planning to do right by you and the baby."

Always looking out for her, she thought with a shot of affection so intense it burned. When he wasn't getting her into trouble, that is. Although it was usually the other way around. It was typically her making rash decisions, and Nick talking sense into her. This time was different. This time she knew exactly what she was doing.

"There is no *who*," she told him, dishing them each out a slice of pizza. "I'm not actually pregnant. Yet."

Nick frowned. "Then why did you say you're having a baby?"

"Because I will be, hopefully within the next year. I'm going to be a single mom."

He sat back in his seat, looking stunned. "How? I mean, who's going to be the father?"

"I'm going to use a donor."

"A *donor*?" His dark brows pulled together. "You're not serious."

She shoved down the deep sting of disappointment. She had hoped he would understand, that he would be happy for her. Clearly, he wasn't. "Completely serious. I'm ready. I'm financially sound, and since I work at home, I won't have to put the baby in day care. The timing is perfect."

"Wouldn't it be better if you were married?"

"I've pretty much struck out finding Mr. Right. I always said that I wanted to have my first baby by the time I'm thirty, and I'm almost there. And you know that I've always wanted a family of my own. Since my aunt died, I've got no one."

"You've got me," he said, his expression so earnest her heart melted.

Yes, she had him, not to mention his entire crazy family, but it wasn't the same. When the chips were down, she was still an outsider.

"This doesn't mean we aren't going to be friends still," she said. "In fact, I'll probably need you more than ever. You'll be the baby's only other family. Uncle Nicky."

The sentiment did nothing to erase the disenchantment from his expression. He pushed away his plate, as if he'd suddenly lost his appetite, and said, "You deserve better than a sperm donor."

"I don't exactly have the best luck with men."

"But what about the baby?" Nick said, sounding testier by the second. "Doesn't it deserve to have two parents?"

"As you well know, having two parents doesn't necessarily make for a happy childhood."

His deepening frown said that he knew she was right. Though he didn't like to admit it, his childhood had left deep, indelible scars.

"I was hoping you would understand," she said, and for some stupid reason she felt like crying. And she hardly *ever* cried. At least, not in front of other people. All it had ever earned her from her aunt—who didn't have a sympathetic bone in her body—was a firm lecture.

"I do," Nick said, reaching across the table for her hand. "I just want you to be happy."

"This *will* make me happy."

He smiled and gave her hand a squeeze. "Then I'm happy, too."

She hoped he really meant that. That he wasn't just humoring her. But as they ate their pizza and chatted, Nick seemed distracted, and she began to wonder if telling him about having a baby had been a bad idea, although for the life of her she wasn't sure why it would matter either way to him.

After they finished eating, they put on their coats and were walking to the door when Nick asked, "Did you drive or take the bus?"

"Bus," she said. If she thought she might be drinking, she always opted for public transportation. If the man who had plowed into her father's car had only been as responsible, she wouldn't be an orphan.

"Walk back to the office with me and I'll drive you home."

"Okay."

The snow had stopped, but a prematurely cold wind whipped her hair around her face and the pavement was slippery, which made the two-block hike tricky. It was how she rationalized the fact that he was unusually quiet and there was a deep furrow in his brow.

When they got to the Caroselli Chocolate world headquarters building, it was closed for the night, so Nick used a key card to let them in. With a retail store taking up most of the ground floor, the lobby smelled of the chocolate confections lining the shelves. Everything from standard chocolate bars to gourmet chocolate-covered apples.

Nick felt around in his pockets, then cursed under his breath. "I left my car keys in my office."

"You want me to wait down here?"

"No, you can come up." Then he grinned and said, "Unless you're an industrial spy trying to steal the Caroselli secret recipe."

"Right, because we both know what an accomplished cook I am." If there were a way to burn water, she would figure it out. Meaning she ordered out a lot, and the rest of the time ate microwave dinners.

They walked past the receptionist's desk and he used his key card to activate the elevator. Only authorized personnel and approved visitors were allowed above the ground floor. And no one but the Caroselli family and employees with special clearance were allowed in the test kitchen.

Nick was quiet the entire ride up to the fourth floor, and while they walked down the hall to his office. She had to smile as he opened the door and switched on the light, and she saw the lopsided stacks of papers and memos on the surface of his desk, leaving no space at all to work. She suspected that this was why he spent so much time on the top floor in the kitchen.

He opened the desk drawer and pulled out his car keys, but then he just stood there. Something was definitely bugging him and she needed to know what.

"What's the matter, Nick? And don't tell me nothing. I've known you long enough to know when something is wrong."

"I've just been thinking."

"About me having a baby?"

He nodded.

"It's what I want."

"Then there's something we need to talk about."

"Okay," she said, her heart sinking just the tiniest bit, mostly because he wouldn't look at her. And he must have been anticipating a long discussion because he took off his coat and tossed it over the back of his chair. She did the same, then nudged aside a pile of papers so she could sit beside him on the edge of his desk.

He was quiet for several long seconds, as though he was working something through in his head, then he looked at her and said, "You really want to do it? Have a baby, I mean."

"I really do."

"What if I had a better way?"

"A better way?"

He nodded. "For both of us."

Both of them? She failed to see how her plan to have a baby could in any way benefit him. "I'm not sure what you mean."

"I know the perfect man to be the father of your baby. Someone who would actually be around. Someone willing to take financial responsibility for the rest of the baby's life."

Whoever this so-called perfect man was, he sounded too good to be true. "Oh, yeah?" she said. "Who?"

He leaned forward, his dark eyes serious. "Me."

For a second she was too stunned to speak. Nick wanted to have a baby with her? "Why? You've been pretty adamant about the fact that you don't want children."

"Trust me when I say that it will be a mutually advantageous arrangement."

"Advantageous how?"

"What I'm about to tell you, you have to promise not to repeat to anyone. *Ever.*"

"Okay."

"Say, 'I promise.'"

She rolled her eyes. What were they, twelve? *"I promise."*

"Last week my grandfather called me, Rob and Tony to his house for a secret meeting. He offered us ten million dollars each to produce a male heir to carry on the Caroselli name."

"Holy crap."

"That was pretty much my first reaction, too. I wasn't sure I was even going to accept his offer. I'm really not ready to settle down, but then you mentioned your plan…" He shrugged. "I mean, how much more perfect could it be? You get the baby you want and I get the money."

It made sense in a weird way, but her and *Nick?*

"Of course, we would have to get married," he said.

Whoa, wait a minute. *"Married?* Haven't you told me about a million times that you'll *never* get married?"

"You know how traditional *Nonno* is. I don't have a choice. But the minute I have the cash in hand, we can file for a quickie divorce. An ironclad prenup should eliminate any complications…not that I expect there would be any."

"That sounds almost too easy."

"Well, we will have to make it look convincing."

Why did she get the feeling she wasn't going to like this? "What exactly do you mean by *convincing?*"

"You'll have to move into my place."

A fake marriage was one thing, but to *live* together? "I don't think that's a good idea."

"I have lots of space. You can have the spare bedroom and you can turn the den into your office."

Space wasn't the issue. They'd tried the roommate thing right after college, in an apartment more than spacious enough for two people. Between the random girls parading in and out at ridiculous hours—and the fact that Nick never picked up after himself and left the sink filled with his dirty dishes while the dishwasher sat empty, and a couple dozen other annoying quirks and habits he had—after two months she'd reached her limit. Had she stayed even a day longer, it would have either killed their friendship, or she would have killed him.

"Nick, you know I love you, and I value our friendship beyond anything else, but we've tried this before. It didn't work."

"That was almost eight years ago. I'm sure we've both matured since then."

"Have you stopped being a slob, too? Because I loathe the thought of spending the next nine months cleaning up after you."

"You won't have to. I have a cleaning service come in three times a week. And for the record, I'm not particularly looking forward to you nagging me incessantly."

"I do not nag," she said, and he shot her a look. "Okay, maybe I nag a little, but only out of sheer frustration."

"Then we'll just have to make an effort to be more accommodating to each other. I promise to keep on top of the clutter, if you promise not to nag."

That might be easier said than done.

"Think how lucky the kid will be," Nick said. "Most divorced parents hate each other. Mine haven't had a civilized conversation in years. His will be best friends."

He had a good point there. "So that means you'll be a regular part of the baby's life?"

"Of course. And he'll have lots of cousins, and aunts and uncles."

Wasn't a part-time father better than no father at all? And she would never have to worry financially. She knew Nick would take care of the baby. Not that she was hurting for money. If she was careful, the trust her aunt had willed her, combined with her growing web design business, would keep her living comfortably for a very long time. But Nick would see that the baby went to the best schools, and had every advantage, things she couldn't quite afford. And he would be a part of a big, loving, happy family. Which was more than she could say for her own childhood. The baby might even join the Caroselli family business some day.

"And suppose, God forbid, something should happen to you," he said. "Where would the baby go if he was fathered by a donor?"

Having lost her own parents, of course that was a concern. Now that her aunt was gone, there was no family left to take the child if she were in an accident or… Although the baby would probably be better off in foster care than with someone like her aunt. She would have been.

"With me as the father, he'll always have a family." Nick said.

As completely crazy as the idea was, it did make sense. "I think it could work."

He actually looked excited, although who wouldn't be over the prospect of ten million bucks? Why settle for the life of a millionaire when he could be a *multi*millionaire?

"So," he said, "is that an 'I'm still thinking about it,' or is that a definite yes?"

Though she was often guilty for jumping into things without full consideration, maybe in this case overthinking it would be a bad idea. Or maybe she just didn't want the opportunity to talk herself out of it. They would both be getting what they wanted. More or less.

"I just have one more question," she said. "What about women?"

"What about them?"

"Will it be a different girl every other night? Will I have to listen to the moaning and the headboard knocking against the wall? See her traipsing around the next morning in nothing but her underwear and one of your shirts?"

"Of course not. As long as we're married, I wouldn't see anyone else."

"Nick, we're talking at least nine months. Can you even go that long without dating?"

"Do you really mean *dating,* or is that code for sex?"

"Either."

"Can you?"

She could. The real question was, did she want to? But to have a baby, wasn't it worth it?

"Maybe," Nick said, "we don't have to."

"Are you suggesting that we cheat on each other?" Even if it wasn't a real marriage, that could be an obstacle. And while she was sure Nick would have no trouble finding willing participants, with her big belly and swelling ankles, she was fairly certain no men would be fighting for the chance to get into her maternity jeans.

"I'm assuming you plan to use artificial insemination," he said.

She felt a little weird about discussing the particulars, but he was a part of this now. It would be his baby, too. "That or in vitro, which is much more reliable, but crazy expensive. Either way it could take several months."

"Or we could pay nothing at all," he said.

She must have looked thoroughly confused, because he laughed and said, "You have no idea what I'm talking about."

"I guess I don't."

"Think about it." He wiggled his eyebrows and flashed her a suggestive smile.

Wait a minute. He couldn't possibly mean—

"Why pay a doctor to get you pregnant," he said, "when we could just do it the old-fashioned way for free?"

Two

Terri gaped at Nick, her eyes—which were sometimes green and sometimes blue, depending on the light—wide with shock and horror. It took her several seconds to find her voice, and when she did, she said, a full octave higher than her usual range, "That was a joke, right?"

"Actually, I've never been more serious." Nick would be the first to admit it was a pretty radical idea, but on a scale of one to ten, this entire situation had a weird factor of about fifty.

He had given *Nonno's* offer a lot of thought and had come to the conclusion that he just wasn't ready to settle down yet. It wasn't so much the idea of being a father that put him off—he loved kids—but the marriage end of the deal that gave him the willies. His parents had gone through hell, and put Nick and his two older sisters through it, too. Now with his sister Jessica's marriage in trouble, as well, the idea of marital bliss was nothing more than a fairy tale to him. And not worth the pain of the inevitable divorce. Not even for ten million dollars.

It had never occurred to him that the actual marriage could be a sham. Not to mention so mutually advantageous. And who in his family would question the plausibility that after twenty years of devoted friendship, his and Terri's relationship had moved to the next level? The women in his family ate up that kind of romantic garbage.

Terri tucked her long dark hair behind her ears. He'd only seen her do this when she was nervous or uncomfortable, and that wasn't very often. She was one of the most centered, secure and confident people he'd ever known. Sometimes this led to her being a touch impulsive, but in this instance could only work in his favor.

"The sooner this kid is born, the better," he told her. "So why would we spend a lot of time and money on procedures that could take months to work?"

Indecision wrinkled the space between her brows and she picked at the frayed cuff of her sweatshirt. "Aren't you worried that it might make things weird between us?" she asked.

"Maybe a little," he admitted. "But, haven't you ever been curious?"

"Curious?"

He gave her arm a gentle nudge. "You've never wondered what it might be like if you and I..."

It took an awful lot to embarrass her, but there was a distinct red hue working its way across her cheekbones. That was a yes if he'd ever seen one, even if she didn't want to admit it. And he couldn't deny that he'd thought about it himself more than a time or two. She was funny and smart and beautiful, so who could blame him?

"I've never told you this," he said. "But there was a time when I had a pretty serious crush on you."

She blinked. "You did?"

He nodded. "Yep."

"When?"

"Our junior year of high school."

She looked genuinely stunned. "I—I had no idea."

That's because he'd never said a word about it. Up until then, he'd never viewed her in a sexual way. Nor, it seemed, did many other boys. She had been a late bloomer, a typical tomboy, lanky and tall—taller than all the other girls and even a fair share of the boys—and as far from feminine as a girl could be. But she'd spent the entire summer after their sophomore year in Europe with her aunt and something intriguing had happened. She left Chicago a girl, and returned a woman.

Boys in school began paying attention to her, talking about her in the locker room, and he wouldn't deny that she became the subject of a few of his own teenage fantasies. Not that he would have acted on those feelings. They were, after all, only friends, though that fact did little to erase the jealousy he felt when he saw her with other boys, or would hear the rumors of the things she had done with them. And as much as he liked how she changed, he resented her for it. He wanted the old Terri back. But he got over it, of course. What choice did he have?

"Why didn't you tell me?" she asked.

"Aside from the fact that I thought it would probably freak you out?" He shrugged. "It was a crush. I had them all the time. And our friendship was too important to me to ruin over raging teenage hormones."

"But you would be willing to ruin it now?"

"Maybe if we were sleeping together just for the sake of doing it, but this is different. We have a legitimate reason to have sex."

In his experience, romantic love and friendship occupied opposite sides of the playing field, and he would never let one interfere with the other. Which is why he was so sure that if they approached this situation logically, it would work. And when all was said and done, everyone would get exactly what they wanted.

"It's a means to an end," he said. "It wouldn't *mean anything*."

She shot him a look. "That's just what every girl wants to hear when she's considering sleeping with a man."

"You get my point. And yes, it could potentially change our relationship, but not necessarily for the worse. It might even bring us closer together."

She didn't look convinced. Maybe she was opposed to the idea for an entirely different reason.

"Do you have moral objections?" he asked. "Or is it just that you find the idea of sleeping with me revolting?"

She rolled her eyes. "You are *not* revolting. And though it's embarrassing to admit, I had kind of a crush on you once, too."

If that was true, she'd done one hell of a job hiding it. "When?"

"It pretty much started the day I transferred into Thomas Academy school in fourth grade."

He recalled that day clearly, when she'd walked into his class, bitter, sullen and mad as hell. It was obvious to everyone in the elite private school that she was an outsider. And trouble. A fact she drove home that very first day when she had come up behind Nick on the playground and pushed him off his swing, knocking him face-first in the dirt. He wanted to shove her right back, but he'd had it drilled into him by his mother to respect girls, so he'd walked away instead. Which only seemed to fuel her lust for blood.

For days he'd tolerated kicks in the shin, pinches on

the arm, prods in the cafeteria line and endless ribbing from his buddies for not retaliating. With his parents in the middle of a nasty divorce, he'd had some anger issues of his own, and the unprovoked attacks started to grate on him. A week or so later she tripped him on his way to the lunch table, making him drop his tray and spill his spaghetti and creamed corn all over the cafeteria floor and himself. The other students laughed, and something inside Nick snapped. Before he realized what he was doing, he hauled off and popped her one right in the mouth.

The entire cafeteria went dead silent, everyone watching to see what would happen next, and he'd felt instantly ashamed for hitting a weak, defenseless girl.

He would never forget the way he'd stood watching her, waiting for the tears to start as blood oozed from the corner of her lip and down her chin. And how she balled her fist, took a swing right back at him, clipping him in the jaw. He was so stunned, he just stood there. But she wasn't finished. She launched herself at him, knocking him to the floor, and there was nothing girly about it. No biting or scratching or hair-pulling. She fought like a boy, and her fists were lethal weapons. He had no choice but to fight back. To defend himself. Plus, he had his pride, because to a nine-year-old boy, being accepted meant everything.

It had taken three teachers to pry them apart and haul them to the dean's office, both of them bruised and bloody. They were given a fourteen-day in-school suspension, though that was mild compared to the tirade he'd endured from his father, and the disappointment from his mother, who he knew were miserable enough without any help from him.

He spent the next two weeks holed up in a classroom alone with Terri, and as the black eyes faded and the split lips healed, something weird happened. To this day he wasn't sure whether it was mutual admiration or two lost souls finding solace in each other, but they walked out of that room friends, and had been ever since.

"So, you beat the snot out of me because you *liked* me?" he said.

"It wasn't even a conscious thing. Until I looked back at it years later did I realize why I was so mean to you. But once we became friends, I never thought about you in a romantic way."

"Never?"

"Why would I?" she said, but a hot-pink blush crept up into her cheeks. She pushed herself off his desk and walked over to the window, looking out into the darkness, at the traffic crawling past on icy roads.

If she hadn't, why the embarrassment? Why was she running away from him?

He knew he should probably let it go, but he couldn't. "You never thought about what it might be like if I kissed you?"

With her back to him, she shrugged. "You kiss me all the time."

"Not a real kiss." But now that he'd gotten the idea into his head, he couldn't seem to shake it off. He *wanted* to kiss her.

He pushed off the desk, walked over to the window and stood behind her. He put his hands on her shoulders and she jerked, sucking in a surprised breath. "Nick…"

He turned her so she was facing him. She was so tall they were practically nose to nose. "Come on, aren't you the least bit curious?"

"It's just…it would be weird."

He propped a hand on the windowpane beside her

head, so she was blocked in by his arm on one side and the wall on the other. "How will you know until you try?"

He reached up to run his finger down her cheek, and not only was it crimson, but burning hot.

"Nick," she said, but it came out sounding low and breathy. It was a side of her that he didn't see often. A softer, vulnerable Terri, and he liked it. And it occurred to him, as he leaned in closer, that what he was feeling right now wasn't just curiosity. He was turned-on. And it was no longer the childish fantasies of a teenage boy who knew he wanted something, but wasn't quite sure what it was. This time Nick knew exactly what he wanted.

"One kiss," he told her, coming closer, so his mouth was just inches from hers. "And if it's really that awful, we won't ever do it again."

Heat rolled off her in waves. Her pulse was racing, and as she tentatively laid a hand near the collar of his jacket, he could feel her trembling. Was she afraid, or as sexually charged by this as he was? Or was it a little of both? With her hand strategically placed on his chest, she could either push him away, or grab his lapel and pull him in.

Which would it be?

He leaned in slowly, drawing out the suspense. When his lips were a fraction of an inch away, so near he could feel the flutter of her breath, as her fingers curled around the lapel of his jacket…a loud noise from the hallway startled them both and they jumped apart.

Damn it!

Nick walked to the door and looked out to see a member of the cleaning crew pushing her cart down the hall toward the conference room.

He turned, hoping they could pick up where they left off, only to find Terri yanking on her coat. "What are you doing?"

"I really need to get home."

"Terri—"

"This was a mistake, Nick. I think we're better off using a doctor, like I originally planned."

"If that's what you really want," he said, feeling disappointed, but trying not to let it show.

"I'll cover the cost."

As if he would let her do that. "I insist on paying at least half."

She looked as if she might argue, then seemed to change her mind. She nodded and said, "That sounds fair."

He grabbed his coat and shrugged into it. "I'll drive you home."

She didn't say a word as they walked to the elevator, and rode it to the underground parking garage, but he could practically hear the wheels in her mind moving. As much as he wanted to know what she was thinking, he knew better than to ask. If she wanted him to know, she would talk when she was ready. If he tried to drag it out of her, she would clam up. He'd seen her do it a million times. As close as they were, there was always a small part of herself that she vigilantly guarded from everyone, and could he blame her? His parents' relationship may have been a disaster, but at least he had parents. Despite their dysfunctional marriage, they loved him and his sisters. From the time she moved to Chicago, all Terri ever had was an aunt who only tolerated her presence. If she had loved Terri, she had been unable, or unwilling to let it show.

Though he knew it irked her, Nick opened the passenger door for Terri. Normally she would make a fuss about being completely capable of opening her own door thank-you-very-much, but she didn't say a word this time. Anyone who knew Terri was well aware she always had something to say, or an opinion about pretty much everything. Tonight, she was quiet the entire ride to her condominium complex on the opposite side of town.

Nick pulled up in front of her unit and turned to her, but she was just sitting there, looking out the windshield. "Everything okay?" he asked.

She nodded, but didn't move.

"Are you sure? You can talk to me."

"I know. I just..." She shrugged.

Whatever it was, she wasn't ready to discuss it.

"Well, you know where I am if you need me," he said, even though as long as he'd known her, Terri never truly *needed* anyone. She wrote the handbook on self-sufficiency.

He leaned over to kiss her cheek, the way he always did, but she flung open the car door and jumped out before he had the chance. As he watched her dart into the building without looking back, he couldn't help thinking that in her attempt to keep things between them from changing, they already had.

Three

Though she had hoped getting a good night's sleep would make things clearer, Terri tossed and turned all night, then woke the next morning feeling just as confused as she had been when Nick had dropped her at home.

She didn't want their relationship to change. But what she realized last night while he drove her home was that it already had changed, and it was too late to go back. They had opened a door, and there would be no closing it again until they both stepped through. Unfortunately, she had no idea what was waiting on the other side.

After a long and unproductive workday spent wondering what to do next, how they could pull this off without killing their friendship—if they hadn't already—she realized that she'd made her decision last night in his office. She'd just been too afraid to admit it. Not only to him, but to herself. Which was what led her to his apartment this evening. He hadn't tried to contact her all day, by phone or even email, meaning that he was smart enough to realize she needed time to work this through on her own. He was always there when she needed him, but he also knew when she needed space. She realized it said an awful lot about their relationship.

He opened the door dressed in jeans and a T-shirt, with a chef's apron tied around his waist and smudged with what looked like chocolate batter. The scent of something sweet and delicious reached out into the hallway to greet her.

"Hey," he said, looking not at all surprised to see her.

"Can we talk?"

"Of course." He stepped aside to let her in, and she gazed around the high-rise apartment that would be home for the next nine months or so. It was painted in rich, masculine hues, yet it still managed to feel warm and homey, in large part due to the casual-comfy furnishings and the dozens of framed family photos throughout the space.

Nick may have had an aversion to marriage, but when it came to his family, he couldn't be more devoted. She was also happy to see that most of the clutter that had been there last week was gone.

"Come on into the kitchen," he said. "I'm trying a new cake recipe."

A culinary genius, he spent much of his free time cooking and baking. He'd often said that if it wasn't for Caroselli Chocolate, he would have opened his own restaurant, but he would never leave the family business.

On her way through the living room, Terri dropped her purse and coat on the sofa, then followed Nick into his state-of-the-art kitchen, half of which she wouldn't have the first clue how to use. Nor did she have the desire to learn.

"Whatever it is, it smells delicious," she told Nick as she took a seat on one of the three bar stools at the island.

"Triple chocolate fudge," he said. "Jess wants me to make something special for Angie's birthday party next Saturday."

"She'll be eleven, right?"

"Twelve."

"*Really?* Wow. I remember when she was born, how excited you were to be an uncle. It doesn't seem like twelve years ago."

"It goes by fast," he said, checking the contents of one of the three top-of-the-line wall ovens. Then he untied the apron and draped it over the oven door handle—where it would probably remain until someone else put it in the broom closet where it belonged. He leaned against the edge of the granite countertop, folded his arms and asked, "So, enough of the small talk. What's up?"

That was Nick, always getting right to the point. "First, I want to apologize for the way I acted last night. You just…surprised me."

"It's okay. You were a little overwhelmed. I get it."

"But I've been giving it a lot of thought. In fact, it's about the only thing I *can* think about, and I just have one more question."

"Shoot."

"If we do this, if we make the baby the old-fashioned way, can you promise me that afterward things will go back to the way they were? That nothing will change?"

"No. I can't promise that."

She sighed. Did he have to be so damned honest? Couldn't he just humor her into thinking she was making the right choice? But that wasn't Nick. He was a straight shooter, and the only time he sugarcoated was in the kitchen.

"The best I can do is promise you that I'll always be there for you," he said. "We'll always be friends. Whether we use a doctor or do this conventionally, we're going to have a child together. That alone is bound to change things."

He was right, of course. She'd been so focused on the idea of how sleeping together would affect their relationship, that she hadn't truly grasped the enormity of having a child together. She'd wanted a baby so badly, she hadn't let herself fully consider the consequences. She realized now that *everything* would change. The question was, would it be a good change?

"I guess I didn't think this through completely," she told Nick. "Big surprise, right?"

"And now that you have?"

It scared her half to death. She'd been friends with Nick longer than anyone. Longer than she knew her own father. "I'm still hopelessly confused."

"Then we aren't going to do it. You can stick to your original plan and use a donor."

"And what will you do?" The idea of him entering a fake marriage with someone else, having a baby with her, left a knot in her belly.

"I won't do anything," he said.

"What do you mean?"

"I'll admit, I was sort of excited about the idea of having a baby, but only because I would be having it with you."

"But, what about the money?"

"Terri, our friendship means more to me than any sum of money."

She was too stunned to speak.

Nick laughed. "Why do you look so surprised?"

"It's just…I think that's probably the nicest thing anyone has ever said to me."

"I didn't say it to be nice. I said it because it's the truth."

And she felt ashamed that she hadn't trusted him, that she never realized just how much her friendship meant to him. "Let's do it," she said. "Let's have a baby."

Now he was the one who looked surprised. "Maybe you should take a little more time to consider this."

"I don't need more time."

"Are you sure?"

She couldn't recall ever feeling more sure about anything in her entire life. She didn't know why exactly. She just knew. "I want to do this."

"The wedding, the baby, moving in with me. Everything?"

"Everything."

"I guess the only question now is, how soon can we get started?" he asked.

"Well, I'm due to ovulate in two weeks, give or take a day or two. I'd rather not wait another month. The sooner I get pregnant, the better."

"The question is, can we plan a wedding in fourteen days?"

"I guess it depends on the kind of wedding you want."

"I would be happy to do this in front of a judge with a couple witnesses."

"That works for me," she said. Terri hadn't spent her adolescence dreaming of and planning her wedding. And why drop a lot of money on a marriage that was guaranteed to end in divorce?

"There's only one problem with that," he said.

She knew exactly what he was going to say. "Your family would have a fit." If there was one thing that the

Carosellis loved, it was a party. They would never pass up the opportunity to gather together, overeat and drink too much.

"Exactly," he said.

"So, how big are you thinking?"

"Immediate family only, maybe a few people from work."

"Two weeks would be the Saturday before Thanksgiving. I can guarantee most places will be booked."

Nick considered that for a moment, then his face lit up. "Hey, how about *Nonno's* house? It would definitely be big enough. We could have the ceremony in the great room, in front of the fireplace."

"He wouldn't mind?"

"Are you kidding? He would be thrilled. The whole point of this is to get the three of us married off and making babies as soon as possible."

It seemed like a logical choice to her, too. "Call him and make sure it's okay. On such short notice, I'm thinking we should keep it as simple as possible. Drinks and appetizers will be the best way to go."

"My cousin Joe on my mom's side can get us a good deal on the liquor. Make a list of what you think we'll need, then remember that it's my family and whatever you plan to order, double it. And we should call the caterer we use for business events. The food is great, and their prices are reasonable."

"Email me the number and I'll call them." There was so much to do, and so little time. But she was sure they could pull it off. She knew that as soon as his mom and his sisters heard the news, they would be gunning to help.

"You understand that my family has to believe this marriage is real, that we have to look like two people madly in love?"

"I know."

"That means we'll have to appear comfortable kissing and touching each other."

The thought of kissing and touching Nick, especially in front of his family, made her heart skip a beat.

"Can you do that?" he asked.

Did she have a choice? "I can do it."

"Are you sure? Last night when I touched you, you jumped a mile."

"I was just nervous. And confused."

"And you aren't now?"

"I'm trying to look at it logically. Like we're just two people…conducting a science experiment."

Nick laughed. "That sounds fun. And correct me if I'm wrong, but didn't you almost blow up the science lab in middle school?"

Which had taught her the invaluable lesson that when a teacher said chemicals aren't to be mixed, she actually meant it. That, plus a week of suspension, and a month of summer school to make up the failing grade she'd more than earned in the class, drove the message home.

But what Nick seemed to be forgetting was she'd only done it because he'd *dared* her.

"I didn't think it was supposed to be fun," she said.

He frowned. "You don't think sex should be fun?"

"Not *all* sex. I guess I just thought, because we're friends, we would just sort of…go through the motions."

"There's no reason why we can't enjoy it," Nick said.

"What if we're not compatible?"

"As far as I'm aware, we both have the right parts," he said with a grin. "Unless there's something you haven't told me."

She rolled her eyes. "I don't mean *biologically* compatible. What if we get started and we don't get, you know… turned-on?"

"Are you saying you find me unattractive?"

"No, but in twenty years, I've never looked at you and had the uncontrollable urge to jump your bones. I just don't think of you that way."

"Come here," he said, summoning her around the island with a crooked finger.

"Why?"

"I'm going to kiss you."

Her heart skipped a beat. "Now?"

"Why not now? Before we go through the trouble of getting married, shouldn't we know for sure? Besides, what if we wait until our wedding day, and it all goes horribly wrong? Suppose we bump noses, or we both tilt our head the same way. And what about our honeymoon? Are we just going to hop into bed without ever having touched each other? Doesn't it make more sense for us to ease into it gradually?"

He definitely had a point. The problem here was that she was trying to play by a set of rules that didn't exist. They were making it up as they went along. "I guess that does make sense."

"So, what are you waiting for?" He tapped his lips with his index finger. "Lay one on me."

The idea that they were really going to do it, that he was going to kiss her for real, and not his usual peck on the cheek, gave her a funny feeling in her head. Her hands went all warm and tingly, as if all the blood in her body was pooling somewhere south of her heart.

It's just Nick. She had no reason to be nervous or scared or whatever it was she was feeling. But as her feet carried her around the island to where he stood, her heart was racing.

"Ready?" he asked, and she nodded.

Nick leaned in, but before their lips could meet, a giggle burst up from her chest. Nick drew back, looking exasperated.

"Sorry, I guess I'm a little nervous." She took a deep breath and blew it out, shaking the feeling back into her fingers. "I'm okay now. I promise not to laugh again."

"Good, because you're bruising my fragile ego."

Somehow she doubted that. She'd never met a man more secure in his prowess with women.

"Okay," he said. "Are you ready?"

"Ready."

"*Really* ready?"

She nodded. "Really ready."

Nick leaned in, and she met him halfway, and their lips just barely touched.

She couldn't help it, she giggled again.

Backing away, Nick sighed loudly. "This is not working."

"I am so sorry," she said. "I'm really trying."

Maybe this wasn't going to work. If she couldn't feel comfortable kissing him, what would it be like trying to have sex?

"Close your eyes," he said.

She narrowed them at him instead. "Why?"

"Just close them. And *keep* them closed."

Even though she felt stupid, she did as he asked, and for what felt like a full minute he did nothing, and she started to feel impatient. "Any day now."

"Shush."

Another thirty seconds or so passed and finally she felt him move closer, felt the whisper of his breath on her cheek, then his lips brushed over hers. This time she didn't giggle, and she wasn't so nervous anymore. His lips were soft and his evening stubble felt rough against her chin, but in a sexy way. And though it wasn't exactly passionate, it wasn't merely friendly, either.

This is nice, she thought. Nice enough that she wanted to see what came next, and when Nick started to pull away, before he could get too far, she fisted her hands in the front of his shirt and pulled him back in.

He made a sound, somewhere between surprise and pleasure, and he must have forgotten all about their ease-into-it-gradually plan, because it went from *nice* to *holy-cow-can-this-guy-kiss* in two seconds flat. He must have been sampling the cake batter earlier, because he tasted sweet, like chocolate.

Oh, my gosh, she was kissing *Nick,* her *best friend.* It was Nick's arms circling her, Nick's hand cupping her cheek, sliding under the root of her ponytail and cocking her head to just the right angle.

Her internal thermometer shot into the red zone and her bones began a slow melt, dripping away like icicles in the hot sun. And only when she heard Nick moan, when she felt her fingers sink through the softness of his hair, did she realize that her arms were around his shoulders, that her body was pressed against him, her breasts crushed against the hard wall of his chest. It was thrilling and arousing, and scary as hell, and a couple dozen other emotions all jumbled up together. But more than anything, it just felt...*right.* In a way that no other kiss had before. And all she could think was *more.*

For the second time Nick was the one to pull away, and she had to fight the urge to tighten her arms around his neck and pull him to her again. But instead of letting go completely, he hooked his fingers in the belt loop of her jeans.

"Wow," he said, searching her face, almost as if he were seeing her for the first time. "That was…"

"Wow," she agreed. If she had known kissing Nick would be like that, she might have tried it a long time ago.

"Are you still worried about us being incompatible?" he asked.

"Somehow I don't think that's going to be a problem."

"Do you feel weird?"

"Weird?"

"You said before that you were afraid things might get weird between us."

The only thing she felt right now was turned-on, and ready to kiss him again. "It's difficult to say after one kiss."

"Oh, really?" he said, tugging her closer. "Then I guess we'll just have to do it again."

Four

Their second kiss was even better than the first, and this time when Nick stopped and asked, "Feeling weird yet?" instead of answering, Terri just pulled him in for number three. And she was so wowed by the fact that it was Nick kissing her, Nick touching her, that she didn't really think about *where* he was touching her. Not until his hand slid down over the back pocket of her jeans, then everything came to a screeching halt.

She backed away and looked at him. "Your hand is on my butt."

"I know. I put it there." He paused, then said, "Am I moving too fast?"

Was he? Was it too much too soon? Was there some sort of schedule they were supposed to follow? A handbook for friends who become lovers to have a baby? As long as it felt good, as long as they both wanted it, why stop?

And boy, did it feel good.

"No," she said. "You're not moving too fast. If you were, would I be thinking how much better it would feel if my jeans were off?"

He made a growly noise deep in his chest and kissed her hard, but despite that shameless invitation into her pants, he kept his hands on the outside of her clothes. And no matter where she touched him, how she rubbed up against him, or encouraged him with little moans of pleasure, he didn't seem to be getting the hint that she was ready to proceed.

When he did finally slide his hand under her shirt, she felt like pumping her fist in the air, and shouting, "Yes!" But then he just kept it there. It wasn't that it didn't feel good resting just above the waist of her jeans, but she was sure it would feel a whole lot better eight inches or so higher and slightly to the left.

She pulled back and said, "If you felt the need to touch my breast, or pretty much any other part of my anatomy, I wouldn't stop you."

Looking amused, he said, "It's not often a woman tells me I'm moving too slow."

"I could play coy, but what's the point? We both know we're going to end up in bed tonight."

His brows rose. "We do?"

"Can you think of a reason we shouldn't?"

When most men would have jumped at the offer, he actually took several seconds to think about it. Which for some strange reason made her want it even more. It was crazy to think that on Wednesday she wouldn't have even considered a physical relationship with him, but two days and a couple kisses later, she couldn't wait to get him out of his clothes. And if he turned her down, she was going to be seriously unhappy.

After a brief pause he shrugged and said, "Nothing is coming to mind."

The way she figured it, their friendship had been leading up to this, even if they hadn't realized it. That equated to about twenty years of foreplay. Technically, no one could say they were rushing things. "So why are we still standing in the kitchen?"

He opened his mouth to answer her, when they heard the apartment door open. Terri's first thought was that it was another woman. Someone he was dating that he'd given a key to. Then she heard Nick's mom call, "Yoo-hoo! Nicky, I'm here!"

Nick muttered a curse. And here he thought the days of his mom interrupting while he was with a girl had ended when he moved away from home.

"In the kitchen," he called, then turned to Terri to apologize. But he never got the words out. Her hair was a mess, her clothes disheveled and she had beard burn all over her chin. Unless his mom had forgotten to put her contacts in that morning, it would be obvious that they'd been fooling around. He could hope that she wouldn't notice, but she noticed *everything,* and typically had an opinion she always felt compelled to share. Terri was a lot like her in that way.

Terri's eyes went wide, and she glanced at his crotch, but she didn't have to worry. He'd lost his erection the second he heard the door and remembered that his mom was stopping by.

"I can't believe this weather," his mom said, her voice growing louder as she walked toward the kitchen. "Two days ago we get a blizzard—" she appeared in the kitchen doorway, a five-foot-three-inch, one-hundred-and-two-pound ball of energy dressed in the yoga gear she wore ninety-nine percent of the time "—and today it feels like spring." She stopped short when she saw Terri standing there beside him. Then she smiled and said, "Well, hello there! I didn't know you were—"

Whatever she was going to say never made it out. Instead, she looked from him, to Terri, then back to him again. "Oh, my, it looks as if I've interrupted something."

He could see the wheels in her head spinning, and he knew exactly what she was thinking—that all the while they were posing as friends, he and Terri had been hitting the sheets together. Friends with benefits. And while he didn't care what she thought of him, he didn't want her to think Terri was like that. And he was pretty sure, by the crimson blossoming in Terri's cheeks, she was worried about the same thing.

Terri always said that his mom was the mom she should have had, and his mom said Terri was the third daughter she'd never had. Sometimes Nick could swear that if forced to ever choose, she might actually pick Terri over him.

"It's not what you think," he told his mom.

"Sweetheart, what you do in the privacy of your own home is none of my business."

"But we're not…I mean, we haven't been—"

His mom held up a hand. "No need to explain," she said, but underneath her blasé facade, he could see disappointment lurking there. And he was sure that it was directed as much at him as it was at Terri.

He turned to Terri and said, "So, should we tell her now?"

Terri looked over to his mom. "I don't know, what do you think?"

"Tell me what?" his mom asked.

"Well," Nick said. "She's going to find out eventually."

Terri grinned, enjoying this game as much as he was. There was no better way to drive his mom nuts than to make her think someone had a juicy secret and she'd been left out of the loop.

"I guess that's true," Terri said. "But are we ready to let the news out?"

"What news?" Though she was trying to sound nonchalant, he could see she was practically busting with curiosity.

"Because you know that as soon as we tell her, everyone will know."

"Nicky!" his mom scolded, even though they all knew it was true. She couldn't keep a secret to save her life. And oftentimes she told him things about family, or her "man-friends" as she called them, that he wished he could permanently wipe from his memory.

His mom folded her arms and pouted. "I know someone who's getting a big fat lump of coal in his stocking this year."

"Terri and I are getting married," Nick said.

"Married?"

"Yep."

"Really?"

"Yes, really."

She narrowed her eyes at him. "You're not just saying that because I caught you fooling around?"

He laughed. "We're *really* getting married."

His mom shrieked so loud he was sure the apartment below heard her through the industrial soundproofing. She scurried around the island to pull Terri—not him, but Terri—into a hug.

"Oh, honey! I'm so happy for you. I always hoped. You know I would never interfere, but I did hope."

Curiously, her idea of not interfering was telling him,

after meeting whatever girl he happened to be dating at the time, that "She was nice, but she wasn't Terri."

His mom held Terri at arm's length, tears shimmering in her eyes, looking as if it was the happiest moment of her entire life. Then she turned to Nick, the tears miraculously dried, and said, "It's about damn time."

Yep, she would definitely choose Terri over him.

"Have you set a date? And please don't tell me that this is going to be one of those ten-year engagements so that you can live together and not feel guilty. You know that you'll never hear the end of it from *Nonno*. He put your poor cousin Chrissy through hell when she moved in with David."

"We're getting married in two weeks."

She blinked. "Did you just say *two* weeks?"

"Yep."

She sucked in a breath and turned to Terri, asking in a hushed voice, even though there was no one around but them, "Are you pregnant?"

"No," Terri said, sounding incredibly patient under the circumstances. "I'm not pregnant."

Looking baffled, she shrugged and said, "Then what's the rush?"

"Neither of us sees any point in waiting," Terri said, shooting him a quick sideways glance filled with innuendo. "My plan has always been to be pregnant by the time I'm thirty, and I'm almost there."

"You want kids, Nicky?" his mom asked, beaming with joy.

"We want to try for a baby right away," he told her. "And we figured it would be best to get married first. We both prefer a small wedding, with a ceremony that's short and sweet. Immediate family and close friends *only*."

"You know that your father's family will have something to say about that."

"We'll videotape it and post it on YouTube," Nick said, earning him an elbow in the side from his fiancée. It also reminded him that they would need to hire a photographer, which then had him wondering if the studio that did the company's promotional shoots did weddings, too.

"Nicky, where's your laptop?" his mom asked.

"On my desk. Why?"

"With only two weeks, Terri and I need to start planning this thing right now. We have to pick out your colors and find a florist and I know just the place to get the cake." She exhaled a long-winded sigh. "There's *so much* to do!"

"But Mom…"

Ignoring Nick, she grabbed Terri by the arm and all but dragged her in the direction of Nick's office. Terri looked back over her shoulder, shrugging helplessly. So much for having a little premarital fun.

On the bright side, he doubted that after tonight they would be uncomfortable kissing and touching, so convincing his family that they were crazy about each other would be a breeze. And he was willing to bet that until he got her alone and into his bed, touching her again was all he would be able to think about.

Though Nick would have preferred to announce their engagement himself, his mom called his sisters, and his sisters called their cousins, and after that the news went viral. So it was no surprise when Tony and Rob cornered him as he was on his way to the test kitchen the next Monday morning.

"Is it true?" Rob asked.

"If you're referring to my engagement, then yes, it's true."

Tony gestured them into a room that wasn't much more than a glorified closet.

Oh, boy, here we go, Nick thought, doubting they were there for a friendly chat.

Boxes of old files lined metal shelves on either side and the air smelled musty. Tony switched on the light and shut the door behind them. "This seems awfully convenient, don't you think?"

Nick frowned, playing dumb. "What do you mean?"

"You know exactly what I mean."

"You've been friends with Terri for all these years," Rob said, "and you just happen to pick now to ask her to marry you?"

Nick leaned against a shelf and it shifted slightly under his weight. "What are you suggesting?"

"You know damn well what he's suggesting," Tony said. "And I don't think a marriage of convenience is what *Nonno* had in mind."

"I don't recall him ever saying that."

Rob shot him a look. "It was implied, and you know it. He wants us all to settle down and have big families. Lots of male heirs to carry on the Caroselli name."

"I love Terri," he said, which wasn't a lie. He just wasn't *in* love with her.

"Is she pregnant?" Rob asked.

With such a short engagement, he had the feeling he'd be getting that question a lot. "Not that it's any of your business, but no, she isn't. Not yet."

"Then why the big hurry to get hitched?" Tony said.

Though his family had many good qualities, they sure could be nosy.

"Again, not that it's *any* of your business, but we want

to start a family right away, and we want to be married first," he said, using the explanation Terri had given his mom last night, which was truly brilliant because none of it was untrue. They just left out a few pertinent facts.

Tony didn't look convinced. "Yeah, but two weeks is pretty fast, don't you think?"

"Terri is almost thirty and she has a ticking biological clock. And you know why *I'm* in a hurry."

Tony lowered his voice, even though they were alone. "Does she know about the money?"

Nick grinned. "What's the matter? Are you jealous that I'm going to get my cut of the money first?"

"Don't forget, it has to be a *male* heir," Rob said. "It could take more than one try. You could end up with three or four kids."

Of course, having a girl was a possibility, and whether or not they decided to ride it out and try again would be up to Terri.

"I think I speak for Rob when I say that we've always really liked Terri. And if either of us finds out you only married her so she'll have your offspring, and you hurt her, I will personally kick your ass."

Hurting her was definitely not on the agenda. They both knew exactly what they were getting into. What could go wrong?

"Honestly, Tony, I figured you would be making an announcement soon, too," Nick said. "You and Lucy have been together a long time now."

A nerve in Tony's jaw ticked. "It would have been a year in December."

"*Would* have been?" Rob asked.

"We split up."

"*When?*"

"Last week."

"Dude," Nick said. "Why didn't you say anything?"

Tony shrugged. "It didn't seem worth mentioning."

Nick couldn't say he was surprised. Lucy was never what anyone would consider a devoted girlfriend. In all the time they were together, she had been to no more than two or three family functions, and Tony rarely mentioned her. They seemed to lead very separate lives. "What happened?"

"I honestly don't know. I thought everything was fine, then I stopped by her place after work one night and she was gone. Her roommate said she moved back to Florida."

Rob shook his head in amazement. "Without saying a word?"

Tony shrugged again, but underneath the stoic facade, he was tense. Nick could feel it. "If there was a problem, she never mentioned it to me."

"I'm really sorry, man," Nick said.

"It's her loss."

Though Tony would never come right out and say it, Nick could tell that deep down he was hurting. But neither he nor Rob pushed the subject.

The door to the room opened and all three jumped like little boys caught playing with matches. A woman Nick didn't recognize stood in the open doorway, looking as surprised to see them as they were to see her. She was in her mid-forties, with short, stylish dark hair peppered with gray and striking blue eyes. She was very attractive for a woman her age, and there was something oddly familiar about her.

"I'm sorry, I didn't know anyone was in here," she said, looking nervously at them.

"It's okay," Tony said. "We were just talking."

She retreated a step. "I can come back."

"It's okay," Nick said, shooting his cousins a look. "We're finished."

"Nick, I don't think you've met Rose Goldwyn. Her mom, Phyllis, worked as *Nonno's* secretary for years, up until he retired."

"For almost twenty years," Rose said.

Nick was struck with a distinct mental picture of a youngish, attractive woman seated outside *Nonno's* office. That was why she looked familiar.

"I remember your mom," Nick said. "You look like her."

She smiled. "That's what everyone says."

"How is she doing?"

"Unfortunately mom passed away this September," Rose said. "Cancer."

"I'm so sorry. I remember that she was always smiling, and gave me and my sisters candy whenever we visited *Nonno* at his office."

"She always loved working here. Being here makes me feel a little closer to her."

"And we're happy to have you," Tony said.

"I heard this morning that you're getting married soon," she told Nick. "Congratulations."

"Thanks. You should come."

"Me?" she said, looking surprised.

"Sure. At Caroselli Chocolate, we like to think of our employees as extended family. I'll tell my fiancée to put you on the guest list. It's a week from this coming Saturday."

"I'll definitely be there," she said.

"Gentlemen, why don't we get out of her way," Tony said, nodding toward the door.

"Nice to have met you," Nick said, shaking her hand.

They headed back down the hall in the direction of

the kitchen, and when they turned the corner Nick asked, "When did we hire her?"

"A few weeks ago. We didn't actually need anyone, but because of the family history, they found a place for her in accounting. When she saw the condition of the file room, she offered to scan in the old files and take us completely digital."

"Correct me if I'm wrong," Nick said. "But isn't there a lot of sensitive information in there?"

Tony shrugged. "Mostly old financial records and employee files. Maybe some marketing materials. Nothing top secret."

"No old recipes?"

"Not that I know of. Why, do you think she's a spy?"

Corporate espionage certainly wasn't unheard of, especially with a world-renowned product like Caroselli Chocolate. "Doesn't hurt to be cautious."

Nick's cell phone rang and his mom's number popped up on the screen. "Sorry, I have to take this," he said, then told Tony, "If you need to talk…"

Tony nodded. Enough said.

Even if they weren't buying his story—because in all honesty, if the tables were turned he would have the same suspicions—Nick doubted they would rat him out to *Nonno*. Still, he planned to keep up the charade. If anyone else figured out that the marriage was a sham, it could definitely mean trouble.

"Hey, Mom, what's up?" he answered.

"White lilies or pink roses?"

"Excuse me?"

"Which do you prefer?" she said, sounding impatient, as if he should have known what she meant. "I'm at the florist with Terri and we can't decide between the lilies and the roses."

Not only did he not know the difference, he didn't care, either. "If you like them, why not pick both?"

"That's what I suggested, but she says it would be too expensive."

"And I told her that I didn't care what it costs. To get what she likes."

"Then you talk to her. She won't listen to me."

He heard muffled voices, then Terri came on the line. "Nick, the flowers are going to be really expensive."

He sighed. She was frugal to a fault. "It doesn't matter. Get whatever you want."

She lowered her voice. "For a fake wedding? I already feel horrible about this."

"Why?"

"Because your mom and your sisters are *so* excited. I feel like we're deceiving them."

"We are getting married, aren't we?"

"You know what I mean."

"Well, it's too late to back out now," Nick said.

There was a pause, and he wondered if she actually was reconsidering her decision. Then she said, "I guess you're right."

"And, Terri, get the flowers you want, regardless of the cost, okay? As long as we're married, what's mine is yours."

"Okay. I have to go, I'll call you later," she said. Then the line went dead.

They weren't doing anything wrong, so why did he get the feeling Terri still had doubts?

Five

Terri rummaged through her toiletries bag, checking off in her mind everything she would need for their honeymoon. When she was sure she had all the essentials, she zipped the bag and laid it in her suitcase. If she had forgotten something, she could pick it up when they got to the resort in Aruba.

She never realized just how much planning went into a wedding—even one as small as hers and Nick's—and thank goodness his mom and sisters were more than happy to tend to the details, leaving Terri time to finish up a high-profile web design job that was due to be completed while they were in the middle of their honeymoon. And since they already had to cut their trip short to be home in time for Thanksgiving, she doubted Nick would appreciate her bringing work with her. Which translated into five consecutive eighteen-hour days in front of the computer, until she was sure her eyes would start bleeding.

Nick had been developing a new product—one so top secret he couldn't even tell her about it—that they hoped to have in production before Easter, so he had been just as busy. Other than brief, nightly phone conversations to keep him up-to-date on the wedding progress, in which one or both of them started to doze off, their contact was minimal. They'd even had to skip their weekly Thursday dinner.

They hadn't discussed practicing for their wedding night since that evening in his kitchen, but it was never far from her mind, and she couldn't help but wonder if he'd been thinking about it, as well. Had he been having sex dreams about her, too? Fantasizing about their first time when he was supposed to be working?

When they finally did get a free night together the Wednesday before the wedding it was too late. According to her doctor it was best to refrain from sex at least five days before she ovulated, to keep Nick's sperm count high, which would make conception more likely. So after a short make-out session that only heightened the sexual tension, they decided it would be safer if they kept their hands to themselves until their wedding night. He helped her pack instead, which included dismantling her entire computer system so she could set up an office at his place. Then later, as they were relaxing by the fire, Nick got down on one knee and pretend-proposed—to give her the full experience, he'd said—but the four-carat, princess-cut diamond solitaire he slid on her ring finger was very real and stunningly beautiful, and hers to keep as a token of his affection even after they divorced.

While she thought it was a sweet gesture, it was a little heartbreaking that the best she could do in thirty years was a fake marriage proposal. But she knew he meant well. It wasn't his fault that she had lousy luck with men.

"All packed?" Nick asked from the bedroom doorway, and she turned to find him leaning casually against the jamb, thumbs hooked in the front pockets of his jeans.

"I think I may have over-packed," she said, tugging at the zipper in an effort to close the bulging case.

"You really think I'm going to let you wear clothes?" he said with one of those sizzling grins that made her heart flutter and her face hot. And though she probably wouldn't have noticed a couple weeks ago, in faded jeans that were ripped at the knees and a white T-shirt that enhanced his dark complexion, he looked sexy as hell. When they had first hatched this plan, the idea of sleeping with him wasn't just unusual, it really scared her. She didn't want their relationship to change. But then he'd kissed her, and touched her, and other than the fact that she was itching to get her hands on him and she couldn't wait to jump his bones, she didn't feel any differently about him than she had before. They were friends, and they were going to have sex—simple as that.

According to her temperature she should have started ovulating today, but the test she took this morning was negative. If the test had been positive, she didn't doubt that they would have consummated their marriage tonight, tradition be damned. And if she didn't start ovulating tomorrow? After two weeks of anticipating their first time making love, could they really hold out another day or two? She might have to say to hell with it and jump him, anyway.

"Anything you still need to do for tomorrow?" he asked. He'd already perfected his new recipe that would go through taste testing and marketing and whatever else they did with a new product, so they were free to spend the next five days relaxing and enjoying each other's company.

"I talked to your mom a couple hours ago and it sounds as if they have everything covered. I seriously don't know what I would have done without them. And I can't help feeling guilty."

"Why?"

"If they knew we're going to be getting divorced as soon as we have the baby, do you really think they would have spent all this time, and gone through all this trouble?"

"If we were getting married for real, who's to say it wouldn't end in divorce, anyway? There are no guarantees, Terri."

She knew that, but it still felt underhanded. Their current circumstance aside, she would never marry a man if she thought the relationship might end in divorce. Of course, would anyone? And there were definite advantages to being married, even if it was only pretend. It meant having someone to talk to without picking up the phone, and not eating dinner alone in front of the television watching *Seinfeld* reruns.

The best part, though, was that having Nick's baby meant always having someone to love—and someone to love her—unconditionally. Though her aunt had probably done her best raising Terri, she hadn't been much of a kid person. She'd never had children of her own, much less expected to have a great-niece she'd never even met dumped in her care. It had been a lonely way to grow up, but when the baby was born, Terri would never be lonely again. She would give her child all the love and affection her aunt had failed to show her. Terri would never make her child feel as if he was inconsequential. She wouldn't travel abroad for weeks at a time and leave him in the care of a nanny. She would be a good mom, and she hoped Nick would be a good dad. Either way, she had enough love to give for both of them.

"Are you nervous?" he asked.

She shrugged. "Should I be?"

"I hear that brides often are the day before their wedding."

Well, she wasn't a typical bride. "I'm just hoping everything goes well."

"Did my mom say what the final guest count will be?" Nick asked.

"Forty-eight."

"That's not bad. Maybe we'll get lucky and my dad won't show."

It broke her heart that Nick and his dad were so at odds. He didn't realize how lucky he was to have both his parents, even if they could be trying at times. She would have given anything to have her dad back. Her mom died when Terri was a baby, and it was harder to miss something she never really had, but she still regretted not getting to know her.

"I'm sure he'll behave," she told Nick. Or at least she *hoped* he would. His sister's wedding had been a disaster thanks to Nick's dad, Leo, who got into it with his ex-wife's date. The argument became so heated, shoves were exchanged, and though they never knew for sure who threw the first punch, fists began to fly. Eventually other family members from both sides of the wedding party had gotten into the scuffle, until it became a full-fledged brawl that resulted in a handful of arrests for drunk and disorderly behavior, several people requiring medical attention and an enormous bill for the damage from the banquet hall.

Never a dull moment in the Caroselli family.

But that had been more that thirteen years ago. His parents had been apart now for more years than they had been married, and had each wed and divorced again—in his dad's case twice. Terri would think that any issues they'd had back then would be resolved by now. Yet she couldn't deny worrying about what might happen if she was wrong.

"Everything will be perfect," she told him, hoping she sounded convincing.

"I hope so," Nick said. "I unpacked the last box of books and set up your computer system. I checked it and everything seems to be working correctly."

He had insisted that they get her moved in *before* the wedding, so the impending task wouldn't be in the back of their minds during their trip. She'd felt a little weird moving her things in before they were actually married. What if during their honeymoon something went terribly wrong? Sexually they seemed compatible enough, but suppose after four days in close quarters, they realized that they couldn't stand living together? She would have to fly home and move all her stuff back to her place.

That isn't going to happen, she told herself, but every now and then she thought about when they were roommates and doubt danced around the edge of her subconscious. There was also the question of sex. Not whether it would be good, but how often they would have it. Would they sleep together once, and hope she conceived, or the entire time she was ovulating? Would he be content to go an entire nine months without sex? The truth was that she liked sex. A lot. Even mediocre sex was better than none at all. And while she was perfectly capable of taking care of things herself, it was so much more fun to have a partner. But for her and Nick to have a full-blown affair would be a mistake. They had to keep this in perspective.

"Thanks for all your help today," she said, tugging the case off the bed so she could roll it out to the foyer. It weighed a ton.

"Let me get that," he said, taking it from her. He lifted it with little effort, then carried it to the entranceway and set it beside his own, which she noticed was half the size of hers and not nearly as stuffed. Maybe he really was expecting to spend the majority of their time naked.

This just kept getting better and better.

She looked over at the clock on the mantel, surprised to see that it was already after ten. "I should probably get home."

"Are you sure you don't want to sleep here?"

"In two hours it will be our wedding day, and it's bad luck for the groom to see the bride."

He gazed at her with tired eyes and a wry grin. "You don't really believe that."

Not really, but she'd be damned if she was taking any chances. "I think we should stick to tradition. Just in case."

He laughed. "And how is what we're doing *traditional?*"

"How many couples our age do you think still wait until their wedding night to consummate their relationship? That's a tradition."

"But we're only waiting because we *have* to. And I'd be happy to break that one right now."

Oh, man, so would she. But as much as she wanted to get him naked and put her hands all over him, she wanted to get pregnant even more, which meant they had to do this by the book.

"Everything that I need for tomorrow is at my place. It'll be easier if I stay there. But before I go, there is something I wanted to show you."

His brows rose. "Is it your breasts, because I'd love to see them."

She folded her arms and glared at him.

"That's a no, I guess."

"It's something I picked up at the doctor's office."

He followed into her bedroom and sat down beside her on the bed. She grabbed a manila folder off the nightstand and pulled out printed sheets, handing them to Nick.

He read the first line and his brows rose. "Methods for conceiving a boy?"

"I mentioned to the doctor that we were hoping for a boy and he gave me this. He said it in no way guarantees a baby boy, but there are some parents who swear by it. I highlighted the important parts."

The first couple pages were about ovulation and cervical conditions, and the differences in the mobility of the X and Y sperm.

"The male sperm are smaller and faster, but not as robust as their larger female counterparts," he read, giving her a sideways glance. "While trying to conceive a male, deep penetration from your partner will deposit the sperm closer to the cervix giving the quicker moving 'boy' sperm a head start to fertilizing the egg first. In addition, female orgasm is important as the contractions which accompany orgasm help move the sperm up and into the cervix. It also makes the vaginal environment more alkaline, which is favorable for the boy sperm." He turned to her, looking intrigued. "Deep penetration? How deep?"

"The next page has examples, actually."

Nick turned to the next page, which contained several vividly graphic illustrations depicting the positions they should use for the deepest penetration. His brows rose and he said, "Wow."

Along with a couple of tried-and-true positions, there were several that she was pretty sure only a contortionist could perform. And they had weird names like The Reverse Cowgirl and The Crab on its Back.

Nick narrowed his eyes, cocking his head to one side, then the other. "Huh, it looks like they're playing Twister."

"I admit some of them are a little…adventurous," she said. And not terribly romantic, if that's the mood they were going for. But they did look fun, and he had said himself that it should be fun. She liked to experiment and try new things, but maybe he was more conservative. Maybe his idea of fun was the missionary position. "They're just examples. I understand if you don't want to try them."

He looked at her as if she were nuts. "Are you kidding? Of *course* I want to try them."

Or maybe he *wasn't* conservative.

He pointed to one of the illustrations. "I like this, but do you really think you can get your legs over your head like that?"

She grinned. "I'm *very* flexible."

He cursed under his breath and handed the papers to her. "I think it would be best if I stopped looking at these. Because now I'm picturing you in all those positions."

What a coincidence, because so was she. She slid the papers back into the folder.

"I have to say, I'm a bit surprised by how open you are about this," he said.

"Why?"

"Over the years we've both made off-the-cuff comments about people we've dated, but we really never talked about our sex lives."

"Why do you think that is?"

"In my case, I consider it disrespectful to kiss and tell."

Good answer. While she was aware that he'd dated a lot of women, and *assumed* he'd slept with the majority of them, she really didn't have a clue how many. And frankly didn't want to know.

"In your case," he said, "I figured you were uncomfortable talking about sex."

"Repressed, you mean."

"Just…private. Like it probably took you a while to get to know someone before you would be comfortable being intimate with them. But then the other night, you were so…"

"Slutty?"

He shot her a look. *"Aggressive."*

"You don't like aggressive women?"

"Do I honestly strike you as the type who wouldn't like an aggressive woman?"

She wouldn't have thought so. But his perception of her, and reality, were two very different things.

"First you propositioned me," Nick said, "then you sat me down for a talk about sexual positions. And I'm not suggesting I don't like it. I think it's pretty obvious that I *do*. I'm just surprised. I thought I knew everything about you, but here's this side of you that I didn't even know existed."

It was odd, after all these years, there was still a part of her that he didn't know. But that was her own fault. "So you're seeing me differently than you did before?"

"A little, but in a good way. It makes me feel closer to you."

What she liked about their friendship was that it had always been very straightforward. There were no overblown expectations, and none of the games men and women played when they were physically involved. She didn't want that to change, though she couldn't deny that the idea of someone knowing her that well scared her a little. Especially now that sex was about to be part of the equation.

Six

Though he never thought he would see the day, Nick was a married man.

Legally, anyway.

He gazed down at the polished platinum band on the ring finger of his left hand. It was a brand, a warning to women that he was now taken, a tourniquet placed there to cut off the lifeblood of his single life. And while he'd expected that to bother him on some level, to make him feel caged or smothered, he actually felt okay about it. Maybe because he knew it was only temporary, or he was looking forward to collecting ten million dollars.

Or maybe he was looking forward to the honeymoon.

He'd received a text message from Terri at 6:00 a.m. this morning that read simply: The eagle has landed.

Which he knew was her way of saying that she was ovulating, and right on time.

Aside from the occasional random and fleeting fantasy,

he hadn't really thought about her in a sexual way since high school. The past two weeks, he had barely thought of much else, and after their conversation last night, it was *all* he'd thought about. Since the ceremony, he'd kept one eye on their guests—who were drinking champagne and expensive scotch, snacking on bacon-wrapped sea scallops, artichoke phyllo tartlets and gorgonzola risotto croquettes—and the other eye on the clock.

He heard Terri laugh, and turned to see her by the bar with his cousins, Megan and Elana. He rarely saw her in anything but casual clothes, but for the occasion she wore a calf-length, off-white dress made of some silky-soft material that flowed with her body every time she moved. Her long, dark hair was up in one of those styles that looked salon-perfect, yet messy at the same time.

His sister Jessica stepped up beside him and propped her hand on his shoulder. In three-inch heels, she was still a good eight inches shorter. She had their father's olive complexion and naturally curly hair, and took after their mother in height, but she had been struggling with her weight since she'd had her first of four babies. Right now she was on the heavy side, which usually meant she'd been stress eating, a pretty good indication that her marriage was once again on the rocks.

"She looks gorgeous," Jess said.

"Yes, she does," he agreed.

As if she sensed him watching, Terri looked over. She glanced up at the clock, then back at him and smiled, and he knew exactly what she was thinking. Soon they would be on their way to the airport, and after a five-hour flight, and a short limo ride, they would reach the resort.

It would be late by then, but he figured they could sleep on the flight, then spend the rest of the night making love in a variety of interesting ways.

"So, how does it feel?" Jess asked him.

"How does what feel?"

"To be a married man."

He shrugged. "So far so good."

"I never thought you would do it, but I'm glad you chose Terri."

"Me, too," he said. "And thank you again for everything. You and mom and Mags did an amazing job putting this all together."

With a satisfied smile, she gazed around the room. The decorations were simple yet elegant, and included both the lilies and the roses—even though Terri still insisted that it had been excessively expensive. And in lieu of the typical wedding band or DJ, they'd hired a string quartet.

"Considering you only gave us two weeks to plan it, I think so, too," she said.

"How are things with you and Eddie?"

Her smile slipped away. "Oh, you know, same ol' same ol'. We have good days and bad days. The marriage counseling seems to be helping. When I can get him to go."

Nick heard a screech, then Jessica's seven-year-old twin boys, Tommy and Alex, tore through the room like two wild animals, bumping furniture and plowing into guests.

Jess rolled her eyes and mumbled a curse. "Excuse me, I've got children to beat."

Nick knew that, physically, the worst she'd ever done was give them a quick love-tap to the back of the head, which was a long-running Caroselli family tradition. Only according to his father and his uncles, depending on what they'd done, and how angry they'd made *Nonni* Caroselli, hers were more like whacks, and were anything but loving. Nick still had a hard time picturing his *Nonni* as anything but sweet and gentle and unfailingly patient.

Terri crossed the room to where he stood, sliding her arm through his and hugging herself close to his side. He knew it was only for show, but he liked it. There was something nice about having the freedom to touch her, and be close to her, without having to worry that she would read into it, or take it the wrong way. She wouldn't smother him, or demand more than he was willing to give. He would call it friends with benefits, but that seemed to cheapen it somehow. What he and Terri had transcended a typical friendship. They were soul mates, but the platonic kind.

"So, I just had an interesting conversation with your cousins," she told him.

Uh-oh. "By *interesting* I take it you mean *not good*."

"Well, no one is questioning the validity of our wedding."

"That's good, right?"

"Yes, but only because apparently your *entire* family thinks I'm *pregnant*."

He sort of saw that one coming. "Did you tell them that you aren't?"

"Of course. And the reply I got was, 'Sure you aren't,' wink, wink, nudge, nudge."

"Let them think what they want, in eight months or so, when you don't give birth, they'll know you were telling the truth. Besides, I'm betting not everyone thinks it." His mom and sisters knew she wasn't, as did Rob and Tony.

"The limo will be here soon," she told him. "We should say our goodbyes so we can get upstairs and change."

Nick heard his dad's booming laugh, and turned to see that he and Nick's mom were standing together by the bay window talking. He muttered a curse under his breath.

The last time they had been in the same room, face-to-face, the evening had ended with a 9-1-1 call. And though they seemed to be playing nice, that could change in the span of a heartbeat if tempers flared. At least neither had brought a date, since that was what had set them off last time.

"Brace yourself," he told Terri. "I think there's going to be trouble."

"What's wrong?" Terri asked, following his line of vision until she spotted his parents.

Oh, hell.

Up until just then, their wedding had been perfect. So perfect that when *Nonno* walked her into the great room, and she saw everyone standing there looking so genuinely happy and willing to unconditionally welcome her into the family on a permanent basis, she had never felt so loved and accepted. If she wasn't careful, she could almost let herself believe it was real, that when Nick spoke his vows, he actually meant them. That when he promised to love and keep her, in sickness and in health, till death parted them, he was sincere. That the love in his eyes as he slipped the ring on her finger was genuine. If she never found Mr. Right, never married anyone for real, she still could say that she'd had the wedding of her dreams.

She didn't want his parents to ruin it by starting a brawl.

Her first instinct was to shove Nick over there to run interference, but then she noticed that his parents were both...*smiling*. Okay, that was a little weird.

"Is it me, or do they look as if they're actually getting along?" she said.

"Yeah, but for how long? All it will take is one snarky comment from either of them and the barbs will start flying."

Call her selfish, but she hoped they would wait until

she and Nick left for the airport before they decided to duke it out.

"Do you think I should go over there?" he asked, but before she could answer, his uncle, Tony Senior, joined his parents, then looked over at Nick and Terri and winked. Clearly they weren't the only ones concerned. And if anyone could keep hotheaded Leo Caroselli in line, it was his big brother.

"Thank you, Uncle Tony," Nick muttered under his breath, looking relieved. "Let's get the heck out of here. If there's going to be an explosion, I don't want to be around to see it."

Neither did she.

They made the rounds to aunts, uncles, cousins and friends from work, most of whom Terri knew on a first-name basis.

When they got to Tony and Rob, who were standing by the bar, Nick shook their hands and said, "Thank you for coming today."

"Yes, thank you," Terri said. "It meant so much to us to have you here."

"Wouldn't have missed it," Rob said, giving Terri a hug and a peck on the cheek. He smelled expensive, like scotch and cologne, and as always his suit was tailored to a perfect fit, his dark hair trimmed and neatly combed, and his nails buffed to a shine. She would bet her life that he probably got pedicures, too. He was so serious all the time, so…uptight. Even when they were kids, she had often wondered if he ever relaxed and had fun.

Tony was attractive in a dark, brooding sort of way, with his smoldering eyes and guarded smile. She'd never told Nick, but when they were in high school she'd had a short-lived crush on Tony. She was quite sure that, being six years her senior, he hadn't even noticed she was alive.

But now he kissed her cheek and said, "May you have a long and happy life together."

"We plan to." Terri smiled up at Nick and hugged herself close to his side, laying it on thick, since according to Nick, his cousins both had doubts the marriage was real.

"Think you can keep this guy in line?" Rob asked.

"The question is, can he keep *me* in line?"

Nick grinned. "I'll give it my best shot."

"I suppose you noticed your parents are talking," Tony said.

Nick shot a glance their way. "Yeah, but your dad seems to have it under control for now."

Terri could see that he was still nervous.

"I haven't seen your mom in a couple years," Rob said. "She looks great. Very...hip."

Nick's mom had always had her own unique style, so it was no surprise that she had substituted the typical conservative mother-of-the-groom dress for a long, flowing 1970s–style number that she could have picked up—and very likely *did*—at the vintage resale shop. In contrast, his dad looked like the typical executive in his thousand-dollar Italian suit. It's no wonder their marriage failed. Two people couldn't have been more different.

Terri glanced up at the clock and realized they were on the verge of running late. She gave Nick a nudge and said, "Our ride is going to be here soon."

"Again, gentlemen, thanks for coming," Nick said, and after another round of handshakes and hugs, with his arm firmly around her waist, they walked over to his parents. Tony Senior had left to stand by his wife, Sarah, leaving the two of them alone again.

"There's the happy couple," Nick's mom said with a bright smile as they approached.

"We're getting ready to leave," Nick told them. "We just wanted to say goodbye."

"Can't wait to get the honeymoon started, huh?" Nick's dad said, his booming voice making Terri cringe inwardly, as did his overly enthusiastic hug.

"Dad," Nick said in a tone that stated *back off.* But Leo ignored him. It wasn't that she disliked Nick's dad, she just didn't know him very well. And yes, he intimidated her a little, too. A far as she could tell, Nick had always been his polar opposite—at least in every way that mattered. Which is probably why they didn't get along.

"Thanks, Mr. Caroselli," she said when he let go.

He laughed heartily, drawing the attention of the entire room, and boomed, "You're my daughter now! Call me Dad!"

She actually preferred *Mr. Caroselli,* but didn't want to hurt his feelings.

Nick's mom—whom she had been calling Mom for the better part of twenty years—took Terri by her hands and squeezed them hard. "I know I've said this a dozen times in the past couple weeks, but I am so thrilled for the two of you. You are exactly what this guy needed." She smiled and gave Nick's jacket sleeve a playful tug. "Everyone in the family knew you were prefect for each other. I'm so happy that you both finally figured it out."

Terri braced herself against a jab of guilt. Though she liked everyone in Nick's family, his mom held a very special place in her heart. She had been the surrogate mother that Terri had desperately needed as a young woman.

She had taken Terri for her first bra, explained menstrual cycles and feminine hygiene products. And when Terri was finally asked out on her first date at the geriatric age of sixteen, Nick's mom had talked to her about the virtues of waiting, not necessarily for marriage, to have sex—she was far too progressive for that—but at least be until she was love. Then she took Terri to the clinic for birth control pills six months later when Terri decided she might take the leap sooner rather than later.

Nick's mom kissed him on the cheek, and gave Terri a hug, squeezing so hard it was difficult to breathe for a second. Her hugs were always warm and firm and full of love. She was so petite and fragile-looking, Terri was a little afraid to hug back too hard, for fear that she might crush her. But Terri had never known a tougher woman. Tough enough to stand up to—take no crap from—her brawny, loud and opinionated ex-husband. And when her second husband's dark side had emerged, and he took a swing at her, she swung right back. When all was said and done, she spent a few days in the hospital, but he spent those same days in jail with a broken nose and some deep scratch marks on his face so he would, as she phrased it, always have something to remember her by.

"Thank you so much for your help with the wedding," Terri said. "It was perfect. I couldn't have done it without you and Jess and Mags."

"Oh, honey, it was my pleasure. Any time you need my help, all you have to do is ask. And no pressure, but I throw a mean baby shower."

"We'll get right on that," Nick said, shooting Terri a glance that was so hot and steamy, she could practically feel it sizzle.

"So," Nick said, looking warily between his parents. "This is…different."

"What? That we're talking?" his mom asked.

"That you're not screaming at each other, and no fists are flying."

Another hearty laugh burst from his dad, propelling

his head back. "Water under the bridge, son. No hard feelings, right, Gena!"

Nick's mom smiled. "We were just saying that it's time we put the past behind us. That our whole problem was that we're just two very passionate people."

That was definitely one way to look at it. Although Terri always thought that is was simply that they didn't like each other.

Nick winced. "I have to admit, you're creeping me out a little."

"I would think you'd be happy," his mom said.

"Don't get me wrong. It's not that I don't want to see you bury the hatchet. I'm just afraid it's going to wind up protruding from someone's back."

"Not to worry, son," his dad assured him. "Everything is fine."

"Well, we've got to get upstairs and change," Nick told them. "Thanks again, Mom, for all your help."

"You two have fun on that honeymoon," his dad said with a wink that unsettled Terri more than a little bit.

His mom kissed and hugged them both. "Text me when you get there so I know you're safe. And have a good time."

Terri was forced to endure another overenthusiastic hug from his dad. As they were heading up the stairs Nick said, "Sorry about that. I know he can be obnoxious. And you don't have to call him Dad if you don't want to."

"He means well," she said. She didn't want to hurt his feelings, so she would probably force herself to call him Dad since it was only going to be for a short time.

They were running behind schedule, so Terri was thankful that she'd laid out her travel clothes ahead of time. There was nothing she hated more than being late, a virtue hammered into her by her aunt, who was intoler-

ant of tardiness. Not that being on time had ever earned
Terri any love and attention. In fact, back then, bad attention seemed favorable to being ignored, so she had been
late a lot as a kid.

As they reached the top of the stairs and turned, a
woman Terri had seen downstairs earlier, but hadn't yet
met, was walking toward them from either the study or
the master suite.

"Oh, thank goodness," she said, looking embarrassed.
"I was looking for the bathroom but I must have made a
wrong turn."

"It's the other way," Nick said, gesturing in that direction. "Second door on the left."

"Thanks. Your grandfather's house is really beautiful.
My mother's descriptions don't do it justice."

"Terri, this is Rose," Nick said. "She was recently hired
and her mom used to be *Nonno's* secretary."

"Pleasure to meet you," Terri said, shaking her hand.
"Thanks for coming today."

"It was an honor to be invited," she said, but the smile
she wore didn't quite reach her eyes. She seemed almost...
nervous, as if they had caught her doing something underhanded.

"Well, we have a plane to catch," Nick said.

"Have a great honeymoon and a safe trip," she said,
then headed swiftly down the stairs, bypassing the bathroom altogether. Call it intuition, or maybe she was just
paranoid, but Terri had the feeling this woman was looking for something. And it wasn't the bathroom.

Nick gestured Terri into the spare bedroom where
they'd left their things. She was about to voice her suspicions, but Nick closed the door and the next instant, he
had her backed her against it, pinned with the weight of
his body, his lips on hers.

Oh, man, could he kiss, and as much as she wanted to keep kissing him, they had to go. After a moment she laid her hands on his chest and gently pushed him away. "You know we don't have time."

"I know," he said. "But getting you naked is pretty much all I've thought about since last night."

His words thrilled her, and she liked the idea of him taking her right here, up against the door.

"Don't you think it would be nice if our first time wasn't rushed?" she asked. "And happened in bed?"

Nick gestured over his shoulder. "There's a bed right there."

"Nick—"

"Okay, okay," he said backing away. "But the second we get to Aruba, Mrs. Caroselli, you're mine."

Seven

Keeping his hands off Terri while she changed into jeans and a T-shirt, seeing her in her bra and panties, was the worst kind of torture, but Nick knew that if they were going to make their flight, the fooling around would have to wait. On sheer will he managed to restrain himself, but the image of her standing there mostly naked was emblazoned in his mind.

They arrived at the airport with an hour to spare, only to find their flight had been delayed due to a line of storms that spanned the entire southeast. As a result, they spent the next four hours stuck in the terminal playing solitaire on their phones, and sharing a less-than-gourmet meal at a fast food restaurant. When their flight was finally called, and they did get in the air, the ride was so bumpy neither of them could sleep. Terri sat beside him the entire five hours, her white-knuckled hold on his hand so tight that he had to let go every few minutes to shake the blood flow back into his fingers.

When they finally landed in Aruba, because of the flight delay, they had to wait another hour for their ride. By the time they reached the resort, and were shown to their suite—which was as luxurious as the description on the website, and about the only thing that had gone right so far—the sun was rising.

After a tour of all the amenities that at the moment Nick didn't give a damn about, he gave the bellboy a generous tip, hung the do not disturb sign on the door, then closed and locked it. "I thought that guy would *never* leave."

"It's official," Terri said, looking as beat as he was feeling. "I've been up for twenty-four hours."

So had he. He'd been known to pull all-nighters at work, then function reasonably well the next day. Maybe the stress of the past two weeks had finally caught up with him, or the miserable flight had worn him out, because his body was shutting down. Though he wouldn't have imagined it possible, he was too exhausted for sex. "Maybe we should take a nap."

Without hesitation Terri walked straight to the bedroom, yanked back the covers on the king-size bed and flopped facedown onto the sheet. She sighed and said in a sleepy voice, "Oh, that's nice."

Nick climbed in next to her and stretched out on his back, felt the mattress conform to his body as he relaxed.

Terri scooted close to him and cuddled up to his side, one arm draped across his chest, her breasts nestled against him. He'd been anticipating this day for two weeks, and now he was too damned tired to move.

"I want to jump you," Terri said, "but I don't have the energy."

"Me, neither," he said. "Can we at least sleep naked?"

She was quiet for a second, then sighed and said, "As nice as that sounds, I don't think I have the strength to take my clothes off."

He imagined all the movement getting undressed would require and said, "Come to think of it, neither do I."

"You know, I never imagined how stressful it could be planning a wedding, even with so much help. It was really nice, but I'm kinda glad it's over."

"I'm sorry if it wasn't your dream wedding."

"I was never one of those girls."

"What kind of girl?"

"The ones who start planning their wedding when they're barely out of diapers. I've always been more interested in finding the perfect *man*."

"Well, I'm sorry I couldn't be that, either." For a fleeting moment, he almost wished he could be. Because for him, she would be as close to the perfect woman as he would ever find. The problem was, he had no desire to be any woman's perfect man.

"You're helping me fulfill my dream of having a child," she said. "That's pretty huge."

If he wasn't so damned tired, he would be helping her fulfill that particular dream right now, but he could feel himself drifting off. She was still talking but the words weren't making it through the fog in his brain. He tried to keep his eyes open, but they refused to cooperate.

He finally gave in and let them close, and when he opened them again he was in bed alone. He looked at the time on his watch, surprised that he'd slept for over four hours.

He sat up, looking around the room, taking in the decor that he'd been too exhausted to notice earlier. The tropical theme was typical for the area, and could be a little too touristy for his taste, but here it was done well. He could smell the ocean, hear the water rushing up to meet the sand.

He rolled out of bed and went searching for Terri. Her bag lay open on the sofa, but she was nowhere in the suite. He opened the French doors that led out onto a small portico, then a narrow stretch of private beach. The air was warm but dry, and the sun so intense he had to shade his eyes. Guests sunned themselves in lawn chairs and swimmers dotted the crystal-clear blue water. Farther out was everything from sailboats and luxury yachts to commercial cruise ships.

He didn't see Terri anywhere, and figured she had probably gone for a walk, or maybe down to the pool.

He stepped back inside, thinking he would call her cell phone, until he noticed it sitting on the table by the couch.

He would take a shower instead, and if she wasn't back by the time he was finished, he would go looking for her.

He grabbed what he needed from his suitcase and stepped into the bathroom. The opened toiletries on the shower shelf, and wet towel hanging on the rack, told him that she'd already been there, and the remnants of moisture still clinging to the tile shower wall said it hadn't been that long ago. Too bad she hadn't woken him; they could have showered together.

He imagined how she would look, all slippery and wet, those long gorgeous legs wrapped around him, pressed against the shower wall. He wondered if that was a position that qualified as deep penetration. And decided right then that they would have to try it and find out.

He had just stepped out of the shower and was toweling off when he heard the suite door open.

"Nick!"

"In here." He fastened the towel around his waist and

exited the bathroom. Terri stood by the bed, dressed in nothing but a white bikini top that seemed to glow against her sun-kissed skin, and a pair of frayed, cutoff denim short shorts that showcased her slender legs, making them look a mile long. Her hair hung loose and damp around her shoulders, and the only makeup she wore was a touch of lip gloss.

It wasn't that he hadn't seen her dressed this way before. But those other times, he hadn't really *seen* her—not the way he was now. He had the feeling it was the same for her, because she hadn't peeled her eyes from his chest since he'd entered the room.

"Good nap?" she asked, her eyes finally lifting to his. They had a hazy quality that said she was already turned on. And knowing she was, thrust his libido into overdrive.

"Yeah. How long did you sleep?"

She shrugged. "A couple hours."

"You should have woken me."

"That's okay. I want you well rested."

He would ask why, but the way she was sizing him up, he was pretty sure he already knew. "So I guess this is the official start of our honeymoon."

"Then I guess it would be a good time to mention that I'm not wearing any underwear."

Damn. "What a coincidence, because neither am I."

Her gaze dropped from his chest to the towel and her tongue darted out to wet her lips. "Show me."

Terri watched as Nick gave the towel a quick tug, then let it drop to the floor. She looked him up and down, shaking her head. There was no getting around it—physically, the guy was perfect. "Wow. That is so not fair."

"What?"

"No one should look that good naked."

"And I'm all yours," he said, walking toward her with no modesty or shame, wearing that I'm-going-to-eat-you-alive look.

Her heart skipped a beat.

"Ready to make a baby?"

A baby. They were going to have sex, and try to make a baby.

Her heart gave a sudden, violent jerk as the reality of what she was doing, and who she was doing it with, hit her hard. Was she really ready for this? "We're going to make a baby," she said.

"Yep." He stopped in front of her and made a twirly gesture with his index finger. "Turn around."

"Together," she added, turning.

"That's the idea," he said, and with a quick tug, untied her bikini top. "Of course, we could do it alone, but that wouldn't be nearly as much fun."

Though she'd never been particularly shy about anyone seeing her naked, as her top fell away, she had to fight the urge to cross her arms over her breasts. What was wrong with her? For two weeks she'd been preparing herself for this, thinking about this exact moment over and over. When it came to sex, she always knew exactly what she wanted, and she'd never been shy about asking for it. So why, now, did she feel like a virgin, about to make love for the first time?

He must have sensed something was wrong, because he asked over her shoulder, "Are you still okay with this?"

"Of course," she said, but it was difficult to sound convincing when her voice was trembling.

"Are you sure? Because you sound a little nervous." His arms slid around her and cupped her breasts in his palms, easing her backward against his wide muscular chest. His skin was still warm and damp from his shower.

And even though it felt amazing, and she wanted more, her heart was in her throat.

"We could stop right now," he said.

Would he really? If she told him that she had changed her mind, that she was scared, he wouldn't be upset?

But she wouldn't get scared. Not about sex of all things. "I don't want to stop."

He ran the backs of his fingers slowly down her stomach to the edge of her shorts, and her skin quivered under his touch. One part of her was saying, *don't stop there,* while another said, w*hat do you think you're doing, pal? We're* friends. *You aren't supposed to touch me this way.*

"As long as we don't consummate the marriage," Nick said, tugging the snap open on her shorts, "we can still have it annulled."

She wasn't sure if he was serious or teasing her. What if he was serious? What would his family think? How would she explain that they'd gone through all that trouble planning a wedding for a marriage that lasted twenty-four hours?

"Terri?" he said, sounding unsure, his hands dropping away.

She turned, arms folded across her breasts. "What if I said I want to stop? That I thought we were making a mistake?"

He blinked, his expression a mix of confusion and surprise. "You're serious?"

She nodded.

He was quiet for several seconds, then said, "If you really don't want to do this, we won't."

"After everything we've been through the past couple weeks, you wouldn't be mad?"

"I would be disappointed, but our friendship comes first, always."

She could see that they weren't just words. He meant it. She wasn't just another woman he was sleeping with, or a convenient way to make ten million dollars. He really cared about her feelings. And she *knew* that. The truth was, this had nothing to do with him. This was about her insecurities.

When it came to relationships, love—or what she perceived love to be—always managed to elude her. And while sex, if she was lucky, was usually fun, she'd never felt the intense emotional connection that she was experiencing right now, with Nick. The *need* to be closer to him. She never *needed* anyone, and it scared her half to death. What if he let her down?

But this was Nick, the most important person in her life. The man she had barely gone a day or two without speaking with in the past two decades. He would *not* let her down. He wouldn't do anything to hurt her. And she refused to ruin what could very well be one of the most significant days in her entire life, just because she had intimacy issues. It was time she grew up, and let go of the past. Time she really trusted someone.

"Do you want to stop?" he asked. "We can."

"No. I don't want to stop."

He eyed her warily. "You're *sure*. Because once we get started, there's really no going back."

"I want this," she said, and she really did, even though she was scared. "I want *you*."

She dropped her arms, baring herself to him, and the hunger in his eyes as he raked his gaze over her made her heart beat faster.

"You had me worried there for a minute," he said. "Although I have to admit, I sort of like you this way."

"What way?"

"Not so confident. A little vulnerable."

Weirdly enough, she sort of liked it, too. She liked the idea of letting someone else take care of her for a change. Within reason, of course. She didn't want him getting the idea that she was a complete pushover.

She slid her arms around his neck and kissed him, then whispered in his ear, "Lay down."

"Now that's the Terri I know," he said with a grin, climbing into bed, watching as she shoved down her shorts and got in with him, straddling his thighs.

"You're so beautiful." He reached up, cupped her breasts in his palms, watched her nipples pull into tight points as he circled them with his thumbs. "I want to take my time, touch and kiss every inch of your body."

She smiled. "Well, if you have to…"

He pulled her against him, wrapped his arms around her and kissed her…and *kissed* her, disarming her with the rhythm of his tongue, his hands sliding across her skin, kissing and stroking away the last of her reservations, until she couldn't recall why she'd been afraid in the first place. And the more she responded, the bolder his explorations became. Still, she could tell he was taking his time, trying not to push too hard or too fast.

She just wanted to touch him—wanted *him*—and as close as he held her, as intimately as he touched her, it wasn't enough. She ached for something, but she wasn't sure what. She just knew she *needed* more. And though she preferred to have the upper hand, when Nick took control, rolling her over onto her back, she let him. Being so tall, logistics in bed could sometimes be a problem for her, but as he settled between her thighs, she and Nick were an ideal fit.

"That's better," he said, his weight pressing her into the mattress.

This was it, she thought, knowing that she would remember this moment for the rest of her life—the exact second when, with one slow deep thrust, they went from being friends to lovers.

She gazed down between them, to where their bodies were joined, thinking it was the most arousing, erotic thing she had ever seen. "Nick, we're making love," she said. "You're inside me."

He followed her gaze, transfixed for a moment, then he wrapped his arms around her and kissed her, started to move inside her.

She really thought she'd been prepared for this, that because they were friends, she could maintain a level of detachment, or objectivity. That it would be "fun" without those pesky feelings of affection to muddy things up. Boy, had she been wrong.

This wasn't supposed to change things, but deep down she knew they would never be quite the same.

"Deeper," she said. "You have to be deeper."

"I can't," he said, thrusting slow and steady, his shoulders tense, his eyes closed in concentration. "I'll lose it."

As it was, she was barely hanging on, and they needed to do this together, and not just so they would have a boy. She...*needed* it. "Nick, look at me."

He opened his eyes and looked down at her. The instant their eyes met, she was toast, and apparently so was he. With a growl, Nick grabbed her legs and hooked them over his shoulders, bending her in half, groaning as he thrust hard and deep, and her body went electric. It was shock and pleasure and perfection, and watching Nick's face, seeing him lose control, reaching their peak together, was the single most erotic experience of her life.

Afterward, Nick dropped his head against her shoulder, his forehead damp with perspiration. He was breathing hard. *"Wow."*

No kidding.

Nick eased her legs off his shoulders and she winced as her muscles, mostly the ones in her butt, screamed in protest. She stretched out her legs and her left cheek started to cramp up. She winced and said, "Ow! Charley horse!"

"Where?" Nick said, rolling off her.

"Left butt cheek."

"Turn over," he said, and when she did, he straddled her thighs and rubbed the knotted muscle, using his thumbs to really work it loose. "Better?"

"Hmm...that feels good," she said, as the pain subsided. She folded her arms around the pillow and tucked it under her head. "I'm going to have a talk with my personal trainer. All those hours spent in the gym, and I'm not nearly as flexible as I should be."

"I guess we'll just have to work on that," he said.

She sighed and closed her eyes. Though she was typically the one doing the pampering after sex, it was nice to be spoiled a little. Only problem was, she was getting a little *too* relaxed, to the point that her body was shutting down.

"Hey," Nick said. "I hope you're not falling asleep."

"Nope," she lied as the world started to go soft and fuzzy around her.

"We're not finished." He gave her a gentle shake. "Wake up."

"I'm awake," she mumbled, or at least she thought she did. It didn't matter because it was already too late. She gave in to the fatigue and drifted off to sleep.

Eight

Nick gave Terri a poke, then a harder poke, but it was useless. She was out cold.

He sighed. Wasn't it the *guy* who was supposed to roll over and fall asleep after sex? His plan had been for them to spend the entire day in bed, trying out many different positions. But he supposed he should be happy that they'd had sex at all.

It was a little difficult to reconcile the Terri from two weeks ago, who propositioned him in his kitchen, and the one who froze up today when he touched her. He wasn't sure what had happened, why she had suddenly gotten cold feet. At first he thought she was teasing him, playing coy, until he saw her face, then the metaphorical ball came out of left field and smacked him right between the eyes.

Was it something he did? Something he said? Did he hurt her feelings? Or was it something he'd had no control over whatsoever?

Damned if he knew.

She was ovulating, so her hormones were probably out of whack, and he knew from growing up in a house with three females, a hormonal woman could be unpredictable—and at times downright scary. But weren't ovulating women supposed to want sex more, not less?

Or was it possible that she didn't find him as appealing as she said she did? Was she so desperate to get pregnant, she would have told him anything?

Nah, that definitely wasn't it, because when they did finally get the ball rolling, it had been pretty freaking amazing. To put his hands all over that lithe, lean body, to feel those incredible legs wrapped around his waist. Over his shoulders.

Damn.

Even so, when he looked at her now, lying there, naked and gorgeous, she was still just *Terri,* his best friend. And other than wanting to put his hands all over her again, he couldn't say that he felt any differently about her now than he had yesterday. Which was exactly how he'd expected to feel.

He assumed, since she would be ovulating for at least a few more days, there was no reason they couldn't have fun until then, or better yet, for the duration of their honeymoon. But he knew that when they returned to Chicago, they would go back to their previous platonic status. The truth was, they hadn't really talked about it. And that had probably been a mistake. But everything had happened in such a rush, they really hadn't had time.

Terri mumbled something in her sleep, then rolled over onto her side, curling up in a ball, as if she were chilled, so he tugged the covers up over her. As long as he'd known her she'd talked in her sleep. There were times, when they lived together, when he would pass by her room at night and hear her babbling incoherently. He would sometimes stop and listen, catch a random word here or there, but it usually didn't make any sense. If she seemed distressed, as if she were having a nightmare, which had happened often, he would push open her door a crack and peek in on her, just to make sure she was okay.

Sometimes he would hear her say his name, wondering what role he played in her dream. There were even times when he imagined crawling into bed with her. How would she react if he did? He never would have done it, though. She wanted the fairy-tale happy ending. A thing he could never give her, and after all the heartache in her life, she deserved to get exactly what she wanted. Even now he hated that she'd had to settle, that he couldn't give her everything her heart desired. But he just wasn't wired that way. Anyone he dated knew that from the start, although that didn't necessarily stop them from believing that they were different, that they would be the one he fell hopelessly in love with.

But Terri knew better. Didn't she?

He was sure she did. They had agreed this situation would be temporary. So why her mixed feelings today? Maybe it would be in everyone's best interest if they had a serious talk about the situation, and set some boundaries to prevent any future confusion. Just in case.

Nick's stomach growled, and he considered ringing for room service, but then he looked at the empty space beside Terri—and the cool sheets and fluffy pillows called out to him. She had said she wanted him well rested, hadn't she?

He stretched out beside her, his eyes feeling heavy the second his head hit the pillow. He rolled over on his side, draping an arm across her hip, wondering, as he drifted off to sleep, if it would be smooth sailing from here on out. Or would she have a change of heart again?

He got his answer when he woke from what he'd thought was an erotic dream. He opened his eyes, looked down at his crotch, and saw the top of Terri's head.

"I'm toast," Terri said.

She dropped face-first onto the sheets, sweaty and out of breath, and Nick fell on top of her, his weight crushing her against the mattress, making it hard to breathe. She was too exhausted to protest. They had been going at it, on and off, for three hours now, and she was ready for a break.

"Do you feel pregnant yet?" he asked, his voice muffled against her hair, which she was sure was probably a knotted mess.

"I think it takes a couple weeks for that part," she said. If she hadn't conceived the first three times they'd made love, she was pretty sure this last time would have done it. Their position, while slightly awkward at first, gave a whole new meaning to the phrase *deep penetration*. Plus, her thighs had gotten one hell of a workout.

She shifted under his weight, feeling light-headed from lack of oxygen. Gathering all her strength, she elbowed him in the ribs. "Hey, you're squishing me."

"Sorry," he said, rolling onto his back. "So, what do you want to do now?"

"Sleep?"

He looked over at her. *"Again?"*

Or not. "I don't know. What do people usually do on their honeymoon?"

He looked over at her and grinned, wiggling his eyebrows.

Good heavens, the man had stamina.

"Something besides intercourse," she said.

He thought about it for a minute, then said, "Oral sex?"

"Funny," she said giving him a playful poke, and he grinned.

"We could sit in the sand and watch the sunset," he said. "I hear they can be pretty spectacular."

"Which I suppose would necessitate me getting up and putting clothes on."

"Personally, I wouldn't mind if you went out there like this, but the other guests might object." He leaned over and kissed her shoulder. "If I could bring the sunset to you, I would."

Wow, that was probably one of the sweetest, most romantic things a man had ever said to her. She smiled and said, "I appreciate the thought."

"Come on," he said, giving her butt a playful smack as he rolled out of bed. "Get up."

She forced herself to stand and walk on jelly legs to the bathroom. It seemed strange that just this morning she'd been uncomfortable with him seeing her naked, and now it seemed perfectly natural. Not only had he seen it all, but there wasn't an inch that he hadn't touched in one way or another. When he told her that he thought sex should be fun, he wasn't kidding. And boy was he *good* at it. He seemed to take pleasure from giving pleasure, which she knew was rare.

She stepped into the bathroom and cringed at her reflection in the mirror. "I look like a beast. I need to do something with my hair."

He appeared in the doorway dressed in shorts and a T-shirt. "Yikes! You do look like a beast."

She glared at him.

"Kidding," he said, flashing her that disarming grin and planting a kiss on her cheek. "I'll meet you out there."

She wrestled a brush through the knots in her hair and brought it back into a ponytail. Not great, but it would suffice. She pulled a light sundress out of her bag and slipped it on, then stepped outside.

The air felt cooler. A gentle breeze rustled the the palm trees, their branches swaying in time like a tropical nature dance. And Nick was right about the sunset. Red-and-orange streaks above the horizon gave the illusion that the sky was on fire.

Nick was on a blanket in the sand a few yards from the water. He sat with his knees bent, his arms wrapped around them. She walked over and sat down beside him.

He smiled at her, nodding to the sky. "Nice, huh?"

"Beautiful."

He leaned back and looped an arm around her, and she rested her head against his shoulder. It felt…comfortable. She wondered if it would be okay to do this after they went home to Chicago, or if any sort of physical contact would be off limits.

"So," he said. "About earlier today…"

She cringed. It was embarrassing, really, the way she'd acted. And she still wasn't quite sure why. "Can we just forget about that?"

"I wanted to be sure that everything is okay now."

"It is, I promise." That should have been obvious the minute she woke him up from his nap, which was exactly why she'd done it. Well, that and he'd looked really good laying there naked.

"You were pretty freaked out," he said.

So apparently they *were* going to talk about it. "I know. I thought I had worked it all out in my head, but then you asked if I was ready to make a baby, and I guess I thought, *I don't know, am I?* It's a huge step. My entire life will change."

"And you were worried about it changing our relationship." It was a statement, not a question.

"That, too."

"Do you think it has?"

"Sort of. But not in a bad way."

"We never really talked about what will happen after the honeymoon."

Which she took to mean that they should talk about it now. "I just assumed we would go back to the way things were. Aside from the fact that we'll be living together, I mean. And, of course, your family will have to believe that we're…you know…*together*."

"So, no sex after the honeymoon?"

Was that disappointment she heard in his voice? Did he want to keep having sex? Or was she just imagining what she wanted to hear? Because she liked sleeping with him. Liked it too much for either of their own good.

"I think that would be best," she said. "Under the circumstances, an intimate relationship could get complicated. Don't you think? I know you don't want to settle down."

He thought about that for a minute, and her heart picked up speed. Was he going to say he wanted to keep sleeping with her? And how would she respond if he did? Even if she wanted it, too, would it be wise to tempt fate?

"You're right," he finally said. "I think it would be better if we went back to the way things were."

She was a little disappointed, but not surprised. And she was sure, when things went back to normal, they would be just as happy being friends.

"What if you don't get pregnant?" Nick asked.

"We try again next month. But not until I'm ovulating."

He nodded, as if that made sense to him, too. "And

if you don't get pregnant then? I mean, for all I know, I could be sterile."

"That's highly unlikely. And it would be fairly easy to determine."

"Even if we're both fine, it could still take months, right?"

"So what you're asking is, how long do we keep this up before we call it quits?"

He nodded.

"As long as we're both comfortable with it, I suppose."

An older couple, who looked to be close to Nick's parents' age, walked by, holding hands. Something about the way they moved together, the way they smiled at one another, made Terri think they had probably been married a long time, and were probably still deeply in love.

They smiled and said hello as they passed, and Terri actually felt a twinge of jealousy. As much as she wanted that for herself, and while most of her friends from college were already happily married and starting families, she had begun to believe that, for her, it would probably never happen. That maybe she was just meant for different things. The only thing she did know for sure was that until she became a mother, she would never feel truly complete. So whatever she had to do to make that happen, wasn't it worth the risk?

Terri woke the next morning to the sound of rain against the windows. Through the filmy curtains, she could see lightning slash across the sky. She glanced over her shoulder at Nick, who was curled up behind her, his arm draped across her hip. Though he was still asleep, certain parts were wide awake and pressed against her. She grabbed her phone and checked her weather app, which called for scattered thunderstorms all day. So much for their plans to rent a car and drive to Arikok National Park.

"Is that rain I hear?" Nick mumbled behind her.

"Yeah. It's supposed to rain on and off all day."

"Darn." Nick slid his arm around her, cupping her breast. "Guess we'll have to stay inside today."

She was sure they could find some indoor activity other than sex, but honestly, why would they want to? They only had a few more days before they went back to being just friends. Besides, newlyweds were supposed to have lots of sex on their honeymoon. Right?

They stayed in bed most of the day, and later that evening when the sky finally cleared, they showered together, then attended a party by the pool with the other resort guests. They played the role of the loving newlyweds, even though they would likely never see any of these people again.

They spent the following day in Arikok National Park. They rented a car, and quickly discovered that very few of the roads in Aruba were marked. They got lost a couple times, but it was worth the hassle when they got there.

Their first stop was Boca Prins, which they were told by another guest at the resort was the most beautiful thing in Aruba. With its beach cliffs, dunes and rocky shore, Terri had to agree. Although the sunset that first night definitely rated a close second.

They stopped for lunch at a local cantina, then drove to Fontein Cave and on to Guadirikiri Cave. Nick found her fear of the the lizards scurrying around incredibly amusing.

In the early evening they dropped off the car and took a taxi to downtown Oranjestad. They did a little shopping as they made their way to Fort Zoutman where they stopped to listen to a steel band and browsed the various local craft booths. They bought souvenirs for Nick's niece and nephews, and Terri found a pair of earrings she knew his mom would adore. She liked them so much she got a pair for herself, too.

Without street signs, it took a while to find the restaurant where they had made reservations for dinner, but the food was incredible. They ate and danced until they were exhausted, but not so much that it stopped them from making love when they got back to their room. After all, it was after their last night together.

Wednesday morning they packed and took a taxi to the airport for their flight home. They made it through security without a problem, found their gate and sat down to wait. That was when the reality of the situation hit home, and suddenly she wasn't ready to leave. Wasn't ready for this to be over.

The longer you wait, the harder it will be, she reminded herself. If they didn't end this now, what would they do? Continue on as lovers until the baby was born, or for the rest of their lives, yet never be in a committed relationship? She wasn't naive enough to believe that any friendship, even one as strong as theirs, could survive that. Besides, she wasn't quite ready to give up on the fairy tale. Finding Mr. Right, and living happily ever after.

But as Nick sat silently beside her, reading an issue of *Time* magazine, she couldn't help but wonder what he was thinking—if he was ready for this to be over or if he had regrets, too. Not that it would make a difference. So why was she obsessing about it?

Their flight was called right on time.

"I guess this is it," Nick said, stuffing the magazine into his carry-on bag. "The end of our honeymoon."

"I guess so." She grabbed her bag and started to stand, but Nick wrapped his hand around her arm.

"Terri...wait."

She sat back down, turning to him. "Is something wr—"

Nick hooked a hand behind her neck, pulled her to him and kissed her. It was slow and deep and bittersweet, and packed with so much raw emotion, she knew he was just as sorry to see this end. But like her, he knew they had no choice.

"Sorry," he said, closing his eyes and pressing his forehead to hers. "I just had to do that one more time."

They were doing the right thing, so why did she suddenly feel like crying? She was too choked up to say anything. If she tried, she would probably burst into tears, and where would that get them? It would just make him feel bad, and her feel stupid.

She pressed one last quick kiss to his lips, then stood and said, "We'd better go."

In the past five days she had grown used to touching and kissing Nick whenever she wanted. Now she would just have to get unused to it. Unless they were around his family, since it was necessary to keep up the ruse.

They boarded the plane, stored their bags and took their seats. With any luck, she was pregnant. She couldn't imagine how she wouldn't be, considering all the unprotected sex they'd been having. And though she almost hoped she hadn't conceived, so they could have honeymoon number two in about four weeks, she knew that dragging this out another month or so would only delay the inevitable. That it would probably be even harder next time.

After they were in the air, she reclined her seat and closed her eyes, pretending to sleep. It was easier than trying to make cheerful small talk, when she felt anything but happy. Nick kept himself amused reading his magazine. At some point she must have really fallen asleep, because suddenly Nick was nudging her and saying that the plane was going to land in a few minutes.

They didn't say much to each other during the miserably long wait in customs. What she wanted was to go back to her own place, curl up in her own bed and be miserable all by herself, but her home was at Nick's apartment now.

"You've been awfully quiet," Nick said, when they were in the car and heading for the city. "Is everything okay?"

She looked over at him and forced a smile. "Fine. I'm just tired. And not looking forward to all the work I have waiting for me."

It wasn't a total lie, but not exactly the truth, either.

"You will take tomorrow off, right?"

"Of course." She hadn't missed Thanksgiving with his family in years. "And maybe I'll do some Black Friday shopping with your mom."

"You're sure everything is okay?" he said.

"I'm sure." She pulled out her cell phone and checked her email. Nick took the hint and didn't ask any more questions.

The car dropped them off around dinnertime, and they rode the elevator up in silence. Though she continued to pretend that everything was fine, there was tension in the air, and she knew that he felt it, too.

She hated for their relationship to take this turn. As long as they had been friends, they had barely even had a fight.

It will just take a little time for things to go back to normal, she assured herself. After that, everything would be fine.

The elevator doors opened and sitting in the hallway outside the apartment door, a suitcase at her side, was

Jess, Nick's sister. She looked tired, and her eyes were red and puffy, as if she might have been crying.

"Hi, there," she said with a weak smile. "How was the honeymoon?"

Nine

"Jess, what are you doing here?" Nick asked, but considering the suitcase beside her, he could make an educated guess.

Jess pushed herself to her feet. "Can we go inside and talk?"

"Sure." He unlocked the door and they all rolled their luggage in. When everyone was inside, he shut the door and turned to his sister.

"Eddie and I are taking a break," she said. "Or, I am, anyway."

"What happened?"

"He blew off counseling for the third week in a row. Knowing I have that to look forward to, that it might make things better eventually, is the only thing that's kept me going the last couple months. He obviously doesn't feel the same way. So I left."

"What about the kids?"

"They're spending Thanksgiving in Indiana with Eddie's parents. They'll be there a week. I'm hoping we can work something out by the time they come back."

"What are you doing here?" Nick asked.

"Honestly, I couldn't bear the thought of staying alone in a hotel for the next week, and I know you guys have the extra bedroom." She smiled hopefully.

"What about Mom's place?"

"I didn't want to worry her. Also, I'd like to keep this quiet, and you know how she is. If she knows, *everyone* will know."

Nick was about to make up some excuse about him and Terri being newlyweds and needing their privacy, but before he could, Terri said, "Of course you can stay here."

"Thank you," Jess said, looking as if she were fighting tears. "You have no idea how much this means to me. And I won't get in the way, I promise."

"That's what family is for," Terri said, hugging her. "Just give me a few minutes to clear my clothes out of the spare room."

Jess frowned. "Why are your clothes in the spare room?"

Nick thought for sure Jess had her stumped with that one, but Terri didn't miss a beat.

"Have you ever looked in your brother's closet?" she asked Jess.

"If it looks anything like it did when he was a kid, I see your point."

"There's beer in the fridge," Nick said. "And the hard stuff is in the bar in my office. I'm going to help my wife."

Jess headed to the kitchen, while Nick and Terri walked to what was supposed to be her bedroom. When they were alone, he whispered, "You realize what you just did, right? You really think it's a good idea for us to share a bedroom? And a *bed?*"

"*No,* but what were we supposed to tell her? Sorry, you can't stay because *I'm* sleeping there? How would we explain *that?*"

If she had just given him a minute to think, he would have come up with something.

"Besides, it's only for a week." She opened the closet and grabbed an armful of clothes. "Do you have room for these in your closet?"

"I'll make room," he said, opening one of the drawers. Of course, with his rotten luck, it was full of lingerie. Damn. "And for the record, my closet looks nothing like it did in high school. Or college."

"I don't care how it looks, as long as it doesn't smell like sweaty sports gear."

He opened his mouth to argue, but realized it probably had smelled pretty awful.

"It doesn't," he said, as they dropped her clothes on his bed. "I keep my gym bag in the utility room behind the kitchen."

"I'll be sure to avoid it," she said, sounding annoyed.

She started to walk away and he grabbed her arm, turning her to face him. "Hey, this was *your* idea."

She looked as if she were about to say something snarky, then it seemed as if all the energy leaked out of her instead. "I know. I'm sorry. I just…I don't even know what's wrong. I'm tired, I guess."

"Just try to cut me a little slack, okay? This isn't easy for me, either."

"I know."

Maybe this scenario of pretending to be married wouldn't be quite as simple as they had imagined, or maybe they just needed a few days to adjust. One thing was certain—having Jess around wasn't going to make the transition any smoother.

They got the rest of Terri's clothes moved into his room and put away in his closet—which she made a point of observing was very tidy—and when they walked out to the kitchen, Jess had made them all dinner. After they ate, they put a movie on, but his sister clearly needed to vent. She alternated between complaining about Eddie and apologizing for complaining.

Around eleven Terri started yawning, which set him off. Once they got started it was a vicious cycle.

"You two must be exhausted from your trip, and here I am talking your heads off," Jess said.

"That's what family is for," Terri told her.

"Well, I'm going to stop whining now and let you two get to bed. And I'm sure I could benefit from a good night's sleep."

Nick was skeptical that she would get one, considering the state of her marriage, and he knew he and Terri wouldn't. Not if they were sleeping in the same bed.

Jess hugged them both good-night, thanked them again for letting her vent then went to bed. When Nick heard her bedroom door close, he turned to Terri. "I guess there's no point putting this off."

"I guess not."

He used the bathroom first, and while she took her turn, he undressed and climbed into bed. She came out wearing a nightshirt that hung to her knees, her hair loose. If it were still their honeymoon, she would be naked, and instead of climbing into the opposite side of the bed, she would be climbing on him.

"So how is this going to work?" she said, pulling the covers up to her waist.

He shrugged. "I stay on my side, you stay on yours."

She shot him a skeptical look. "You can do that?"

Did he have a choice? "It's a king-size bed. You won't even know I'm over here."

She still didn't look completely convinced, but she switched off her light, rolled away from him and pulled the covers over her shoulders.

"What, no kiss?" he said.

She glared at him over her shoulder.

"Kidding." The way she was acting one might have thought that letting his sister stay here had been *his* idea.

He turned off his light, settled onto his back and closed his eyes. He was physically exhausted, but his mind was moving about a million miles an hour, which could make for a very long and sleepless night. The last time he looked at the clock, it was one-thirty, but he must have drifted off because before he knew it, he heard Terri say his name, felt her nudging him awake. He didn't want to wake up; he was too content and comfortable curled up against something warm and soft. It took several seconds to realize that the thing he was curled up against was Terri, and she was looking at him over her shoulder.

"What are you doing on my side of the bed?" he asked.

"I'm not."

He let go and sat up. Sure enough, he had invaded her side of the bed by several feet.

He scooted back onto his own side. "Sorry about that."

"Habit," she said. "Not a big deal."

"It won't happen again." He looked over at the clock and saw that it was only two-thirty. He rolled on his side facing away from her, determined to stay that way the rest of the night.

An hour later she woke him again. He was curled up against her like before, but this time his hand was up her nightshirt and cupped around her bare breast, and he was aroused. In fact, he was horny as hell.

"Um, Nick, maybe you should—"

He yanked his hand from inside her shirt and scooted away from her. "Why didn't you stop me?"

"Don't blame me," she snapped, rolling to face him. "I woke up that way."

He took a deep breath and blew it out. "Sorry, I didn't mean to accuse you."

She sat up. "This is not working. Maybe I should sleep on the floor, or in the bathtub."

"You know what the problem is," he said. "I usually sleep hugging a pillow, but you're lying on it, so I'm hugging you instead."

"Do you have a pillow you could hug instead of me?"

He switched on the light and started to get up, then turned back to her and said, "You may want to look the other way."

Her brows rose. "You don't want me to see you in your pajamas?"

"I wouldn't care if I were wearing any."

Her mouth fell open in surprise. "You're *naked?*"

He shrugged. "I've always slept naked. I don't even own pajamas."

"You own underwear, right? I mean, I've seen you wear it."

He sighed. "I'll put some on."

He hadn't slept with anything on since he was fifteen, but he would just have to get used to it, he supposed.

Terri turned away from him as he got out of bed. But he could swear, as he walked to the closet, he could feel her eyes on him, specifically his ass. He tugged on a pair of boxer briefs, grabbed a pillow from the top shelf, switched off the light and walked back to bed. "Got it."

"And you're not naked?"

"Nope." He climbed into bed. With the skivvies on, he was instantly uncomfortable. Fantastic.

"Well, good night," she said.

"Good night." Though it probably wouldn't be. He curled up with the pillow between them, and must have fallen asleep pretty quickly, because when Terri nudged him awake the next time, it felt like minutes, when in reality a couple hours had passed.

"Nick, you're doing it *again*."

She was right. His arms were around her, his hand was back up her shirt and he was as aroused as he had been the last time.

"Sorry," he said scooting away for a third time, feeling around for the pillow. When he couldn't find it, he asked Terri, "Where did the pillow go?"

"I don't have it," she snapped.

And she was clearly annoyed with him. Not that he could blame her. He switched on the light, and Terri grumbled in protest, covering her head with her pillow. As his eyes adjusted, he looked all around the room and discovered it lying on the floor at the foot of the bed. He must have lobbed it in his sleep. "There it is."

"Awesome."

"I said I was sorry." He threw off the covers in frustration and shoved himself out of bed.

"Nick!"

He turned to her and realized she was staring at the front of his…well, not his underwear, because at some point he'd apparently taken it off. And she was getting an eyeful.

She sat up in bed. "You said you put underwear on."

"I did! I guess I must have taken them off again." He pulled back the covers, and sure enough, there they were, kicked down near the foot of the bed. He grabbed them and said, "Got 'em."

"This is ridiculous," Terri said.

"I'll put them on."

"And what, *staple* them in place?"

Preferably no. "No need to get vicious. And keep your voice down. Jess is going to hear you."

"Do you have any idea what it's like to wake up with someone fondling you?"

It sounded pretty good to him, but by her tone, he was guessing that she disagreed.

"Look, I'm doing my best."

She sat there in silence for a few seconds, just staring at him—mostly at his crotch—then shook her head and said, "Screw it."

He thought her next move would be to grab her pillow and a blanket and charge off to sleep in the tub. Instead, she pulled her nightshirt over her head and said, "Get over here."

Confused, he opened his mouth to speak, then closed it again.

"What are you waiting for?" she asked, tugging off her panties.

"But...I thought we weren't supposed to—"

"Hurry, before I change my mind."

He climbed into bed, and she pushed him onto his back, straddling his thighs.

"For the record, this is it," she said. "This is the last time. Got it?"

"Got it," he said, then sucked in a breath as she leaned over and took him in her mouth.

This pretending to be crazy-in-love thing was going to be harder than Terri originally thought, and maybe telling Jess she could stay hadn't been such a hot idea, after all. Nick was curled around her again and sound asleep—from the waist up, at least. Sure, it never should have happened, and they were only delaying the inevitable, but Terri couldn't deny that after she had jumped him, she had slept like a baby the rest of the night. Which technically hadn't been all that long, since it was eight now and they hadn't gone to sleep until five. But it was definitely going to be the last time, even if that meant sleeping on the couch. She would come up with some plausible excuse to tell Jess. Like Nick snored, or…well, she would think of *something*.

She slipped from under Nick's arm and got out of bed. He grumbled for a second, then went right back to sleep. She grabbed her nightshirt from the floor and pulled it over her head, then shrugged into her robe. As she walked to the kitchen, the aroma of freshly brewed coffee met her halfway there.

Jess was sitting on one of the bar stools, dressed in what Nick referred to as her mom-clothes—cotton pants and an oversize men's button-up shirt—sipping coffee and staring off into space, looking tired and sad.

"Good morning," Terri said.

Jess looked over at her and smiled brightly. "Happy Thanksgiving! I made coffee."

"It smells delicious." She crossed the room to the coffeepot and pulled down a cup from the cupboard.

"It's a fresh pot. I made the first when I got up and it was getting a little funky. I forget that not everyone is on a mom schedule."

Terri poured herself a cup and added a pinch of sugar. "When did you get up?"

"Five-thirty."

"Yikes! The earliest I ever manage to get up is seven, but usually it's closer to eight-thirty."

"One of the benefits of working from home," Jess said. "You roll out of bed and you're there. Of course, that will change when you have kids. For the first year, you'll barely sleep at all." She grinned and added, "Not that you seemed to be getting much sleep last night."

"I'm sorry if we woke you."

"Don't apologize. You're newlyweds. It's what you're supposed to do. And I'd be lying if I said I wasn't jealous. I can barely remember the last time Eddie and I had sex. And the last time we had really *good* sex? It's been ages."

Terri couldn't fathom why Jess would stay married if things were so bad. It's no wonder Nick and Maggs were so against tying the knot. First their parents' marriage ended in disaster, now Jess was turning it into a family tradition.

"So, speaking of kids," Jess said. "I noticed you didn't drink wine with dinner last night. Does that mean...?"

"I'm pregnant?" She shrugged. "I hope so, but I won't know for sure for another week and a half. I'm trying to be cautious just in case. Which means I shouldn't be drinking coffee, either, I guess."

"Or you could start drinking decaf. I think it still has a trace of caffeine, though."

Well, then, this would be her last cup of real coffee, she supposed. She would have to remember to pick up some decaf tomorrow.

Terri sat beside her. "So, how are you doing?"

She shrugged. "Everything about this situation sucks. I'm just so tired of dealing with it. Sometimes I wonder if it's even worth fighting anymore. It's not fair to the kids." She laid a hand on Terri's arm. "But you and Nick, you're different. I've never known two people who were more suited for each other. I mean, look how long you've been friends."

If only that were true. If only they loved each other that way. Because if things could stay just like they were now, she could imagine them being happy together. Of course, there was the slight problem of Nick not wanting to be married. "That doesn't necessarily mean we were meant to be married."

"Terri, are you having second thoughts?" Jess whispered, looking concerned.

"No, of course not. I'm just trying to be realistic."

"As long as you don't let your fears get in the way of your happiness. If you convince yourself it won't work, it won't."

"Was there a time when your marriage was good?"

"The first couple years were great. I mean, we had our disagreements, no marriage is perfect, but we were both happy."

"What do you think went wrong?"

"Marriage takes hard work. I think we got lazy. Between work and raising the kids, we forgot how to be a couple. Does that make sense?"

"I think so." Being friends could be a lot of work, too. It required compromise and patience. Twenty-year friendships, the ones as close as hers and Nicks, were probably as rare as twenty-year marriages. In a way it sort of was like a marriage. Just without the sex. And honestly, they probably talked as much as or more than most married couples.

"Plus, we have a few other issues…" Jess started to say, but her brother walked into the kitchen, and she clammed up. Did that mean it was something she didn't want him to know about?

Dressed in jeans and nothing else, his hair mussed

from sleep, Nick looked adorable. But when didn't he, really? Too bad last night—or, technically, this morning—had been the absolute last time.

"Good morning ladies," he said, sounding way too cheerful. He gave his sister a peck on the cheek, then scooped Terri into his arms, dipped her back and planted a slow, deep kiss on her.

"*Ugh,* get a room," Jess teased, walking to the sink to rinse her cup.

Nick grinned and winked at Terri. "How did you sleep, sweetheart?"

She flashed him a stern look, and gave him a not-so-gentle shove. It was one thing to be affectionate with each other, and quite another for him to molest her in front of his sister. Okay, maybe she did hesitate a few seconds before she pushed him away. But still...

He walked around the island to pour himself a cup of coffee. "So, when are we supposed to be at Mom's?"

"Eleven," Jess said, sticking her cup in the dishwasher. "Dinner is at five at *Nonno's*. Would you mind if I tag along with you guys? I get the feeling the only way I'll make it through dinner this year is by consuming copious amounts of alcohol."

"I won't be drinking," Terri said. "I can be the designated driver."

"So I can get hammered, too?" Nick said with a hopeful grin.

She shrugged. "If you really want to."

It didn't matter to her. She'd known guys who were quiet, brooding drunks, reckless and irresponsible drunks, and downright mean drunks. The worst she'd seen Nick do when he was really hammered is act a little goofy and get super-affectionate. Although not creepy, molester affectionate. He would just hug her a lot, and tell her repeatedly what a good friend she was, and how much he loved her.

"In fact, why don't we start right now?" Nick said. "We have almost a case of champagne left over from the wedding. I could go for a mimosa."

"Oh, that sounds good!" Jess said, rubbing her hands together. "I'll get the glasses and the orange juice."

"I'll open the champagne," Nick said.

And I'll watch, Terri thought, feeling left out. But she knew that having a baby would take sacrifice, and as far as sacrifices go, this one would be minor. And if nothing else, it would be an interesting day.

Ten

Nick's sister Maggie called asking if she could tag along with them to their mom's and then *Nonno's*. She drove over to Nick's place and they all piled into his Mercedes, with Terri driving, since Nick and Jess had already polished off a bottle and a half of champagne. And it was barely ten-thirty.

Nick's mom served Bellinis with brunch, a traditional Italian cocktail made up of white peach puree and prosecco, an Italian sparkling white wine.

Terri lost track of how many pitchers the four of them consumed, but by the time they left for *Nonno's* house, no one was feeling any pain. At one point Nick leaned over, touched her cheek, gazed at her with a sappy smile and bloodshot eyes and said, "I love you, Terri."

He was rewarded with two exaggerated *awww's* from the backseat. They didn't realize he meant that he loved her as a friend.

"I love you, too," she said, taking his hand and placing it back on his side of the front seat so she could concentrate on the road. But before she could pull away, he grabbed her hand and held it tight.

"No, I mean I *really* love you."

She pried herself free and patted his hand. "I really love you, too."

"It's not fair," Maggie whined from the backseat. "I want what you guys have."

"Me, too," Jess said.

Nick looked over his shoulder at his sisters. "You've told me a hundred times that you would never *ever* get married, Mags."

"And you actually *believed* me? Every woman wants to be married, moron. I only say I don't to spare myself the humiliation of being thirty-three and still single."

"I'm going to be forty," Jess said.

Nick scoffed. "In *three* years."

"Besides," Maggie said. "You're *married.*"

"But for how long? I keep telling myself things will change, but they never do." Jess sniffed. "He's not even trying anymore."

"So leave him," Maggie said. "You deserve to be happy."

"I can't."

"Why not?" Nick said.

"There are certain things I'm not willing to give up, like private school for the kids. And do you have any idea how much sports programs cost? I would have to take out a third mortgage."

"Third?" Nick said, and Terri didn't have to see his face to know that he was frowning. She glanced back at Jess in the rearview mirror, and it looked as if all the color had drained from her face. Was she going to be sick?

"You know, forget I said anything," Jess said.

"No," Nick said. "That house was a wedding gift, there shouldn't be a mortgage."

"Can we please drop it?" she asked, sounding nervous.

Nick apparently didn't want to drop it. "Why did you mortgage the house, Jess?"

"Raising a family is expensive."

"You both make good money, and you have your trust to fall back on."

When she didn't answer him, Nick said, "Jess, you do still have your trust? Right?"

"I have enough socked away to put the kids through college, but I won't touch that."

"And the rest?" Mags asked.

Her cheeks crimson, she said, "Gone. It's all gone."

"Where?" Nick demanded.

She hesitated, then said, "Bad investments."

"What kind of investments?"

"Well, it depends on the season. Football, basketball…"

Nick cursed again and leaned back against the headrest, staring straight ahead. "Jessica, why didn't you *tell* someone?"

Jess sniffed again. "It was humiliating. I hoped that the marriage counseling might help him work that out, too, but whenever the subject comes up, he gets furious and denies that there's a problem. That's why he stopped going. I'm not sure what to do now. If there's anything I *can* do."

"Maybe he just needs a little persuasion," Nick said.

Jess paled even more. "What are you going to do?"

"He works for Caroselli Chocolate, and if he wants to keep his job, he'll play by our rules. Either he goes to Gamblers Anonymous, or he's out of a job."

"And then where will the kids and I be? We have so much debt, we're barely hanging on as it is."

"If Eddie won't take care of you," Nick said, his jaw tense, "then the family will."

Terri felt so awful for Jess. She couldn't even imagine what it would be like if someone lost all of her money, and to something as careless as gambling. She wouldn't even waste her money on a dollar scratch-off ticket.

The mood in the car was pretty somber the rest of the way to *Nonno's*, and when they got there, Nick and his sisters went straight to the bar. Wishing she could join them, Terri said hello to everyone—trying not to cringe as Nick's dad gave her one of those cloying hugs—then headed upstairs to use the bathroom. As she reached the top of the stairs, she heard voices coming from *Nonno's* study. A man and a woman. Curious, she stopped to listen, but couldn't make out what was being said, only that they both were angry.

She stepped closer, straining to hear, even though it was none of her business. My God, she really was becoming a Caroselli.

"We have to tell him," the man was saying.

The woman, sounding desperate, said, "But we agreed never to say a word."

"He deserves to know the truth."

"No, I won't do that to him."

"I've kept this secret, but I can't do it anymore. The guilt is eating away at me. Either you tell him or I will."

"Demitrio, wait!"

The doorknob turned and Terri gasped, ducking into the spare bedroom, her heart pounding. She hid behind the door and watched through the crack as Nick's Uncle Demitrio, Rob's dad, marched out, followed a second later by Tony's mom, Sarah. Terri had no clue what they could possibly be fighting about, though she could draw several conclusions from the small snippet of conversation she'd heard. Then again, she could be completely misconstruing the conversation. She could ask Nick, but if he told Tony and Rob what she'd heard, and they confronted their parents, all hell could break loose and she didn't want to be responsible.

When she was sure they were both gone, she used the bathroom, then rushed back downstairs before anyone could miss her.

Elana, Tony's younger sister, stopped her in the great room just outside the dining room door. She had been labeled the family genius after graduating high school at sixteen. She earned her masters five years later and passed the CPA exam shortly after that. She worked in the international tax department of Caroselli Chocolate, and according to Nick, would probably take over as CFO some day.

"So, how are you?" she said, shooting a not-so-subtle glance at Terri's stomach.

"Good." *And by the way, I think your mom is having an affair with your uncle.*

"How was Aruba?"

"A lot of fun. I'd like to go back some time." Maybe after the divorce, she and Nick and the baby could go for a non-honeymoon there.

"I see you don't have a drink. Can I get you something?"

"Thanks, but I can't. I'm the designated driver tonight."

"Oh, right," she said, but Terri doubted she believed her. "I did notice that your husband and his sisters seemed to get an early start this Thanksgiving."

By the time the evening was over, the rest of the family would be hammered, too. It was a Caroselli holiday tradition.

She heard Nick laugh, and spotted him, drink in hand, leaning on the bar. "Excuse me, Elana, I need to have a word with my husband."

Elana grinned. "Sure. Say hi to Gena for me when you see her."

"I will," she said, heading in Nick's direction.

"Hey," Nick said, smiling brightly as she approached. "Where'd ya go?"

"Bathroom. How are you?"

"Just standin' here holdin' up the bar," he said, his speech slightly slurred.

"You mean, the bar is holding you up?"

He nodded, his head wobbly on his neck. "Pretty much."

"Maybe you should give me that," she said, gesturing to his drink, and he handed it over without argument. She set it on the bar, out of his reach. "Why don't we go sit down? Before you fall over."

"You know, that's probably a good idea."

He hooked an arm around her neck and she led him to the sofa. If she hadn't been so tall and fit, he probably would have gone down a couple times and taken her with him.

She got him seated on the couch, but before she could sit beside him, he pulled her down onto his lap instead.

"Nick!"

He just grinned, and whispered in her ear, "Everyone needs to believe we're crazy in love, remember?"

Yes, but there were limits.

She thought about what she'd heard upstairs, and curiosity got the best of her. She doubted Nick would remember much of this night, anyway. "So, what's the deal with your Uncle Demitrio and Aunt Sarah?"

"What do you mean?" he asked, fiddling with the bottom edge of her dress.

She moved his hand to the sofa cushion instead. "I saw them talking and it sounded...strained."

"Well, they do have a history."

"They do?"

He laid his hand on her stocking-clad knee instead. "I never told you?"

If he had, she couldn't recall. "Not that I remember."

"They used to date."

Uh-oh. "Seriously?"

"In high school, I think." His hand began a slow slide upward, under the hem of her dress. "But Demitrio enlisted, and dumped Sarah, then Sarah fell in love with Tony instead."

And in light of what she'd heard upstairs, Terri would say it was pretty likely that Sarah and Demitrio had rekindled their romance. But since it was none of her business, she would keep it to herself.

Nick's roaming hand was now pushing the boundaries of decency. She intercepted it halfway up her thigh.

"Behave yourself," she said, and before he had the chance to do it again, Nick's dad announced that dinner was served.

She assumed she would be relatively safe at the dinner table, but thanks to a tablecloth that hung just low enough, she spent a good part of her meal defending herself against his sneak attacks.

She knew he could be affectionate when he drank, but she'd never known him to be so...hands-on. Of course, the last time she saw him this drunk, they weren't sleeping together. And as much as it annoyed her, she liked it, too.

The food was amazing, and the wine flowed freely, but Terri was able to limit Nick to two glasses. Unfortunately no one was keeping an eye on Jess and Mags, and by the time people started to leave for home, they were so toasted, Terri needed the assistance of Rob—whom she'd never seen even the slightest bit intoxicated—to get the girls in the car, and wondered how the hell she would get them in the building and up to Nick's apartment.

When everyone was buckled in and the doors were closed, Rob asked, "You want me to follow you and help get them upstairs?"

"Would you?" she said. "That would be so awesome. Unless his building has a flat-bed cart I could borrow, it would probably take me half the night to get them up to the apartment."

And just in case she had conceived, it would probably be better if she didn't lift anything too heavy.

"Let me go get Tony and we'll swing by Nick's—I mean, your apartment, on our way to Tony's place."

When she climbed in the car, Nick looked over at her, that goofy grin on his face. "Thanks for being designated driver."

"No problem." She buckled up and started the engine.

He let his head fall back against the rest and loll to one side. "I had a lot to drink today."

"You certainly did."

"Are you mad?"

"A little jealous maybe, but not mad."

He closed his eyes as she pulled away from the curb. They hadn't even made it to the corner when, his eyes still closed, he said, "Are we there yet?"

She laughed. "I bet you were a riot as a kid."

He grinned, and must have fallen asleep after that, because he didn't make another sound all the way to his building. Rob and Tony were a few minutes behind her, and they each took a sister while Terri led Nick—who thankfully was able to walk with little assistance—upstairs.

Rob and Tony got the girls into the guest room, and Terri got Nick undressed—all the way down to nothing because he would end up that way eventually—and into bed.

She leaned down to give him a kiss on the cheek, and discovered that even intoxicated, he was lightening fast. He looped an arm around her neck and pulled her in for a kiss. A long, slow, deep one. He smelled so good, felt so nice, that she let it go on longer than she should have.

He looked up at her, brushing her hair back and tucking it behind her ears. "Do you have any idea how long I've wanted to do this?"

"Um, since the last time you kissed me?"

"For years," he said. "And I wanted to do more than just kiss you."

"Uh-huh." That was definitely the alcohol talking.

"Terri, I mean it. When we lived together, I would meet girls and bring them home—"

"I *remember.*"

"But what you didn't know was that when I was with them, I would be wishing it was you."

Her heart took a dive, then shot back up into her throat. "Come on, Nick. You did not."

"No, I did," he said, his eyes so earnest she could swear he was actually telling the truth. But he couldn't be. He was only saying it to soften her up, so she would sleep with him again.

"If you wanted me so much, why didn't you tell me?"

"I should have," he said. "I wish I would have."

"No you don't." He was clearly confusing her with some other woman.

"Yes, I *do*. In the car, when I said I love you, I meant it."

"Of course you did. We're best friends. I love you, too."

"No. I mean, I *really* love you."

In a way she wanted to believe it, but she knew it was just the alcohol making him sentimental. She'd seen it happen before.

"I think I always knew it was inevitable," he said, his eyelids heavy.

"What was inevitable?"

"That we would end up together. And Jess was right, we are perfect for each other. Now I can't believe we didn't figure it out a long time ago. Maybe we just weren't ready."

"You should go to sleep," she said. "We can talk about it in the morning, okay?"

"Okay," he said, letting his arm drop from around her neck, his eyelids sinking closed.

She stood up, knowing that despite what she'd said, this was not a conversation they would be continuing. She doubted he would recall a single word of it.

She switched off the light and walked out to the kitchen. Rob sat on one of the bar stools, drinking a bottled water. Tony had helped himself to a beer and leaned against the fridge drinking it.

"What a night," Terri said, sitting beside Rob. "Thanks for helping me."

"So, what's going on?" Tony asked.

"What do you mean?"

"I've seen Nick and his sisters get pretty drunk, but never all of them at the same time. Is everything okay with Gena?"

"Gena is fine."

"Does it have something to do with Eddie not showing up for dinner?"

"Maybe you should ask Jess about that."

"So it is about Eddie," Rob said.

"I can't really say one way or the other." But they would find out soon enough if Nick followed through and gave Eddie that ultimatum.

"You know," Rob said. "You'll never survive in this family if you don't learn to gossip."

Your dad is sleeping with Tony's mom, she wanted to say. How was that for gossip? "Let's just say it's been a tough day for everyone."

"Everything okay with you and Nick?"

"Great. We're great."

"He mentioned that you guys wanted to start a family right away," Rob said. "And I noticed that all you drank tonight was water."

He and half a dozen other people had noticed. And inquired.

"A preemptive precaution," she said.

She was under the distinct impression that she was being pumped for information. Had Rob and Tony agreed to *Nonno*'s offer, too? Would they be making engagement announcements of their own? And if they did, would this turn into some sort of race to the finish line?

Eleven

Last night's overindulgence had taken its toll, and when Terri returned home around eleven the next morning after a few hours of Black Friday shopping with Nick's mom, she encountered a gruesome scene. Jess and Mags were sacked out in the living room, the curtains drawn, the television off, looking miserable.

"Good morning," Terri said, setting her packages on the floor beside the door so she could take off her coat.

"Not really," Jess said weakly, a compress on her forehead, eyes bloodshot and puffy. "Is it physically possible for a head to explode? Because it feels like mine might."

"I don't think so," Terri said.

"Shhh," Maggie scolded. The previous night's makeup was smeared around her eyes, giving her a raccoon appearance. "Do you two really have to talk so loud?"

"Did you guys take anything?" Terri asked, and both nodded. "Are you drinking lots of water?"

"Yes, Mom," Maggie said.

"Hey, I've gotta practice on someone. Where's Nick?"

"He got up and took some ibuprofen then went back to bed," Jess said.

"How did he look?"

"Have you seen the movie *Zombieland?*" Maggie asked.

"That bad, huh?" Terri had been a little jealous last night to be the odd man out, but in the aftermath, she was glad she hadn't been able to let loose. "I'd better go check on him."

Terri hung her coat in the closet and gathered up the other three coats that had been dumped in various spots throughout the room and hung them up, too. Then she tiptoed into the bedroom. The blinds were closed, all the lights off and Nick was sprawled out diagonally, facedown on the mattress naked, as if he had collapsed there and didn't have the strength to move another inch. He may have been hungover, but he sure did look good.

There were two empty water bottles on the bedside table—so at least he'd had the good sense to hydrate—and a pair of jogging pants on the floor. She picked them up and draped them across the foot of the bed. During their honeymoon, he'd been pretty good about picking up after himself. He left an occasional wet towel on the floor, or whiskers in the sink, but so far he was nowhere near as bad as he used to be.

She was about to turn around and leave, when Nick mumbled, "What time is it?"

"After eleven. You okay?"

He lifted his head and gazed up at her. Only one eyelid was raised, as if he just didn't have the energy to open them both. The eye she could see was so puffy and red-rimmed it almost hurt to look at it. "What do you think?"

"Is there anything I can get you?"

"A gun?"

She laughed. "Anything else?"

He sighed and dropped his head down. "Another bottle of water? And a promise that you'll never let me do that again. I must be getting old, because I'm not bouncing back like I used to in college."

"That happens, I guess." The last time she'd overdone it with a pitcher of margaritas, she'd paid severely the following day. "I'll be right back."

She walked to the kitchen for his water, stopping to ask his sisters if they wanted one, too. They both moan-mumbled an affirmative, and she grabbed an armful from the fridge. She set two beside each sister, then returned to the bedroom, where Nick was actually sitting up in bed. She sat on the edge of the mattress beside him and handed over the water.

"Thanks." She watched his Adam's apple bob, the muscles in his neck flexing as he guzzled down the first bottle in one long gulp. He set the second one on the bedside table for later. He sighed, letting his head rest against the headboard. "Thanks."

"No problem."

"How are the girls doing?"

"In a little better shape than you, but not by much."

"Thanks for taking care of us last night."

"You would have done the same for me. And if I recall correctly, you have a time or two."

He slipped down, flat on his back. "Like the time in high school when you broke up with Tommy Malone and you went a little crazy with the peach Schnapps."

"It was peppermint Schnapps, and I didn't break up with him. He dumped me for Alicia Silberman because

I wouldn't put out. And apparently she was more than happy to."

"I did offer to kick his ass for you."

She smiled at the memory. He would have done it, too. "He wasn't worth the trouble."

"So when did you finally do it?" he said.

Confused, she asked, "Do what?"

"Have sex."

The question took her aback. Not that she was ashamed of her past—not all of it, anyway—but it just wasn't something they had ever talked about. "Why do you want to know?"

"Just curious. I was a junior in high school."

"I heard," she said. "With Beth Evans, in her bedroom when her parents were both at work."

"Who told you?"

"I overheard Tony and Rob talking about it a couple years ago. And, of course, there were rumors around school at the time." Which she had rarely put any stock in, but apparently this time they were right. "I hear you gave quite the performance."

Nick laughed. "Not exactly. I was so nervous I couldn't get her bra unhooked, and the actual sex lasted about thirteen seconds."

"That's not the way Rob tells it. He said that you said you had her begging for more."

"I may have exaggerated a tiny bit," he said with a grin. "Sexual prowess is very important to a teenage boy. The truth is, it was a humiliating experience."

"Well, if it's any consolation, you've perfected your methods since then."

He laughed. "Thanks. When was your first time?"

She cringed. "It's embarrassing."

"Why?"

"Because it was so…cliché."

"Tell me it wasn't a teacher."

It was her turn to laugh. "Of course not! It was the night of senior prom."

"You're right, that is cliché." He paused, then said, "Wait a minute, you went to prom with that guy from the math club. Eugene…something."

"Eugene Spenser."

"Wasn't he kind of a…*geek?*"

"A little, but so was I." And that *geek* had moves that she later realized put most college guys to shame. He actually *did* have her begging for more.

"I don't remember you dating him."

"Um…I don't think you could call what we did dating, per se."

His brows rose. "What *would* you call it?"

"Occasionally we would…hook up."

The brows rose higher. *"Hook up?"*

"You know, have sex."

He sat up again, his hangover temporarily forgotten. "Really?"

"Yes, really."

"You would just…have sex. No relationship, no commitment?"

She nodded. "That's about it."

"Were there *other* guys that you 'hooked up' with?"

"A few."

"But they weren't boyfriends."

"They were friends, but not boyfriends."

"And you had sex with them?"

"I had sex with them," she said, unsure why he found the scenario so unbelievable. "What can I say, I liked sex."

"So did I, but…"

"But it's supposedly different for you?"

"Yes."

"Why? Because you're a guy? Or because you were madly in love with every girl you slept with? I'm recalling the parade of females in and out of your room when we lived together, and I can't say I remember seeing the same face more than once or twice." Which made her think about what he'd said last night. How he would be with a girl but think of Terri. But he'd been so drunk he probably hadn't meant it. He probably didn't even know what he was saying.

"Well, we know you didn't sleep with *all* your friends," he said.

"Not any of my girlfriends, if that's what you mean. Although one did invite me into a three-way with her boyfriend once, and I might have if the guy hadn't been such a creep."

"You never slept with *me,* either."

She shrugged. "You never asked."

His brows perked up again. "If I had, would you?"

At first she thought he was teasing, but his eyes said that he was serious. Had he really wanted to sleep with her back then? Were those not just the ramblings of a drunk man last night? And did she really want to know? It's not as if they had any kind of future as a couple now, so what difference did it make?

"No. Our friendship was too important to me."

"And theirs weren't?"

"Not like ours. For me sex was…I don't know. I guess it made me feel in control. And special in a way. Definitive proof of how much my aunt screwed me up, I guess."

"Do you still feel that way?" he asked, looking intrigued.

"No, not anymore." She also didn't like the direction

this conversation was taking. It was too...*something*. "Well, I should let you get back to sleep."

"I'm feeling better now. I think I'll take a shower instead."

"Are you hungry? I could pick up lunch."

"Something light, maybe? I have soup in the pantry."

As long as he didn't mind her potentially burning down the building. "Sure. It'll be ready when you're done."

"Unless you'd like to join me," he said, wiggling his brows.

"I thought you were hungover."

"Not *that* hungover."

She couldn't help but laugh, and wonder if there would ever be a time before the divorce when he would stop coming on to her. Or a time when she stopped wanting to say yes. "Well, the answer is no."

He shrugged. "Thought it couldn't hurt to ask."

He rolled out of bed, deliciously naked, and walked to the bathroom. Terri watched him, trying her best not to drool, noting that he'd left the door wide-open.

It was a good thing he didn't realize how little persuasion it would take to change her mind, or she would be joining him.

She heard the shower turn on and before she could even be tempted, or think how good he looked naked and soapy, how his body felt all slippery and warm against hers, she hightailed it to the kitchen, stopping to see if Jess and Mags were hungry.

"I can barely choke down saltines," Jess said. "But thanks."

"I'll pass, too," Maggie said. "I need to get home soon, anyway."

"Let me know if you change your minds."

In the kitchen she opened the door to the walk-in pantry, which was remarkably well organized for a man who used to leave his canned goods in the bag on the kitchen table for days after a trip to the store.

There was an entire shelf dedicated to a dozen brands and types of soup, but she didn't have a clue what he would prefer. Under normal circumstances he liked tomato, but she wondered if that might upset his stomach.

Crap. That meant she would have to go ask him. She would stand outside the bathroom and shout to him, so she wouldn't have to see him through the clear glass shower doors. It would just be easier that way.

That was exactly what she did, and Nick did in fact want tomato, but as she started to walk away, he called, "Hey, Terri, would you grab a washcloth from the cabinet for me?"

Crap.

"Okay," she called. She planned to just throw it over the top of the shower door and run, but before she could, Nick swung open the door. Of course he was wet and soapy, and sexy as hell.

She held out the cloth to him, but he grabbed her wrist instead, tugging her, fully clothed, into the shower and under the hot spray.

"Nick!" she shrieked, trying to pull away, but he wouldn't let go.

"Well, gosh," he said as water saturated her sweatshirt and jeans, her hair. "Looks like now you *need* a shower."

Water leaked out of her hair and into her eyes and her wet clothes were weighing her down. She wanted to be mad, wanted to feel like slugging him, but all she could manage was a laugh.

His hand slid down to cup her behind and he wedged one thigh intimately between hers. A moan slipped out and her head tilted against the tile, giving Nick access to her throat, which he promptly began to devour.

She should be telling him no right now, but damn it, she didn't *want* to. Instead, she said, "This is it," as he kissed his way upward, nibbling the shell of her ear. "This is the *last* time."

He pulled back, eyes black with desire. "Take off your clothes."

Terri pushed her cart through the produce section of the grocery store, dropping in the items on the list Nick had put together last night for her. When she lived alone, she did the majority of her shopping in the frozen food section, so the gourmet meals Nick had been making every night were pretty cool. They also made up for the fact that, although he'd improved a lot, Nick hadn't quite lost all his slob tendencies. He often left newspapers or magazines on the coffee table, or dirty clothes on the bedroom floor, and he never seemed to clean up after himself after using the bathroom in the morning.

But those things didn't bother her nearly as much as they used to. She'd been living alone for a long time now. She had worried that having someone there, having to share her space, would feel suffocating. She also thought she would miss her condo, but that wasn't the case at all. Now that Jess was back home trying again to work out things with Eddie, and Terri had the guest room to herself, she missed sleeping with Nick. And not just the sex, which they agreed would stop the day she moved out of his bedroom.

She'd grown awfully fond of cuddling, and she missed lying in bed with him and just talking. There were so many little things that she realized she'd taken for granted. And she was starting to get the feeling that she and Nick just being roommates might not cut it anymore. Maybe she wanted more than that.

But then she always reminded herself that despite what she wanted, Nick was perfectly content with his life just the way it was. He didn't want to be tied down. And whatever happened with the baby, she knew that in time she would be okay with that. Knowing he was her best friend, and always would be, would be enough for her.

She hoped.

Right now, though, as the date approached when she could take a pregnancy test, she became more and more obsessed about it. She was ultra aware of any changes in her body, any signs of pregnancy. She would check her reflection to see if she was glowing, poke her breasts to see if they were tender. She even started eating foods that she'd read could aggravate morning sickness to encourage signs of pregnancy, but so far, nothing. She tried not to let it discourage her, but she was nervous. Suppose it didn't work this month, or the next, or the next? What if she discovered that she couldn't get pregnant?

Every time her thoughts started to wander in that direction, she forced herself to stay positive. Even if the first try was unsuccessful, it didn't mean the second would be, too. She just had to be patient.

On her way to the dairy section, Terri passed the aisle with the feminine products, and took a detour. Though she had to wait until after her period was late to test, it couldn't hurt to buy it a few days early.

She grabbed the most expensive one—thinking it would be the most accurate—and read the back, both stunned and excited to see that the test could be performed as soon as four days before her period was due, which coincidentally was today.

Heart jumping in her chest, she tossed the box in the

cart. She hurried through the rest of her shopping and paid for her groceries, so nervous and excited she barely recalled the drive home. She forced herself to wait until she got all the groceries upstairs and put away, then she opened the box and pulled out the instruction leaflet.

Her excitement fizzled when she read the line that said to take it with the first urine of the day, which she had flushed away almost *ten* hours ago. *Damn.* If she wanted an accurate reading, she had no choice but to wait until tomorrow morning.

She stuck the test in the cabinet in her bathroom and tried to forget about it, but failed miserably.

Later that night, after the tenth time of not hearing Nick ask her a question or make a comment about the movie that she wasn't really watching, he seemed to realize something was up.

"Is everything okay?" he said. "It's like you're here, but you're not really here."

At least if she told him, she wouldn't be the only one crawling out of her skin. "When I was at the grocery store today, I went down the feminine products aisle."

He frowned. "Is this something I really want to know about?"

She rolled her eyes. "The pregnancy test aisle, Nick."

"I thought we had to wait until your period was due to test."

"So did I, but the directions said you can take the test as early as four days before your period is due."

"When is that?"

"Today. But it was too late in the day, so I can't test until tomorrow morning."

"How early?" he asked, and it was hard to tell if he was excited, or nervous, or really didn't give a crap. His face gave nothing away.

"As soon as I wake up."

He pulled his phone from his pocket and started to fiddle with it.

"What are you doing?" she asked.

"I'm setting my alarm for tomorrow morning."

"For what time?"

He looked at her and grinned. "Five."

Twelve

Nick paced outside the bathroom door, like an expectant father waiting for news on the birth of his child, not the result of a pregnancy test. And what was taking so long? Weren't they supposed to give results in minutes?

The door opened and Terri stepped out, still in her pajamas.

"Well?" he said.

"It's still marinating. I just couldn't stand there watching it."

"How much longer?"

She looked at her watch. "Three minutes."

"Don't worry," he said. "It'll be positive."

"You realize that if it is, that's it. For the rest of your life, it will no longer be about you, you'll always have this person depending on you."

Hadn't they been over this before? Why did he get the feeling she was trying to scare him? Or maybe she was the one who was scared. She had to carry the baby for nine months. The one making the most sacrifices. "I'm ready," he assured her. "And I'm here for you. For whatever you need. No matter what the results are."

"Meaning, if it's negative, you still want to try again?"

"Terri, I'm in this for the long haul."

"For the money."

"Don't you think it's a little late in the game to be questioning my motives?"

She sighed. "You're right. I'm sorry. I guess I'm just nervous."

"We're in this together. If you don't trust me—"

"I *do.* I don't know what my problem is. Maybe I'm hormonal."

She looked at her watch again and said, "It's time."

Here we go.

She took a step into the bathroom, then stopped. "I can't do it. I'm too nervous. You look at it."

"What am I looking for?"

"A plus sign is positive, a minus sign negative."

"Okay, here goes." He stepped into the bathroom and picked up the little stick off the counter. He turned it over and looked in the indicator window for a plus sign...

Damn.

"Well?" she asked hopefully from the doorway.

Damn, damn, damn.

He looked up at her and shook his head, watched her face fall. "Are you sure you did it right?"

"Yes, I'm sure. It's not as if it's the only one I've ever taken."

That surprised him. "Really?"

She nodded. "I had a few scares in college."

"Why didn't you tell me?"

"What difference does it make?" she snapped, and he realized he was being insensitive.

"I'm sorry. Come here." He held out his arms and she walked into them, laying her head against his chest. "Is there anything I can do?"

She shook her head. "The directions do say that I could get a false negative taking the test this early. They say to try again the day my period is due."

"So, you could still be pregnant?"

"There's only a twelve percent chance, so more than likely, I'm not."

"Twelve percent is better than zero percent. You'll test again Tuesday and then we'll know for sure."

Nick tried to keep a positive attitude all day, tried to keep Terri's mind off anything having to do with pregnancy or babies, did everything he could think of to cheer her up. He made her favorite dinner, but she only picked at it. Then he suggested they rent the chick flick she'd been bugging him about, but she looked so lost in thought, she probably hadn't absorbed the plot.

They said good-night at eleven, and it was almost midnight when Terri appeared in Nick's bedroom doorway. "Nick? Are you awake?" she whispered.

He sat up. "Yeah. Are you okay?"

She took a few steps into the room. "Can't sleep. Would it be okay, just for tonight, if I sleep with you? And I mean, actually sleep, not—"

"I get it." He pulled back the covers on the opposite side of the bed. "Hop in."

She climbed in beside him and he laid back down, facing her.

"Sorry about this," she said, shivering and burrowing under the covers. It did seem particularly cold, which meant she had probably been messing with the thermostat again. At her condo, she kept her thermostat at a balmy sixty-three degrees. He could swear she'd been an eskimo in a past life. Or a reptile.

"Don't apologize. I like sleeping with you."

"For years I've managed to fall asleep just fine on my own," she said, sounding disgusted with herself.

"It's been a rough couple of days. You don't have to go through everything alone. We're in this together, remember?"

"For now, but there could come a time when you're not around, and I have to be able to stand on my own two feet."

"Where is it you think I'm going?"

"Like my aunt used to tell me, if you don't let yourself depend on people, they can't let you down."

Nick could hardly believe she'd just said that, that she would even *think* it. He knew she had trust issues but if she really believed that, her insecurities ran much deeper that he had ever imagined.

"Have I ever let you down?"

"No."

Why did he get the feeling there was an unspoken "not yet" tacked to the end of that sentence? "So, who? Your parents? I really don't imagine they *wanted* to die."

"No, but they did."

He sighed. "Terri—"

"I'm not wallowing in self-pity or looking for sympathy. It just is what it is. You never know what might happen, so it's important to be self-sufficient. That's all I'm saying."

"''Tis better to have loved and lost, than never to have loved at all,'" he said.

"And after you lose someone, see if you still believe that."

She said it not as if it were a possibility, but a predestined event. He didn't even know how to respond to that, what he could say to change her mind. If it was even possible to change it. But the real question, the thing he needed to decide first was, did he want to?

Unfortunately, they never needed that second pregnancy test. Terri started her period Monday morning. As long as he'd known her, he'd seen her cry maybe four or five times total, but when she called him that morning at work to tell him the bad news, she was beside herself.

"Do you want me to come home?"

"No," she said with a sniff, her voice unsteady. "I'm being stupid. I knew this would happen, but I guess I was still hoping. I shouldn't be this upset."

"It's okay to be upset. I'm disappointed, too. But we try again in a couple weeks, right?"

"You're sure you want to do that?"

"Of course I'm sure." He'd only told her that a dozen times since Saturday morning. Was she really worried that he would back out, or was *she* the one having second thoughts? "But you realize that means being stuck living with me for an extra month. Think you can handle that?"

"Well," she said, her tone lighter, "you are pretty high maintenance."

He laughed, because they both knew that couldn't be farther from the truth. "So, when does act two start?"

"I haven't figured that out yet. I'll do that later today."

"What sounds good for dinner? I'll make or pick up anything you want."

She paused for a second, then said, "Pizza. From the little Italian place around the corner. With ham, mushrooms and little hairy fish."

"Pizza it is," he said. He heard a knock and looked

up to see his dad standing in the open doorway, and he didn't look happy. Nick's gut reaction was to immediately wonder what he'd done this time, but that was just a holdover from his childhood. He didn't answer to his father anymore, and sometimes he still forgot that, still got that sinking feeling when he walked into the room. "Terri, I have to let you go."

"Okay. I...I love you."

"I love you, too. I'll see you around seven." He hung up and looked over at his dad. "What's up?"

"Sorry to interrupt, but I need to talk to you."

"Come in."

He stepped inside and shut the door behind him, which was probably not a good sign.

He took a seat across from Nick, his brow furrowed, far from the happy-go-lucky facade he wore most of the time. Even if he were smiling now, it would have no bearing on what he'd be doing five minutes from now. He had a hair-trigger temper and could turn on a dime.

"I've noticed something lately," he said. "And I thought maybe you knew what was going on. That Tony and Rob may have mentioned something."

"About what?"

"Your Uncle Tony and Uncle Demitrio."

"No, they haven't said anything. Why? Is something wrong?"

"All I know is that something feels...off. They hardly talk anymore, and when they do, it's obvious there's tension. I asked them both individually but they swear nothing is wrong."

Nick debated telling him what Terri had seen at *Nonno's* house, but it didn't seem fair to drag her into this. "I don't know, Dad. Have you talked to Rob or Tony?"

"You're close with them. I thought it would be better if you did."

Nick sighed. Unlike most of the rest of the family, Nick had no burning desire to stick his nose into someone else's business. "No offense, but if there is something going on, I don't want to be in the middle of it."

"I'm not asking for much," he said sharply.

"Maybe they told you everything is fine because they feel like, whatever is going on, it's none of your business."

"If it starts to affect this company it is."

"You're the CPA. Is it affecting the company?"

"Not yet, but—"

"Instead of jumping to conclusions, maybe you should just ride it out for a week or two and see what happens. *Nonni* used to tell us that when you and Tony and Demitrio were kids, you had fights all the time."

"This is different," he said.

"Just give it some time, okay? Then if you're still worried, I'll mention it to Rob and Tony."

He nodded grudgingly. "So, how are things with you and Terri?"

"Good." At least he hoped so. She'd been…off lately. She'd been quieter, more closed up than usual. They used to talk on the phone nearly every evening, and the conversations would sometimes last for hours. But lately, they could be sitting in a room together and she barely said two words to him. Sometimes she was so lost in thought, she would seem to forget he was even there.

Maybe it was that she'd been anxious about getting pregnant. Or they just needed time to get used to living together. Whatever it was, he hoped that she would be back to her old self soon. He was beginning to miss his best friend.

"Your mom mentioned that the two of you are planning to start a family soon."

"When did you talk to Mom?"

He hesitated, then said, "At your wedding."

Why did Nick get the feeling that wasn't the only time? And why would he be contacting Nick's mom? Was he harassing her?

Nick made a mental note to ask his mom about it.

"Yes, we're planning on starting a family, but it looks as if it might take a bit longer than we'd hoped."

"So, Terri really isn't pregnant?"

"You shouldn't listen to gossip, Dad. It's beneath you."

He pushed himself to his feet. "If my son would talk to me once in a while, I wouldn't have to."

Maybe, he thought, as his dad stalked out, slamming the door behind him, *if you hadn't been such a rotten husband and father, I would.*

But those words would mean nothing to him, since the great Leonardo Caroselli took no responsibility for his past bad behavior. It was always someone else's fault.

Nick stewed about it for the rest of the day, and began to think that it would ruin his entire evening. When he got home later with the pizza and a bottle of wine, he went searching for Terri, worried that he might discover her curled up in bed crying. Instead, he found her in her office, so focused on her computer screen and the design she was working on, she hadn't even heard him come in.

"Pizza's here," he said.

She turned, surprised to see him, then smiled and said, "Hi, is it seven already?"

In that instant the stress of the day, with his mounting frustration seemed to melt away until all he felt was... happy. And content. But hadn't she always made him feel that way?

He hadn't fully appreciated that until just now.

"I have something to show you," Terri said. "But first…"

She got up from her chair, put her arms around him and hugged him hard. And damn did it feel good to hold her. So good, he didn't want to let go when she backed away.

"What was that for?"

"For being so patient with me, and for being such a good friend. We've gone through some pretty huge changes in the last month. Everything happened so fast, we didn't have much time to prepare ourselves. But at the same time, in the back of my head, I had this idea that we had to hurry, that if I didn't get pregnant right away, if I missed the deadline I set for myself, it would never happen. I think maybe that's why I didn't get pregnant. I was anxious about *everything.*"

"I've noticed that, the past week or so, you haven't been yourself. Like you're here, but you aren't really here."

"I know. And I'm sorry I've been so self-absorbed. But from now on, I'm back to being my old self. I promise."

"Good, because I've missed you."

She smiled, then gestured to the calendar on the wall above her desk. "See that highlighted week?"

She had marked the twenty-third to the twenty-seventh in blue. "Yeah."

"Do you know what it is?"

"Um…Christmas vacation?"

"That's the week I'm due to ovulate."

Nick laughed. "Are you serious?"

She smiled and nodded. "That would be a pretty awesome Christmas present, don't you think?"

"It certainly would."

"I think this time it will work."

"And if it doesn't?" He hated to see her get herself all stressed out again.

"If it doesn't, we try again in January. I just want to relax and let things happen naturally."

"And they will," he said. He had a really good feeling about this.

But just when he thought he had everything figured out, thought he knew the plan, a few days later she threw him another curve ball.

Terri's car was parked in the garage when Nick got home from work a few days later, but the apartment was quiet. He looked in the obvious places. Her bedroom, her office, even the laundry room behind the kitchen, but he couldn't find her, or a note explaining where she'd gone. He was about to grab his phone to call her, thinking she may have gone down to the fitness room for a quick workout before dinner, when he swore he heard the sound of running water from the direction of his bedroom.

He walked down the hall to his room and stepped inside. "Terri?"

"In here," she called from his bathroom, and he heard what sounded like the hum of the sauna jets in the tub. Was she cleaning it, maybe?

The bathroom door was open, so he walked in.

Unless she liked to do housework naked and submerged in the water, she was not cleaning anything.

He stopped beside the tub and folded his arms. The water came up to her neck, and with the jets on high, he couldn't see more that a blurry outline of her body, but that was enough to kick his libido into gear. "Something wrong with your tub?"

She smiled up at him. "Nope."

Okay. And she was in his tub because…

"I've been thinking about it, and if we want to get it right this time, if we really want me to get pregnant, maybe we could use a little more practice."

"If you'll recall, I actually suggested that we practice first. You said no."

"I guess I was wrong."

Though it would be all too easy to pretend that he believed her just to get laid, they were both better than that.

"That's an interesting theory. Now, you want to drop the bull and tell me why you're *really* here?"

Terri should have known that Nick would call her out, that he would demand total honesty from her. And as annoying as it could be at times, he kept her honest.

"It's not like you to play games," he said, looking disappointed in her. "If after twenty years you can't be honest with me—"

"I miss you," she blurted out, hating how vulnerable the words made her feel. "I know I'm not supposed to, that we're just friends unless I'm ovulating, but I can't help it."

"Are you saying that you want a sexual relationship outside of baby-making?"

Honestly, it was all she could think about lately, and she was tired of fighting it, tired of feeling as if something was missing. But maybe he didn't feel that same way. "If you think it's a bad idea—"

"I didn't say that." He shrugged out of his suit jacket and hung it on the hook next to the shower stall.

"I know it wasn't part of the plan," she said. "But I've begun to think that the two of us going nine months without any sex is a slightly unrealistic goal. I like sex, and we do it really well together, so why not?"

"You don't think it will complicate things?"

"Why would it? We both want the same thing—to have a baby without getting tied down."

He closed the lid on the toilet and sat. "I thought you were still looking for Mr. Right eventually."

"Instead of trying to find him, I think I may just sit back, relax and let him find me. There's no rush."

"So what happens with us after the baby is born?"

"We get divorced, like we planned."

"And we start seeing other people?"

She shrugged. "I don't see why not."

He looked skeptical. "It wouldn't hurt your feelings, or make you jealous to see me with someone else?"

"I've seen you with lots of women and it never bothered me before." At least, not enough to impact their friendship. Sure, it might be a little strange at first, but they would adjust. Hell, for all she knew, they could be completely sick of each other by then. Going back to a platonic friendship might be a huge relief for them both.

But considering how long it was taking Nick to respond, maybe he didn't think it was such a hot idea. He had been pretty hands-off lately, not so touchy-feely as before. Even when they slept together in his bed the other night, he hadn't put the moves on her. Maybe he was only interested in sleeping with her when they were trying to make the baby.

He rested his elbows on his knees, his hands folded under his chin. He was deep in thought, as if maybe he was trying to come up with some way to let her down easy.

A knot formed in her stomach, and she started to get the distinct impression she had just made a big ass of herself. But it was too late to back out now. Not without making herself look like an even *bigger* ass. The one time she took a chance and put herself out there on a limb—

"You're sure about this?" Nick said.

She nodded, feeling a slight glimmer of hope.

"*Really* sure?"

"Really sure."

"Because not touching you the past ten days has been hell on earth. So you can't just sleep with me once, then change your mind again. Either you're in or you're out. There's no middle ground. Agreed?"

Whoa. "Agreed."

"Now that we have that settled," he said, grinning and tugging his tie loose, "scoot over."

Thirteen

"Earth to Nick!"

Nick's attention jerked from the notepad he hadn't even realized he'd been doodling on. Everyone at the conference room table—his dad, his uncles, plus Rob, Tony and Elana—was looking at him.

"Sorry, what?"

"Have you heard anything we've said?" his dad snapped, as if Nick were a stubborn child and not a capable adult. Well, maybe not so capable right now, but that really wasn't Nick's fault.

"Currently sales for the quarter are down," Nick said, regurgitating the only snippet of the conversation he'd heard so far.

"Is that it? You didn't hear anything else?"

"Sorry, I didn't get much sleep last night."

"Have you tried a sleeping pill?"

"Leo, he's still a newlywed," Demitrio said, winking at Nick. "He's not supposed to sleep."

Yeah, and Terri had kept him up particularly late. They made love after the nightly news, then at 2:00 a.m. he woke to find her buried under the covers doing some pretty amazing things with her mouth. But starting today they had to abstain until she ovulated. And though he never thought he would catch himself thinking it, he was ready for a break.

Since the first day of their honeymoon, the sex had been great, but this past week she had been *insatiable*. They made love in the morning, either in bed or in the shower, and if he had no meeting scheduled for lunch he would come home for a quickie. Yesterday he'd asked her to bring him a report he'd left on his home office desk, and when she got there, she'd had that look in her eye. Then she locked his office door and he knew he was in trouble.

They did it some evenings right when he got home from work, and always when they got into bed at night. They had done it in the tub, on the sofa, in his office chair and about a dozen other places. It seemed as if every time he turned around, she was poised to jump him.

Not that he was complaining. But, *damn,* he was getting tired.

"We're considering bringing in a consultant," Demitrio told him. "Someone to view our line with a fresh set of eyes. Someone who could help us update our marketing without losing the essence of who we are as a company."

"Who are we thinking of?" Nick asked, noticing that Rob, as marketing director, did not look happy.

"Her name is Caroline Taylor. She's based on the West Coast, and she comes highly recommended. She's not cheap, though."

"Which is why I think we're wasting our money and our time," Rob said.

Nick was sure it had more to do with Rob's bruised ego. If they brought in another chocolatier to develop new products, Nick would be insulted, too.

"Son, this in no way reflects on your job performance," Demitrio said. "It's quite common for companies to bring in outside consultants. We've been talking about a fresh look for the company, and I believe the time is now."

Rob clearly wasn't happy about it, but he didn't argue, either.

"I take it we've contacted her already," Nick said. Undoubtedly, someone had mentioned this, but he'd missed it.

"Yes, and we got lucky," Demitrio said. "She's typically booked up for months, and sometimes years in advance, but the company she was supposed to start with in January went bankrupt. She's all ours if we want her. And I have to give her an answer by the end of the week."

Everyone, except Rob, of course, thought it was a good idea.

"Great!" Demitrio said. "We wanted to run it past everyone first, and the board will make a final decision tomorrow."

Uncle Tony was up and out the door before anyone else had a chance to stand up. Though Nick tuned out most of the meeting, during the parts he did catch, his uncle Tony hadn't said a word. Maybe his dad was right, and there was something going on between his uncles.

Nick knew that his uncle Tony had always followed the rules. He went to the right schools, graduating with honors and worked his way up through the ranks. Uncle Demitrio, on the other hand, had been a hell-raiser, uninterested in the family business, in and out of trouble with the law until he joined the army. Nick had heard his dad mention that while everyone else in the family had to earn their position, Demitrio had everything handed to him. Maybe that was causing hard feelings between Tony and Demitrio. But then, how did Aunt Sarah factor into that?

As Nick walked back to his office, Rob caught up with him in the hall. "So, any baby news to report?"

"First try was a bust."

"I'm sorry. How did she take it?"

"Not well at first, but she's okay now. We're just going to take it one cycle at time."

"Besides work, Tony and I haven't been seeing much of you lately."

"That's married life, I guess." Nick stopped in front of his office door and leaned on the jamb. "Maybe after Christmas we can all go out. Maybe even for New Year's."

"We could do that."

He was quiet for several seconds, and Nick asked, "Something on your mind, Rob?"

"I feel as if I owe you an apology."

"For what?"

"When you told us you were marrying Terri, instead of congratulating you, we accused you of doing something underhanded."

"And threatened to kick my ass, if I recall correctly."

"And it was a lousy thing for us to do. A person just has to see you two together to know that you really love each other, and not only that, it's obvious you're best friends. Which I think is really cool. If only it could be that way for everyone, there would never be another divorce. You really don't know how lucky you are to have her."

"Believe me, I know." And the more he thought of divorcing Terri, the less he liked the idea. He was beginning to wonder if the feelings of love that he'd been having for her were the romantic kind. And he had the distinct feeling that she was wondering the same thing. In their entire relationship he had never felt so close, so…connected. Not to her, and not to anyone else for that matter.

Most of his relationships—the semi-serious ones—rarely lasted much more than a month or two before he started to feel restless and smothered. With Terri, it felt as if there weren't enough hours in the day to spend with her. But at some point, they were going to have to make a decision. In his mind, he was pretty sure the decision was already made.

"Did you get her a Christmas present yet?"

"Not yet," Nick said. "But I have something in mind."

"First Christmas as a married couple. It better be special."

"Oh, it will be," he said, although he had no clue how he was going to wrap it.

On the Saturday before Christmas, which was two days before she was due to ovulate again—yeah, they were both climbing the walls in anticipation—Nick and Terri braved the crowds and four inches of freshly fallen snow to finish up their holiday shopping. They had both been so busy with work, they hadn't had time to get a tree. It seemed silly to go all-out so late in the season, so they picked up a pre-lit, battery-operated tabletop version to set on the coffee table.

She bent and fluffed the artificial branches into what sort of resembled a real tree—a real, *small* tree—switched the lights on then sat back on her heels to admire her work. "Not too shabby."

"What are we going to hang on it?"

She sat beside him on the sofa. "Your mom has a box of stuff that's made for a small tree. She put it aside for us."

"You want me to go pick it up?"

"Would you mind?"

"We're supposed to get another six inches tonight. If we wait, we may not get the ornaments until after Christmas."

"In that case you should probably go."

"Did you want to come with me?"

She sighed. "I can't. I have about fifty gifts to wrap. And if I recall correctly, you were going to help."

"You choose. Decorations or wrapping, which would you prefer?"

She though about that for a second, then said, "Decorations, I guess."

He pushed himself off the sofa. "I'd better go now, before the snow starts again."

She followed him to the door and watched as he put on his coat and checked his pockets for his wallet and keys. "Anything else you need me to pick up while I'm out?"

"Dinner?"

"You don't want to fix something?" He'd been making her watch him cook every night, yet she hadn't tested out what she'd been learning.

"Would you prefer a microwave frozen dinner, or burnt grilled cheese and tomato soup?"

"Fine, I'll pick up dinner. Thai okay?"

"Sounds delicious."

She kissed him goodbye. What shouldn't have been more that a quick peck, lingered. Then her arms went around his neck and her tongue was in his mouth, as one of her legs slid between his.

"Hey!" he said, pulling away. "That was an illegal move, lady. Two more days."

She flashed him a wicked smile. "Just keeping you on your toes."

He opened the door to leave, looking at their pathetic excuse for a tree. "Are you sure you don't mind having this tiny fake thing? You always get a real tree."

"So we'll get a real one next year," she said. "Drive safe."

Nick was in the elevator, on his way down to his car before Terri's words finally sank in.

So we'll get a real one next year....

Did that mean she was planning on them having a next year? That she thought they would still be married? Did she *want* to stay married? He'd been considering bringing up the subject, just to test the waters, but he hadn't yet figured out what he wanted to say. Was this it, handed to him on a silver platter?

And now that he knew she was thinking about it, too, how did he feel?

Nick got in his car and sat there for several minutes, thinking about what it would mean to both of them to make this a real marriage. To spend the rest of their lives together.

That was a really long time.

He drove to his mom's condo on autopilot, but as he turned the wheel to park in the driveway, he saw it was already occupied. *By his dad's car.*

Aw, hell, this couldn't be good.

Hackles up, Nick hopped out of his Mercedes and jogged through an inch of fresh snow to the door. He rang the bell, and when she didn't answer, he knocked briskly. Still no answer.

This was *really* not good.

He used his key and opened the door. He stepped inside, expecting to hear shouting, or furniture crashing. Instead, he heard the faint sound of a radio playing a clas-

sic rock song—which his mother favored—then a muffled moan of pain, all coming from the back of the condo.

Oh, hell, they've gone and done it now, he thought, picturing one of them with an actual hatchet in their back.
Or possibly missing a limb or, God forbid, some other
protruding part.

He rushed down the hall, tracking snow all the way.
Realizing the noise was coming from his mom's bedroom, he burst through the partially closed door. And
when he got an eyeful of his dad's bare rear end, he realized that no one was feeling any pain. At least, nothing
they didn't want to feel.

Nick cursed and covered his eyes, realizing that he'd
just walked in on every child's worst nightmare—his parents in bed doing it.

He heard the rustle of the covers and then his mom
said, "Nick, what on earth are you doing here?"

He dared move his hand, relieved to find that they
had covered themselves, and were in a less compromis-
ing position.

"What am *I* doing here? What is *he* doing here? And
why in God's name were you…" He couldn't even say
the words. He knew the memory of the whole gruesome
scene would be eternally burned in his memory, and
would haunt him until the day he died. "What the hell
is going on?"

"What do you think is going on?" his mom asked,
sounding infuriatingly reasonable. "We're having sex."

Ugh, it was bad enough to see it, but to have verbal
confirmation was just too much. "You can't do this."

"Obviously, we can," his dad said, looking amused.

"Nicky, we're two single, consenting adults. We can
do whatever we want. Within the boundaries of the law,"
she said, giving Nick's dad a wink.

Nick sniffed, catching just a hint of something that had been burning…. "What the… Have you been smoking *marijuana?*"

"Like you never have," his mom said. "Besides, it's medicinal, for your father's back."

The nightmare just kept getting worse. "You *hate* each other."

"We've certainly had our differences, I won't deny that, but we don't *hate* each other. And though we may have had a bad marriage, we had a good sex life."

He always knew that his mom's mother-earth, hippie-child attitude would come back to bite him. And speaking of that, were those teeth marks on his dad's left biceps…?

He closed his eyes, wishing the vision away.

"Why don't you put on the kettle for tea," his mother said. "We'll be out in a few minutes."

"Sure," Nick said, hoping they weren't planning to finish what they started.

He headed to the kitchen, shrugging out of his coat and draping it across a chair. Then he pulled out his cell phone and dialed Jess's number. When she answered, he could hear the kids screaming in the background, and Jess sounded more than a little exasperated. "What's up?" she shouted over the noise.

"I need to talk to you," he said, keeping his voice low so his parents wouldn't hear.

"What?" she shouted. "You need what?" She paused then said, "Hold on, lemme go somewhere quieter."

While he waited, Nick filled the kettle and set the burner on high. The screaming on the other end of the line faded, and Jess said, "Okay, now I can talk."

"Where did you go?"

"Front hall closet, so it's only a matter of time before they find me or I run out of oxygen."

"I just walked in on Mom and Dad doing it. And they were smoking pot."

She was silent for a several seconds, then said, "To-gether?"

"Yes, together."

"How did you manage that?"

He explained everything, expecting her to express the same horror he was experiencing. Instead, she started to laugh.

Irritated, he said, "It's not funny. It was...*horrifying*."

"No. It's pretty funny."

"I think you're missing the point. Mom and Dad are *sleeping* together."

"No, I got that. I'm just not sure why you're so freaked out. Would you rather have walked in on Dad chopping Mom into little pieces?"

"No, but...they hate each other."

"All evidence to the contrary. And you should be happy that they're getting along."

"And if he hurts her again?"

"Do you really think she was the only one who was hurt when they divorced?"

That's the way Nick remembered it, but before he could say so, his dad walked into the kitchen.

"I have to go," Nick told Jess. "I'll call you later." He hung up and asked, "Where is Mom?"

"You mother is getting dressed."

Nick's dad walked past him to the sink, pulled down a glass from the cupboard and filled it with tap water. He seemed to know his way around pretty well, which led Nick to believe that this wasn't the first time he'd been here. How long had this thing been going on?

"What the hell do you think you're doing?" he asked his dad.

"Getting a glass of water," he said, taking a swallow. "Would you like one?"

"You know what I mean. After what you did to Mom, what you did to me and the girls, you have no right."

He dumped the rest of the water down the drain, set the glass in the sink then turned to Nick and said, "You're twenty-nine years old, son. Don't you think it's time you grew up?"

The words struck Nick like a slap in the face, rendering him speechless.

"I realize I wasn't the greatest father and I was a pretty lousy husband, but you've been holding this grudge for twenty years. Enough already. Let it go. Everyone else has."

Nick was at a loss. Anything he could say at this point would just come off as immature and petty.

The kettle began to howl as his mom walked into the kitchen, dressed in hot-pink workout gear. "Who would like a cup of tea?" she asked, sounding infuriatingly cheerful. Who wouldn't be cheerful after an afternoon of sex, drugs and rock 'n' roll?

"Rain check," his dad said, then gave Nick's mom a kiss. It was disturbing to watch, but almost…natural in a weird way. They seemed like two people who were perfectly comfortable with each other, and happy to be so.

When the hell had that happened? And how had he missed it?

Fourteen

"Tea?" his mom asked Nick after his dad left.

"Sure," he said when what he really needed was a stiff drink.

"Have a seat," she said, gesturing to the kitchen table. He sat down and watched as she got out the sugar and cream and placed them on the table. When the tea was ready, she set a cup in front of him, then sat down across from him with her own. "So, to what do I owe this unexpected visit?"

For a minute he couldn't remember why he was there, then he remembered. "Decorations for our ugly little tree."

"Well, for future reference, if you ring the bell and I don't answer, come back later."

Yeah, he'd learned that lesson the hard way. "I'm sorry. It was inappropriate of me to barge in like that. But when I saw Dad's car, I was concerned."

"About what? You didn't honestly believe that I was in some sort of danger? That your father would hurt me?"

When she said it that way, it did sound sort of stupid. "I guess I didn't know what to think. Everything has gotten so...jumbled up lately. I don't know what to think about anything anymore."

"Oh, honey." She reached out to cover his hand with her own. "Are you and Terri having problems?"

"Not exactly."

She gave his hand a firm squeeze. "Take it from someone who knows. Marriage is tough. You have to keep the lines of communication open. You have to really work at it."

"And if it's going *too* well?"

Confused, she said, "*Too* well?"

He should shut his mouth now, since she was never supposed to know about this, but who else could he talk to?

"Despite what everyone believes, my marriage to Terri was never supposed to last."

She blinked. "I don't understand."

"Terri wanted a baby, and she was going to use a donor."

"I know. She and I discussed it."

"Well, the gist of it was, why use a donor and not be sure what she was getting, when she could use someone she knew? Specifically me. That way the baby would have lots of family, and if something were ever to happen to Terri, she knows he will be well taken care of."

He didn't dare tell her about the ten million. He could live with the entire family knowing about their baby arrangement, but if his mom blabbed about *Nonno*'s offer, he was a dead man.

"Well," she said stiffly. "It sounds as if you have it all figured out."

"You're angry?"

"No… Yes." She stood so fast her chair almost fell over backward. It teetered on two legs, then landed with a thunk upright.

"Mom—"

"I'm mad. I'm disappointed." She paced back and forth behind him, her puny little hands balled up, as if she might haul off and pop him one. Which would probably hurt her more than it would hurt him. "How could you lie to your family that way?"

"It's not as if I could tell everyone the truth."

That's when he felt it, a firm crack against the back of his head so hard he could swear he heard his brain rattle. She must have been channeling *Nonni* for that one.

"Jeez, Mom." He rubbed the still-stinging part of his head.

His mom sat back down, looking much calmer. "I feel better now."

"I'm sorry, okay? We didn't do it to hurt anyone. You know how much Terri wanted a baby. And you've said a million times that you love her like a daughter. Would you prefer her baby be your grandchild or the product of some random sperm donor?"

"But you two seem so happy, so in love. You can't fake that."

"Maybe we weren't."

"You love her?"

"I think I do."

"And how does Terri feel?"

"That you can never depend on anyone, because eventually they'll let you down."

She sucked in a quiet breath. "Oh, that's not good. But I'm not surprised. She's been hurt a lot."

"But since she said it, things have been really great. And today she was making plans for next Christmas, so I'm thinking maybe that means she wants to stay married, too. I just want to be sure of my own feelings before I make a move, because two years from now, I don't want to wake up one day and realize I've made a terrible mistake. Because I will have lost my wife *and* my best friend."

"Not all marriages go bad, Nicky."

"Mom, you can't deny that our family hasn't exactly had an impressive track record when it comes to successful marriages. You and Dad were a disaster. Jess is miserable."

"There's a reason for that, you know."

"A Caroselli family curse?"

"Nicky, what you have to understand is that your dad and I, we were never friends. When it came to sexual compatibility, we were off the charts, but you can't base a marriage on sex. It just doesn't work. At least, not long past the honeymoon. And your sister, she was so determined to prove that she was different than her parents, that she would never make the same mistakes, she rushed into a relationship before she was ready. And when it started to go south, she didn't have the skills to know how to fix it. Which unfortunately, is partly my fault. I wasn't much of a role model. It's taken me until very recently to get my head together and realize what a real relationship should be. And you know who helped me?"

He shook his head.

"You and Terri."

"Seriously?"

"Maybe you two don't see what everyone else does, but you really are perfectly matched."

"Maybe this is a stupid question, but if your marriage was that bad, and you were that unhappy, why have kids?"

"Because you think it will change things, bring you closer together. And it does for a while. Which is why, when things get bad again, you have another baby, and then another."

Which explained why Jess had four kids of her own, he supposed. "So what you're saying is, you only had us kids to save your marriage?"

"Of course not. I was thrilled when I found out I was pregnant with all three of you. You kids were the light of my life, and sometimes the only thing that kept me going, when I thought I couldn't take another second of being miserable." She reached up, touched his cheek. "You and your sisters always made me happy."

"If you were so miserable, why did you stay married for so long?"

"I came from a broken home, and I wanted better for you. I thought that if I couldn't be happy, the least I could do was give you kids a stable home with two parents."

"Our home was anything but stable, Mom."

She sighed. "I know. But I had to try. And you will never know how sorry I am for what I put you kids through. And so is your father. We were both doing the best we could, or what we thought was best."

"And what you two are doing now, is that for the best, too?"

She shrugged. "All I know is, we have fun together. We talk and we laugh, and he seems to understand me in a way no one else ever has. And the sex—"

Nick held up a hand to stop her. "TMI, Mom."

She grinned. "The point is, right now, he makes me happy. Maybe it will last, maybe it won't. Maybe we both just needed to grow up. Who knows? What I do know is that after all this time, we've finally become friends. With you and Terri, it's different. You're already friends. What you have to decide now is if you love her."

"We've been friends for twenty years. Of course I love her."

"But are you *in love* with her?"

He shrugged. "I guess I don't know the difference."

She looked at him like he was a moron. And she was probably right. Maybe what he needed was another good hard whack in the head.

"Okay, let me ask you this. Who is the first person you think of in the morning when you wake up?"

That was easy. "Terri."

"And when you're not with her, how often do you think about her?"

Lately, too many times to count. "If there was a way I could be with her twenty-four hours a day, I would do it."

"Now, think about when you're with her and find a single word to describe how she makes you feel."

He thought that would be a tough one, since she made him feel so many things lately. But with barely any thought, the perfect word came to him. "Complete," he said. "When I'm with her I feel complete."

"And has anyone else ever made you feel that way?"

"Never," he admitted. Not even close.

"Now, imagine her with someone else."

There was no one else good enough for her. No one who knew her the way he did. Who could ever love her as much…

The answer must have been written all over his face, because his mom smiled. "What do you think that means, Nicky?"

What it meant was, he didn't just love Terri, he was *in* love with her. Looking back, there was hardly a time when he hadn't been. He sighed and shook his head at the depth of his own stupidity. "I am such an idiot."

His mom patted his hand. "When it comes to relationships, most men are, sweetheart."

"What if Terri is still afraid to trust me? How do I convince Terri that I love her, and that I won't let her down? How do I make her trust me?"

She shrugged. "It may take some sort of grand gesture to convince her. But if you know her as well as I think you do, you'll figure it out."

When it came to things like grand gestures, he was clueless. He could barely get his own head straight, and now he was supposed to figure her out, too?

"And while you're at it," his mom said. "Maybe you could cut your dad a little slack. Everyone makes mistakes."

"Some more than others."

"And goodness knows you can hold a grudge. But haven't you punished him enough? Couldn't you at least *try* to let him make amends? Would you do it for me?"

Maybe Nick had been a bit bullheaded—a trait he had inherited from his father, of course—but to be honest, he was tired of carrying around this pent-up animosity. After all his parents had been through, if she could forgive him, shouldn't he at least make an attempt?

"I'll try," he told her.

His mom smiled. "Thank you."

"I'm sorry I barged in on you like that," he said.

"Well, considering the look on your face, it was much more traumatic for you than it was for your father and me."

No kidding.

When he left his mom's condo, he went straight home, still completely clueless as to what he would say to Terri.

With any luck, he would have some sort of epiphany, and the right words would just come to him. That was bound to happen at least once in a man's life, right?

When Nick got home, Terri was sitting on the living room floor amid a jumble of wrapping paper, ribbon and bows.

"I'm home," he said, even though that was pretty obvious, as he was standing right there. He was off to a champion start.

She just looked at him and smiled and said, "How are the roads?"

"Getting bad," he said. "How's the wrapping?"

"I've been doing this every year for over twenty years now, and I still manage to suck at it."

He reviewed the pile of presents she'd already finished, and it did sort of look as if a five-year-old had done them.

"Plus my knees are about to pop." She pushed herself to her feet and watched him expectantly. "So where is it?"

He hung up his coat. "Where is what?"

"The decorations."

"Oh, crap." He'd been so rattled when he left his mom's he'd forgotten to grab the box.

"You drove all the way to you mom's and *forgot* them?"

"I'm sorry."

"I don't suppose you picked up dinner, either."

Dammit! "No, I forgot that, too. But I have a very good excuse. I walked in on my parents having sex."

Her eyes went wide, and she said, *"Together?"*

He repeated the story to her, and by the end she was laughing so hard tears were rolling down her face.

"It is *not funny*," he said.

"Yeah," she said, wiping her eyes. "It is."

"I'm traumatized for life. Did I also mention that they were smoking pot?"

"Like you've never done that," she said. She walked into the kitchen and he followed her. "So what are we going to eat? I'm starving."

"We could order in."

"In this weather, it will take forever."

"I could throw together a quick tomato sauce, and serve it over shells. It wouldn't take more than an hour."

"After shopping all day, then living through the horror of seeing your dad's naked ass, do you really think you have the energy?"

Shaking his head in exasperation, he snatched his apron from the broom closet. "Get me two cans of crushed tomatoes and a can of tomato paste from the pantry."

He tied the apron on and grabbed the ingredients he needed from the fridge. He chopped onions, celery and garlic, and sautéed it all in a pan with olive oil. When the onions and garlic turned translucent, he stirred in the crushed tomatoes and tomato paste, then added oregano, basil and salt. He ground fresh pepper in next, then added the slightest pinch of thyme, which his *Nonni* had always taught him to use sparingly, warning that too much would overwhelm. Nick had learned a lot in culinary school, but the really valuable things he'd learned from her.

"How do you do that?" Terri asked from the bar stool where she sat watching him. "You don't measure anything. How do you know it's the right amount?"

"I do measure it. Just with my eyes, not a spoon. When you make something as many times as I've made *Nonni's* tomato sauce, a recipe becomes obsolete."

She sighed. "I can't make toast without screwing it up."

"It's just a matter of following the directions and using good judgment."

"Well, there you go, I have terrible judgment."

"You married me," he said, hoping to break the ice. Maybe she would say it had been the best decision of her life.

She smiled at him and said, "I rest my case."

He laughed in spite of himself. He set the burner on medium and took off his apron. "So, I was thinking maybe we could—"

His cell phone buzzed in his pants pocket, startling him. Then it started to ring. He pulled it out and saw that it was Rob. "Hold on a minute, Terri.

"Hey, Rob," he answered.

"Hey, have you got a minute?"

"Um, I'm making dinner."

"It'll just take a minute."

"Okay, sure, what's up?"

"Something kind of weird happened yesterday, and I'm really not sure what to think. I thought maybe your dad said something to you about it."

"You know me and my dad, always chatting."

"I know it's a long shot, but I thought maybe he mentioned it."

"Mentioned what?"

"What's going on between my dad and Uncle Tony."

"Actually he did mention it, but only to ask if I knew what was going on. Which I don't. He wanted me to ask you and Tony Junior if you knew anything."

"All I know is that I stopped by my parents' house tonight and Uncle Tony's Beemer was there. I heard shouting from inside, and when my mom answered the door, she looked as if she'd been crying, and Uncle Tony looked pissed. He left just a few minutes after I got there. When I asked what happened, my parents wouldn't talk about it."

"What about Tony? Have you talked to him?"

"A few minutes ago. He didn't have a clue what I was talking about."

He considered mentioning what Terri saw on Thanksgiving, and that whatever it was, Aunt Sarah was involved, too, but he was a little fuzzy on the details. Besides, it wouldn't be fair to bring Terri into this without first asking her if it was okay.

"I'll ask around and see what I can come up with, but I'm sure it's nothing to worry about," he said, even though that was the opposite of what he was actually thinking. Something was up, and he had the feeling it was bad.

Fifteen

"Everything okay?" Terri asked when Nick hung up, but she could tell by the look on his face that something was wrong.

"I'm not sure. According to my father and Rob, there's some sort of friction between Uncle Demitrio and Uncle Tony. Didn't you say that you heard Uncle Demitrio and Aunt Sarah fighting at *Nonno's*?"

He *remembered* that? She wondered what else he recalled from that night. "I don't know if I would call it *fighting,* but it seemed…heated. But like you said, they used to date, so maybe there are still hard feelings."

"Why now, after thirty-some years?"

She shrugged. This was not a can of worms she wanted to be responsible for opening.

"Do you recall what they were fighting about?"

"I didn't hear the whole conversation, just bits and pieces."

"Like what?"

"Something about telling someone something."

"That's vague."

She shrugged. "She said she didn't want to, and then they walked downstairs."

"You didn't hear them mention a name?"

"No. It was probably nothing. Honestly, I figured you would have forgotten all about it."

"I remember a lot of things from that night." Something about the way he said it, the way he looked into her eyes, made her heart skip a beat.

"Wh-what do you remember?" she asked, her heart in her throat, unsure if she really wanted to know.

"Bits and pieces."

"Do you remember saying anything to me?"

"If I recall, I said a lot of things to you. To what specifically were you referring?"

He wanted her to tell him, so he clearly *didn't* remember. She felt an odd mix of relief, and disappointment. "Never mind."

"Was it when I commented on the stuffing?" he asked. "Or when I expressed my unrequited and undying love for you?"

He said it so calmly, so matter-of-factly, that for several seconds words escaped her. She couldn't even breathe. Then she realized that he was just teasing her. She refused to feel disappointed. "I want you to know that you shouldn't feel weird or uncomfortable for saying it."

"I don't."

"All that stuff about you wishing other girls were me. I know you didn't mean it."

"What makes you think I didn't mean it?"

"Because…" She paused, unsure of what to say next, because he had to be messing with her. It was the only explanation. "Nick, come on. You were completely hammered."

"Just because I was drunk doesn't mean I didn't know what I was saying or mean what I said. In fact, that's probably the most honest I've ever been with you. And with myself for that matter."

Suddenly she was having a tough time pulling in a full breath again, and the room pitched so violently she clutched the counter to keep from falling over.

Nick loved her? *Love* loved her? And didn't she want that?

It was one thing to fantasize about it, but she was totally unprepared to actually hear him say the words.

"Besides," he said. "I'm not drunk now. And I still feel the same way, so I guess it must be true."

A small part of her wanted to jump for joy, while another part—a much bigger part—was having a full-blown panic attack.

Slow, shallow breaths. In and out.

What was *wrong* with her? This was a good thing, right? Shouldn't she be happy? A rich, handsome man who just happened to be her best friend in the world love-loved her. Shouldn't she be *thrilled*?

She should, but why wasn't she? Why instead was every fiber of her being screaming at her to run?

"Terri, are you okay?" Nick looked as if he were getting his first inkling that something was off. Specifically, her.

"I'm just a little surprised," she said. "I mean, this definitely was not a part of the plan."

"Plans change."

Not this one.

He sat beside her and took her hands. "Look, I know you're scared."

She pulled her hands free. "It's not that."

"Then what is it?"

"You don't want to be married. You've said it a million times."

"I was wrong."

"Just like that, you changed your mind?"

"Pretty much."

"And how do I know you aren't going to change it back? That five years from now you won't get restless or bored? How do I know you won't die?"

"Okay, Terri," he said calmly, as if he were speaking to a child. "Now you're being ridiculous."

"Am I? Have you forgotten that you're talking to a woman whose parents have both died? Like you said, they probably didn't want to die. I'm guessing they didn't plan on it, either. But they still did."

"I never meant to imply that I'm not going to die. Everyone dies eventually. And, of course, I'm hoping my death occurs later rather than sooner."

"Why are you doing this now? Everything was going so well."

"That's why I'm doing it. After what you said about Christmas, I figured you wanted this, too."

"What did I say about Christmas?"

"That next year we would get a real tree. Which I took to mean that there would be a next year for us, that you're planning for the future."

How could a few innocent words get so dangerously misconstrued? "That wasn't what I meant."

"So what did you mean?"

"I don't know!" She wished he would stop pushing and give her a minute to organize her thoughts. "There was no hidden agenda, they were just words."

"Terri, I am in love with you. I know what I want, and

that isn't going to change. Not a year from now, not five years from now, not a hundred. As long as I am alive, I'm going to want you."

"I want you, too," she said softly. "But I just don't know if I'm ready for this. If you could give me a little time—"

"How much time? A year, two years? Twenty years? Because that's how long it's taken us to get this far. You can't live your life in fear of what might happen."

"This isn't going to work."

"What isn't going to work?"

"The marriage, the baby, none of it. It's not fair to either of us. You want something from me that I just can't give, Nick."

For a minute he didn't say anything. He just sat there staring at the wall. Finally, he said, "You know what I could never figure out? You're beautiful and intelligent, yet you insisted on dating jerks and losers. Men that I— and pretty much everyone else—knew were all wrong for you. And now I realize that was the whole point. Because for all the talking you do about finding Mr. Right, you didn't *want* to find him. You would rather play it safe by getting into a relationship you knew would fail, or one that was just about sex. Because if you didn't care, they couldn't hurt you. But how many people do you think *you* hurt, Terri?"

She bit her lip.

"How many men really cared about you, maybe even loved you, and you just tossed them away? And now you're doing the same thing to me."

He was right, she knew he was, but she couldn't do anything about it. She didn't know how. Those self-defense mechanisms he was referring to were so deep-seated, she didn't know how to be any other way.

"If you could just give me a little more time—"

"Terri, we have been best friends for *twenty* years. If you don't trust me now, you're never going to." He pushed off the bar stool and started to walk away.

"What about the ten million dollars?" she said, only because she wasn't quite ready to let him go. Not yet.

He stopped and turned to her, his face blank, even though she knew he had to be hurting. "There are plenty of other fish in the sea."

He didn't mean it, she knew he didn't, but as he turned and walked away, his words cut deep. If only he could give her a little more time. But he was right, she was damaged goods and he deserved better than her.

When Nick woke the next morning, when he and Terri were supposed to be trying to make a baby, he walked into the spare bedroom to discover that all her clothes were gone. He walked to the kitchen and found "the" note. She said she was sorry and she would be back in a few days to get the rest of her things. Simple, to the point.

And that was it.

Numb, he made a pot of coffee that he never drank, warmed a bagel that he forgot in the toaster, opened a beer that then sat on the coffee table untouched and stared most of the day at a television he never bothered to turn on. And for the first time in years, he did not talk to Terri. He wanted to, though, which surprised him a little. It felt unnatural not telling her about his day, even if all he did was sit around wallowing in self-pity.

On Christmas Eve, at his mom's house, he told everyone she had to flu, knowing that if he told them the truth it would ruin everyone's Christmas. And since this entire mess was his fault, since he was the one who talked Terri into this, and assured her everything would work out great, he deserved to suffer alone. Although he didn't doubt she was suffering, too. And he wished he could take back some of the things he had said to her.

He told himself he wasn't going to miss her, yet caught himself expecting her to be there, because she hadn't missed a holiday with his family in years. Because she had no one else.

He was miserable, but at least he was with people who loved him. She was miserable, too—he didn't doubt for a second that she was—but on top of that, she was alone. Guilt gnawed at him all evening. He hardly slept. By Christmas morning, he knew what he had to do, what he *needed* to do. And yes, what he wanted to do.

From the outside, Terri's condo was the only one that was bare of holiday decorations. It looked so...lonely. A misfit among units draped with twinkling lights and fresh pine wreathes and nativity scenes. They hadn't exactly gone all out at his place, either, but at least they had their scrawny and unadorned little tree that sat for a couple days on the coffee table looking as lonely and pathetic as he felt.

He trudged through two inches of freshly fallen snow to her door and rang the bell. Terri opened it wearing flannel pajamas, due, he had no doubt, to the sub-zero temperature where she kept the thermostat. She was stunned to see him, of course, just as he'd expected she would be. So stunned that for several long seconds she just stared openmouthed at him.

"It's really cold out here," he said, and she snapped into action.

"Sorry, come in."

She held the door for him and he stepped inside. He stomped the snow from his shoes and shrugged out of his coat, surprised to find that it was reasonably warm. "This is nice," he said.

"Nice?" she asked.

"The temperature. It's usually so cold."

"I decided last night that I'm sick of being cold."

It was about time.

"What are you doing here?" she asked as he walked through the foyer into the living room. Her laptop sat open on the coffee table and the television was tuned to what he recognized as some cheesy made-for-television holiday flick she'd forced him to watch a couple years ago.

"I'm picking you up," he said, making himself comfortable on the sofa.

"Picking me up for *what?*"

"Christmas at *Nonno's.*"

"But…"

"You better hurry. You know how he hates it when people are late."

She stared at him, dumbfounded. "I'm sorry, did I miss something?"

"I don't think so. It's Christmas day, and on Christmas day we always go to *Nonno's.*"

"But…the other day…?"

"I'm really sorry about that."

Just when he thought she couldn't look any more confused. "*You're* sorry."

"What I did to you was really unfair. I basically forced you into doing this, assured you repeatedly that everything would be great, and work out exactly according to plan, then I changed my mind and got angry when you were surprised. I tried to make you feel guilty when it was my fault, not yours."

"Nick, you had every right to be mad at me."

"No, I didn't."

"And now you're here to take me to Christmas dinner?"

"Did you honestly think I would let you spend Christmas alone?"

Tears pooled in her eyes, but didn't spill over. "Actually, I sort of thought I deserved it."

"Well, I don't think so. So go get ready."

"So we're just going to be friends again? Like before?"

"If that's my only option. I won't say that I don't love you, because I do. I think I probably always have, even if I was too stupid to realize it. But you're too important to me to let you go, and if friendship is all you want, I'm okay with that."

One minute Terri was standing in front of him looking thoroughly confused, and the next she was sitting in his lap, arms around his neck, hugging him harder than she'd ever hugged him before.

"I love you, Nick."

Now he was the confused one. "Okay, what just happened?"

She sat back on his thighs and laughed. "I don't know. All of a sudden I just…knew."

"That constituted a grand gesture?"

"A what?"

He shook his head. "Never mind."

"I have a confession," she said. "Something I've been wanting to tell you for weeks."

"What?"

"When we lived together, and you brought girls over, I used to wish it was me in the bedroom with you."

"No, you didn't."

"I *did*. I always wondered what it would be like."

"And now that you know?"

She grinned. "I really like being the girl in the bedroom with you. And the idea of another girl being there instead of me…"

"How would you feel?"

"Like ripping out her throat with my bare hands."

He laughed. "Well, you'll never have to, because there's no one else I want there, either. Because despite what I said, those vows meant something to me. And I was meant to say them to you."

She grinned. "Wow, that was so sappy, I don't know if I should laugh or cry."

"Why don't you kiss me instead?"

She did, and then she started to unbutton his shirt.

He caught her hands. "We really don't have time. *Nonno* is expecting us."

"Well, *Nonno* will have to wait. We have business in the bedroom. We're already two days behind schedule."

He'd completely forgotten that she was ovulating. "Well, just a quick one I guess. If you're sure you still want to. We can wait a month."

"I don't want to wait. I know what I want, and besides, aren't you looking forward to all the money?"

"Oh, well, don't even worry about that."

"Why?"

"I told him I didn't want the money anymore."

Her mouth dropped open. "What? *When?*"

"Right after we got back from the honeymoon."

"Why?"

"It just didn't feel right taking it."

"What did *Nonno* say?"

"Not much. I thought he would be really surprised, but it was almost as if he was expecting it."

"But it's ten *million* dollars! You just gave that up?"

"I'm having a child with you because I *want* to, not because I *need* to."

She cupped his face in her soft hands. "Have I mentioned that I love you?"

He grinned. "Why don't you tell me again?"

"I love you, Nicolas Caroselli."

"What about that perfect man you were looking for? Are you ready to give him up?"

"I don't have to."

"You don't?"

"Heck, no," she said with one of those wicked grins. "I already married him."

* * * * *

MILLS & BOON®

Why shop at millsandboon.co.uk?

Each year, thousands of romance readers find their perfect read at millsandboon.co.uk. That's because we're passionate about bringing you the very best romantic fiction. Here are some of the advantages of shopping at www.millsandboon.co.uk:

* **Get new books first**—you'll be able to buy your favourite books one month before they hit the shops

* **Get exclusive discounts**—you'll also be able to buy our specially created monthly collections, with up to 50% off the RRP

* **Find your favourite authors**—latest news, interviews and new releases for all your favourite authors and series on our website, plus ideas for what to try next

* **Join in**—once you've bought your favourite books, don't forget to register with us to rate, review and join in the discussions

Visit **www.millsandboon.co.uk**
for all this and more today!